THE RIGHT HAND OF SLEEP

THE RIGHT HAND
OF SLEEP

JOHN WRAY

ALFRED A. KNOPF   NEW YORK   2001

THIS IS A BORZOI BOOK PUBLISHED BY ALFRED A. KNOPF

www.aaknopf.com

Knopf, Borzoi Books, and the colophon are registered trademarks
of Random House, Inc.

Library of Congress Cataloging-in-Publication Data
Wray, John.
The right hand of sleep / by John Wray.—1st ed.
p.   cm.
ISBN 0-375-40651-4
1. Austria—History—1918–1938—Fiction.   2. Gamekeepers—Austria—Fiction.
3. Villages—Austria—Fiction.   4. Murder—Austria—Fiction   5. Jews—Austria—
Fiction.   I. Title.
PS3573.R365 R54   2000
813'.6—dc21   00-020309

Manufactured in the United States of America

First Edition

A message was taken ahead for me
By the right hand of sleep:

"Blue ruined hills,
  Right-handed sky,
  Coming home to you fills me
  With a vast sickness."

—P. Lederer

. . . and in the matter of the as-yet-unresolved murder
case in Niessen bei Villach, the direction of inquiry will
come as no surprise to keen followers of history . . .

—*Villacher Tageblatt,* September 8, 1938

The Right Hand of Sleep

NIESSEN

OCTOBER 12, 1917

A boy came out of the house first, the crumbling, sun-yellowed house with the dark tiles and ivied sides, the peaked roof and sandstone steps down which he went stiffly, nervously, adjusting the plaid schoolboy's backpack on his shoulders. A tall stooping boy in his middle teens, smiling to himself as he waited by the gate, breathing quickly. It was a bright fall day and he closed his eyes for a moment, feeling the sunlight through his eyelids there at the garden's edge.

Soon the others came, a man and a woman, the parents of the boy. The man moved slowly, his cream-colored suit well ironed but billowy, as though cut for someone larger. His features like his clothes seemed oversized or borrowed, a loose cluster of tics behind which his eyes hung uncertainly, moving from the boy to the trellises to the old house behind them. The woman walked half a pace behind the man, guiding him by the elbow down the steps. She was still young. She carried herself proudly and severely. Hearing them the boy opened his eyes. He was still smiling slightly, and looking at them as he smiled, but the smile was not meant for them and when he realized this he drew his lips together. He stood at the gate for what seemed a very long time, watching them coming. Finally they reached him and the three of them went out onto the street.

Linking arms they walked toward the mortared gray wall of the canal and the brightly colored rooftops behind it. A smell of woodsmoke was in the air. At the canal they left the road and turned onto a narrow lane. The woman was watching the boy silently, her left arm braced against her husband. He and the boy were talking to each other in low, even tones, but she was not listening to them. The man's eyes as he spoke were not on the boy or on the ground ahead of them but instead on some far-off thing, as they always were. The boy talked on, not listening to the talk itself but talking only to fill the minutes, eyes rarely leaving his father's face. From time to time he let out an embarrassed laugh.

After some minutes they came to a wide gravel avenue curling out from town over a mortared bridge. They stayed there awhile looking down into the water. Before long a young, doughy-faced man came up the avenue on a bicycle. The woman waved to him and he pulled up in front of them.

—Well, Oskar, said the man, grinning down at the boy. —Your number's come up at last, has it?

—Yes, Uncle.

—Yes. Well, we're damn proud, all of us. Hopping proud.

—We're not proud at all, Gustl, said the woman.

The man on the bicycle grinned again. —Mothers take these things hard, old man, he said, tapping the boy's shoulder. —"We have all of us our burthens," as the ditty goes.

—Why aren't you in Italy yet, Uncle? said the boy.

—Palpitations, Oskar. You know very well. Palpitations, damn them. He sighed. —Still. There's need of good men on the home front as well, as the Kaiser says. Eh, Karl?

The boy's father made a low sound, possibly of assent, looking down the avenue through the lines of whitewashed willow trunks toward the station.

—We'd best be going on, Gustl, said the woman quietly. —You'll be round tonight for supper?

—Yes, yes, Dora. He drew in a breath, looked down at the boy and gave a wink. —Well, Oskar: do your duty by those greasy olive-pickers. Stack 'em straight for your nearest and dearest.

—That's enough, now, Gustl, said the woman. —God in heaven.

—Good-bye, Uncle. I'll do my best.

—Damn right you will.

—The train, Dora, said his father, stepping forward.

Walking down the Bahnhofstrasse with his parents on either side of him, hurrying to the station, the boy was struck for the first time by the significance of what was happening to him and looked back often over his shoulder. Framed by the cut-back willow rows, encircled and held toward the sun by the mountain behind it, the town looked like nothing so much as an antique jeweler's miniature, sliding away with a clicking of wheels and cogs into the pines. He realized that it was beautiful and at the same time that it was vanishing from his life. His mother was talking to him now, rapidly, urgently; his father was walking as quickly as he was able, wheezing and opening his eyes wide with every breath. It occurred to the boy that he hadn't looked at his mother since they'd left the house and he knew this must hurt her but still he could not do it. I know what she looks like, he thought. I know what she looks like right now. I don't need to see her.

—Have you taken enough warm things, Oskar? she was saying. —Have you taken enough winter clothes?

—Maman, he said, laughing a little. —I can't wear just whatever I like, you know. They'll be wanting me in a uniform. He looked over at his father, who nodded gravely.

His mother's voice resumed immediately, tight with worry, humorless. —Do you find this so very funny, Karl?

—A little funny, Dora. Not so much.

—I was thinking more about your underclothes, Oskar, his mother said, pulling him forward. His father let out a quiet laugh behind them.

At the station the boy presented his conscription card and was issued a ticket. There were a number of other families on the platform but he stood with his parents a small distance away, looking in the direction from which the train would come. One of the women was sobbing noisily and clutching at her two sons, twins with thick shoulders and flattened reddish hair who muttered and made faces at each other.

—Who are these people? the boy's mother said. —Who is that woman, Karl, with those two boys? She frowned. —I swear I don't know one single person here at all.

—You do know them, Maman, the boy said, looking at his father and rolling his eyes. —Franz and Christian Rindt. Their brother, Willi, runs the new gasthaus across the square from Ryslavy's. And you know the Hoffenreichs behind them. Erich, Maria and Peter.

—Well, his mother said, straightening herself. —For me there will always be one gasthaus in Niessen: the Niessener Hof. She looked over at her husband, who stared resolutely up the tracks. Her lips were tightly drawn and she looked prim and comical. As though she's just eaten a piece of wax-dipped fruit, the boy said to himself. Everything she is is joyless, and not just because of Père. She was like that before, too, when he was better. Your finest country lady. He thought again that if the war hadn't called him he'd have found another way to leave, with or without their blessing, before very long.

—We're all cut from the same cloth in times of war, Maman, said the boy. —Our Kaiser tells us so.

His father raised a hand to cover his mouth. —Go on, his mother said. —Go on, Karl. Laugh at that. But she was smiling now as well.

At that moment someone pointed and the three of them turned to see the first jet of steam coiling over the trees. —Well, Oskar, said his mother calmly. She had taken hold of him by his shoulders and was looking him over exactingly and slowly, studying him, her eyes wide and determined. In case I don't come back, the boy thought, turning the thought back and forth in his mind to get the feeling of it. He looked past her at his father who was watching the train approaching, motionless and enraptured, as if this were the inescapable thing he'd been awaiting. It isn't this, all the same, the boy thought. It isn't this. But this reminds him of it.

For the space of a minute none of them said a word. Behind

them Frau Rindt was still weeping and shouting in her heavy hill-town drawl against the war.

—Keep a journal, Oskar, his father said when the train was almost to the station. —Will you do that for me? All the inane details, *les temps absurdités* . . . yes? I'm sure there'll be plenty. Send it to me in installments, with your letters. I did that for my own Père, when I had my time in Dalmazien. He was smiling now. —Will you? His voice was very mild, almost beseeching.

The boy glanced at his mother. —Would that help you, Père? he said slowly.

His father nodded. —I'd consider it a kindness. It saved your old grandfather, in his day, from expiring of boredom. He raised his shoulders slowly, doggedly, as though resisting a pull upward. —You'll spare me that, won't you, Oskar? Wasting slowly away in this pretty backwater, decaying into dust?

—Now, Karl, said the boy's mother, suddenly severe again.

—I'm sorry, Dora. A little joke.

—We can't have this, Karl. Not now. Are you listening?

—It's all right, Maman, for Christ's sake, said the boy. —Let it alone, he said, already hearing the noise of the train behind him.

—I'm sorry, Dora, said his father. —A little joke with the boy, that's all. We'll never see him again, you know.

—Karl! she said now, beginning to tremble.

—Please, Maman. Let him be. Please.

—Oskar, she said, laying hold of his arm. Then the train was beside them.

THE FUTURE

MARCH 4, 1938

There were two in the compartment: the smoking man and Voxlauer. The nub of a cigarette leapt and hovered in the pane and glimmered there over the reddening pastures and towns. The man smoked carefully, tapping lightly with his shoe heels. The smoke rose in a coil from his lips to a vent in the ozone-stained glass. Outside, to each side of them, dark fields were passing and glittering in places with the last rays of daylight. Lights were coming on in the houses and men and wagons were moving toward them across the turned fields. As on any other day.

Heaving a pack down onto the floor Voxlauer took out the last of the food he'd brought with him, a scrap of bacon wrapped in cabbage and a loaf's-end of pumpernickel. He was grateful now to have taken the canteen he'd found a few weeks earlier at the bottom of a drawer, wrapped in army drabs. —Was this Andrei's? he'd asked Anna. He'd been standing at the foot of the bed. She had nodded, raising her head tiredly and letting it fall. A few days later she'd reminded him of it, saying he might need it if he were to travel soon. And in fact he'd needed it sooner than either had thought and it had been a great comfort, that last week of traveling, filled with light sweet brown tea or fresh water with a dried wedge of lemon.

Finding the canteen he unstopped it and poured the last dregs of tea into a cup with the word "plenty" stamped along its rim in edged Cyrillic script. The smoking man stubbed out his cigarette and proceeded to roll another in the fold of a newspaper. Every so often the train wound closer to the river, rising along its bank through stands of willows lit in passing by the compartment lights.

At the border they waited a long time in silence. Two Hungarian officers inspected the crates in the passageway, making jots in thick vellum notebooks. They handed the conductor a receipt and stamped the train's crumbling freight log and moved on. After another, briefer wait the Pass-Kontrolle came on board. The Austrian officials were better dressed, less capable and more friendly than the Hungarians had been. The head of the station came to visit the passengers personally. He was a little drunk and before he asked to see their passports he sat down in the compartment and retied his shoes. —The good of winter boots that let in the damp is a puzzle, he said, smiling. The young guard behind him remained standing. —A puzzle for the ages, said the inspector, shaking his head sadly. When the boots were tied to his satisfaction he straightened himself and in a more formal tone of voice inquired after their papers.

Voxlauer looked out at the rails and the crossties beneath them, counting the pins and seams. The smoking man's passport was examined and found to be in order. He was a lighting-fixtures manufacturer and salesman from Vienna. He slid the passport back into his briefcase and offered the inspector rolling paper and tobacco. —No thank you, Herr Silbermann, said the inspector, still smiling, and the tobacco in turn was offered to the guard, who accepted enthusiastically and set about rolling a cigarrette against the greasy wooden door of the compartment. Strands of tobacco spilled onto his coat and clung there among the epaulets and folds. The inspector turned to Voxlauer and eyeing his threadbare overcoat asked again after his papers.

Voxlauer dug into a pocket and handed the little book, unscuffed and green, to the inspector. Although the inspector was a younger man than Voxlauer, and younger too than the salesman, he already bore the slight stoop of a life spent on trains. As he flipped through the passport, his face clouded slightly. —There's not one of our stamps in this booklet, he said.

—I know that, said Voxlauer. —I applied for it while living abroad.

—What became of your previous passport?

—It was taken from me.

—When?

—In the war.

A brief silence followed. —You are a veteran? asked the inspector.

—Yes.

—Place of residence?

—Niessen bei Villach.

—Where were you living, while abroad?

—In the Ukraine.

Another silence. Voxlauer looked up at the inspector. The salesman shifted uneasily in his seat. After a moment more the passport was handed to the guard, who had finished with the rolling of his cigarette, to be stamped. Then it was returned to Voxlauer and the two men made to exit the compartment. —Good-bye, Eli, said the inspector. —We'll be seeing you again at Easter?

—With a butterlamb under each arm, said the salesman. —And Mark'esh for your dyspepsia.

—I beg of you, Herr Silbermann, laughed the inspector. —This state of affairs cannot possibly continue. The salesman laughed also. The two men standing regarded affably the two seated men before turning to go. The inspector paused a moment at the door.

—Welcome home, Herr Voxlauer. Give the south a great warm kiss from me.

—I'm so surprised you're not Russian! said the salesman as the train began moving. —You look the part, if I may say so.

—Well. I'm sorry to disappoint you.

—Are you a nihilist?

—What?

—A nihilist. You've been in Russia for some time. He paused. —That's a fair enough question, isn't it?

Voxlauer smiled. —Call me a sympathizer.

The salesman nodded. —Are you from the Steyrmark?

—Near enough. Kärnten.

—I thought either Kärnten or the Steyrmark. Elias Silbermann, from Vienna.

—Oskar Voxlauer. He shook the hand offered him.

—Any relation to Karl?

—Who?

—Come now, Herr Voxlauer! The composer.

Voxlauer looked at him. —Karl the composer, he repeated.

—Operettas. Sentimental airs. All the rage when we were little. Surely you must remember! The salesman began to hum a waltz.

—Yes, I remember now. I've been away for some time. No relation, I'm afraid.

—What sort of name is that, "Voxlauer"? I'd always wondered. Is that Bavarian?

—Austrian, I think, said Voxlauer.

—Oh. I'm not sure of that, the salesman said.

—What did you say your name was, Herr . . . ? Voxlauer said tonelessly.

The salesman didn't answer. They rode awhile in silence. —I served, myself, he said after a few minutes, almost apologetically. —In the Tyrol. He leaned forward and raised a trouser leg to disclose a mottled blue scar. —The last great time. He smiled.

Voxlauer didn't answer. The lights in the passageway leapt and flickered as the train clattered over a rail switch. After a sudden lurch leftward the wheels became quiet again, or near to quiet.

—Those godforsaken kits are all mine, said the salesman, pointing at the crates. —Blood of my brow.

—What's inside them? said Voxlauer.

—Tungsten ingots.

—Ah.

—Yes, said the salesman. He laughed. —Exactly. What's your trade then, Herr Voxlauer?

Voxlauer sat looking out the window. —My trade? he said. —Nothing.

—There's a great many folk in that profession nowadays.

—That is to say, farming, Voxlauer said after a few seconds' pause.

—Nothing or farming? said the salesman, blinking.

—Whichever you'd prefer.

—Well: I think I'd prefer nothing to farming, if it's all the same, laughed the salesman—and anything to life as a peddler of lighting fixtures. He paused a moment. —Fortunately that's not my sole vocation. I'm a pianist by training.

Voxlauer rubbed his eyes. —Tough times, I suppose.

The salesman regarded him a moment through the smoke and the gloom of the compartment. —Have you not been home since the war? he said finally.

—No.

—A great deal has changed, Herr Voxlauer. A very great deal.

Voxlauer didn't answer. The first low steeples and clusters of light heralding the approach of the suburbs of the capital appeared along the south side of the train. To the north was the river and beyond the river identical clusters ever growing in density. Lights signifying buildings and families and German and books and machinery. The numbness he could no longer remember not feeling made itself noticed again, like the whine of a gaslight. He made no effort to take in what Silbermann was saying to him.

—Many of us simply fear for our livelihoods.

—Excuse me?

—Because of events in the north.

—I know nothing at all about that, said Voxlauer.

—I thought maybe you were an illegal. Many of them are coming back now.

—An illegal?

Silbermann nodded. —An illegal. A Black Shirt. He raised his left arm stiffly in salute.

—Ah, said Voxlauer. —I wouldn't very likely be coming from the Ukraine in that event, would I?

Silbermann shrugged. —I suppose not.

They were very close to the river now and the packed sand under the rails dropped straight into the water. —It's taken as a bad sign, Silbermann said after a pause. He was passing the tobacco back and forth between his hands and looking the whole while out the window, or at his reflection in the glass. To stop him fidgeting Voxlauer asked for a cigarette.

—With pleasure, said Silbermann distractedly, spreading the newspaper over his lap. Voxlauer closed his eyes and listened to the sound of Silbermann's fingers on the newsprint and the sound of his own breathing, deliberate and calm. The steady turning-over of the gears. The rattle of the door.

—Here you are, Silbermann said brightly after a minute or so had passed, twisting the paper ends nimbly with his fingertips as he cast about after the matches. They were soon recovered from the floor and the cigarette lit. Voxlauer exhaled and watched his breath snake upward along the glass as Silbermann's had done.

The cigarette drew evenly and smoothly. Voxlauer stared up at the vent. Silbermann was rolling another, glancing every few moments out the window, measuring their distance from the station. —Twenty minutes, he said, looking up and smiling.

—Twenty for you. I'm continuing south.

—I'd forgotten. You have family waiting?

—Of a sort, said Voxlauer. —A mother.

—Mothers. One wonders how they manage.

—They manage very well.

Silbermann looked up from his paper. The tracks were rising now to the level of the lowest houses and in the middle distance the stolid fin-de-siècle apartment buildings of the inner city came into view, monochrome and bright, with St. Stephen's spire rising bluely behind them. —How long have you been a farmer, then, Herr Voxlauer?

Voxlauer sat back from the window. —For as long as I can remember.

. . .

They marched us into the Isonzo in the early morning, twenty miles up from the station in loose oilskin coats and jackboots brought back from the front and hurriedly reblackened for us. It was October and a wet, heavy snow was falling. When we reached the back lines a few bewildered trench cutters stared at us, then waved us up the hill. No one seemed to have been expecting us. Everywhere men were cursing the snow and dragging crates and canvas sacks up and down the hill on runners. The war was ending, though we didn't know it yet. My battalion was put together of frightened aging men and homesick boys with hurt looks on their faces; we were the replacement for a battalion that had been utterly routed that September in the hills outside Caporetto. I was the youngest, turned sixteen that past December. I had no ideas of my own yet about anything. I felt no homesickness for my family, or for Niessen. I was happy to be in the war.

They set us to work right away gathering spent mortar casings and firewood. An advance trench was opened a few meters below the tree line and we were moved into it that same day, with eight twenty-millimeter mortars and three or four dozen machine-gun posts. The gunners were all officers between twenty-five and forty and had been on the line for near to a year already; most were months past their leaves. They barely seemed to register our arrival.

The first night was very quiet. A lieutenant came round to our newly dug positions and yelled at us for letting the trench floor fill with water. He was bleary-eyed and stooped and apologized a few minutes later for losing his temper. Later that night I saw him slumped over on a crate outside the officers' mess, twitching and mumbling in his sleep. In the morning we learned seven men had deserted.

Things had begun unraveling by then, but quietly, without any noticeable change. I stared saucer-eyed at everything around me, as though at any minute I'd be found out and ordered back to school. As the shelling began that second day a cluster of officers crawled from one post to another down the lines, thanking us for not leaving our positions. The Germans were coming, they told us, in two or at most three weeks' time. We were to hold to our dugouts, return modest fire at intervals, and wait.

In late November six German battalions arrived. We had barely advanced at all, ten or twenty meters at most up a steep snowfield under near-to-constant mortar fire. The excitement I'd felt at first had given way to a steady nervous tiredness, an impatience for something definite to happen. Since I'd been on the lines there had been no true offensive. The trenches we'd abandoned over the last few weeks had filled completely with mud and castaway food tins and cartridges; to reach us the Germans had to lay a network of planks over them and inch their way forward in their caterpillar-treaded trucks. Things must have looked desperate to them because they stayed in the transports until their officers had finished their tour of the lines, coming out only when given the direct order. Maybe it's comfortable for them in there, I thought. I watched raptly as the infantry and gunners let themselves down one by one from out of the covered beds, surefooted and serene. That was the first of many times I envied them.

The Germans had new, lightweight artillery and quick-loading mortars and shells filled with chlorine gas; they moved among us like royalty the next few weeks, clean-shaven and imperious, giving lessons in the loading of shells. Everyone was talking about a last big offensive before the snow made it impossible to move. The general opinion among the Germans was that we were an unqualified disgrace and would have stayed where we were for the rest of the war if not for the new artillery. Tullberg, their commanding officer, compared us to a mouthful of rotten teeth, crying whenever the wind blew. Most of the others resented the Gemans but I, for one, was eager to learn everything I could from them, especially about the guns. My father had often explained to me that while our empire was unsurpassed in the sophistication of its arts, he credited his time in Berlin and Leipzig with whatever understanding of the modern world he might possess. "The Germans are our rule-and-compass-toting cousins, Oskar," he was fond of saying. "Regrettable as it seems to us, we must study them."

The new shells were black around the seams and flew off soundlessly when you fired. I remember that best, out of every-thing: the soft, flat report of the firing gun and the faint click just after, muffled and bright at once, like a cup or a spoon falling from a low height onto the carpet. Gas burns were blue and white and began under the skin. The gunners were all German and wore down-quilted anoraks and yellow cowhide gloves to protect their hands.

By the time of the twelfth offensive the snow had begun in earnest and the new trenches we dug were set slantwise into the drifts. We were closer to the Italians now than we'd ever been. Mortars tore into the walls as though they were confetti paper and burst through in great pillars of twisting smoke, scattering us like pigeons up and down the line. The Germans had brought an entirely different war with them from the one we'd been in; even the Italians seemed to have noticed. I tried to imagine them hud-dled up the hill in their own dugouts, feeling the same fear I was beginning to feel, but I could never manage to picture them as any-thing other than flat, gray-faced caricatures. Occasionally voices would carry down to us in the pauses between shellings but they always had a smoothed-over, lifeless quality to them because of the snow and the trees and the near-to-constant wind. Sometimes at night we'd hear the sound of singing.

Two days before the offensive the shelling stopped almost completely. It was clear to everyone that the Italians knew what was coming and when, but the Germans were relaxed and confi-dent. On the day of the offensive we sat in a long row against the uphill wall, pounding on our feet through the toes of our boots to bring the feeling back into them, waiting on the order. Finally late at night the word came through.

The bombardment lasted more than seven hours. I was feeder to a German fusilier, a taps sergeant named Wachmann who was patrician and friendly and spat whenever he had to give an order. His sense of humor reminded me of my Uncle Gustl's, self-serving and full of bluster; he also had Gustl's same Kaiser Wilhelm mus-taches. I found myself wanting very badly to please him. We fired at eight-minute intervals, sowing cover for the infantry, pausing to give them time to reach their next point of shelter, then firing again. After three and a half hours of loading my hands were numb and white with cold and Wachmann sent me down for padded mittens. The walls of the back trenches made the firing seem very far off and the narrow strip of sky overhead was patterned by clouds with streaks of thin, rust-colored smoke across them. I was a long time getting the mittens.

When I came back to the post I saw that the wall had fallen in and an instant or two later I saw Wachmann himself, pressed down backward into the snow with his eyes shut and bleeding and violet scalloped burns over his face and shoulders. He rocked from side to side, arms pushed tightly down against his legs, murmuring something through his blackened teeth I couldn't decipher. His mustache and eyebrows had been burned away and his face looked to have been lifted up somehow and shifted slightly off its bones. I knew as I looked at him that the noise of the bombardment was all around me and that I myself was saying or shouting something but all I could hear was the noise of Wachmann trying to speak. It was a sickening noise. I stood without moving for a few moments longer listening to it and deciding whether or not to touch him or to take his pistol from its holster and kill him with it before the sound of the shelling and my stuttering voice returned all at once and I ran back through the trench and the columns of infantry that were suddenly filling it, screaming for an officer. The taps sergeant's been hit, I gasped to the fusilier in the next gunner's post. He turned round and looked at me as though I'd just asked him whether he could spare a schilling. Get back to your position, you idiot! he yelled, shooing me away with his yellow gloves.

I ran back through the smoke to find the wall fallen further in and the mortar canting over against the pile of shells. Wachmann was still there with his head lolling back and a cord of thickened mucus jutting like a tusk from his mouth into the snow. I watched him for a little while, waiting for him to move, then crossed to the far side of the dugout and vomited. Afterward I sat back against a heap of spent shell casings and did nothing for a long time with the guns booming all around me. I knew my leaving for the mittens had had nothing to do with the rest but it was exactly that, the *thought that nothing I did could have made any difference, that made me feel I should have been in the dugout when the shell came down. Wachmann was just on the other side of the casings but I couldn't look at him anymore. I felt very small and very light. A strange smell hung in the air, a smell like the tips in a box of wooden matches that has gotten wet. The air was clotted thickly in my mouth and it was hard to breathe. I stretched myself out on the ground and tried to lie completely still, looking up at the play of clouds and smoke across the sky. Hours passed. The returning fire grew fainter and fainter, like the clatter of a departing train, then vanished altogether. For the next half hour there was no sound along the line but a wet, muffled buzzing. Then even that ended. Everything was silent, palpable and alive, like the air between pealings of an enormous bell.*

Voxlauer awoke late that night as the train entered the last limestone gorge curving down onto the plain. His pulse quickened instantly and he felt a cold weight pressing against his forehead and shoulders. He put his face to the window. The passageway now empty of freight threw its light onto the closing rock walls, leaded over and sheer. They could of course have been any walls but he knew it was the last gorge and memories fought for precedence in his brain and he felt bewildered and childlike in his fear. Why he should be afraid now, so groundlessly, he had no idea, but he was helpless in the face of it. With a great effort he brought the walls into focus. Fifty-odd meters down ran the brook, soon to vanish under the rubble of its bed only to reemerge two kilometers downstream in the pools of the old spa at Brunner's Cross. His breath clung to the windowpane but he made no effort to clean the glass, looking out instead through the ebbing and gathering fog as the pines flew past. The bloodless white lights of the spa when they came marked the opening of the gorge into fir-shrouded eaves curving off to each side like the pages of an album, falling away and turning. Then came the river and the bend by which the bell towers were visible for the first time, the ruin looming up behind them like the hull of an immense capsized ship. To the left was the toll road to Italy running south between the willow rows; to the right the canal which held the half-moon-shaped town fast against the foothills, laddering up into the pines. He could feel the breath clutching in his throat like a baby's, close-gutted and strange. But the air, when it came, was a nectar to him.

He chose not to enter by the front gate where Maman was sure to be waiting for him on the verandah, a little smaller than he remembered but otherwise unchanged with the ancient house behind her. At the last bend of the canal he turned down the narrow side lane into the orchard. The trees were still much as he'd pictured them, though they seemed a bit sparer, and the gravel of the lane was near to vanished under scrub. He gathered from this that the old gardener, Greiss, had died or else grown too old finally and moved down to Judenbach, where his son had a small property. Then it occurred to him that Greiss had already been old, very old, twenty years before and that his son had been called to duty three weeks before he, Voxlauer, had been. The son had been five or six years older than Voxlauer with thick orange hair and milk-colored skin and when his sister brought the news to his table at the Niessener Hof he had wept and taken off his shoes and refused to go home. And the old man had come and dragged him back to the garden and had beaten him with a split poplar cane until Maman threw open the shutters and shouted Enough! in that imperious way of hers. And the son had apologized to her and to everyone and had set off for the Isonzo the very next morning.

Coming to the back gate he found it locked and mortared shut at both its joinings. He kicked his pack under the lichened fence boards and proceeded to haul himself over it, no differently than he had in distant summers when he'd come home from Ryslavy's after she and Père were already in bed. Coming down he landed on a cart leaning against the wall and his right foot drove clean through the cankered wood. He cursed sharply in the dark, pulled his foot back up through the planks, then crouched and felt around him for the pack. Finding it, he stood up carefully and walked as quietly as he could around the barn.

She had heard him crossing the plank footbridge over the creek and the house lights came on as he passed the old wine trellises. He'd not imagined it this way, when he'd still imagined it at all: arriving furtively in the middle of the night with only the empty house and her to greet him. As if nothing had happened in the world. When he came to the front gate she was waiting for him on the steps. She looked at him a full minute up and down pretending not to recognize him before smiling a little, almost ruefully, and leading him up to the verandah.

—Hello, Maman, he said, trying to find in her the person he remembered. She looked old, terribly old, older than even she had a right to look after all she'd lived through. She must be sick, he thought suddenly. The thought broke slowly over the next few moments, spreading inside him with a coldness that seemed to reach back over decades. I wonder how long she's been like this, he thought. I wonder when it started. It seemed to him now, in the cold light that shone over everything, that he could remember a change in her letters of three or four years past, a sharper sense of reproach, shriller, more urgent. But I never thought she would look like this, he thought. She's only just past sixty, for the love of God.

Yes. And Anna was only forty-eight, a few months over, and she died. The coldness washed over him again and he stood speechless, motionless, staring at her.

She was still studying him in silence, making the same frightened concessions, the same adjustments that he was making. Gradually a light began to kindle in her crumpled features and she broke into a smile. She pulled him to her and embraced him and he felt her withered arms and the lightness of her body.

—You've been away so long, she said finally, almost apologetically, in a voice far kinder than he'd expected.

—Don't you know me anymore, Maman?

—*Ach!* I know you, Oskar. She was still studying him, her face knit strangely together, out of sorrow or bemusement or some other long-preserved and near-to-forgotten emotion he could not have said. It was hard to say one thing or the other for the lines and the grimness around her bright, hard eyes. The smile still held somewhat flickeringly to her mouth.

—I'd had things to say, she said finally, slowly. —But I can't remember any of them. It doesn't matter. I'm happy I've lived to see you back, that's all. I'm happy to see you, anyway, she said, blinking.

—I'm happy to see you too, Maman.

—But not to be back?

He looked around him at the verandah and the garden. —I don't quite feel back, as yet.

—You will. She looked at him now without smiling but more comfortably, more confidently than she had before. —You do recognize your mother, don't you? The woman who gave you life?

He grinned. —I thought you'd disavowed that act, Maman.

She laughed at this. —Only so I could keep my place in church, Oskar. You'll not begrudge me that, I hope. She smiled again and took his arm. —Are you tired from the train? Hungry? Shall I make you something to eat?

—Thank you, Maman. I'm tired, mostly. Don't warm up the stove on my account.

She laughed again quietly. —I've been keeping that stove warm for nigh to twenty years, you wandering Judas.

—*Maman! J'ai mort de faim!* said Voxlauer the next morning, crossing to the kitchen table. Outside the sky was a vibrant blue and the sunlight shone full on the back of his chair as it had on those Sundays when they'd taken breakfast late, coming up hungry from service with the meal warming in the oven and his father playing brightly through the parlor door. While Maman busied herself around the table Voxlauer would stand with his ear to the paneling listening to the music and the squeak of Père's stool as he leaned in and away from the keys and picture him on the other side, elegant and intent, oblivious to small things like service or the setting of the table for breakfast. Sometimes the music would stop abruptly and he would hear the scratching of a fountain pen on paper for a moment or the sound of his father humming to himself, a little flatly, before it began again. —For God's sake, Karl! Maman would shout when breakfast was laid out and the music would shift from allegro to adagio and shortly afterward Père would come cheerfully to table.

—It's like a Sunday today, said Voxlauer, pulling out the chair. —I've slept late.

She smiled. —You've slept clear to Sunday. But I suppose you're entitled.

He looked at her. —I've come a long way, this week.

—I know, Oskar. So you're entitled. How did you sleep?

—Very well.

—Good.

—A bit cramped, maybe.

She smiled again. —You've grown. And I suppose the guest room hasn't.

He nodded. —Not much has changed.

—More than you think, Oskar.

—What do you mean?

—Well, she said, crossing to the stovetop. —In town.

—Oh. That. He stared out the window at the slate wall with the canal behind it. —Is there really such a difference, now to then?

—I know, Oskar! she said, wiping her hands with a washcloth. —I know about your fine ideas. I read the books you told me to read. I read your letters, what few there were of them. Did you read mine, I wonder?

Voxlauer didn't answer. —Those were some time ago, those fine ideas, he said finally.

—Certainly they were. She watched him for a while. —There's a difference now, in town.

Outside the window the canal was brightening even further in the growing light and plate-sized pieces of ice here and there revolved slowly, as if in a gentle current. He wondered idly what sort of fish were underneath them.

—You've made it just in time for elections, she said, setting down the coffee and a plate of rolls. —Irma Gratzer's coming at eleven.

—Elections?

She shrugged. —Elections. The town council no-accounts. She winked.

—I'm not registered.

She clucked brightly, waving a hand. —We'll take care of that first, then.

—I'm not going into town yet.

—Oskar.

—Yes?

She paused a moment, looking at him looking back at her. Her expression softened. —Suit yourself, then.

As he heard her footfalls on the gravel his breath came easier to him. His worn face had shocked her. He'd sent photographs but those were now years out of date. One of the house, one of the horses. One of himself and Anna, taken on the occasion of their third anniversary. He went into the parlor to look for them.

The parlor gave no sign that so much as a saucer had been shifted those twenty-odd years. The watercolors hung palely in their gilt-edged frames on three sides of the dining table and the table itself was covered by a dust-heavy cloth. It had the smell of a room long since sealed against time, shut away and forgotten, though he knew she must pass through it daily to reach the veranda. A line of wash was strung through the open door and he recognized his own linen dangling from it, steaming in the mid-morning sun. He sat himself down with the sun at his back and his feet on the warm clay tiles and spread open a folio of photographs.

The folio held several bundles of varying sizes randomly bound together. He undid the twine from each bundle and organized them into heaps, oldest to newest, along the yellow-glazed wall of the verandah. The first to catch his eye was a large overexposed picture of his father on the steps of the opera in a wide-brimmed fedora and a loden jacket, pointing at the ground. On the back of the photograph the words "new shoes" were scrawled in his father's crimped, fastidious hand. A woman who might or might not have been Maman stood laughing in the middle distance, waving a patterned shawl.

In the next picture she was more clearly visible. She stood frowning at the camera in mock displeasure, the playful curl of her lips wholly alien to his conception of her. In the third his father had removed his fedora and sat cross-legged on the steps, grinning and gesturing at the sky with his baton. On its back he had written "the fool." Voxlauer looked at this picture for a long time, trying to imagine his mother and Père's life before his birth, before she'd left the opera, before Père had stopped composing and become ill. He thought of their slow, courtly promenades along the canal, acknowledging the greetings of the passersby, and tried to imagine them much younger still, on a similar walk in Arnstadt, or in Teplitz-Schönau, or in Berlin. But the memory of Père in his last year came to him instead, as it always did: on his bench in the farthest corner of the orchard, hollowed out and unsure of his surroundings, aged beyond measure by his sickness and by the slow corruption of everything, the murders of the Kaiserin and of Archduke Ferdinand, the workers' strikes and the revolutions and the Kaiser's own idiocies and lastly, most of all, by the unforeseeable vastness of the war. Voxlauer laid the print down carefully by its edges.

There followed in the pile a number of photographs well known to him of Maman in various of the roles she had performed in the years before her marriage, carefully composed publicity shots taken against a painted drop of Grecian tombs and arbors. *La Bohème, Turandot, La Traviata*. Names he'd been entranced by as a child. The gilt edges of the daguerreotypes muddied and discolored by thumbprints. Maman at seventeen, barely distinguishable behind crepe veils and sequins in a large-scale cast portrait for *Aída*. The opera house in Arnstadt, weather-stained and somber. A picture of his father visibly older and ill-of-health, reclining in a loose-fitting summer shirt on the verandah—fifty years of age, possibly a little more, reading to him from a tattered paper copy of James Fenimore Cooper's *Pioneers*.

Later he found the pictures of Anna taken on the farm and at the market in Cherkassy. In the first she was in front of the house, her face to the hard, flat sun, the bright puddles of snow-thaw behind her bleeding into her outline. Her hair hung in two thick plaits and shone warmly through the sepia of the print. Her plain straight mouth was open slightly, as though she'd been talking as he fidgeted with the borrowed camera, and her hands were clasped tightly at her waist. In the photograph from Cherkassy they stood an arm's length apart, both regarding the camera suspiciously, as though it were an unwelcome witness to their happiness. His cheeks were drawn and sunken from his vagrancy and his beard was growing in uneven, downy patches, like an adolescent's or a beggar's. Already these photographs, too, were taking on the quality of publicity shots for a wholly imaginary life. And this parlor and verandah which in past years he'd not been capable of remembering clearly formed the model again for all he knew or understood, as it had from his earliest days.

Sometime past noon he fell asleep on the carpet. When he awoke he found that a blanket had been draped over him and a half-opened snowbell set on a kerchief near his head. Maman's voice and the voice of another woman carried through the hallway and across the open stairwell.

—The wages of immodesty.

—What was it exactly?

—Liver.

—Ah. The liver. I see.

The woman's voice was high and reedy and cut into his mother's even tones like a schilling cast into a puddle of water. It seemed familiar to Voxlauer but he made no effort to place it. He listened to them awhile discussing him and his prospects in town as he might have listened to news of a foreign disaster on the radio, or as a child half-asleep listens to the talk of adults at ease and smoking after dinner. He drew the blanket over his head.

—I never once gave my approval of the "arrangement," as he called it.

—What became of the first man?

—I haven't the slightest. Liver most likely.

—Now Dora.

A brief pause. The sound of tea being poured, and the smell of it. He was still very tired and allowed himself to drift in and out of waking with their talk always liminally addressing him along the seams and the margins of his memory.

—Like a Bolshevik, with that face of his.

—Yes. Well, you definitely should shave him before bringing him to anybody.

—*Ach*, Irma. As if he'd once let me near him.

—Well. A silence. —Where will you take him, then?

—I don't know. Herbst's.

—With that face? In a gasthaus?

—He's a good boy for all that. They know our family still, in town, I believe.

—Of course they do, Dora. There's nothing to say in that regard.

—And they remember him, too, some of them.

Another pause. —Some of them do, yes.

—Paul Ryslavy does.

—He's been away so long, Dora. And with the Russians the whole while.

—Because of that woman. She cursed quietly. —That turnip picker.

—Well.

—What?

—Well, Dora—

—It was cancer of the liver, said Voxlauer, stepping in from the stairwell.

—You'll never guess who I saw today, Maman said cheerily, reaching past him for the soap brick. —At the elections.

—Who?

—Sister Milnitsch. She looked over at him. —Kati.

—No. Is Kati a Dominikanerin now?

—These twenty years.

Voxlauer let out a low whistle. —I must have made quite an impression on her.

—Ha! Don't flatter yourself, Oskar.

—Well. I'm only saying. He wrung out the dish towel and took three chipped Meissen saucers from her. —Let them out now, do they?

—Only at elections. They drive them down the hill in one of the bishop's cars. Drive them back up when they're finished.

—Kati Milnitsch. I haven't thought of her in ages.

—Well, neither have I, Oskar. She looked lovely in a habit. You'd be surprised.

—No I wouldn't.

—All right then. All right. She poured the dishwater slowly from the tin basin into the drain. —You missed something there, though, Oskar! she said.

Voxlauer set the plates down and made a face. —Maman. I was sixteen years old.

—I was barely eighteen when your Père and I were married.

Voxlauer didn't answer.

—Oskar?

—I don't want to talk about Père.

She was quiet awhile then, staring down at the plates. —You're so old, now, Oskar, she said finally. —Who would have you? She paused again. —You were beautiful once. Beautiful. I don't mind saying so.

—I've already had a wife.

She took the plates from the counter in front of him and stacked them and took them over to the cupboard and put them in carefully, one after the other. The plates squeaked loudly as she stacked them.

—I won't hear a word about her, Maman. He paused a moment, looking at her. —Not a word. I'm warning you now.

—What can we talk about, then, Oskar? She was quiet for a time. —I haven't said anything, she said, still facing the cupboard door. —I haven't said anything yet.

—That's a lie, Voxlauer said simply.

. . .

After dinner he shaved off his beard with his father's straight razor and let her cut his hair in front of a full-length mirror she'd saved from her opera days. Then he went out into the twilight, still dressed in his traveling clothes, and walked down through the garden.

When he came to the bridge he turned and followed the creek for a minute or so till he reached the southern boundary stone. Then he went left, stepping over the creek, and made his way through the tight-woven bracken till he'd traced the property line east to the orchard. In places he barely recognized the garden and full-grown trees appeared suddenly before him where none existed in his memory. The birchwood pavilion at the northwest corner of the orchard was badly decayed and the floorboards felt spongelike and slippery beneath his feet. The house where Greiss and his son had lived was now locked and shuttered. The open barn next to it was empty except for the cart he'd fallen onto the night before. He wondered who had moved it. Had she? No, she was too old to do such things. Not too old, he reminded himself. Still.

—Still, she looks old, said Voxlauer aloud.

The vegetable garden lay under a thin shirt of ice where the slate wall shadowed it and skeletons of the last year's wine hung in curls from the trellises and rattled with an angry tenacity as he brushed past them. When he rounded the house Maman was waiting for him on the verandah. —Don't be too late, she called down. He said nothing in reply but went out through the gate and shutting it behind him made a small gesture, more an acknowledgment than a wave, and set off up the snow-guttered road to the ruin.

Past the canal the road curved sharply uphill to the hump of pocked granite the ruin rose from, black and crumbling, like scaffolding for a vanished building. Three quarters around the outcrop the houses fell away and a trail wound through snarls of winter bracken to the summit. From there the ruin was like an immense stage set, gothic and fragile, behind which the entire plain lay shuttered against the cold. A ladder led up through the remains of the sacristy and he climbed to the roof and looked across the hillside.

St. Michael's and the square lay bare and unpeopled except for a few sedans and delivery cars spaced evenly in the snow and a pack of dogs circling the fountain, dry and crated over for the winter. The Niessener Hof and Gasthaus Rindt faced each other sullenly across the square, the Bahnhofstrasse lolling out between them. The avenue itself was largely unlit and he noticed that many of the shops he remembered toward the station had disappeared. A train was just pulling out and beyond it the alleys and lanes of town gave way to a belt of newer, more landed properties and beyond those the first modest farms. He cast about for the creek and found it where it forked at the canal and followed it with his eyes down into the garden and past the house where a light was still burning and further out still along the toll-road through the willows southward. The train passed silently between them, its twin taillights fluttering. He turned and clambered back down the ladder. The sky overhead was clear and cold.

The fusilier came by a short time later and looked the sergeant over. He asked me if I had been wounded and I shook my head. He looked at me a moment, then told me to put my helmet on. I searched for it around me in the snow but couldn't find it. Come over here, Private, the fusilier said. He motioned to me to take the sergeant's legs and, leaning stiffly over, took hold of him by the sheepskin collar of his coat and pulled. The sergeant came away from the wall with a noise like tearing crepe and a little ravine of yellow snow tumbled after him onto our boots. We went with the body to the back lines, stumbling and slipping on the wet planks laid in pairs over the trenches. At the halfway point two men appeared with a stretcher and took the sergeant from us. We were within shouting distance of the tents of the rear line and I wanted very badly to keep going. If I remember rightly I started crying then, a steady breathless shudder that I made no attempt to keep the fusilier from noticing. The nausea came back and I took a few steps to one side, watching the men lurch forward with the stretcher around and between the shell craters toward the tents. The fusilier gave a light pull on one of my sleeves and we turned and began to walk back up the slope to the deserted front.

As we reached the line we saw the last column of men scrabble over the ridgetop and disappear. The fusilier's battalion had advanced without him and he was suddenly afraid they might think he'd deserted. It seemed to me the offensive must have been a great success: only a small part of a battalion had hung back, to oversee the transport of the remaining guns. We stood on the last footbridge looking down at the empty trenches. Do you have a weapon? asked the fusilier.

Yes sir.

Well?

Sir?

Did you slip it down your breeches, Private? Where in God's name is it?

It was in the pit, sir, I said.

He cursed. Go and find it, then.

I walked back to the ruins of the turret and cast around in the drift and rubble for my rifle. The mortar had been taken away. Not finding anything, I sat down again against the empty casings; at some point I got to my feet and looked down the line. The fusilier was gone. Far off down the slope a team of mules was hauling six or seven coupled mortars up a track. I watched them slowly pass out of sight and after that stared a long time off into the woods, not thinking about anything.

I spent that night in a snowed-in supply tent on the former Italian side of the lines. The front had been abandoned hurriedly and very little looked to have been taken. In among the stacked crates of flour and beans and salted meat were two piles of winter uniforms, slate-colored and quilted, with the Venetian lion recumbent over each lapel. I pushed the piles together and fashioned them into a sort of bed and crawled underneath it and felt the weight of the coats pressing me down into the floor. I thought of the way the sergeant had been pressed into the snow and imagined the force of the explosion something like the weight I felt on top of me, but vast and on every side and all at once. Then I laughed at myself, seeing an avalanche of uniforms exploding into the dugout. That's not the way it was, I thought. It was a shell that did it. He was burned all over.

The roof sagged steeply on the uphill side of the tent and standing on some of the crates I was able to slip my head through a hole in the fabric and look back down the slope. The sky was high and clear and as night fell a line of fires sprang up behind the tents where the sergeant's body had been taken. Now I will remember him that way, I thought, picturing his black and running face. The family and the friends will remember him one way and I'll remember him the other. I felt giddy thinking this. Wachmann's face and the sight of his body as it died suddenly seemed a privileged and secret knowledge. Only I had seen it. The fusilier had seen something, perhaps, but I had seen the whole of it. Everything but the explosion. I thought again, more vaguely now, that I should have been there when the shell hit. I thought very briefly about a letter I'd gotten that morning with news about my father. The firelight looked beautiful thrown back onto the tents but I couldn't picture myself going to them. A ringing and shuddering was passing through my body, rattling the crates under my feet, but I felt nothing unpleasant, only giddiness.

After a time it grew too cold to watch the fires any longer and I ducked my head inside and buried myself down in the coats until only my eyes and nose were showing. I lay very still, imagining being discovered by the Italians in the middle of the night. I thought about Wachmann again and how the snow had clung to his back like the bristles of a pig when we pulled him away from the wall. The wind grew louder and snow fluttered down steadily from the hole in the roof. Eventually I fell asleep.

When I woke my nose and eyelids were coated with drift but the rest of me was warm for the first time in weeks and I felt forgotten and content. I got up and went outside to piss; it was already late morning and blindingly bright. Down the hill I saw a ring of men in what looked to be Turkish uniforms talking quietly and smoking. When my vision cleared a little I recognized them by their peaked hats as our own Kaiser's hussars. I went back into the tent and took up my rucksack and slid down the steep clear-cut slope toward the men. The drifts made the going slow and strenuous between the stumps, and I was a long time getting down; at one point I stumbled and tore the shoulder of my coat. I came out of a cluster of pines a few yards farther on and heard a shot at the same moment but by then it was too late to turn back. I looked up and saw a man in an open flannel shirt totter a few steps and then fall face-forward into the snow. A second or two later the man who had fired noticed me. He called to me to raise my arms and come slowly down the hill. The others turned round at this and watched me as I came. When I reached the even ground I laid my rucksack down, very gingerly, then raised my hands again. I hadn't seen the man who had fallen clearly but I knew that he was not an Italian and that I was not going to make it anymore to the tents.

Two hussars came forward and led me by my elbows into the circle. They asked me the name of my battalion and my regiment and I told them. The officer with the pistol, a captain, gestured at my shoulder. How did that happen, Private? he asked.

Just now, sir. I fell.

How did you lose your battalion?

During the shelling, sir. I was feeder to a mustard-shell battery. The taps sergeant died.

The captain frowned. What taps-sergeant?

Taps Sergeant Wachmann, sir. A German.

Were you hit?

No sir.

There was silence for a moment. How did you lose your battalion? the captain said, as matter-of-factly as before. A shaking had begun along my left arm. The others were closer to me now and I could see the steam of their breath rising up behind the captain's head. He was looking at me as a gymnasium teacher might to an able student and I wanted very much to tell him again about Wachmann and the fusilier and everything that had happened since but I saw in the same instant that he hadn't put away his gun and the look on his face had changed. How did you lose your battalion, Private? he said again.

I stayed with the taps sergeant. At my position sir.

There was another silence. Someone sniggered.

Shoot this man, the captain said flatly, handing me his pistol.

The circle widened to show another man on his knees in the snow, stripped to his underclothes. Tears were running down his cheeks and guttering in his beard and in the folds of his face. I stood for a few seconds without moving or speaking. Who is he? I asked.

A deserter, said the captain. Behind me in the circle someone spat. A voice was screaming now behind my eyes, not my voice or the voice of any other living thing but a voice just the same, high and piercing as a steam jet. Things began to swim together. I took a half step backward to steady myself and felt a hand against the small of my back. I know you, said the man on the ground, tilting his head up toward me.

I stared down at the man. I know you, he repeated. He had stopped sobbing now and was looking up at me or at something just behind me with wide-open unblinking eyes. The thought entered my head for the smallest part of an instant that he was not talking to me at all, or to anyone in the circle, but directly to God. I know you, he said again, breaking into a smile.

Shut your mouth! screamed the officer. The scream was thin and bright like the noise that was sharpening each second behind my eyes and I drew back automatically. The man on the ground was staring at me and swaying from side to side as if in a rapture. Mucus clotted in his beard and on his lips. He made no motion either to raise himself or to lie back down onto the snow. He was raising his left arm to me, open-handed, as if asking me to help him onto his feet.

Do you know this man? said the captain, turning round to look at me.

No sir, I said. I raised the pistol and fired.

When he reached the front gate Maman was sitting exactly as she'd been when he had left her. As he came up the steps she sat forward with a start and he realized she'd been asleep. —You haven't forgotten how to startle a body yet, she muttered.

—I'm sorry.

—Well. That's all right.

He stood beside her awhile, looking up at the treeline. —Does old Ryslavy still run the Niessener Hof?

—No. Alban died last winter. Pauli runs it now.

—Pauli.

—He's asked about you.

—How is he?

—Well. Knock on wood, Oskar.

He was quiet for a time. —When did this start happening, these changes? he asked. —How long ago?

She sighed quietly, more a contraction than a sound. —Nothing has really happened yet.

—But you're worried about Pauli? Truly worried?

She shrugged. —He has a little girl.

He squinted again at the hillside, frowning slightly, remembering Pauli and Old Ryslavy and the Hof and his favorite table there, then all at once remembering his age, every year of it. Even the war seemed long ago.

—I did read your letters, Maman. I didn't believe about the changes, that's all. She watched him as he said this. He couldn't make out her face in the dark but her head had turned toward him. He took a breath.

—There was so much exaggeration everywhere around us. This whole time. He paused. —I can't explain it. We didn't get very much news. Not much that was clear. There were rumors. I wanted to believe there had been changes. If there had been changes I could have come back. He paused a moment. —Or I wanted nothing to change, if you prefer. That could be. He laughed.

She looked at him. —How do things seem to you now?

He frowned again. —Well. They seem the same.

—They're not the same, Oskar.

He stood close beside her, leaning slightly over. —What is it with Pauli? he said. —Trouble with Rindt?

—Mmm.

—Rindt's thick with the Black Shirts, is he?

She didn't answer.

—That greasy bastard.

—Yes, Oskar. She sighed.

He laid his hand on her shoulder. There was precious little under the wrap to indicate it held part of a living human being. He felt her breathe in, a slight shifting of the bones. —Having you away did nothing to lighten the years, she said almost in a whisper.

—I was ill, Maman. And then I was married.

—If you choose to call it that.

He took his hand away and laid it against the pane of the door. —Come in off the verandah now, for God's sake.

—In a minute.

—In a minute, then. He stepped into the parlor and shut the door behind him, leaving her there, swaddled tightly in her blankets, motionless and austere.

Gasthaus Rindt on closer inspection appeared much the worse for wear. Voxlauer recognized in passing some of the drunks of his youth splayed in wicker chairs on the patio and men who might possibly have been their sons equally drunk beside them, basking sleepily in the noonday light. A dry snow wisped around the tables. Many of the window frames were boarded over and paper sacks of cement lay like sandbags in the foyer. A woman in *Trachten* watched him from the entryway. He wished one man he remembered a good morning and crossed the avenue to Ryslavy's.

The Niessener Hof by comparison still seemed more or less hale, though a few windows on the upper floors had been nailed shut and some tiles looked to have loosened along the gutters. The façade had recently been given a fresh coat of lime and the vestibule as he entered it appeared in good repair. Most of the tables were empty but a fair-sized crowd stood parceled along the bar. He leaned over as unobtrusively as he could and asked the girl drawing drafts where he might find Herr Ryslavy. —In his office, said the girl with a lazy wave behind her.

Ryslavy was in a small windowless room just off the kitchen, slumped deep in an old cowhide chair with his back to the door, shouting into a telephone. The room itself seemed barely an office at all but rather a storeroom for wine crates and bottles of pilsner.

Voxlauer watched from the kitchen for a while, then tapped lightly on the doorframe. Ryslavy turned at the sound and looked up at him a moment, then mumbled his excuses and hung up the receiver. He regarded Voxlauer a few seconds further, scratching his round stubbled chin, then rose slowly from the chair. —I'd expected a Cossack, he said, stepping forward.

—You should have seen me yesterday. I looked like Genghis Khan.

—Much better, said Ryslavy. His teeth as he smiled were the color of weathered pinesplints. He shifted restlessly from foot to foot. —The least you might do is look your age, for the love of God.

—You should have seen me yesterday, said Voxlauer.

The floor was carpeted in varicolored receipts, some of them still bearing the blue K&K of the imperial notary. A fly rod of red lacquered bamboo hung in a corner above an oliveskin tackle bag. The air stank of pipe fumes and carbon ink. Ryslavy stood a moment longer, then slipped around the desk. —A cautionary note: I've done nothing since you left but get fat. And go fishing.

—Two not unrelated pastimes.

—And breed. I have a daughter now. The fair Emelia.

—Maman told me. I believe I passed her at the bar.

—Yes.

—Or was that the missus?

Ryslavy made a face. —Ecch! The missus. Run off with an American, two years ago this April.

—An American?

—A stinking unwashed bugger.

—I'm sorry to hear that.

Ryslavy kept quiet.

—Sorry to have missed it, actually.

—A Baptist, believe it ot not, said Ryslavy, smiling. —The genuine article. A preacher of some stripe or other. If I wasn't an atheist beforehand I definitely am one now.

. . .

They sat at a table in a hall off the kitchen, sipping pilsner from wide ceramic mugs, looking out across the square. Ryslavy packed his pipe fussily. He looked over at Voxlauer. —You look tired.

—I am. I'm perpetually tired.

—What was her maiden name?

—Rhyukina. Voxlauer turned his mug back and forth. —We were never married.

Ryslavy chewed his pipestem. —Of course I heard all of this from your mother, he said carefully. —I've felt like your older brother through this whole affair. I feel that way now.

—I know it.

—It's a complicated time you've chosen. For Emelia and me especially.

—I know. I didn't choose it.

They sat quietly awhile. Ryslavy lit his pipe. —Do you need money?

—Thank you. No.

—We'd love to take you on here if you did, now that you've been shaved and powdered.

—I don't need any money. I've been here half a week and already I'm sick to death of this place.

—I don't believe you.

—Well, I can't stay in town.

They sipped at their beer. Ryslavy drew his lips together.

—I don't understand, Oskar. Your mother—

—I was hoping to hire on somewhere near to here. As a cowsenner, maybe.

—Never come to town?

—Just to see her.

Ryslavy smiled. —And the rest of us can go to hell? Is that it?

Voxlauer looked out the window toward the patio at Rindt's.

—Your silence has been duly noted, said Ryslavy. He took a swallow of beer. —You've not changed as much as one might have hoped. That is very obvious.

Voxlauer shrugged. —I never had much love for this town, Pauli.

—But the people in it, Oskar! said Ryslavy, setting down his mug and frowning. —The people in it.

—Yes. The people in it. My father and my mother. Well, my father is dead and you know that very well and everyone here knows it. And they know one or two other things about me, too, or so I gather. But they couldn't know less about why I left or why I came back. He paused to breathe, leaning forward in his chair.

—Of course they couldn't, Oskar. I didn't mean you owed them anything.

—Or you, either. Or her.

—No.

Voxlauer closed his eyes. The breath was coming hard to him again, as it always did when things began to reel. He was right that he had to leave but he knew at that moment that they might not let him, Maman and Pauli and the rest. Uncle Gustl, Irma Gratzer, Kati Milnistch, all the others he'd not yet seen. He felt unsteady on the chair and lowered one arm carefully along the chairback. He expected to see Ryslavy staring at him when he opened his eyes but Ryslavy was looking quietly out the window, puffing on his pipe. Voxlauer closed his eyes again. After a time Ryslavy cleared his throat.

—I'm sorry about your father, Oskar.

—That's all right.

—I'd heard you've been sick.

—Yes.

—I never found out exactly what it was. Something from the war?

Voxlauer smiled. —Yes. Something from the war.

—What was it, exactly?

—It was attacks. He scratched the back of his neck. —Is attacks, I suppose.

—Attacks?

—Breathing trouble. That sort of business. Sometimes I see things.

Ryslavy raised his eyebrows. —What sort of things? Things from the war?

Voxlauer smiled. —Catholic things. You wouldn't understand, Pauli.

—The hell I wouldn't. I'm an honorary Catholic, on account of my firm belief in alcohol. Ask any of your papist brethren.

—I don't like talking about it much.

—Oh, said Ryslavy. They sat quietly again.

—Has it gotten any better? said Ryslavy after a time.

Voxlauer dug his hands into his pockets and hunched forward, the toes of his boots pressed together under the table. Outside in the square a sparse dry snow was falling. —I thought it had, he said.

In the evening they drank on and played tarok and ate from huge heaping platters of cutlets and tatterbread dumplings. The girl came to clear the table and sat in on a few rounds. —Emelia, this is your old Uncle Oskar, said Ryslavy. —Oskar, Emelia.

—Pleased to meet you, Uncle, said the girl, smiling down at her cards.

After the round was played she stood up from the table and returned a short while later with a tray of prosciutto and melon and smoked sections of trout. They laid the fish on small wedges of oven-crusted bread, spattered the wedges and the fish with butter, then laid them whole onto their tongues.

—Ah. That's lovely, said Voxlauer, leaning back.

—Fish want swimming, as they say, said Ryslavy, producing a thin yellow wine bottle from under the table. He poured the wine into two tall-stemmed glasses and proceeded to tell Voxlauer about stickle trout and river trout and the subtleties between them, in the water and in the pan, and his lease of spawning rights to the ponds in the valley above Holzer's Cross. How word of his fish had spread to such a degree that it had grown necessary to install a pensioner in the valley as a warden, and, later, how the old man had become erratic with drink and for the last winter of his life could most often be found across the square at Rindt's, splayed out cold across the benches. Voxlauer listened to it all patiently and closely.

—In October we caught three boys buckshotting from the poor bugger's own boat, said Ryslavy with a gesture of absolution. —With his own damned shotgun.

—What happened to him?

—We found him in a snowdrift last January. In his overcoat and drawers. Daughter still collects his pension. She's a something, said Ryslavy, smiling.

—What does that mean? said Voxlauer.

—A queer one. Used to teach school down at Brunner's Cross. Looks a bit Yiddish, which is a fine thing, I'll tell you, because the old drunk was a bastard of a Yid-hater all his days. Hated Papa something fierce. Not enough to refuse a little schnapps money now and then, of course.

—Of course.

Ryslavy grinned. —She's a something, anyhow.

—I'm sure she is. What about this cottage, then?

—A room with a roof over it. Ryslavy shrugged. —A chimney.

—How far up valley?

—By the farther pond. You remember, Oskar. On that soggy piece of marsh by the runoff.

—I might remember.

—Well, there you have it.

—Well: if I have it already, then I'll take it, I suppose, said Voxlauer. —You've talked me into it.

Ryslavy looked at him uncertainly. —Beg pardon?

—Thank you, Pauli, said Voxlauer. —I'll take it. He said it again over Ryslavy's slurred objections and repeated his decision with a violence that startled even the girl who'd returned and stood watching them from the swinging doors, holding aloft a tray of candied pears.

—He refused me the same thing, she said sullenly.

Maman's face as he told her betrayed little or no surprise. She looked past him as he spoke, over his shoulder toward the gathering dusk over the ruin. —I suppose I couldn't have hoped for more than one week, she said.

—It's only up at the ponds, Maman. It's work.

She smiled. —We'll never see you anymore down here. Once a week for butter, maybe.

—It's work, he repeated.

She was already busy with the table for supper. —Gustl's coming tonight, she said brightly.

Gustl arrived on his bicycle punctually at seven. Voxlauer heard him cursing through the open parlor window and came out onto the verandah. —Hello, Uncle, he called down. Gustl waved up distractedly. He was pulling a grease-blackened length of chain from a tartan satchel, cursing to himself and spitting onto the gravel.

—Hark! the Bolshevik speaks. Wait till I get my hands on *you,* my boy.

—There's no need for the chain, Uncle, surely, hereabouts?

—Chancy days, Oskar. Chancy days. Gustl snapped closed the little padlock and tucked the key into his hatband and nodded. He squinted up at the verandah. —Where's that infamous beard?

—Growing in.

—Aha!

—Maman! Gustl's here.

—I hear him, she said, coming out onto the stairwell. —Tell him to bring some pilsner up from Gottschak's.

—I have it already, Dora, laughed Gustl.

They sat on three sides of the parlor table over which a white cloth had been spread eating noodles and cabbage and boiled halved potatoes and bitter canned peas in watered butter. Every now and again Maman kicked him hard under the table.

—Ah! I see what you mean, Uncle.

—Do you, Oskar? A damn lot's come clear these last few years. Not that it helps the poor serf any.

—It hasn't helped you, then.

—Not a scratch. The flour-jew takes my grain same as always.

—If you're lucky, Gustl, said Maman.

Gustl rotated his head wearily. —Luck, my dear sister, doesn't enter into the equation. In thirty-five years of groveling for a fair-set price and getting pulled by the prick every time it never once has.

Voxlauer smiled. —Ouch! How does that feel, Uncle?

—Don't set him going again, Oskar.

—I'm only saying. Sounds like out-and-out bad luck to me.

Gustl set his fork down carefully. —Was it bad luck the Jew invaded this country, not as an army but by stealth, and connived through ceaseless intrigue to leach the bounty from our German soil? It was not. Gustl stopped to clear his throat, paused briefly for effect, then recommenced. —Was it bad luck he brought Bolshevism—if you'll pardon me, Oskar—into Europe? Not at all. Rather it was the result of a thousand years' inveterate scheming. You, I suppose, can be excused your confusion. He raised his fork augustly to his lips.

Maman's chair back creaked loudly as she straightened in it. —Good Lord, Gustl. You sound just like a hut-country Schönerer. What do we care about German soil, of all things?

Gustl looked back and forth between them, eyes wide open and compassionate. —I don't know which of you is more in need of a contemporary newsmagazine, he said finally.

The next morning she found him in the linden grove working the hard smooth ground with a loose-handled rake. What scrub there was among the trees had been piled in a clearing and weighted down with stones from the creek bed. —What's that scrub pile for? she asked.

—I don't know, said Voxlauer.

—When will you be going?

—I don't know.

She stood for a few moments beside him without moving or speaking, not looking at him, not looking away. —Don't you? she said quietly.

—Tomorrow, said Voxlauer.

The sun was just inclining over the verandah wall as he made ready to go. He asked if he might borrow some books from the parlor to read in the evenings and she nodded her head yes. He took an old animal lexicon, a guide to butterflies and moths, and a clothbound *Selections from Goethe,* fraying along the spine and edges. He wrapped the books in waxed paper and took the provisions she'd bought for him and folded his linen and packed everything down with a green oilcloth tarpaulin in the bottom of his pack. He asked if he could take some of the photographs and she stood still a moment, frowning. —I can't imagine what you'd be needing those for, she said. Instead she brought him two cabled wool sweaters that had once been his father's and a green pressed wool cap. —Is he letting you fish, at least?

—As much as I like.

—Père's reel is under the roof.

—I won't need it.

—Well, she said.

—Well.

—I hope you'll shave before coming to town.

—I'll need Père's razor, then.

She went to the kitchen and returned with the razor and a brush. She looked younger for a brief moment, coming out onto the verandah. He remembered her face the day he'd left for the Isonzo and realized with a start he was nearly older now than she'd been then. She was looking past him. —I don't know what I was expecting, she said. —Not this, though. That's for certain.

—There's a road now, Pauli tells me. Up from Pergau. You could have Irma drive you sometime.

—Werner's car is in the shop.

—Maman.

—You're right. She smiled and kissed his cheek. He bent down to receive it and felt the dry press of her lips and the crepe-paper folds of her skin against his face. Then he stepped past her and shouldered his pack and left the house.

After stopping in at the Niessener Hof for breakfast and the key he walked up past the old gymnasium with Ryslavy close beside him. —There's a snake rifle and shotgun in a locker by the stove, Ryslavy was saying. —They'll both need some cleaning. There's oil and forty shells, I think, in one of the cupboards. And a can of loose shot somewhere, if I remember rightly.

—I could use that for fishing, said Voxlauer.

—Please use the rods, Oskar. Please. The green spoons are best for the fast water between the beds. On the slow current use something fatter. Try the orange tags.

—Don't mother me, Pauli. Anything but that.

—I'll visit, said Ryslavy. —Next week. He slapped Voxlauer on the back and waved him on where the road wound past the last empty barns. Voxlauer couldn't help noticing that his expression as he stood in the road looking up and waving was one of relief.

The valley was little more than a saddle of damp earth hung at three-quarters height between the humped Birker hills to the north and a crescent of yellow cliffs to the southwest and west. It began at a wooded pass above a shingle-roofed reliquary on the old Holzer property and sloped down in a lazy bend along the steep muddy feet of the cliffs. The walls of the valley were high and pine-covered, but the banks of the creek that began below the pass turned a brimming green in summer and drew legions of butter-flies. As a boy he'd spent hours by the ponds with a whisk and a canning jar, chasing damselflies low along the water only to see them vanish in a sudden spray and flash of copper. He'd fix his eyes firmly on the spot until another flew past him, oil-colored in the slanting light, and the game would begin again.

After an hour's walk through the pine-bound soil of the woods under Holzer's Cross he came onto a road of crushed tile leading up to the farm. A little farther on he found the entrance to the val-ley, bare and blown clear of snow under the dull white sky. The road to the ponds broke away to the left and set its curve in the shelter of a dense spruce plantation. He kept on past the crum-bling reliquary and the down-valley fork to a blue-plastered house from which a line of smoke was rising. He left his pack at the gate and swung his legs over the fence and called up a good day to the house.

A woman in a felt jacket came to the door and opened it and called to him to come up. She nodded to him as he climbed the steps and led him without speaking into a water-stained anteroom. Her hair was drawn back in a dark silk babushka and her shoulders were wrapped in a woolen shawl. How like Anna's mother she looks, thought Voxlauer. Resigned and kindly. I suppose they look the same everywhere, these old farmers' wives. Maman could never be mistaken for one of them. —I'm sorry to trouble you, he said, bowing slightly.

—Ach! said the woman. She took his coat and ushered him into the kitchen matter-of-factly. —Come in out of the weather, young Herr.

—Oskar Voxlauer, said Voxlauer, bowing again and smiling.

—Elke Mayer, said the woman. —Fine to meet you. Rest your legs a bit, if you'd care to, Herr Voxlauer.

—Thank you. I'm Paul Ryslavy's new gamekeeper, he said, sitting down at the window table.

—I know. Herr Ryslavy telephoned just this morning.

—You have a telephone here?

—This is not Russia, said the woman, smiling.

—No it isn't. I was hoping to buy some bacon from you. Or sausage.

—We have bacon and ham. Would you like some fresh cream?

—Thank you kindly.

She brought out the ham and a jar of cream and set it on the table. Then she poured milk from a blue steel pitcher into a crockery mug and measured out a thimbleful of schnapps and poured it into the mug and set the bottle down. The milk was still warm from the udder and a skein of yellow cream clotted at its meniscus. The schnapps gave the milk a warm pink opalescence, like firelight on a snowdrift. She poured a second cup for herself.

—Prost, he said, lifting his glass.

—Prost.

From a scrap of butcher's paper at the end of the table she unwrapped a small pumpernickel roll and a quarter of twice-smoked bacon. She cut the bacon into long fatty strips just thin enough to let light through and laid two cuts apiece on thick slices of roll. —Mahlzeit, she said. Voxlauer thanked her again. The bacon was wonderfully chewy and well salted and mixed gloriously with the schnapps. They ate awhile in silence, watching the light brightening and dimming over the treetops and roofs of the town far below them.

—Old Ryslavy was clever to buy land when he did, said the woman after a time. —Lumber's near the only sure money trade nowadays. She refilled his cup.

—There's the Niessener Hof, besides, said Voxlauer.

—We'll see where that gets him, said the woman. He looked at her again. She had the look of someone past worrying about other people's affairs, but only just. He thought again that she reminded him of someone, not Anna's mother now, but someone else. An aunt possibly. He felt very young sitting there in her kitchen drinking his schnapps in milk. She looked out the window now, smiling a little. —All stripes of people are moving onto the mountain lately. It's becoming quite a settlement.

—What do you mean?

—Well, the colony, firstly, down at Pergau. Ice baths and nakedness and so forth. She shook her head. —And then there's all the people come to fish Herr Ryslavy's ponds.

Voxlauer laughed. —What's this down in Pergau? A retreat or some such?

The woman rolled her eyes. —The good Lord knows, Herr Voxlauer. We poor fools can only gossip.

—Who else is there?

—Well, the schoolteacher is another. On the Pergauer saddle.

—Pergau is a good few miles off.

—Tell that to the nudists, said the woman. She laughed. —They're great ones for marches.

They sat awhile longer in the darkening room, talking about the colony and a similar group down in Villach whose members had been arrested that fall for parading in the Stadtpark wearing nothing but fig leaves and winter slippers. They talked about their families and discovered they were distantly related to one another on their fathers' sides. Voxlauer paid her for the jar of cream and the ham and attempted to give her something for the schnapps but she refused. Outside the window the light was slowly leaving the hillside. She stood after a time and left the room and returned a moment later with a paraffin lamp which she lit and set down on the table. —You'd best be going soon, she said. —My sons will be coming in and they're sure to be unpleasant. They're no friends of Ryslavy's.

—Why not?

The woman hunched herself over and made a hooking gesture with two fingers from the bridge of her nose. She looked at him and shrugged.

—I see, said Voxlauer. He thanked her for her kindness and left.

By the time he came down off the pass it was drizzling and dark and a yellow mist rose from the ditch along the roadside. The road passed between two fenced pastures unused in winter and entered a second grove of close-set spruce trees. At the far end of the grove three beehouses marked the border of Ryslavy's land.

The beehouses had once been painted red, green and orange respectively, and strips of curled enamel still clung here and there to the buckling wood. Voxlauer opened the door of the first and looked inside. The interior was arranged like a cabinet with four deep-set shelves, the upper two mortared thickly over with honeycomb. Now and then a sluggish brown drone emerged and dragged itself from one chamber to another. Voxlauer followed one in with his thumb and drew out a long gray-brown splinter of honey.

When he arrived at the last turning above the ponds he caught a faint scent of smoke and the scant lights of Pergau came briefly into view. The road dipped all at once into a pine-filled depression and emerged just as quickly along the ice-covered water. A kerchief of new snow floated over the ice, diffusing the dim light of the stars into milk. The noise of his steps was likewise diffused by the snow and he passed through the low trees in silence. At the far end of the pond he found a rowboat frozen to its mooring, nearly invisible in the darkness under its snow-covered wrap. The ice against the boat's side was black and clear of snow and held pebble-sized globes of air fixed in rows within it like schools of tiny fish. He leaned against the boat, then kicked it, but it refused to move.

The lower pond was separated from the upper by a thin line of rapids. The road cut along the south bank in three quick turnings and crossed on cemented plank pilings to the broad northern lee of the water just above the pond's mouth. Set against the slope on this wedge of flat ground was a cottage. It glowed bonelike in the dark with the tall trees behind it and its round, porthole-shaped windows set like sockets into the blank white plaster. The door had been barred with two heavy barrels, one of which now lay overturned, spilling food tins and newspaper in a fan-shaped confusion over the snow. Fox tracks and weasel tracks scattered in all directions over the powder and showed clean as picture negatives on the gravel underneath. Voxlauer righted the fallen barrel and moved it to the left of the lintel and took the key from his pocket and turned it in the corroded lock chamber. The hinges of the door complained loudly as he forced it open. A smell of sweat and sour woodsmoke greeted him as he stepped inside and slid the door shut behind him on the blossoming cold.

The room Voxlauer had entered was damp and low-ceilinged and bent at its middle around a crockery stove. A narrow bench ran along the stove and he set his pack on it and fumbled in the dark after matches. He found a kerosene lantern and turned it on its side until he could smell the gas, then struck a match and righted the lantern and surveyed the cottage by its light.

To the left of the stove under a deep, ventlike window a table had been propped against the buckling wall. A chair lay beside it, thrown back onto the floor as though stood up from hurriedly. A hunting locker stood open in a corner. The crick of the room formed an alcove of sorts, hidden from his sight, and crossing to it he found a packed straw pallet bearing the imprint of a small, huddled body, like a thumbmark in tallow. A film of silver hair lined the topmost depression. The heaped woolen blankets reeked cloyingly of urine and he pulled them from the bed and went to the locker and stuffed them inside. The blankets, too, were covered in hair, short and stiff as a terrier's.

With great effort he managed to pull the mattress from its wooden bedframe and taking a poker from the floor he began to beat the shape out of the canvas in a flurry of straw, hair and dust. The old man looked to have been very slight, from the width of the silhouette, and crook-backed. Voxlauer pictured him there asleep, drawn in under the blankets, the steady rasp of his breathing filling the little room. I'll be like that soon, he thought. But my hair will be white. Père's was near to it when I left. He remembered a letter to the front, the last from both of them: *Maman is getting shrew-ish. She's frowning at me, but it's so. We're both gone senile with worry. Can it be true things on the lines are as desperate as you say? This pains me very badly. The feelings you mention are under-standable but you must never doubt in the eventual victory of Franz Josef our Kaiser. To disbelieve this is a terrible thing Oskar and you must not do it. The Germans started this godawful war in their pride and their death-mysticism but by Christ we will end it for them. I wish above all else I could sit with you in your tunnels but I know you are not a coward and will do your duty come what may and return to us quickly. I miss you My Heart more than I can say. Please send only the best news for a time as I don't think I can bear the other.* That was all. And, later, in her hand: *Keep your head low in the trenches. Irma's Leo was killed last Saturday north of Udine lighting a cigarette. Père is feeling braver. Je t'aime, mon petit soldat! Maman.*

He went to the door and opened it and stood for a moment, breathing in the cold air, then propped it open and returned to the alcove. He sat for a while on the frame in the half-darkness, mut-tering to himself.

He felt worn and brittle, far older than his years. Older than Père had ever been. He sat without moving for a while. —Not quite, Oskar, he said aloud, leaning forward into the quiet. —A few years yet, for that. He looked carefully around the room. I won't make those mistakes, he thought. No children. No wife. I could do it now and not trouble anybody.

Except Maman, he thought suddenly. Except her. He pictured her then as he had when he'd first gotten her hysterical sheet of scribble twenty years before: dressed in unbrushed black silks and veil with the pale sky above her, not listening to the apologetic sparrow-voiced peeping of the priest, all of Niessen crowding in behind, staring down at the long hole cut into the grass. Was that what she was expecting now? He breathed in effortfully and thought of Anna. She had wondered about him, expected it for a time, after he'd told her about Père.

In a way I have done it already, he thought. Not like Père, but worse: I have done it twice. Taken myself away. Again the crumpled and snow-sodden letter appeared before him, and he himself appeared, lying on a damp horsehair blanket the day before the twelfth offensive, reading her letter and feeling the inevitableness of it rising tidelike under him: *He has done the most bastard thing. The most hateful. The most selfish. The worst, only thing left my dear little boy* . . . And on and on in tight blank circles without meaning, not sparing him anything, every detail of that day down to the arrangement of the papers on the writing table, the cane-backed chair thrown down onto the floor, the tipped-over inkwell. And he thinking to himself in that first instant She's made poetry out of this, out of this thing, too . . . The boy in the upper bunk was leaning out into the crawl space and looking down at him, half smiling, curious.

—*What is it, Voxlauer?*

He hadn't moved or spoken, but gathered in his breath, weakly and raspingly, with a sound like a brush passing over a leather strap: *Ahhh. Ahh*

—*Voxlauer? Hey?*

—*What?*

—*You made a noise.*

—*Yes.*

—*What is it?*

—*It's my father.*

—*What?*

—*He's shot himself. Ahh. He's shot himself, do you hear*

Then a silence, blanketing and deep.

—*Oskar?*

—Ahhhh, said Voxlauer aloud, listening to the sound give out into the cold.

He rose and worked the mattress with the poker until the smell again made it difficult to breathe. He crossed the room to the door and caught his breath and returned to the mattress. When he had finished he hung the lantern from a hook above the door and went outside to the woodpile and brought in six quartered logs and an armful of kindling. Taking a broom and a dustpan from under the bench, he swept up the loose straw and emptied it into the stove mouth. The stove itself was thick with ash but he had no strength left to clean it. He laid on the kindling and the splints and started a fire and opened the stove vents. Then he spread his coat over the sour-smelling mattress and slept.

That night the hussars gave me a coat and a felt blanket and sat me among them round the fire. The images of my father as I imagined him, and the taps sergeant and the deserter, mixed and separated again until I couldn't think of any one of them without the other two crowding in behind. There was no difference, finally, between them: all three had died. They had each died badly and I'd had a part in their deaths and I had come away alive. The knowledge of this made me feel ghostlike and transparent and I wondered that no one around the fire seemed to notice. I had been solid and fully in my body before shooting the deserter but he had died very badly, slowly and in great pain, and I hadn't been able to fire a second time. Once he'd died and I knew that I was safe I'd been able to step away from the fact of myself a little and not think, only follow the hussars back to the tents. But now night had fallen and I was still not back in my body properly and in fact was trapped outside of it as the rest of them drank and cursed their superior officers and gossiped about the war.

They were a young regiment, excepting some of the officers, and a few of them were from Kärnten. One boy in particular, Alban I think his name was, was kind to me and shared a dram of watery schnapps and a little flake of chocolate. I found that in spite of what was happening I could drink and eat and talk to him very amiably. We exchanged addresses and promised we'd meet at the Niessener Hof for a drink sometime after the war, and he found me a bedroll and a coat and space in a tent with three other enlisted men. The captain came round a short time later and promised to have me restored to my company by six-o'clock the following evening. The front's moved on some eighteen-odd miles, he said. We took Caporetto this morning in less than an hour. He was standing over me at the opening of the tent and speaking evenly and unexcitedly with the clear starry sky behind him. Appreciative murmurs rose up from the others. That's good, I said after a time, not thinking that it was, particularly, or thinking anything at all but saying it was because that was simplest. There was silence for a moment. I looked up at the captain; he seemed to be waiting for me to say something more.

That's good, I repeated. I suppose it's the Germans, sir?

It's the gas, he said, turning on his heels and leaving.

The next morning as we climbed through a dense belt of firs I broke off from the column and struck down into the trees. The company had thinned into loose clusters of men beating paths through the brush and my leaving went unnoticed. I felt indifferent to this, whether or not I had been seen, feeling that I was dead already. I'd been killed by the gas or the cold or the smell in the air or by the man I had killed; how I'd died made not the slightest difference. Where I was to drop, when eventually I did, made no difference either except that I knew it should not be in the snow in a trench like the taps sergeant, with the smell of gas and burnt powder all around me.

At the lower edge of the firs the slope steepened and the cover spread apart and I half slid, half stumbled downhill over the tamped snow, brushing tips of buried saplings as I went. One hour later I reached the old front and a few hours after that I was standing at the gate of the first farmstead leading down to Laibach. From where I stood I could see the empty plaza and the kapelle and the station behind it where we'd begun our march. It was just past midday, breezy and mild. I followed the fence to the back of the house.

The yard seemed deserted, empty of stock and people, and I approached the house cautiously and rapped on the door. After a while I pushed it open and stepped inside. Standing around the kitchen in various poses of laziness and disinterest were seven men

*carrying repeating rifles, dressed in tattered blue fatigues. I looked
at them for a moment or two, then put up my hands.*

*The men looked me over for a time. We thought maybe you
were the milkmaid with the milk, said one of them. He spoke with
a slow, heavy accent I took at first to be Hungarian. He watched
me a little while longer, then motioned to me to lower my arms. I
let them fall, saying nothing. What are you doing here? asked the
man. He was looking at my private's coat and holster.*

Looking for breakfast, I answered.

*He snorted. Well, you won't find any here, little man. Believe
me, we should know already. Just an old whore strung up by her
garters in the cow shed. One of the men made a sign of the cross
behind him. The first man shrugged.*

I don't believe you, I said.

Do we look like we've eaten? he said tiredly.

*I looked from one to another of them around the little room.
One by one each of them returned my gaze out of droop-eyed,
jaundiced faces. Not much, I said. The man smiled again and
nodded.*

*There were nine of them in all, deserters from a Czech battery spe-
cializing in minelaying. A number of them had kept their wire-
stripping and cutting tools and we used these to cut locks and
chicken wire in a long chain of farms running north and east into
Hungary. As the Czechs could no better return to Bohemia than I
could to Kärnten we decided to continue east over the wide rolling
plain to Budapest. We slept during the day in windbreaks or in little wooded depressions and traveled after dark, stealing here and
there from farmers as we went. When anybody saw us we chased
after them a little, waving our guns and yelling.*

*We kept due east, more or less, skirting the towns, our only
idea to get as far from Austria as we could before the war ended.
We were all convinced we would win the war with the new gas
from Germany and that afterward deserters would be hunted*

down and murdered. The man who had first spoken to me, Jan Tobacz, a dentist from Prague, had a wife and child staying with relatives in Budweiss and was terrified they might be shot. This was the first time I'd thought about the Empire as something altogether different in the east than we thought of it at home, something vast and full of strange designs, a thing to keep well clear of. Jan himself came from a wealthy Prague family and had never questioned the architecture of things, as he termed it, until going to the war. He'd been on the Isonzo front for nearly two years and had spent the better part of his second year planning his desertion. We became friends over the following weeks and talked about the war and our decision to leave it until we were both of us free of any doubt. I came to see the restlessness of my last few years as the inevitable response to the smallness of Niessen, to its baubles-and-penance religion, to borrow another of Jan's phrases, and to the way we'd had of living at a remove from things, discouraging all but a few friendships, keeping my father's condition hidden as long as we could. Jan was something of a socialist and under his direction I came to view my past life as an haut-bourgeois evil and my father's filigreed, salon-ready compositions as its most grotesque flowering. I began to blame the music, Niessen, the war, and anything else I could think of for my father's death. The farther east we traveled the more my disgust grew at all that I had been raised to cherish and admire, from the French we had spoken each night at the dinner table to my mother's cultivated fondness for Italian sweets.

I had my seventeenth-birthday supper in a field by an open well for oxen, somewhere just southwest of Budapest: two autumn hares in a little brass tureen with a carrot and a spoonful of rancid butter. Welcome to the rest of life, Jan said proudly. I felt old, looking at him, and terrifyingly clear-headed. I knew even then that I'd not see Niessen again as a young man.

Two or three nights later we came to a small farm on the city's outskirts, a few low plaster buildings with sloping roofs set around a pond on a parcel of steep, muddy ground. We hadn't eaten for two days and stared across the dull brackish water at the lights of the house. We waited a long time for them to go out, sitting on our rucksacks in the damp grass. There seemed to be a party going on. Finally Jan muttered something in Czech to two of the men and they stood and walked around the pond to the gate. We watched them go. Isn't it a little dangerous, with everyone awake? I asked.

Jan laughed. I've only sent them to beg, Oskar.

We waited in silence. Suddenly there was a shout and the gate clattered open and the two Czechs came galloping full tilt around the pond. What the hell is it? Jan shouted once they'd reached us.

We're to come right in, they said, half in disbelief. Every one of us.

When we came to the house we found that a huge plank table had already been cleared and pushed into the middle of the kitchen, and long benches dragged out from the pantry. The farmer and his three sons greeted us warmly as we entered and motioned to us to sit down and begin. They told us in cheerful patchwork German that the lady of the house was boiling potatoes and cabbage and had gone to the smokehouse for another yard of sausages. We looked at them in blank confusion, sheepish in our hunger, not daring to ask any further questions or touch any of the food. After a few minutes of painful, friendly silence, broken only by the growling of our stomachs, the farmer's wife returned with a platter of smoked meats and a thick loaf of bread and set them down in front of us with a pitcher of pond-cooled beer. We must have sat dumbfoundedly for another moment blinking up at her because she laughed and lifted her upturned hands, saying Eat! Eat!

We looked at each other for a few seconds and then set in, all of us grinning now like idiots.

The wife spoke better German than her husband and as we ate she stood watching us proudly. She asked which regiment we'd deserted from and where we were headed. She was particularly curious as to how I'd come into the company. How did you happen east, then, little soldier? she asked me.

By accident, ma'am, I said, buttering a roll and smiling.

I know better, she said coyly.

What do you mean, please? said one of the Czechs. I looked up at the farmer's wife. Excuse me, ma'am? I said, my mouth full of bread.

She laughed, taking us all in with her sparkling black eyes. Come come, gentlemen! We're not so far as all that from the city. This country is very flat, she said, winking at her husband. News gets about.

I still don't understand, I protested.

She shrugged. There's a big strike tomorrow, in favor of the Seven Points. In Dzizny Square. Surely you knew about this? My husband will be going, and my sons. You may ride with them. To save yourself the marching, she said, breaking again into a grin.

I still sat staring at her blankly. Strike? I said.

The Bolsheviks, the farmer said loudly. The Bolsheviks, good gentlemens.

It was the first time many of us had heard that word.

The whining of the door hinges woke him early the next morning. The room was bright and cold. Bits of straw he'd missed in the night danced in spirals on the knotted clapboard floor and around the little table. The last of the fire had long since burned to ash and he felt small and frozen on the bed. He went to the stove and built another fire, shut the door and put on his coat and took out the provisions he'd bought at the farm and boiled some water and made a pot of coffee. He drank two scalding cups and felt the cold in his hands and legs slowly receding. Then he stood and crossed the room to the open locker.

In the locker were twenty-five rounds of bullets and a large box of shells for the shotgun. The shotgun and the rifle were both filthy with grease and the rifle's stock was badly pocked with shot holes. The fly rods, by contrast, looked pristine and chaste bundled carefully in cotton sheeting in a separate compartment. The flies were packed in narrow cork boxes, one to each box, and gave no sign of ever having been used. They shone against the mute brown of the cork like specimens from a South Seas expedition, bright and gaudy and mysterious. He lifted a blood-red fly and felt its weight-lessness and the curve of its tiny hook. He brought it to the window and marveled at its redness and tickled his nose with its feathers.

Out the window the forest was in sunshine and the surface of the pond sparked and glimmered where the furrowed ice gathered the snow-thaw. The barrel he'd righted lay overturned again and a fresh layer of garbage decorated the turf. A wetness in the air that could have been either the wetness of late fall or early spring gave the world an iridescence and a light in all its corners. But a cold current ran through the air still and quivered along the ground and above the water.

As he sat on the stoop a short while later working a rag through the chambers of the shotgun a figure appeared on the far side of the pond. It was dressed in a dark coat and heavy woolen pants and might have been mistaken for the figure of a man but for the hair which hung down from a gray loden cap and hid her face entirely. She held to the tree line and stepped briefly out into the sun by a stand of young birches before disappearing into the pines.

Voxlauer sat quietly for a moment. Then he picked up the rag and finished cleaning the shotgun, taking care to wipe the grit from around the hammer and pin. He took the hatchet from the wood-pile and picked out three quartered stumps and split the stumps into narrower splints and hacked the splints in half across their length and carried the stack inside to the stove bench. A few scraps of bark lay around the stove's grate and he gathered them up absently and heaped them into a little pile for kindling. Then he took up his hat and went outside.

The tracks came down out of the slope above the pond and hatched back and forth as the ground steepened. The boots were heavy enough to leave clear prints in the needle cover and he fol-lowed them up to an old logging road running west below the cliffs. He scrambled onto the road and headed east until it joined with another he recognized as leading up to the reliquary, then turned and carefully retraced his steps. Where she had stepped out into the sun a cut showed in the snowbank and beyond it were three deep, sharp-edged prints in the yellow mud. Her boots were new and thick-soled and threw small clots of dirt to the side with each step. A tear in a branch showed where she'd left the cover of the birches. Voxlauer walked back through the loose-flung trees to the bridge and the cottage, looking back every few steps over his shoulder.

That night Voxlauer lay awake and thought about the woman. She'd been coming from Pergau, or from the colony, possibly. She moves like an old man, he thought. Cautiously and tiredly. But she dresses like a member of the Red Guard. He felt his face wrinkle itself into a smile. A vision of Anna came to him then unbidden: Anna in her crepe dress, relic of better years, laughing at his parodies of the Kaiser. Ah, Franz Josef, she would say, nodding soberly. A terrible man, I'm sure. And he, Voxlauer, would say: No, not a terrible man, but a fool, and they'd talk awhile, without much interest or urgency, about the war or some other long-past thing. Anna in her dead husband's army clothes bent over stiffly behind the house, saluting tiredly as he pulled up in the battered trap. Voxlauer lay a few minutes longer staring upward in the darkness, then stood and felt his way to the table and lit the lantern.

Above the table were two shelves running the length of the wall, cluttered with tins and empty jars and sacks of nails and plaster. The upper shelf was too high to see onto properly and he pulled the chair over to it. It was filled with tins similar to those on the lower shelf, beans and spinach and pickled herring and others whose labels were torn or illegible from watermarks. At the end of the shelf he found a folio much like the one he'd looked through in the parlor a week before. He took it down and brought it to the table.

The folio held three pencil-and-gouache sketches on heavy paper: one still life and two portraits. The still life was drab and uninteresting to him but the portraits, one of a woman and the other of a long-haired child, were spare and delicate and very beautiful. Voxlauer sat at the table for a long time looking at them, holding them close to the lantern. The faces looked back at him starkly and directly, without reproach but also without any tenderness or goodwill. They were carefully drawn and the resemblance of the one face to the other was unmistakable. I'll ask Pauli about them next time, he thought. The old man, Bauer, must have done them. He sat awhile longer at the table, remembering what few details Pauli had told him, before putting the lantern out finally and going to sleep.

A noise roused him a few hours later and he sat up at once, rigid and stock-still, feeling for the wall with his fingertips. The fire had gone out and he had no idea whose bed he was in or by what force he'd arrived there. All was in blackness and he felt numb and far from things. The sweat ran cold between his shoulder blades and he stripped off his shirt and rose from the bed and listened. The sound came again like the scraping of bootheels over gravel, clear and insistent. He remembered now where he was and looked about him for the rifle, stepping silently toward it in the dark. The steel of the barrel felt cold to the touch and he held it uneasily a moment, shifting from foot to foot. Then he put it down and went to the door.

The door shuddered as it swung open and he heard them scampering away before he saw them, a large fox and two half-grown cubs, pausing a moment at the edge of the turf with their huge eyes reflecting the starlight. They were slender and dark and their ruffed tails stood out straight behind them. They seemed reluctant to leave, out of curiosity or hunger, perhaps, or simply out of weariness from the cold. The nearer of the two cubs held the spine of a trout in its teeth like a diadem. Its tail quivered and beat against the air. It sniffed and bobbed and came nearer to him in slow winding loops. At one point he could have leaned over and blown onto its fur as it let the bones drop and nosed further into the barrel. Voxlauer sat quietly in the snow with his breath twisting upward in little plumes, raveling and curling. Eventually he made to gather in his coat and they bolted as one creature noiselessly into the pines.

The numbness was gone now and he found himself excited and unable to sleep. He lit the lantern and brought it to the table and took the guide to flowers and butterflies from his pack and leafed slowly through it. The illustrations glowed like the flies in

Ryslavy's tacklebox, bright and otherworldly. He sat at the table with his eyes closed, recalling the butterflies of the valley, swallowtails and beys and mourning cloaks, their wings barely heavy enough to cut the air. The colors he remembered were dark and saturated with a muddy fire and the brown of pine resin and standing water. He saw again his arms bare past the elbow reaching deep into the hollow green body of the pond and vanishing among the drab hairlike plants along its bottom. His father or someone else was steering the boat and calling to him not to fall in.

When Voxlauer woke the morning was already showing gray behind the cliffs and a high peeping birdsong limned down to him from the tree line. His bones ached fiercely and he shivered awhile in his coat, keeping his eyes open and listening. The song clattered to its height, broke, then beat its way upward again. He had the feeling of having forgotten a dream and tried for a time to remember it with no success. After a few attempts he stood up from the chair, went to the stove and started a fire. Then he went to the bed and lay down on it and watched the light grow slowly in the little room.

This room hasn't changed in a hundred years, he thought. Longer. Look at it. Four white walls and a table and a stove. A mattress with a body stretched on it. The only change has been that body. And that's no change at all, really, one body to another. This room was unchanged all the years I was with Anna and it was unchanged when I was in Italy and it was unchanged before that. The thought of Italy tightened his throat as always and he guided his attention patiently back to the room around him. The wide uneven floorboards, the roof beams, the cracked and scaling plaster. When was this room last whitewashed? he wondered. I'll see to that in the spring. He closed his eyes. The thought that the room had remained unchanged lulled him into a reluctant calm. I could forget my own name in this room, he thought. Without drink or company. He thought again about the old man. —There's no life here at all, he said aloud. He smiled. He knew this was a lie but he enjoyed it the way a child enjoys telling lies to itself, secretly and slyly. Sometime after that he opened his eyes and got up from the bed.

. . .

We slept that night on bales of hay dragged down from the barn loft and lined up in neat rows in the courtyard. The next morning the sons woke us early and brought us coffee from the kitchen. We went out with our packs and climbed into one of two deep-bedded carts pulled by mules and tried our best to fall back asleep. As we pulled out onto the road the wife's face appeared in the kitchen window and beamed down at us. She called out something in Hungarian to her husband and laughed, then leaned further out the window and waved until the curve of the hill rose up and hid the house.

We rode five to a cart, sitting on stiff, suitcase-sized haybales, smoking our first cigarettes since leaving the Isonzo. The morning sky was just beginning to admit the haze of noon around its edges and I felt easy and content. The flat stubbled fields rose and fell in low humpbacked ridges as we made our way down the long escarpment into the capital. Now and again we'd stop at a crossing or a rail junction where two or three men would be waiting, clutching baskets of bread or cheese or wine with a carefree, festive air, as though going to a picnic.

No one seemed particularly surprised by our presence; if anything, it seemed to be taken as a proof of something. The greatness of the city, I supposed. Talking with the youngest son, who spoke a smattering of German, I gathered people were coming from far and wide to watch the strike. When I asked him about the Bolsheviks he grinned and slapped me on the shoulder. They stopped the war, he said.

When?

Just now.

How? I said sleepily. I didn't believe him about the Bolsheviks or even that the war was over. Someone was always saying that the war was over and everyone was always in a hurry to believe it. How did they stop it? I said again, grinning a little, half in anticipation of a joke.

He shrugged. No tsar, no fighting. He looked proudly over at his father, who sat in front driving the mules. My father says he *maybe march today. Our uncle is in a factory for rubber. But today nobody works in it. You see? He laughed again.*

I didn't answer. The close-cropped fields were gradually giving way to chestnut groves and clusters of clay-roofed houses. That coat is good, said the son, eyeing my woolen field jacket unabashedly. It was very cold in Italy?

Very, I said. I looked at his thick sheepskin vest. Would you like to trade?

Not bad for you, smiled the son. He took off the vest and passed it over to me. He was smaller than I was and my jacket hung tentlike from his bony shoulders. That'll keep you warm in winter, I said.

Or in prison, said Jan. The others laughed.

When we reached the center of town the streets were already full to overflowing. Police and Civil Guardsmen were running around in a panic, trying to coax the massed crowds back against the houses. Half a mile from the river we were forced to tie up the carts and continue on foot. Everywhere people were shouting and drinking and acting as if the war really were over, drumming against streetlamps and house doors and passing carriages, dancing with arms linked on the curbs. I moved forward as if in a trance, watching the people on all sides laughing, howling, bellowing, jeering openly at policemen and files of soldiers as they crowded past, writing insults to the Kaiser and the Crown of Hungary in school chalk on the walls and pavements. For the first time, moving cautious as an ant through the crowds, hidden in them and a part of them at once, it dawned on me that I might actually get away. More than that—I began to think for myself again, crushed and jostled into consciousness by the massing bodies. The idea came to me then, calmly and quietly at first, of the thing that I was going to do.

Closer to the square the crowds grew even denser. The march had already begun and as we crossed Theresien Avenue a huge roar went up in front of us. The farmer and his sons elbowed their way forward, calling out the name of the uncle's factory like a marching hymn: Sol-ya . . . Sol-ya . . . Sol-ya . . . Another roar went up, booming back over our heads. Things were happening close by but we could see next to nothing. People were climbing onto each other's backs, but the sway of the crowd threw them down again just as quickly. The farmer and his eldest son were wide-shouldered and bullet-headed and they pressed ahead ruthlessly, the rest of us falling meekly in behind them. All at once we were heaved forward into the linked arms of a row of terrified policemen. Through their shoulders I could see the wide empty square with the river behind it, slow and austere, and on the far bank the city of Buda curving down on its yellow hill. Across from our street at each corner of the square, identical cordons of police held identical masses restrained. Without warning a shout would erupt from one street or another, often a lone man's voice, and the other five streets would immediately thunder back in answer. In the middle of the square a battalion of K&K cavalry sat in orderly, expectant rows.

For a brief moment the crowd behind us fell back a little and grew still. In those few calm, deliberate seconds it was quiet enough to hear the horses shifting uneasily and shuddering under the riders. Then a new sound began on the opposite side of the square, building and carrying to us over the tops of the trees, and the crowds there pushed forward to each side in blind confusion. Gradually they flattened back against the houses to admit the marchers, who were pouring out now from all of the downtown avenues onto the square. The roaring to every side grew immeasurably louder. The police on the street hesitated a moment, looking over their shoulders at the cavalry, then simply broke rank and let us through.

It was clear from the very first that no one, not even the marchers, had expected such an awesome show of numbers. I was later to hear that it was the largest assembly in the history of the capital. A few minutes after the entrance of the first columns of workers, the square was so filled by the crush of bodies that it became impossible to tell the marchers from the spectators who had broken everywhere through the laughable restraining lines of the police. The noise was deafening, like no sound I'd yet heard; the cavalry unit had all but vanished in the tumult. Occasionally single riders could be seen swaying helplessly over the profusion of heads and fists, shrieking at their horses. The marchers were moving now in a ring around the square, droning one workers' anthem after another, and a song over and over again that I didn't yet recognize as the Internationale. Now and then the whole crowd would join in, monstrously out of key, most of them simply bellowing along with the prevailing din. I looked about me at one point and noticed Jan standing a few paces to my left. Is everyone in this city a Bolshevik? I shouted to him.

Opportunists, Oskar! Opportunists! he called back. He seemed to be enjoying himself immensely. We laughed for a moment across the sea of lowing faces at each other.

Somewhere in the maelstrom a man was crashing a pair of cymbals together. Two isolated shots rang out, one after the other, but no one paid any attention to them. Suddenly the crowd surged forward and heaved us flat onto the pavement. I barely had time to get on my feet before a second surge sent me stumbling out into the street. Marchers and onlookers milled together on every side, the wide-eyed policemen pressed too closely into them even to raise their blackjacks. I looked back over my shoulder and saw Jan's face falling away from me. I'm going east! I called to him. East! He waved once more, shouted something happily and was gone.

The cavalry were now gathered into a ring and huddled defensively on their mounts at the far edge of the park, firing shots into the air. The tide and current of the crowd had grown more violent, falling back from the riders grudgingly at each report and closing in again after only a few seconds. The entire scene was like nothing so much as a wide field of mud shifting in a heavy rain. Panic began to build in earnest now around the square, rocking and funneling the crowds, and in another instant I was thrown back from the cavalry as inexorably as I'd been carried toward them a few moments before. Out of the corner of my eye I saw one rider tilt and fall slowly sideways with his mount into the field of pitching heads. An instant or two later I was rushing down a narrow sloping street with a thousand others, all of us somehow one body and one brain, a column of state police and King's cavalry just behind us. And you thought you'd left the war behind, I thought, grinning stupidly to myself as I ran.

. . .

That same night I boarded a K&K train east from Luzni station to Czernowitz and the border. Everything everywhere was in the same state of witless confusion. There were rumors that the Kaiser was offering all of Hungary as a sop to the Bolsheviks. No one asked to see my ticket.

As we crept rattlingly up into the Carpathians I sounded out the merchants and retired officers in my carriage for news about the October Revolution and the armistice. All I could gather was that the Bolsheviks had formed an alliance with the Russian navy and simply declared the war with Germany to be over. A group of tsarist generals, Commander in Chief Dukonin among them, had refused to give up their armies and continued to fight German forces throughout Poland and Silesia, living in the woods like warlords. I had no idea how much of this could be believed. One old man, a retired taps lieutenant from Graz, swore the Tsar was in northern Hungary. He stuttered as he spoke and twisted the corners of his ash-gray muttonchops excitedly. He was convinced that I was an emissary of some kind until I confessed that I was in fact a deserter.

Well . . . he stuttered, adjusting himself in his seat uneasily. Perhaps you could petition the Tsar for some manner of asylum?

I don't think so, uncle, I answered. It wasn't his army I deserted from.

All the same, said a matronly woman in French-cut silks across the aisle. You can't very well run to the Bolshevists, can you, child?

Why not? I asked.

Well, said the ex-lieutenant, glancing up and down the car with well-intentioned watery eyes. Well . . . he began.

They've nothing to live for, really, interrupted a tiny, well-coiffed lady from across the table, running her plump hands along the teakwood inlay of the window-banks as if by way of exposition.

I'm going to them just the same. I'm a Bolshevik now as well, I said, drawing myself up proudly. Bolshevism, I continued, drawing on notions I'd mastered just two or three days previous, is an international movement. I raised a mud-stained finger. Along lines of class.

But not along yours, child! said the first woman kindly. I had made the mistake of telling them about my family.

There'd be no place for Karl Peter Voxlauers in their movement, I promise you, the ex-lieutenant put in.

Best thing that he's dead, then, I suppose, I said. That quieted them awhile.

They gave me a number of further reasons between them over the course of the afternoon and I listened to them all attentively and cheerfully, as though taking part in an elaborate burlesque. My desertion was taken as nothing more than a romantic breach of decorum; the war had long since grown distasteful to these people. The idea of an Austrian boy of fine Biedermeier stock feeling sympathy for the Revolution, on the other hand, was preposterous to them—inconceivable, in fact. They were forced, eventually, to ignore me.

Voxlauer spent the morning in a clearing on the north ridge, looking to scare up deer bedded down in the loose brush among the pines. Just past noon a buck sprang in a high trembling arc from its cushion of scrub and veered toward him and away again, galloping hard between the stumps. Voxlauer's stiff fingers worked the safety clumsily and the buck was almost out of range when he fired, both barrels discharging in the same instant and ramming the stock into his collarbone so his eyes teared and blurred. The deer stood at the edge of the clearing, quivering and heaving. He unbreeched the shotgun and levered out the smoking cartridges, moving nearer all the while over the uneven ground. The deer remained standing at the edge of the clearing. Its head lolled strangely and from where he now stood he saw the eyes rolling and bulging, witnessing nothing. Fishing two more shells from the pocket of his coat he reloaded the shotgun and raised it to his shoulder again and pulled both the triggers. The buck's head whipped hard to one side as the spray hit it and it staggered a few paces before falling over. By the time he reached it the breath was coming in rasps through its shot-mangled throat and its mouth was a pillow of pink foam. He cast about in the bracken for a rock to crush its skull with and found one of a fair size, but when he returned with it the buck was already dead.

He skinned it in strips and hung the strips from the branches of a leafless white bush close by and opened the belly and uncoiled the intestines and threw them into a heap. Next he cut out the stomach, which burst as he pulled it, the liver, the kidneys and the thick, bruise-colored heart. The stomach he tossed onto the pile with the intestines but the other innards he wrapped in a swath of deerskin tied tightly together with bailing wire. He spent the rest of the day butchering the venison and packing it into cubes bound in broader, heavier squares of the hide. When he'd finished he left the carcass for the foxes to find and fashioned a sack from a bedsheet he'd brought from the cottage and filled the sack with the bundles of meat, then took hold of the sack by its knotted, sodden corner and started awkwardly down the slope.

The sack was too heavy to lift and Voxlauer was forced to drag it behind him through the brush where it caught every few meters on a root or in branches and resisted his pull like a still-living thing. He cursed it steadily as he went, turning on it finally and threatening it, kicking at it with his boots until self-awareness returned to him suddenly and he began to laugh. It was dark already in the pines and he felt light-headed and discovered when he was halfway down the slope that he had no clear idea where he was going. He sat down in the needles with the smell of resin all around him, staring up through the trees at the pink underpinnings of the clouds. The sky drew itself steadily westward.

That night another memory of Père came to him, softly and persistently, like a moth circling a light. He and Père were together on one of their favorite walks, a gently sloping path that began behind the ruin and ran along an avenue of young birches to a little glade. The light filtered grayly through the trees and he was holding Père's hand and stepping over the roots and stones, frowning from the effort. Père was walking too quickly for him to follow; he was staring absently, fixedly ahead of him as he often did, mumbling in a low monotone without moving his lips, like a priest or a nun at their private prayers. —Père, he'd said, stopping in the path. —Père? Can we go slower?

Père had stopped as if struck on the back. —What's that, Oskar?

—You're going too fast.

—I . . . ? No, no, Oskar. No, no, my little Herr. He had smiled then, squinting slightly as he smiled, the look of an adult trying to explain something delicate and complex to a child. —I'm in a hurry, Oskar. That's why I walk so fast. I wish I could walk much faster. I would feel better. It's terrible, Oskar, you know. It's terrible always to be in such a hurry.

He had smiled then, too, looking up at Père, searching for the joke. Père made jokes very often when they were together, instead of giving the answers he wanted. He knew very well that they couldn't be in any kind of hurry. They had finished dinner early and Maman had said that tonight, for once, they could take their sweet time. He liked that expression very much, especially when Maman said it, which was not often. That was why he had remembered.

Père had begun walking again now, quicker even than before, and he had stamped his feet in protest, letting out a squeal of frustrated laughter. —Père! he had shouted. —Père! Stop! Don't walk so fast!

Père had spun about suddenly on his heels and run back to him, gripping him hard by both of his shoulders and shaking him so that his head lolled back and forth like a pocketwatch on a chain. The trees blurred and rocked above him. —I can't! I can't! I can't! I can't! I can't! Père had screamed, shaking him at every word. —I just told you, Oskar! Good God! Let it—

Père had let go of him then and turned round on the path, forgetting him completely, staring at a point far off through the trees. —Let it, Père had said again in a faraway voice, not talking to him any longer.

—Let what? he had said frightenedly, still stuttering in the wake of his first surprise. He'd looked up then and seen that Père was weeping, the tears running freely in bright swift streaks across his face and down the front of his fine white shirt. He had begun to cry then as well. Père was still turning in strong dizzying circles above his head, smiling and laughing and weeping, saying the same four words over and over:

—Let it happen now.

After a few nights of freezing rain in the valley there followed a steady period of warmer days. The snow melted into the dark spongelike turf and the ice on the ponds buckled slowly and sank under a thin layer of oily water. On one of these warm mornings Voxlauer was crossing the bridge when a man appeared at the road's farthest turning. The man was tall and thin and dressed in cowled, flowing robes, like a monk's, and the white bloom of his hair dipped and wobbled as he labored up the incline. Catching sight of Voxlauer he slowed and approached in loping steps marked and measured by a whittled bamboo cane. Reaching the bridge he planted the cane in the gravel and leaned forward slightly and looked out at the water. —Spring is bounteous, he said, smiling.

—I suppose it is, said Voxlauer.

—You are the new gamekeeper.

—That's right.

—Oskar Voxlauer.

—Yes.

—As a gamekeeper, Herr Voxlauer, you must know very well that spring is bounteous.

Voxlauer looked at him squintingly. —With whom do I have the pleasure?

—Forgive me! Professor Walter Adolf Piedernig. He bowed. —Of the Pirestine Collective.

—The what?

—The *Collective,* child. The Disciples of Piraeus. Of the Body's Four Humours as writ by name on the Pirestine parchments and brought westward from Damascus by that most blessed philosopher. He regarded Voxlauer for a moment expectantly. —The colony, he said finally.

—The one down in Pergau?

—Above Pergau. Yes.

—Ah, said Voxlauer. They stood awhile in silence. The older man looked down at the younger man benevolently. Then he turned and looked up the road, shading his eyes. —Were you headed to the pass?

—Only to the beehives.

—Then we can walk together a little while. I'm on my way this morning to the chapel on Birker Heath.

—The chapel? said Voxlauer, raising an eyebrow.

—Well, more to the heath itself, laughed the man. His clay-colored neck and arms glowed even redder where they emerged from his white homespun vestments. His face and jaw were latticed with deep curving furrows, like a sailor's, and his brow where it sloped down from under its snowy crest was the color of turned soil. He stood surveying the pond bank and the water, smiling on it as if giving a benediction, rocking back and forth on his bare feet with his papery eyelids pulled down low against the sun. He seemed in no particular hurry for Voxlauer's reply.

—What takes you up to the heath? said Voxlauer after they had been walking for some minutes.

—The same thing that takes anyone up there, said Piedernig. —The view.

—I'd thought maybe the hunting.

—I'm not interested in your game, Herr Voxlauer, said Piedernig without slackening. —Have confidence in that.

—I'd thought of going myself for that purpose, actually.

—You're no more of a hunter than I am. Piedernig looked at him, then up the road. —Or a gamekeeper either, for that matter.

—I beg your pardon?

—I knew your father at one time. Enjoyed some of his airs.

—Ah.

—What you're after in that tumbledown hovel of yours is an Egyptian mystery, to tell you plainly.

Voxlauer squinted a moment into the woods. —My father never mentioned you that I can recall.

—We went to gymnasium together. In Graz.

—I don't recall him mentioning you.

—I said I knew the man, said Piedernig with a wave of his hand. —I didn't say we cared much for each other.

A brief quiet followed. Voxlauer scuffed his bootheels in the dirt. —What were you before? he said. —Some sort of schoolmaster?

—About as much as you're a gamekeeper, said Piedernig. He smiled.

They walked on until they came to the opening of the clearing at the top of which the beehouses leaned together like a row of stoved-in boats. —Those cabinets are in sorry shape, said Piedernig. —I don't think old Bauer ever opened them. Afraid of getting stung, most likely.

—Did you know him well?

Piedernig shrugged. —Well enough, poor devil. His daughter worked under me when I was gamekeeper, in a manner of speaking, to fair Niessen's pride and hope. He spat cheerily into the dirt. —Well enough to hazard these bees weren't altogether smothered by his attentions.

Voxlauer smiled. —They don't seem to have suffered too much for it, anyhow.

—How's that?

—Well, said Voxlauer. —I was saying—

Piedernig looked at him sharply. —Would you know a happy bee from an unhappy bee, Herr Voxlauer?

—I'm not sure I'd know a live bee from a dead one.

—Pay us a visit at the colony this week. Piedernig stopped and laid a sun-spotted brown hand on Voxlauer's shoulder. —Our bees are in a perpetual state of bliss.

Voxlauer watched him as he gathered his robes together and stepped carefully over a puddle of runoff and disappeared into the spruce plantation. Not until he'd been gone for some minutes did it occur to Voxlauer to ask about the figure.

Arriving in Czernowitz, the last station on the civilian line, I left my smoking-car acquaintances behind as quickly as I could and made my way to the drab little center of town in search of news of the fighting and, if possible, a ride east to the front. I was told by the postmaster, a sad, dignified-looking Jew from the capital, that the fighting had ended three weeks before as far north as the town of Lemberg on the Polish border, six hours away by train, and the only soldiers left were deserters from the Hungarian Civil Guard. Why I'm still here I have no idea, he murmured, wagging his head side to side, as though to keep from falling asleep. In response to my torrent of questions about the east he exhaled soundlessly time and again and shrugged his shoulders, sliding small heaps of mail from one corner of his massive eagle-emblazoned desk to another. He barely looked up to acknowledge me as I wished him a safe return to Budapest and left.

Already I noticed a change in the Hungarians around me, most of them speaking German grudgingly, as if questioning my right to ask it of them. The Empire was fading quickly now, like a lamp running out of oil, and with it the last of the delusions that had kept everything comprehensible. No one seemed particularly surprised when I asked for transport to the border of the Ukraine. Some assumed I was a deserter, others a spy; nobody seemed to care very much one way or the other. In spite of this, I was taken on more and more reluctantly the closer we came to the border, riding the length of a few fields, then getting down and walking, often for hours, until the next cart passed. No one seemed to know any German now at all; I felt I was forgetting it with them.

At Jzerneska I forded the Dniester on a barge hauled across the water on sagging iron cables and midway across the river it dawned on me that I was free. The heavy gray water was tumbling and folding over on itself along the left side of the boat, sloughing over into the hull, and the sheer weight and stubbornness of it seemed to testify to my escape. The idea that I'd crossed bodily over into Bolshevik territory, territory that to me represented the opposite of everything I'd left, made me light-headed and breathless to get to shore. I allowed myself a few thoughts of Maman and Niessen but the thoughts became too big immediately and I concentrated again on the river. Reaching the bank, I gave the ferry driver near to the last of my money, and seeing this he smiled a guarded little smile. To my surprise he spoke in well-schooled German. Yes; I don't think you'll be needing these, he said, holding up the coins. They're on a new system hereabouts.

What system is that? I asked.

Barter, he answered, holding up a palm. This potato for your wife. He laughed. He was grizzle-haired and tanned the color of marsh water and dressed in a skirt of knotted and sewn-together rags, like the Gypsy in Il Trovatore. I guessed him to be a Slovak. That's fine, I answered after a moment. All the possible meanings and implications of his joke, if that was what it had been, revolved weakly in my tired brain. Finally I thought back to what Jan had explained to me about the withering away of capital under true communism and decided the Bolsheviks must have done away with money. That's fine, I said again, more confidently.

The Slovak shrugged at this; not sadly, as the postmaster in Czernowitz had done, or doubtfully, but only blankly. We stood half on the barge and half on the shifting, reed-covered bank, watching the sun sink slowly over the wide planed earth with nothing to hide itself behind. A sudden panic gripped me at the thought of being abandoned there, but the Slovak seemed in no great hurry to push off. With a slow, careless motion of his hand he offered me a wedge of plug tobacco.

Very kind of you, I said. I looked at him again. Could you spare anything further?

He blinked a few times, his face flat and colorless in the weak sun. *Meaning?*

Food. Meaning food, I answered, more quickly than I'd intended.

His eyes slid back to me and he grinned again. *That'll cost you, little Kaiser.*

I thought I might barter.

He nodded to himself and reached down into the hull of the barge and passed me a sodden loaf of bread and some marmalade in a damp brown fold of paper. *Four kronens, Your Eminence,* he said, touching his cap.

I laughed. I don't have four kronens. I have two. My empire's gone a bit to seed, as you might have noticed.

He was quiet awhile, looking past me, studying the horizon intently as though trying to decipher a tiny line of print. *Two kronens, then.*

I handed him the last of my money. He tucked it into his shirt with the same slow, untroubled movement he'd made offering me the tobacco and stepped off the bank. The sun was still sliding sluggishly downward. The feeling of momentousness I'd had while crossing the river had disappeared without my noticing and I felt my solitariness very keenly. A narrow puddle-dotted path ran down from the levee in three short turns and off into the boundaryless sweep of grass without the slightest dip or bend. I looked back a second time at the Slovak, who was watching me for the first time with something approaching curiosity, as though the incongruousness of my being there had only just occurred to him. Will this take me to the Bolsheviks? I half whispered, gesturing sheepishly at the path.

The look of casual curiosity on the Slovak's face changed all at once into one of surprise and delight, as if he'd just been given a small but very charming present. *Eventually, little Kaiser. Eventually it will. You'll have to do a bit of walking on it first, though, I'm afraid.*

I turned slowly back to face him. Why is that?

This territory belongs to the Holy German Empire, he answered, curtsying.

. . .

The cabinets when Voxlauer opened them seemed husked out and deserted. Dry, brittle shells littered the trays. Here and there a live bee crawled among them, confused by the sudden glare. The hives in the yellow house were the least decrepit and he cut into one at its bottom edge and pried off a dark wedge of honeycomb. Going back to the road he paused a moment, looking out toward Pergau in its nest of graphite fields. The snow line had lifted that past week to the bald tops of the hills and a dull green showed ahead of him in the spruce grove. The young trees looked stunted and unnatural in their geometric rows with the older growth behind them, regal and dark, and the shadow of the cliffs spread down over them as though covering a flaw. When Voxlauer came to the pastures he found a cow grazing at the roadside behind a new fence of barbed wire. It lowed at him, raised its head and took a few cautious steps toward the fence. When he made no sign of stopping it turned and lowered its face to the grass again.

He came to the Holzer farm just as the bell to supper was ringing and two men approached the house slowly over the freshly spaded ground. He hung back along the edge of the road and watched them. They were wide rangy men with long legs and large strides and they joked with one another as they passed through the little orchard and scraped together what little snow was left among the trees and threw it at each other and cursed. The older of the two looked to be near Voxlauer in age and wore his long hair tucked loosely into a woolen cap. The younger one was bearded, with wide-spaced, simple eyes, and cocked his felt hat sideways on his head like a beret. A dog loped between them but it appeared not to notice Voxlauer and neither did its masters. When they had almost reached the gate Frau Holzer came out onto the steps and called to them to bring kindling from the woodshed. She remained there with her arms crossed in the manner of a benevolent regent, waiting until they returned a few minutes later with arms full of fresh-cut pine quarters. Then she turned and stepped ahead of them into the house.

Instead of going back by the valley road Voxlauer climbed to the top of Birker ridge and followed it west. To his right a more broken arm ran up to the heath and the higher hills northward, and the valley, now completely in shadow, curved away to his left. After an hour's walk through chest-high brush that clawed at his coat front and his sleeves he came out onto the clearing where the deer he'd killed lay scattered in all directions through the brush. Small black ants spread netlike over the carcass and welled up from the sockets and the heap of the bowels. The coil of the intestines had been bitten through and strung like tinsel over the bracken and it hung now in loose ribbons, yellowing in the sun. The smell was near to overpowering. Voxlauer stepped away and climbed back to the ridge.

In Italy he had seen bodies equally open and picked apart but the cold had always kept them from smelling. The wetness of everything around and the smell made him dizzy now and he fixed his eyes on the ground and walked stiffly onward through the trees. One infantryman he remembered, a Czech, had broken his leg crossing a foxhole and gangrene had set in within hours. He'd reeked so badly under the saltpeter compresses that the stretcher carriers, when they finally came, wound wet rags over their faces and turned their heads away from him as they walked. The deer had had that same smell, or close enough. He shut his eyes and tried to remember it more clearly: the damp of the foxholes, the bright rolling noise, the sulfurous taste of the air during shellings. The trench on the Parese front had had a particular smell, lived in so long that the stench of shell gas and piss sank down into the snow and froze there, seeping out in the slightest thaw. —That much I remember, he said aloud.

He followed the ridge down in the growing dusk, passing the ponds far below, and walked farther out still until by the last light he came to a furrowed spine of rock bare and exposed to all cardinals. Looking out, he could see around the valley's bend and over the Pergauer saddle to the broad plain beyond. The steeple at Pergau was just visible over a pine bank and above it in a bowl of tilled land a cluster of white shacks huddled. —Herr Piedernig, I presume, said Voxlauer, smiling crookedly to himself. A short while later he slipped quietly across the flagged square at Pergau.

He passed a few field hands on the road above the town but no one spoke to him beyond wishing him a good evening. The fields surrounding Pergau were shallow and steep and he was quickly back in the woods. After a quarter of an hour he passed a junction in a small saddle of even ground and came to the border of Ryslavy's land soon after.

In the morning Voxlauer remembered the honeycomb in his coat pocket and ate it for breakfast in a bowl with milk and bread crumbs. Then he took two purple flies from the tackle box and unwrapped the lighter of the two rods from its sheeting and went out and climbed along the rapids till he came to a pool where the current bent itself into ellipses and the surface was clear and untroubled. Trout were hovering there in pockets of weaker current and darting without warning into new configurations only to hover dark and motionless again above the creek bed. Despite the clarity of the water their skins shone a mute copper color against the gravel. Nets of sunlight played over the bed and quivered in time to the surface's rippling. He stepped back from the bank and began casting in high cautious arcs into the whitewater above the pool, letting the fly drift down and into the current and spiral there awhile before drawing back and casting again.

By midmorning he had caught three fish. He brought them in and laid them on the table where they stared up at him with blanching eyes. They were small but very beautiful and the skin which had looked gravel-colored under the water sparkled now in its mucus like a curtain of cut jewels. He gutted and washed them and set one to fry in butter and flour on the stovetop. The other two he wrapped in newspaper with a few sprigs of new grass and set aside. The smell of the butter and the fish perfumed the dank air and settled on his skin and his clothes until nothing could be smelled but the sweet frying meat and his whole body was tense and restless with hunger. He ate the fish directly off the stove and scraped together the burnt flakes from the bottom of the pan and put a forkful into his mouth, savoring its bitterness. It was hot now in the little room. He went out and made a slow, ambling circuit of the pond.

That afternoon he took the remaining two fish and put them into his pack and walked down toward Pergau. The sun was half hidden behind checkered fields of cloud and the woods as he walked were aglow with great hatchings of light brightening and vanishing on either side. When he came to the junction he turned left and walked uphill to the edge of a muddy field. On its far side stood the houses of the colony, loose clapboard huts with damp dirt tracks between them. Broad white sheets hung from clothes-lines and four muddy-faced children playing hoptoad stopped their game when he approached them. A woman in a brown sackcloth dress taking in wash asked his name and what he wanted.

—Oskar Voxlauer. I've come to see Herr Piedernig, if I might.

—You needn't be so formal here, laughed the woman. —My name is Ruth.

—Oskar Voxlauer, he said again, nodding to her.

—Walter's in the big house with the others at supper. She turned and pointed past the children to the tallest of the huts. —Tell them I'll be along soon.

—Thank you, Fräulein, said Voxlauer. —I will.

As he came to the house steps a fragment of music came to him, a low clicking of keys that had no referent in his memory. He waited a moment on the doorstep, trying to place it among pieces of his father's, or among Anna's collection of phonograph albums, but it faded from one moment to the next without giving him time to remember. He came to himself again and pushed open the door.

The room he passed into was bright and high-ceilinged and ran the full length of the house. Ten or twelve women and men of assorted ages, all but a few with identically cropped heads and sunburnt faces, sat cross-legged on the floor around a blanket laden with wooden bowls of walnuts and preserved fruit and trays of cheese and pumpernickel bread. Piedernig stood above the group making rounds with a steaming pewter teakettle. He looked up as Voxlauer entered, put the kettle aside and strode over to him with his arms wide in greeting. —How's this! he said, looking at Voxlauer's hands. —Do you come bearing gifts?

—Spring is bounteous, said Voxlauer, handing over the parcel.

—Amen to that. Piedernig undid the paper and sniffed at the contents. —Damned well met. Children! he said, turning toward the circle. —We have another visitor today from the world. Oskar Voxlauer, gamekeeper. He smiled and looked over at Voxlauer. —Make room for the man. You, Seppl—see what you can do with these. He extended the parcel to a member of the circle, a slight, balding man who rose ceremoniously and withdrew with the fish to an adjoining room.

—Oskar and I met on the road this past Sunday, praise be to spring, announced Piedernig. He motioned to Voxlauer to be seated on the blanket. —He was having a spot of trouble with his bees.

—What sort of trouble? asked a small, redheaded woman to Voxlauer's right.

—Well. They don't seem too lively, said Voxlauer, reaching for a bowl of winter pears.

—You wouldn't either, living in those mausoleums, said a voice from across the blanket. The voice was low and burled, like the rasping together of woolen sleeves. The woman who had spoken was round-faced and dark and looked at him without smiling. Her hair was long, unlike the others', and hung loosely down over her shoulders to the pair of hunter's coveralls she wore over a moth-eaten canvas shirt. Piedernig said something to her amid the general laughter and her eyes shifted tiredly, returning his smile.

—Exactly! Not to mention you woke them from a very fine sleep, the redheaded woman said.

Grudgingly Voxlauer turned his head and looked at her. —I don't know much about bees, he said.

—Oskar's a sort of gentleman's gamekeeper, said Piedernig, winking.

Before long the man called Seppl returned with the trout, fried in butter on a bed of leeks and boiled potatoes. Many around the circle declined their portions but Piedernig devoured his with obvious relish, sighing elaborately and sucking on his fingertips. The red-haired woman and a bearded man next to her seemed to have taken their shares largely out of politeness and sat with the steaming fish in front of them, watching Voxlauer uncomfortably. A sallow, Jesuit-faced man with a startled expression stared fiercely at him from across the blanket.

—We don't eat fish here, as a rule, offered Piedernig between mouthfuls. —Brethren of the stream and so forth. And you, Fräulein Bauer: aren't you having any?

—I'll take a holiday from fish today, I think, said the long-haired woman, not looking at Voxlauer.

—Excellent. Donated to the cause. Oskar, may I present Fräulein Else Bauer, another of our neighbors. Fräulein Bauer inhabits the villa just across from us in these godless foothills.

—That's quite an overstatement, a villa, said the woman, smiling at Piedernig with that same sleepy look. Voxlauer watched her a moment or two without speaking.

—Pleased to meet you, he said after a moment.

One by one, some amicably, some grudgingly, the members of the circle introduced themselves to him. With the exception of Piedernig, who was dressed in the same light-colored robes he'd worn three days previous, they were clothed in identical genderless shirts of brown homespun and fraying sackcloth pants. The man with the startled expression surprised Voxlauer by breaking into a wide yellow grin and shaking hands with him vigorously across the blanket. Piedernig presided over it all like the Gautama Buddha, nodding and smiling fatuously. —And now for the wine, he said, holding up a finger.

Seppl stepped briskly into the kitchen and returned a moment later with two bottles of gooseberry wine stopped with rolled birch-bark corks. The bottles were circulated and each one of the assembled sniffed the stoppers before decanting the wine into crockery mugs. Piedernig rose to his feet.

—Dearest children, he began, holding a wine bottle just below his chin—children and disciples in Christ and his quartered Host, steeped and rebaptized in its four cleansing humours—

The names of the seasons rose up now around the circle in counterpoint to Piedernig's singsong, closely followed by the words *fire, water, fundament,* and *air.* Voxlauer sat quietly, looking down into his mug.

—and the water, and the fundament, and the cleansing fire; amen, said Piedernig. He sighed happily. —Heil be to spring.

—Heil spring, answered the others in chorus. Piedernig sat down with his legs folded under him and raised his mug to Voxlauer. —Prost, Oskar!

—Amen to that, said Voxlauer, much relieved. He raised the wine to his lips and drank deeply. It was powerfully fermented and left a paraffin-like glaze on the back of the throat and a tickling along the gums. Voxlauer smiled and nodded and complimented the wine. He hadn't had a drink in more than two weeks and the liquor quieted him immediately and caused his eyes half to close, as a beam of light might on a summer evening. For a moment he sat contentedly holding the mug, letting the talk go around and over him.

—I did manage to collect some honeycomb yesterday, he said after the warmth had risen between his shoulder blades. No one seemed to be listening. The woman named Ruth had come in and now sat a few places to his left, arguing with Piedernig. It seemed to be about the Nazis. Voxlauer put down his mug reluctantly and tried to pay attention.

—When they come, Walter, why shouldn't they come everywhere at once, in equal measure? Both in the towns and in the hills? Why should it be any different here than it was in the north, or in Bavaria itself, for that matter? Are we so much cleverer here?

Piedernig grunted. —Hardly that, child. But it's always been a rooming-house phenomenon, this "Aryan Socialism"; a disease bred and fostered in the city, like every other idiocy. He took a slow, comfortable glance around the circle. A number of the assembled murmured their assent. He let out a sigh. —Bank clerk's mysticism. The assistant lecturer's ideal of Germanism. To the left of Voxlauer someone laughed.

—They've never been too well received in villages, Piederning continued. —Let alone in the hills, in their starched shirts and fancy collars. We've had enough fanatics and lunatics without them, thank you kindly. Country people have too much sense for that sort of opera. We'll see that, or rather not see any of it, I'll wager, when they arrive. They'll not last long, children. He sat back contentedly and raised his cup to his mouth.

—They seem to be doing all right in these hills, said a round-faced boy to Voxlauer's right.

—If by that remark, Kasperl, you mean those two sot-brained Hirams up there on the Holzer property, spending their days looking for anything warm-blooded to bugger with those pork-tin muskets of theirs, we'll proceed to the next witness. What's your opinion, Herr Gamekeeper?

—Are you so sure they'll come, then? Voxlauer said.

—They'll come, and soon, said the woman named Else who had spoken earlier. Voxlauer looked at her again and felt the same astonishment, not at her beauty but at the sadness which seemed to hover over her like a canopy, enclosing everything else within its quiet. She looked at him steadily from under heavy lids, not unkindly but from a great distance, as though relinquishing him and the knowledge of him in her unhurried relinquishing of everything. Looking at her now he felt the beginnings of something like fear stirring inside him, a vague premonition that might also have been a memory, like the music he'd heard on the steps. He steered his eyes away from her and brought them to focus again on the boy, Kasperl, who was speaking again in low, defiant tones.

—They'll run us out, that's sure. First thing. They'll come and run us out.

—Tsk, Kasperl, said Piedernig. —Steer clear of soothsaying awhile, for all our sakes.

—Maybe they won't, said Else, looking not at Voxlauer now but from one face to another around the circle. —Maybe they'll simply let us alone. They have no plan that we know of that should trouble us. What could they possibly want up here? Let's not judge them entirely just yet, Walter. Let's wait and see what they actually do when they come. She raised her wine mug to her lips and drank, looking around the circle. —Change might actually do us good.

No one spoke for a moment. —Change, Fräulein, is for the chattel in town, said Piedernig. —The steady regression in progress's name we've discussed so often. It's why we're all here. Remember?

—I'm talking about genuine change, Walter. Genuine progress. If that had ever been for Niessen I'd likely still be living there.

—Fräulein Bauer is a retired gymnasium-school instructor, said Piedernig fondly. —Though you certainly wouldn't guess it by her politics. Look at her glowering now! I've embarrassed her. He laughed and turned back to Voxlauer. —What about you, Oskar? What was it you retired from?

Voxlauer didn't answer. —I believe I saw you walking by the ponds a week ago, he said to Else after a moment.

—I can't help it if your ponds happen to lie between my house and town, Herr Gamekeeper, she answered. She was looking not at him but at Piedernig, who sat leaning back with his legs crossed beneath him and his eyes drooping like a house cat's, humming quietly to himself. To Voxlauer's surprise she closed her eyes also, as did the others, solemnly, one by one around the circle. A disembodied humming rose among them, quavering and deep. He looked back at her and saw her mouth's corners curling up as though for his benefit but always with that sadness he'd recognized immediately and which ran through her all features like thread through a raveling dress. Nature is bounteous, spring is bright. Work is chastening. Food is blessed. A half-eaten pear browning in a wooden bowl. A dark purple stain on the blanket near her hand.

—You see, Oskar: our bees are as slothful as your bees. But ours sleep the sleep of the just.

Voxlauer peered in through the blue-painted door of the cabinet. —They do seem more prepossessing, he said.

Piedernig nodded. —Bees were created to make honey as man was created to make excrement. But they'll do as we do in a shithouse.

—And yet they stay in those same houses, year after year, said Voxlauer.

—You'll do as you think best, of course, said Piedernig. —They can do without their honey, can they, at the Niessener Hof?

—For all I care, said Voxlauer. Piedernig chuckled.

Bars of light slanted down among the whitewashed house frames and the lines of wash onto the straw-battened dirt tracks below them. Piedernig began walking and Voxlauer followed him dazedly, nursing a slow, gathering happiness.

Rounding a row of haylofts they came to a small square of flattened ground hidden among the huts with a pen on one side of it and a garden on the other. The children he'd passed before were harrying an ancient goat around the pen and a woman in a homespun dress the same color as the goat sat watching them from the wall of a terraced garden. The children were shiftless and barefoot in spite of the damp and their bones stretched and tautened under their pale dirty skin as they moved. The woman stared sullenly at them as they passed but Piedernig seemed to take no notice of her. He walked bobbingly a half step ahead of Voxlauer and led him out along the perimeter of the huts and across the field to the crown of the road, then stopped short as though penned in by the field. Voxlauer stopped also, waiting for him to speak.

Piedernig turned and raised an arm toward the fractured base of the cliffs. —How sharp are your eyes, Oskar? Do you see that gap in the rock, just at bottom? Where that sulfur-colored band comes down and meets the muddier color?

Voxlauer looked upward. —What about it?

—A man used to live there. We fed him from time to time.

—Fancy that.

—He tried to live as you live. Piedernig looked over at him. —He thought the way you think, give or take.

Voxlauer lowered his eyes from the cliffs and looked at Piedernig. —What would you know about the way I think, Professor?

Piedernig smiled. —Calm yourself, Oskar. Please. I haven't spent these nine years removed from man's and woman's folly without learning more about it than I'd care to dwell on. I've made a study of you in my idle hours, and feel I've come to an understanding of your nature and ambitions. He tapped Voxlauer on the shoulder. —You yourself, of course, believe that you have no ambitions any longer.

Voxlauer smiled. —And that's a delusion, is it?

—The caveman, also, thought he could take off the world as

one might a pair of breeches. And we fed him. Partially out of respect, I suppose, for his convictions. But largely out of sympathy.

—What sort of man was he?

—A well-known type, really. Guarded. Jealous of his past. A fanatic, to tell the truth. He'd have done beautifully nowadays.

—I don't doubt it.

—Yes. Piedernig pursed his lips.

—And now you feed me.

—We feed one another, Oskar. Your predecessor, in his day, brought rabbits and nuts and other welcome offerings. A very friendly unfortunate man.

—What happened to him?

—He died.

—So do we all, said Voxlauer. —Thank you for the supper.

Piedernig bowed. —Bless you for your visit, Oskar. An educated man is a blessing in any wilderness.

—I'm not an educated man.

—As you like, Oskar. As you prefer. The son of an educated man, if you'll accept that title.

A brief silence followed. —You are a charlatan, said Voxlauer flatly.

Piedernig sighed. —Of a sort. I give them perhaps a little less than I allow myself.

Voxlauer smiled. —I'd noticed that at supper.

—I'm not talking about the trout, now, Herr Gamekeeper, said Piedernig shortly.

—Just the same. I don't begrudge you it.

—That's very kind. Piedernig smiled. —But it's true, just the same, that your bees are dying. He turned and, waving once more over his shoulder, strode back through the new grass toward the huts. Voxlauer watched until he disappeared among them. He remained standing some minutes more, watching the afternoon advance across the field and the shadows creep even as he watched them across the open ground from right to left. As he went down the hill the last edgings of light caught here and there among the trunks of the pines on clumps of drab, dirt-encrusted snow. When he arrived at the junction he stopped again and stood for a time staring blankly into the woods. Then he turned and went back up the hill to the colony.

She was just crossing the field as he came out from the trees and he stepped hurriedly back into their shadow so as not to meet her on the open ground. A few moments later she came down to where he was waiting, showing no surprise at seeing him standing at the edge of the road shifting nervously from foot to foot. She nodded to him without smiling and they began walking. When they were not quite halfway to the junction she asked why he had been waiting for her.

—I have some sketches of yours, I believe, said Voxlauer.

She smiled. —I see. I won't ask you your opinion of them, Herr Voxlauer, if that's your worry.

—Two portraits. And a pastel of some Enzians.

—The pastel is mine. I'm not sure that I want it. As to the portraits, you're welcome to them, I'm sure. I can't recall them.

Voxlauer looked down the road a moment. —Thank you. I'd appreciate it if you would take them, all the same.

She laughed a muted, low-strung laugh, her dull eyes regarding him evenly.

—Are they so awful?

—No. No, they're very fine.

—Are the portraits of me?

—Yes.

—Then they're the property of my father. You can do what you want with them. Hang them up. Throw them in the dustbin. Whatever you like.

—What I'd like, Fräulein, is for you to take them. I'd take it as a kindness.

The smile went altogether from her face and she looked at him now with something approaching anger. —I want nothing more to do with that shack you live in, Herr Voxlauer, and I, for my part, would take it as a very great kindness if you didn't force me to. The years I spent in it were the worst of my life and I don't care to relive them. She looked over at him again more closely, as though studying his face for the precise nature and number of words needed to suit his type. —The family you work for, she said carefully—took my father's self-respect and health as sure as if they'd put each individual bottle into his mouth and wiped his chin for him afterward. I imagine they've told you something different, but I was present while it happened. I sat and watched. If you've passed any time at all in that dank hole you ought to know how he lived out his last year. It pained me then, Herr Voxlauer, to think about it, and pains me worse now. She paused a moment for breath. —So please don't trouble me any more about it, for the love of Christ.

—I'm sorry, Fräulein, said Voxlauer, drawing even with her. —I didn't know any of that. I meant no harm about the sketches.

—You knew well enough about my father.

—I knew he drank. Yes.

—Yes, she said, taking in a breath. —And I know about yours.

—I'd think that might make us even.

—Not altogether. Your father was a famous man. Esteemed and successful.

—My father spent the last fifteen years of his life trying to get his music played, said Voxlauer.

—Your father was a king to everyone in town. Everyone! Even I remember him.

—He died as wretchedly as yours did, all the same. And about as many people mourned him.

—Oh yes. We were talking about my father's death, weren't we, Herr Voxlauer. And about the Ryslavys. Your—she paused a moment, searching again for the most fitting word—your *bosses*.

—Old Ryslavy's dead, too. It was Pauli who hired me up here.

—Does it matter? she said quietly, still looking down the road. —Can he be any different?

Voxlauer looked at her until she turned. There was no anger in her expression now, only dullness. —Why did you say that, Fräulein? Because he's a Jew? Is that why?

—Because he's his father's son. For no other reason. She paused a moment.

—He is that, isn't he?

—I beg your pardon?

She looked at him kindly for the first time since they'd begun walking. —His father's son.

Voxlauer nodded gravely. —I've never had any cause to doubt it, Fräulein. They walked for some distance in silence. —I feel the same way you do, about town, he said after a time. —I suppose that's obvious.

—It's obvious to me that you don't like it. Whether you feel the same about it as I do is something else altogether.

—Well. I don't feel the same way about our neighbors to the north, that's certain.

Her eyes opened wide. —Oh? How *do* you feel about them?

—I've never cared too much for Germans. I'd rather not have them putting me in their parades. He drew himself to attention and raised a fist.

Else laughed. —I think you might benefit from a few marching lessons, Herr Voxlauer. Besides, it's not the Germans who make the fist. It's the Italians.

—Maybe so, said Voxlauer. —Maybe so, Fräulein. But the Italians also make gelato, and tiramisù. I can forgive them a bit of silliness.

She laughed again, less harshly now. —All right, Herr Voxlauer. They had come to the junction. —I'll relieve you of the sketches, if they're really such a burden. You can leave them with Herr Piedernig, on your next visit. Will there be anything else?

Voxlauer straightened. —No. Nothing else. Thank you kindly, Fräulein.

—Good evening, then.

—Good evening.

She took a few steps, then half turned toward him, looking over her shoulder. —Were you shooting a few days ago? she said. —Up on the ridge?

—Three days ago. Yes.

She nodded to herself and walked slowly into the woods. Voxlauer turned uphill and began his measured walk up to Ryslavy's land, stopping now and again to look through the treetops at the dwindling sun.

. . .

Over the next seven weeks, drifting eastward through the occupied Ukraine across the nothingness of the steppes, broken every so often by a huddle of mud-colored, windowless huts or a well and a ring of clay-walled pens, usually empty, I came to know true hunger for the first time. It woke me in the morning and pushed me forward irresistibly, long after I'd lost all desire or hope of reaching the Bolshevik territory, and sat me down at night in a state of half-consciousness until the time came to get up and drift listlessly forward again. I ate whatever I could catch, steal, or beg for in pantomime, and most of the people I came across were too curious or frightened to refuse me. I learned a few very helpful words of Ukrainian, enough to make it clear I was not a soldier, though not enough to prevent me from getting beaten regularly for stealing. The beatings were mild, however, little more than symbolic, as the men who beat me were as weak and vague-minded with hunger as I was. They struck me a few times halfheartedly, went through my pockets, then shuffled back into their houses. I was worthless to them.

As I came farther east, the steppes gave way to more sheltered, fertile country, thin tilled fields and squares of rich dark ground along rows of whitewashed cottages, manor farms and trees and teams of mules or horses on the roads. I traveled in constant fear of being caught by the Germans or mistaken for one of them by partisans, but discovered to my great relief that the occupation of the Ukraine was little more than a diplomatic and tactical invention. In a few of the towns, I found the old imperial officials still going about their business, stricken and bewildered as the Jew in Czernowitz had been, and was able to talk to them in French about the Bolsheviks and the occupying army and the war; for the first time I was grateful for my twice-weekly lessons as a child. I learned that the German-Soviet lines, only a few days' travel east, were little more than a ghost front, but that there was no love for the Bolsheviks or any other kind of Russian-imposed revolution anywhere in that country.

In some of the larger towns the Bolsheviks, the White Russians and the German army maintained fully parallel governments; each person I spoke to on the street had a different opinion as to which of the three regimes was in fact in power. The war between the Whites and Reds was already beginning, though the territory fought over was still technically German. I continued east with a vague idea of reaching Kiev, which I'd heard had been liberated a few weeks before. I learned a few more Ukrainian expressions, the commonest questions and insults and turns of phrase, and gradually began to have better luck getting myself fed.

A few weeks after this I found Anna. She was newly a widow, or believed herself one, at least, and had a small estate, or what she blithely referred to as an estate, to live off as best she could. I met her at the market in Cherkassy the morning I arrived, feverish and weak again from hunger. She was standing, tall and out of place in a flowered muslin housedress, in a corner of the market, selling dried radishes at the head of a cart filled with half-empty bags of seed. By some miracle she spoke a few words of German.

I'm starving, I said to her.

I need a worker, she answered, in French. Can you work? Arbeiten?

Yes. Arbeiten, I said. She nodded gravely. Later I found out she was ecstatic to have found me. Most able-bodied Ukrainian men were drunk or far away and those who weren't couldn't have cared less about her seven leached-out hectares. I laughed myself when I first saw her drafty plank house leaning over into the mud. But she brought me inside and put water on the stove for me to wash and cooked a meal over the next few hours the like of which I hadn't seen since leaving Niessen: braised carrots in honey and sliced buttered potatoes and mushrooms preserved in vinegar and four or five precious slices of dried goose breast from the smokehouse covered in pickled cranberry preserves. She watched me closely as I ate, wondering, she told me later, who in heaven's name I was and how I came to be in the town of Cherkassy speaking no more than twenty words of Ukrainian and awkward, gymnasium stu-

dent's French. She sat picking at her plate of carrots and potatoes absently, her small gray eyes never straying from me. At
any moment I expected her to come to her senses; I ate as quickly
as I could, barely tasting the food in my hurry. Eventually she
spoke.

You've come from the war? she asked, in Ukrainian.

I stared at her dumbly. After a moment or two I set down my
fork and shrugged.

She frowned. The war, she repeated. For some reason she was
set on speaking Ukrainian to me, though she must have known I
hadn't a chance of understanding her. She'd learned her French
and her smattering of German at gymnasium in Kiev, had in fact
won a prize, she told me proudly, but her schooling had ended
on her sixteenth birthday and now she was well past her twenty-
ninth. She looked older to me than that, with her hair pulled
straight back and a few streaks of white already showing at the
temples; no longer young at all. But I thought she was beautiful,
like an angel on a veteran's monument—smooth-polished and sexless, proud and severe, indifferent to one's gaze and at the same
time utterly naked under it. I was seventeen then, not much better
than a child, and I suppose all women had that quality to me. But I
see her even now in that cool glow of permanence that statues
have, sitting across from me at the long dining table, waiting
patiently for me to answer. Nothing I learned afterward could dis-
pel that first idea of her.

Seeing that I still didn't understand, she stood up from the
table and crouched down behind it, peering solemnly at me over
the white linen tablecloth, making rattling noises deep in her
throat and gesturing at me violently with both her arms. I stared at
her a moment or two longer in flat stupidity. Oh! The war, I said
finally. Krieg. I smiled uncertainly.

Yes. The Krieg. You come from it? Yes?

Yes, I said.

I ran, I added after a silence.

She nodded, looking at me carefully.

My husband, yes? Andrei. At Krieg, she said.

Yes?

Mmm, she murmured. I sat forward uneasily in my chair, expecting the inevitable, but Anna only smiled. He is dead. They've all decided.

I nodded cautiously. I understand, I said. I'm sorry. I'd begun to feel very ill at ease.

I thought at first she'd misunderstood because she stayed on her feet, shaking a finger at me excitedly, then made a face and disappeared again behind the table. Confused, I stood and leaned forward until I could see her stretched out like a cadaver on the floor, smiling mischievously up at me. No, no, she was saying. No, no. I am happy, she said slowly, in her effortful, deliberate French. Do you understand? I am happy. Ich bin froh.

A few days later Voxlauer took up his pack and the jar now empty of milk and set out in his shirtsleeves in the mist of early morning up the road to Holzer's Cross. By the time he had come out of the spruce grove under the reliquary the mist had largely burned away and the town spires sparkled wetly on the plain. He went with the jar to the door of the farmhouse and knocked. After a short time Frau Holzer came to the door.

—May I come in? said Voxlauer.

—Why not? My sons are on holiday today. They've gone down to Niessen.

He stepped inside. —I'm headed there myself.

Frau Holzer didn't answer. She'd taken the jar from him and was filling it from a large copper pitcher by the stall-side door. —We have fresh-butchered kid today if you want it.

—Is it chamois?

—Of course. She smiled. —But not from Ryslavy's woods. I'd swear an oath.

—I brought down some game myself, a few days back.

—How fine.

—I'd very much like some butter, if you can spare any.

—Of course we can. She stepped into the next room and returned with two small grayish bricks wrapped in waxed paper.

—Could I look by on my way back from town, and get these from you? I won't be long. Three or four hours.

—That will be fine, said the woman. She looked at him kindly. —Why are you going to town?

Voxlauer glanced at her. —To visit my mother.

—I see. She was quiet a moment. —Well. She may not recall me, but please say best wishes to her from Elke. Elke Mayer. It was Mayer when she knew me.

—I will, said Voxlauer. —Thank you kindly. He stepped out the kitchen door into the entryway. —I'll be back by two. Three at the very latest.

—No hurry, said the woman. She looked at him a moment longer, then went in to the pantry and began rattling in a tall chipboard cupboard there. He waited a few seconds to see if she was coming back into the kitchen, but she did not. He pulled the house door shut behind him.

As he came out of the woods above the square a light rain began to fall and the ruin as he passed it paled gradually into the mist. The square was empty save for three olive-colored sedans and behind the square the hillside rose steeply and then vanished in a hard, straight line, as though planed flat by the passage of heavy ships. Rarely had he seen mist so bright and so opaque and he stood for a while at the edge of the square looking back up the slope. As he passed the sedans two men in gray oilskin capes came out of the Amtshaus and walked briskly toward him. They passed him and climbed into a sedan and drove around the shuttered fountain and out the toll road, heading south. As he passed Ryslavy's he caught sight of Emelia through the open doors, drawing a draft behind the long teakwood bar, and called in to her. She held up a hand.

At the grocer's he recognized Frau Mayer's two sons standing with their backs to him, talking to an elderly man he remembered from before the war, the three of them dressed up in loden capes, as if for a state holiday.

—What day is it? Voxlauer asked the grocer's boy. The boy looked at him a moment, then smiled as if acknowledging a private joke. —A March Saturday like any other if you ask me, Herr, he said.

It was too cold and wet on the verandah, it seemed, even for Maman; creeping stealthily upstairs he found her in the kitchen, pounding dough for candied dumplings. She gave a little start as he rapped on the doorframe, then came over and embraced him, holding her flour-covered hands away from him like a boxer. He let go of her and she went back to the table and dipped her hands again into the flour tin. He watched as she ran her hands once up and down the rolling pin and began passing it vigorously over each of the narrow strips, which contracted and curled angrily after each stroke so that the effort of rolling seemed wasted. But as always at some unknowable point she was satisfied and reached for the jar of black plums and laid one pitted halved section in the middle of each strip.

—You're growing your beard again, she said, balling up the strips into dumplings and pinching off the corners between her thumbs.

Voxlauer didn't answer. A kettle began whistling on the stovetop. —Shall I pour you some tea?

—Let's have coffee today, she said, wiping her hands on her apron. He watched as she ranged the dumplings into neat rows on a square of wet linen and folded the cloth over.

—Were you expecting me? he said.

She smiled a little. —Tomorrow is Sunday, Oskar, after all.

They sat with their coffee in the parlor at a low table and he spoke to her about the valley and how it had changed. —The creek is deeper but narrower across the middle, he said. —And though Pauli stocks it in the grand Ryslavy style, there seem to be less fish than I remember. The ice has broken under the bridge and the upper pond is open. The cottage pond will be, too, in a few days.

The old green piers are gone. There's a boat for me to use, and two beautiful rods. Next week I'll bring some venison, Maman, if you'd like.

—That would be pretty, she said. She had been listening attentively in the beginning but now she sat back in her chair and looked out at the street as though waiting for the commencement of some grave state procession. Voxlauer thought again of the sons' loden capes. —The woman up at Holzer's Cross sends her best wishes, he said. —Elke Mayer.

—Who?

—Elke Mayer, said Voxlauer, frowning.

—Yes, yes. Elke Mayer. We went to gymnasium together. She was sitting with her face to the glass. He sat quietly, watching her. After a time she nodded to herself.

—Maman, he said, leaning toward her. —What's the matter?

She looked at him a moment without speaking. Her face was drawn stiffly together.

—They marched into Vienna on Thursday, Oskar, she said, blinking at him. —They've taken our republic.

He sat with a dozen others along the bar. Some shops were open, some were closed. They sat in a row with their drinks while the girl, Emelia, fidgeted with the quartz-band radio. Its green eye wavered fluidly.

We've only just bought this radio, Emelia said. The voice came through faintly, brightening and fading. It sounded sedate and self-assured, not at all as Voxlauer had imagined it. The crowd noise behind the voice rose in high cresting trills cut by momentary bursts of static. A man next to Voxlauer told Emelia to turn it louder.

—That won't make any difference, Herr, she said. She came over to Voxlauer.—Another draft, Uncle?

—Please.

—You. Turn it louder, said the man. He smiled out of the side of his mouth at Voxlauer. —I don't think she wants to turn it louder, he said.

Voxlauer looked at him. He was heavyset and dressed in a blue work coat and knickers. —Turn it louder, he said again to Emelia. He slurred as he spoke, sloughing over his *s*'s in the manner of the Tyrolese. Voxlauer shifted a little on his stool and looked at the man steadily until their eyes met. The man's eyes were green and bloodshot and fixed driftingly on Voxlauer. He raised one eyebrow with a concerted effort. —You in need of something, citizen?

Voxlauer shrugged his shoulders. —A little quiet. He gestured at the radio. —I'm hearkening to our Führer.

The man grinned. —That's fine. He spun on his stool back to the bar.

The voice came in clearly now, rising steadily in pitch. That's static now, behind him, thought Voxlauer. But he knew at the same time that the voice itself was clear and the sound behind the voice was that of a huge number of people screaming. He closed his eyes.

—What's he saying now? said the man.

—Vienna is a pearl, said someone behind them.

—He said that?

—In the crown of the Reich.

The man let out a drawn-out, braying laugh. Emelia had returned with Voxlauer's beer and set it down before him. —You, girl, said the man.

Voxlauer looked over at him again. Emelia had stopped in mid-step and stood waiting for him to speak.

—This is a great day for your people, he said after a pause.

Emelia didn't answer. She stood midway between Voxlauer and the wall, looking past the man at the others behind him. Voxlauer felt the muscles of his neck knitting together. The man leaned toward her slightly, winking at Voxlauer as he did so. He looked at Emelia and grinned. When he spoke he spoke carefully and slowly.

—Back in Innsbruck we'd have stacked you straight by now, you dusky bitch.

The crowd noise was clearly crowd noise now and not static as Voxlauer rose and hit the man across the face with his beer glass so the beer itself sprayed in a high wandering arc over the heads of the assembled. In another moment there were people between them and he could hear his own shouts dying away and the drone from the radio rising and eclipsing everything. As the man was being led away he spat at Voxlauer and made to lunge at him. Blood was running from his nose and from a small bright hole above his right eye but he seemed oblivious to it. He was yelling at the top of his lungs and trying to break away from the two men, both strangers to Voxlauer, who were leading him outside. Voxlauer sat back against the bar and watched them go. Emelia was just behind him and he heard her breathing sputteringly, like a child, cursing herself quietly and telling herself to hush. A short time later she went back down the bar.

Across the square at Rindt's a similar crowd was faintly visible through the frosted-glass panels of the patio and Voxlauer sat and watched it for a while, counting his breaths quietly as he'd taught himself to. After a time he felt Emelia looking at him. He revolved slowly on the barstool to face her.

—Where's your father? he said.

Emelia made a face. —He's drunk.

—He has a right, said Voxlauer, looking at her. —Today, at least.

—Yes. I suppose so, Uncle. She was still watching him, solemnly, as though waiting on him for something. —What is it? he said.

She looked back meaningfully along the bar. Aside from the crackle of the radio the room was absolutely still. No one in the crowd was looking at him but no one was talking to anybody, either. The speech seemed to have ended.

Voxlauer stared at Emelia for a time. —Should I leave? he said finally.

—Please, Uncle, she whispered.

—Let's have another drink first, he said. —Not pilsner.

She brought him a glass of yellow Apfelschnaps and he drank it straight down and called out for another. His voice rang hollowly across the bar. She came back with the pint-sized blue ceramic bottle and put it beside his glass and went down the bar and stood at the far end, near the kitchen door, wiping intently at the top of the bar with a corner of her apron. Gradually the room began to fill again with talk and she went back to the taps and commenced drawing drafts of beer. Voxlauer drank until the little blue bottle was empty, then rose carefully from his barstool and went outside.

In truth, rather than in memory, Anna was nothing like a statue. She was schoolgirlish and talkative and given to sudden fits of extravagance with what little she still owned, her dresses and phonograph albums and tins of French tobacco, sensing that even these few relics of her past life would soon be gone. She was bourgeois in a way I'd never seen before, taking pleasure in things freely and matter-of-factly but feeling no sense of entitlement to them, no resentment when they were taken away from her. Her husband Andrei, a well-to-do country doctor with radical pretensions, had beaten her almost nightly for her lack of progressive thinking. She introduced herself as a Bolshevik when we met, which bewildered me at first; a few weeks passed before I realized it was entirely out of gratitude to the Revolution for taking her husband away to St. Petersburg.

My life with her began slowly and tentatively. There was a great amount of work to be done but we ate in grand style every evening, sitting at the long, warped, reverently polished dining table, gorging ourselves on all manner of tinned and potted delicacies. "Dress rehearsal for better days," Anna would say coyly when I tried to raise objections. It was hard for me most days to imagine anything much better, sitting there across from her. For a time I even forgot my own vague radical delusions. We slept an arm's length apart that first night on her wide, rolled-tin marriage bed, dressed in heavy flannel bedclothes against the chill, and she talked to me drunkenly, earnestly, in pieced-together German and French about her plans for the land and her troubles under the various occupations. She explained things to me patiently, repeating words and phrases often, questioning me sternly from time to time as a sister might an idle younger brother she's decided to improve.

It was as a sister, in fact, that I thought of her for most of that first year. I'd always felt the lack of one, more intensely, almost, than all the commoner wants that followed, and in Anna's company I felt the kind of carelessness and fond indifference I'd imagined brothers and sisters to feel toward one other. To think of someone so proud and adult as my lover would have scared me half to death, there at the beginning of our time. Anna, for her part, had lived so long alone in that narrow, drafty house that my presence in her bed must have seemed as much a terror as a bless-

*ing. Between our paired confusions, then, it was the better part of a
year before we came together finally as man and wife.*

*When we did it was with a great amount of laughter, of hesi-
tancy and of concern on my part to seem as though I'd done it all
before. I'd come in early to the house from turning hay and found
her standing at the window, staring out to where I'd been working,
her housedress loose about her shoulders and a look on her face as
though she'd just been handed down an order. I had no idea at first
what it was she wanted. After a few seconds she raised an arm
solemnly toward me and suddenly I understood and crossed the
room in my loose mud-clotted boots and kissed her. We went up
the stairs together to the pressed-tin bed and lay down on it. Afterward Anna told me we were married and I saw no reason in the
world not to believe her.*

*From that day Anna was my sister and my lover both, never
entirely the one thing or the other, not even in bed. She nursed me
through my attacks when they came, which was often in those first
few months, with a patience that made the most terrible of my
visions seem childish. We talked for hours on end about what happened in the war, the killing of the deserter and the death of my
father and everything that had come before and after, until my
memories began to break apart of their own accord and to take on
distinct shapes, separable from one another and from me. At night
she would draw me to her in a state of curious, impersonal desire,
almost of surprise, as though I were some stranger come entirely
by chance or accident into her bed. Often she called me by the
name of a boy she'd known in Kiev while still a girl, but I knew
very well she was calling out in those moments not to him or
to anything but her own memory-cluttered happiness. Afterward
she'd remember all manner of things with a calm, transported
clarity, bright with foresight and melancholy, and she'd talk in
careful detail about her childhood and youth and her luckless marriage as I lay motionless beside her. I never spoke at those times but
lay back in quiet attention, drawing tiredness and contentment
over me like a quilt.*

Gradually my attacks grew fewer. We worked hard and brought in a fair yield in those first years, when we still thought of the land as ours. Anna taught me Ukrainian stubbornly, almost ruthlessly, refusing for whole days to speak any French or German at all. I was steadily amazed at each successive side of her: her fierceness, her coquettishness, her vanity, her sobriety, her kindness even to those people in the village, and there were more than a few, who hated and envied her for the way she walked and spoke and acted when among them.

Every evening after dinner the phonograph case would be opened, and I'd be privileged with the duty of revolving the crank while she chose that night's opera from her collection of twenty, cleaning each of the three or four disks devotedly with a spit-dampened kerchief. Often as not, the music would be accompanied by dancing lessons, waltzes and polonaises and other equally anti-quated steps, taught with the same tireless severity as the Ukrain-ian but with far less success, as only four of her twenty operas offered music even remotely suitable. Anna favored the works of the German Romantics: Lohengrin, Tristan and Isolde, Weber's Euryanthe, Nicolai's Merry Wives of Windsor. *The irony in her love of German opera was not apparent to her. I often teasingly compared her to* Lohengrin's Elsa, *taking in a mysterious and enchanted stranger, though in fact it was Elisabeth in* Tannhäuser *she'd always most admired, pining away unto death for her despised and banished lover. My arrival in Cherkassy, sickly fugitive that I was, must have seemed to her like the fulfillment of her most fer-vent, opera-besotted dreams. Had I been any less pathetic she'd likely never have desired me.*

Anna's superstitiousness was deeply fixed in her. She kept a sil-ver icon of the trinity over her night table and talked to it when-ever she was alone, day or night, kneeling bare-legged on the floor and speaking in a straightforward, affectless tone of voice about the most minute details of our daily life. She felt no embarrassment when I found her there, smiling up at me contentedly from the far side of the bed, but never tried to get me to kneel beside her, either. She recovered her French quickly and within a few months we were holding long and intricate debates in a pidgin of our three lan-guages that would have sounded like cipher to anyone who over-

heard us. We called it the Tsar's Dutch, our invented language, and kept to it even after my cotton-mouthed Ukrainian had bettered. It seems to me now that even then, during our first few months together, we were practicing for a time when it would provide us with our only privacy. Five short years later, living on a collective farm outside Kiev with two hundred other kulaks and assorted class enemies and meeting only once a day, in the dining hall at a massive plank table with the forty-eight other workers in our section who regarded us, even the most petit-bourgeois of them, with unqualified suspicion and contempt, the Tsar's Dutch was near to all that was left us.

In 1921, in the middle of my third year with Anna, the Ukraine was retaken by the Bolsheviks. Less than a year later, on a September afternoon, the first motorcar I'd seen since crossing the border appeared unannounced and unexpected over the gentle roll of fields between Anna's house and the town and came to a stop twenty meters from where we stood, not doing much of anything, staring up the Cherkassy road as though waiting for just that motorcar to appear. It was a sand-colored G.A.Z. sedan with a folded-down canvas top and four men were sitting in it, dressed in high-collared brown coats and linen caps pulled down hard against the wind. None of them were wearing the Red Army uniforms still in fashion at that time and it was only by the looks on their faces as they crossed the field toward us and the fact that the driver remained behind the wheel staring blankly ahead of him with his goggles pushed down over his eyes that we knew them to be cadres. The smallest of them, a delicate-looking man in spectacles and a bow tie who reminded me of photographs I'd seen of the old Petersburg intellectuals, informed Anna with a crisp, calm, emotionless precision I couldn't help admiring that she had been identified by the Cherkassy soviet and the local village Mir as a kulak, a hoarder of grain and an enemy of the people and as such was to be transferred to a labor camp without delay. Alternatively, she could be sent to a newly inaugurated state farm, a sovkhoz, six hours to the north; the choice was hers. Why such an unusual offer was made we never learned, though Anna guessed it might have been in deference to her husband, who'd fallen in defense of the

*Revolution at the battle of Moscow two years earlier. I was flatly
ignored, though it was made clear I could follow her to either des-
tination if I chose. A truck would come for her or the both of us
that same evening.*

A light rain was falling as Voxlauer crossed the square past the
newly uncrated fountain and walked up into the woods, making
for the curtain of mist above the ruin. The square had been filling
with people all afternoon and as he looked down now policemen
were clearing a wide lane through the traffic and laying pylons
along its two sides and linking them together with lengths of yellow cord. A canvas-covered truck pulled to a halt alongside the
pylons and two men came down from the truck bed and began
unloading iron benches. Voxlauer reached into his pack and took
out a bar of chocolate he'd meant to give Emelia and ate it slowly,
watching the members of the post office band unpack their instru-
ments and tune them under the yellow and white awning of the
Amtshaus. A boy walked along a line of Sterno torches, lighting
them.

Voxlauer turned and continued up the hillside. He felt very
drunk and bewildered from the fight and the speech and swallowed
hard every few steps to keep an attack from coming. He counted
his breaths aloud to himself from one to seven. His voice rose
in front of him into the air. It's happening now, he said to himself. What we've all been waiting on. He remembered hitting the
Tyrolean with the glass of beer. He pictured himself swinging the
glass. It was a reflex, he thought. Anyone might have done it. But
he remembered the silence throughout the room afterward and the
look on Emelia's face, more frightened for what he had done than
for anything the Tyrolean had said to her. I can't go back, he
thought suddenly. I've done something now. It may not have been
so much but I have done it.

He thought for a while about the Tyrolean. If he was a big
Nazi he'd have been over at Rindt's, he thought, trying to calm
himself. Still. Everybody saw me hit him. The thought that the

fight, in itself, could mean nothing to the others at the bar in their excitement and their drunkenness seemed naïve and childish to him. That quiet afterward, that proves it, he thought. The quiet of recognition. They'd been waiting for me to do something and now I've given it to them. Given them cause.

To distract himself he thought about the Tyrolean again. He'll go back to Innsbruck and say he broke his nose murdering a Bolshevik, thought Voxlauer. He laughed. Or a Yid-lover. —He'll make chief of police now, said Voxlauer aloud. —Friends and neighbors! he shouted, flinching at the recoil of the silence all around him. —Children of the Reich! I humbly accept this office . . . Again his voice rose into the trees, warbling and shrill. The sound was painful to his ears and kept on even after the body of the sound had vanished and silence swept back around him like mud filling the groove where the wheel of a cart has passed. He continued up the slope as quietly as he could but the sound traveled with him now and would not leave him.

The dark ground tipped and swelled beneath him and he stumbled every few steps up to the first fields. At the junction with the valley road he remembered Frau Mayer and the cream and bore right along the edge of the spruce groves past the chapel. When he arrived at the house a light was burning in the kitchen, tremulous and gaslit, but no one answered to his knock. He peered in through the window and saw that the kitchen was empty. He crossed the farmyard to the stalls and slid the door open but saw only the crosswalk between the pens, narrow and straw-battened, and the animals shifting heavily in the dark at the sudden draft. He stood quietly awhile in the open door, listening to their breathing.

Returning across the wet ground to the house he called out and waited what seemed to him a very great length of time. He rapped again loudly on the door. After a few minutes more without an answer he stepped inside. To each side of him in the entryway the work clothes and jackets of the sons hung from pegs and lay crumpled among the boots and the hunting tack strewn loosely about the floor. Above the pegs skulls of deer mounted on birch-bark plaques hung one above the other, receding from great twelve-pointed racks to fluted, teacup-sized scalp bones just under the ceiling, more like the skulls of weasels or house cats than of deer. A black grouse over the kitchen lintel regarded him blankly out of one amber-beaded eye. He opened the door to the kitchen and blinked a moment in the light of the lamp set on the window table, then called out warblingly again into the house.

When his eyes had adjusted to the light he stepped into the kitchen and looked about him. There was the oven, there the stove. A cluster of pots and ladles hung over a wooden counter. An unpainted cherry-wood cupboard faced the counter and the stove front. He crossed over to the cupboard and pulled it open.

Squares of bacon wrapped in butcher's paper lined the uppermost shelf, ordered in neat, staggered rows like candles in a sacristy. Below the bacon were bundles of smoked sausage and bricks of cheese and below these were sacks of onions and potatoes and small plug-necked bottles of schnapps. Voxlauer took a few parcels of bacon and sausage and a handful of red onions and stuffed them into his pack. He sniffed at the potatoes, chose two of a good size, then uncorked a bottle and tipped it back and took a long, burning draft. —I'm on holiday today, too, said Voxlauer into the quiet. He stood awhile in the middle of the room, drinking. Then he took up the lamp and put away the bottle and went on into the darkened house.

The pantry behind the kitchen was piled to the rafters with jars of all sizes, cans of compote and preserves, fish and salted meat, vegetables and fruits floating gilded in their preservative brine. Voxlauer turned a jar of pickled eggs back and forth under the light, watching the oil swirl and settle. On his way into the parlor he stumbled over a stool and nearly let go of the lamp. He felt nauseous suddenly and stopped to breathe, setting the lamp down on a newly waxed cabinet covered in trinkets and curling brown photographs laid together end on end, like cards in a game of tarok. The room began to reel under his feet and he held tight to the cabinet's rim, focusing on the white lace dust cover. The faces of the sons smiled up at him from out of dark, patinaed frames. Before the pictures lay a broken-stemmed pipe and a pair of pince-nez and to the right of these, in frames of twisted ironwork, portraits of Georg Schönerer and Adolf Hitler.

The room of the two sons lay just beyond the parlor and Voxlauer entered it cautiously, holding the dying lamp out in front of him. He was standing between the narrow beds, looking at the banners and slogans covering the four walls, when the attack came. A shuddering noise like the sound of air caught by a train window rushed into the room and doubled him over against the bed. His breath exited his chest in one pauseless sweep as though sucked out by a bellows. He clung to the burled, palm-smoothed bedpost and vomited. The banners and swastikas and placards on the walls combined before his sight into a screen of dancing symbols and he cursed at it voicelessly and clenched his eyes tightly shut. But a horizonless field of shifting forms spread itself in front of his closed eyes, heaving and reeling sickeningly, he was forced to open them again onto the room. And still the vision persisted, containing the room too within it now, yawning endlessly before him, cold and gray and inexhaustible, widening even as he watched. I know what it is now, thought Voxlauer. I have a name for it.

—The future, he said into the room.

For an instant all his drunkenness left him and he looked at the density and profusion of color surrounding him with something approaching awe. Then just as suddenly the vision abandoned him and the drunkenness returned. With it came a screeching, directionless anger, rearing and sickening him and doubling him over again until his face was almost to the floor. He stumbled about the room from one wall to another, clawing at the posters and hangings and throwing them down into a heap between the beds. When the four walls were stripped bare he fell back from them onto one of the beds, leaning against the bedpost, sucking air into his lungs. After a time he stood up shakily and went out of the room.

He found the butter and the cream Frau Holzer had left out for him on the kitchen counter and went back to the cupboard, filling his pack randomly with parcels from the various shelves. Stumbling among the coats in the entryway he cursed and kicked a boot hard against the wainscoting. I've done this now, he thought. I've done this thing, too. Even though she was kind to me. He felt clear and lucid again and stood a long time in the entryway, swaying very slightly from side to side.

Like hitting the man in Pauli's bar. I can never come back here, either, he thought, sadly and calmly, as though looking back on himself from a place far removed in time. He began to take the parcels out again, one by one, from his pack, arranging them in a straight white row under the coats. Then he stopped himself, smiling a little. —That won't do anything now, Oskar, he said aloud, picking the parcels up. A short time later he lurched out into the yard and stood watching his breath rise and spread across the sky, icy and black and without end.

The first weeks on the collective Anna moved and spoke and took in the things around her as though asleep. She knew what had happened, in the same sense that she knew her date of birth or her name or the time of year, and was able to learn, with my help, the things she needed to learn to satisfy the sovkhoz bosses, but something had shifted incontrovertibly in her image of the world and its intentions toward her and from then on it seemed as if our roles had been reversed—she was now the exile from a faraway country and I was both her translator and her guide. Most painfully of all to me, she never seemed indignant or resentful as she went about the various absurd and demeaning chores assigned to her to remove her "kulak sense of privilege"; if anything it was her eagerness to please, her blank-faced willingness to do whatever was asked of her, that confused the other workers in her brigade and kept her in regular disfavor with the Women's Council. Each night she'd tell me with a strange, apologetic smile the things she'd done that day and I'd return her smile blankly, idiotically, knowing as well as she did that the jobs had been meant to humiliate her and the next day would bring more of the same.

Yet all during that time, incredible as it seems to me now, I held adamantly to my belief in Lenin and participated in the regular discussion groups on Wednesday and Friday evenings, asking countless questions of the cadre instructors, struggling to see the ideal behind the bleak fact of the collective. Anna began for some reason to believe that our time on the sovkhoz would soon be over and I made every effort not to discourage her, convinced as I was that conditions would soon improve. I began to write letters home to Maman, letters full of Leninist rhetoric and self-righteous contempt for my old life, but in spite of her difficulty understanding the change in me, I saw that she had long since forgiven me for deserting; it was clear from her first reply that she held Lenin and his international horde of terrorists and saboteurs to blame. Her regular rants against "Bolshevikism" provided Anna and me with a great many evenings' entertainment. For a while we recovered something of our former happiness.

Our first three years on the sovkhoz passed more or less in this way. Then slowly, irresistibly, in a succession of lighter and heavier shocks, the last of our belief in things expired. Lenin's death, when it finally came, seemed like nothing to me so much as a token of my own disillusionment. More and more of the collective's yield was requisitioned each year to feed the workers in the cities and fund the first of Stalin's Five-Year Plans; the bosses became more and more irritable and suspicious of everything, fighting openly now among themselves, and our standing in the sovkhoz remained peripheral and suspect in spite of my continuing avowals of enthusiasm and Anna's unceasing efforts at goodwill.

On our brief furloughs home we found ourselves reviled as soviet lackeys by the same people who'd reported us to the cadres five years before; the regime had lost the last of its support in the countryside, and grain-hoarders and suspected rebels were shot daily in the villages. Many of the richer peasants slaughtered their animals in the public markets and burned their houses to the ground so no more could be taken from them. The roads from one town to another began to fill with families with the stricken, uncomprehending look of people in the initial stages of starvation. A saying from before the Revolution came back into common use, even on the collective: "A bad harvest comes from God; famine comes from the Tsar." Already some were predicting the coming famine would be the worst that the country had ever seen.

When the Great Famine hit in the winter of '32 I learned quickly that the hunger I'd known in the time of my desertion had been less than a passing pang. The produce storehouses of the collective were put under round-the-clock watch by an entire company of Red Army infantry and anyone approaching within twenty meters was fired on. The cities were far worse off than the countryside: in Cherkassy the people ate dogs, the bark off trees, even one another. Grain continued to be sent north by train to finance the latest of Stalin's construction drives. Anna fell ill, as did many others on the collective, and I had nothing at all to give her. When it became clear to everyone that she was dying I was allowed to take her home and she bettered slightly there, enough to move frailly through the house from one window to another, watching women from the village sowing cabbage and beets on the narrow strip of land that had once briefly belonged to her.

This and another three years, Père, I would have to tell you

At first light of day Voxlauer was high on the west ridge, shivering in the shadow of the tree line along a strip of clear-cut turf. The tangle of the ridge spread and fell away beneath him and vanished over Pergau into the mist. He leaned back against a knotted pine, staring down along the ridge out of the wet, red corners of his eyes. An hour earlier he'd passed through the clearing where the bones of the deer lay scattered in all directions through the scrub and the silvered bracken, radiating out spokelike from the gutted ribs. At some point in the night he'd been down to the cottage where he'd emptied his pack and put on his coat and stowed the bottle in one of its pockets. At some point also he had vomited and a clotted pinkish oil clung to his collar and beard and crept slowly in a crescent down his shirtfront. He sat back with the chamber of the shotgun across his knees and waited, wheezing quietly from the cold.

The shadow of the pines grew steadily sharper and a high reel of birdsong inclined up the slope toward him. Light was gathering now and the thought of day brought with it a panic he'd not known for years, sweeping over him inescapably, holding his body suspended in its center like a wave of dark gray water. —Mother of Christ, he said aloud. He shut his eyes and felt a shiver run down his leg and a warm trickle of piss a moment after. Reluctantly he allowed his eyes to open. There was a movement in the trees and he leaned over gratefully into the cold wet turf.

It was a doe this time with a very young foal. Voxlauer's hands spasmed as he undid the safety of the shotgun and brought it level, bracing the stock against his collarbone. All along the tree line now the brush seemed alive with furtive movement. He shifted the shotgun slightly and both deer jerked up at once and struck off with loud harsh barks into the pines.

Voxlauer scrabbled to his feet and ran across the slope into the trees. As though down a long corridor he heard the snapping of twigs hush and recede behind a thickening screen of yellow wood. He struck in after the sound, holding the gun barrel crosswise in front of him like a King's Hussar, throwing all the weight of his body forward. Branches clawed at his sleeves then lifted suddenly and spread apart as the ground fell away and he felt himself sliding and tumbling and brought the rifle close to his chest. He was rolling now and let the slope carry him down in loose ragged somersaults, faster and faster, with his legs flying up behind him and the roots gouging into his shoulders and ribs. The light spun and heaved. At a buckling in the slope the gun discharged both its barrels and he felt a pain across his thighs that beat hotly in his throat and against his closed eyes. He came to rest on his back with his head facing downhill and warm wellings of blood pooling under the tails of his shirt. The sky was still turning, buckling, righting itself and buckling again. Somewhere close to his head was the sound of running water.

Voxlauer lay for a long time with his eyes on the raked sky. His mouth felt chapped and blistered and eventually he pulled himself down to the water and drank. Afterward he rolled onto his back again, breathing in soft, musical rasps, and tried to stand. To his amazement he found that he could and that the pain was abstract and far away. His pants and shirtfront were wet and this troubled him vaguely but as he walked he tried hard to think of something else and after a time he succeeded. He felt small and lighter than air and saw himself drifting in a boat on a wide, shallow lake, letting his arms trail down in the water, dragging his fingers through the weeds.

He managed to reach a road before he collapsed again. Close by was a house and the smell of woodsmoke wafted sweetly down to him. He closed his eyes and lay back with his knees drawn into his chest and that was how she discovered him, his legs half in the ditch and his coat bunched and furled around his ankles, his arms trailing off in the dirt to either side. She pulled him upright by the shirt collar and shook him until the color came back into his face and shoulders, then forced him to stand and, one arm braced against his back to steady him, led him up to the villa.

The Valley

———◆———

April–July 1938

Else set the pot and cups on a lacquered tray and brought it in to him where he sat propped up on the bed with his swaddled legs spread in a V over the quilting. There was dust in the room and she couldn't see his face clearly for the sunbeams but she knew he was awake. He shifted heavily as she entered and the loose bed frame creaked under him. —I've made coffee, she said, as though it were the most natural thing in the world for him to be there.

Voxlauer stared at her a moment. She was standing over him, gracious and matronlike, waiting for him to speak. —Thank you, Fräulein, he said finally. He took the cup offered him and levered it slowly up to his mouth. —It's wonderfully bright in here.

She frowned at this. —Should I pull the curtains?

—No. Leave them open, please.

—I thought you might like some air, she said, going to the window. —It's not warm outside, but the air is fine.

—Thank you. Open it if you want to.

—What?

—I said open it if you want to. The window. Please do as you would on any other day.

She turned to him and smiled. —On any other day, Herr Voxlauer?

—I'd like not to put you to any sort of trouble.

—Well, she said, turning to the window again and pulling it

carefully open with both hands, as though a pane might fall—
aside from the trouble of hauling a full-grown body up into my
kitchen and spending a night keeping it from bleeding all over
my bedsheets, and three nights after that listening to it muttering all sorts of horrors, and making my bed here on the parlor
couch, which, as you can see, she said, turning to smile at him—is
losing its stuffing, you've not put me out so very much. Besides,
having put *yourself* to the trouble, Herr Voxlauer, of falling on a
loaded gun, it doesn't seem so much for me to open my own parlor
window.

Voxlauer was quiet a moment. —I thought this was the bedroom, he said.

—Where you are is the bedroom, said Else, opening a second
window. —Where I am, Herr Voxlauer, is the parlor. She brought a
footstool over to the bed and sat down on it. —So.

—So, said Voxlauer. He smiled shamefacedly. —I suppose a
knock on your front door might have been simpler.

She had brought a pair of boots from under the bed and was
working her feet into them, frowning slightly. They closed with
buckles across the ankles and she drew them snug and then raised
her eyes to look at him. The coffee she had given him was cold but
strong and he passed his tongue back and forth across his teeth,
grateful for its bitterness.

—How did you get me up here, Fräulein? With pulleys?

Else shrugged. —I'm heavy-boned, thank you. Built for the
country life. Unlike yourself, if I may say so.

—Yes, Fräulein. I'm sure you're right. He passed a hand over
his forehead. —Have I had a fever?

She nodded, letting out a mock-weary breath. —A right
plague of it. You were very talkative, as I've said, but a bit weak on
specifics. Her fine straight hair wisped outward with her breath
and her head tilted back from him distrustfully. The light behind
her was whorled and dark, like river water. —How on God's earth
did you manage it?

Voxlauer looked down at his legs. A band of black stains tra-
versed his thighs from right to left, fanning out along his left leg,

123

graceful and intricate as a tattoo. He shook his head. —Fool's luck, he said at last, grinning at her.

In the evening she undid the wraps and cleaned the cuts and painted them with Mercurochrome and he saw that they were not very deep. The strangeness of what had happened was dawning on him now, coldly and steadily, but Else seemed perfectly at ease and happy to have him there to complain about and tend to. She showed him some loose bits of shot on a saucer and pointed to the holes each had come from, thin rust-colored grooves bordered by a dull, lifeless white. The skin was flayed in ribbons above his knee-caps and the muscle underneath showed a bright garish red, like the inside of a deerskin, but he found he could move both legs slowly up and down without too much pain. —Sit back now, Else said angrily. —You'll only start them going again. And in fact as he brought his legs together he felt a warmth welling under the bandages and a prickling seeping into the bone just above the cuts. He lay back very carefully and closed his eyes.

When he opened them again the light was ebbing from the room and he saw her highlighted through the glass, working a round patch of earth in the garden with a spade. She had come and gone all day from the room, taking little notice of him as he lay on the bed, rarely staying long in his sight. Her attitude toward him was so different now from what it had been on their walk down the hill, so inexplicably mild and gracious, indulgent and disinterested at once, as though his presence there on her bed were a given, not to be fretted over—his confusion had grown steadily more complete since the morning. Now he watched her in quiet detail as she fussed somewhat coquettishly over the ground, worrying it with sharp quick gouges of the spade. After every few passes she stepped back and surveyed the plot, her round face twisting into a smile as though acknowledging her foolishness. Her hair caught the last weak light in its gloss and darkened her smooth, ageless, nearly sexless features. Voxlauer closed his eyes for a long time and when he opened them she was still in the garden, crouched down pulling roots from the spaded ground, the color almost gone from the windowpanes. As he watched her, the twilight wandered down across them, stooping like a willow bough. A few minutes later she came inside.

She brought supper to him as he lay half awake with his head against the bedboard: tinned tomatoes in an omelette with leeks and gray, rye-seed-speckled cheese. He called to her when he was done and she came down from the kitchen with a mug of sweet brown beer. While he drank she took the dishes and returned with a lamp and a pile of battered books, spines cracked and stained to illegibility. She put the lamp down by the bed on a night table and lit it and sat down with an earnest and businesslike air on the stool. —I've not had an audience in a while, she said, seeing him watching her. —What shall we read?

—You're a schoolteacher, said Voxlauer, putting down his mug. —I'd forgotten.

—Answer the question, Herr Voxlauer, or we'll send you to the corner without your beer. You'd not like that much, I fancy. She smiled.

Voxlauer sighed. —Give us the choices please, Fräulein.

—*Max and Moritz,* Else said reverently. —*Hatschi-Bratschi. King Farú.* Robert Walser—

—Those are all children's reads.

She frowned. —Walser isn't.

—No?

—He's Swiss.

—All right. Let's have the Walser then, said Voxlauer, lying back. Years later her voice would remain clearest in his memory, low-riven and solemn, secretive and measured, the texture and the color of crushed wool. The close, half-drawn breaths, the unspooling sadness of that voice. It's resignedness. She read evenly and slowly, stopping now and again for a sip of his beer, and kept steadily on as his eyes fell closed. The lamp sputtered and smoked behind her.

• • •

Once there was a town. The people in it were merely puppets. But they spoke and walked, had grace and sensitivity and were very polite. Not only did they say "Good morning!" or "Good night!" they meant it quite sincerely. These people possessed sincerity.

In spite of this, they were very much city people. Smoothly, if reluctantly, they'd shed all things coarse-grained and countryish. The cut of their clothes and of their manners were the finest that anyone, tailor or socialite, could possibly imagine. Old worn-out unraveling outfits were worn by nobody. Good taste was universal. The so-called rabble was unheard-of; everyone was completely alike in demeanor and erudition without resembling one another, which would of course have grown tiresome. On the street one met no one but attractive, elegant persons of noble mien. Freedom was a thing one knew well to guide, to have in hand, to rein in and to cherish. For this reason controversies over questions of public decency never occurred. Insults to the common morality were equally undreamt-of.

The women especially were wonderful. Their fashions were as charming as they were practical, as seductive as they were well designed, as titillating as they were proper. Morality seduced! Young men loped after it in the evenings, slowly, dreamily, without falling into greedier, hastier rhythms. The women went about in a sort of trousers, usually of white or pale blue lace, which rose and then wound tightly around their waists. Their shoes were tall, colorful and of the finest leather. The way these shoes clambered up the legs, and the legs felt themselves enclosed by something precious, and the men, in turn, imagined what those legs were feeling, was glorious! This wearing of pants had the further advantage that the women brought a spirit and eloquence into their gait, which, hidden under skirts, had felt itself less noticed and appraised.

On the whole, quite simply everything became "Emotion." The most miniscule things were a part of it. The businesses ran brilliantly, as the merchants were vigorous, industrious and honest. They were honest out of conviction and tact. They had no desire to make life, beautiful and airy as it was, any harder for one another. There was more than enough money, plenty for everyone, since everyone was so responsible, looking first to the fundamentals;

there was no such thing as Sunday, nor any religion either, over whose dictates one might fall into disagreement. The houses of entertainment took the place of churches and the people gathered there devotedly. Pleasure for these people was a deep and holy matter. That one remained pure even in pleasure was obvious, since everybody felt a need for it.

There were no poets. Poets would have found nothing new or high-minded to write about. There were no professional artists of any kind, as a natural aptitude for the arts was commonplace. A fine thing, when people have no need anymore of artists to be artistic. They had learned to view their senses as precious and to make full use of them. There was no cause to look up fine sayings in ancient texts because one had one's own fine-grained and particular perception. One spoke well when one had cause to speak, one had a mastery of the tongue without knowing whence it came . . .

The men were beautiful. Their carriage bespoke their erudition. They delighted in many things, they were busy at many tasks, but everything that happened did so in connection with the love of beautiful women. All of life was drawn into this fine, dreamlike relation. One spoke and thought of everything with deep emotion. Business matters were conducted more simply, more discreetly and more nobly than is now the case. There were no so-called higher things. The very idea would have been an intolerable suffering for these people, who found beauty in everything.

Are you asleep?

Voxlauer woke to dull pains in his legs and Else's still form beside him wrapped in a patterned sheet. He rose and limped to the kitchen in search of a chamber pot and, finding none, stepped out into the early-morning dampness, a bright mist hemming in the pines. The bleeding seemed to have lessened. He hobbled back past the house and leaned over behind a solitary birch, pissing against the white trunk and down onto a skirt of mud-colored drift. Three days now I've been here, he thought, leaning against the tree. Or is it four . . . ? He felt unbearably old suddenly, watching his piss trickle into the snow. And her inside sleeping. Suddenly the past day and evening and above all the fact of her there in the bed asleep served as nothing to him but proof of his own harmlessness, his nonexistence, a photograph projected onto a paper screen. To his own surprise he laughed at this, a rasping, hollow laugh that traveled dully and gracelessly off into the woods. Watch yourself, Oskar, he said. Button up your pants. He shook his head a few times violently from side to side, still smiling at himself without the least affection, then limped back to the villa through the snow. When he came into the bedroom he saw she now lay with half of her body out of the covers, sighing and whispering in her sleep. He sat down on the stool and pressed the heels of his palms against his knees.

An hour later she stirred. —Is it morning?

—It looks to be. Voxlauer smiled. —I had best be going.

—Yes, she said sleepily. —Have you had any breakfast?

—Thank you. How did you sleep?

—Very well . . . You've had breakfast? she said again. She seemed to be making an effort to see him clearly, or perhaps to place him in her memory.

—Yes. There's coffee in the kitchen, if you'd like any.

She sat up all at once, awake now, squinting at him. —You've been walking.

He nodded. —An undeserved miracle. I'll go back to my hut now, if you'll excuse me, and fall over.

She smiled. —Why not fall over here, Herr Voxlauer, and spare yourself the trouble?

—Thank you, Fräulein. You're very kind. I'm ashamed to say that my dignity won't allow it.

—Your dignity? said Else, squinting again. —What does your dignity have to do with anything here, Herr Voxlauer?

—Nothing, I'm sure, Fräulein. I'd rather not incommode you further.

She blinked a few times at this in mock surprise. —Have I been incommoded, sir?

—Well. You've been put out, at least, said Voxlauer, feeling the blood rushing to his face at her joke. He felt adolescent and intensely spinsterish both, sitting there a few feet from the bed looking down at her, unable to laugh or reply or even to force his mouth into a grin. An innocent enough joke, a simple joke, he told himself, not meeting her eyes now but looking down absurdly at the floor. He thought suddenly then, quite naturally, of Anna, not with any sense of shame but with a sharp pang of longing for their effortless way together.

—I'll be going then, Fräulein, he managed after an extended silence.

—You're sure you can manage? Else said, looking at him doubtfully.

—I think so. Yes.

—Well. I'll stay where I am, then. She fell back and drew the blanket ends closer around her, turning over into the sheets.

—I'll bring those sketches down sometime soon, if you like, said Voxlauer, rising cautiously from the stool.

She made a small flapping gesture with her fingers. —Yes. The sketches, she said, drawing herself farther into the blankets.

—Good morning then, Fräulein, said Voxlauer quietly. He took the smoke-blackened kettle off the stove as he went out.

By the time he arrived at the cottage new pains had begun and his frayed pants were stiff and sodden to the ankles. Wine-dark tracings of blood rose upward along the seams and his socks had sloughed off inside his boots. He undressed in the cool of the little alcove and rebandaged his legs carefully, brushing flakes of dried blood and Mercurochrome onto the floor, then lay back on the pallet and watched the light gather into a porthole-shaped mass and travel down the wall toward a hand-shaped smudge above the bed. Through the window came the high, twiglike clatter of a rail.

click click click

A shape spun down from somewhere overhead, throwing sparks onto his eyes. —Père? whispered Voxlauer. His eyelids fluttered and the balls of his eyes moved sluggishly back and forth under their weight. As he turned his head the shape spun off to the left, humming quietly, like a mortar shell arcing into a drift. A soft, dull *ping!* followed, like a spoon dropped from a low height onto the floor. Then the click. Voxlauer sat up, suddenly wide awake again. —She asked me how I managed it, he said. *Ping!* came the answer from above the bed. He ignored the noise and focused his attention on remembering. Else turning onto her side, face into the sheets, right arm twisted back behind her. Sitting up in bed to see him better, frowning slightly as she spoke. The fluttering of her fingers as he'd turned to go.

It grew warmer in the room and the column of light trembled and began to bend. Voxlauer turned his head and looked through the porthole at the sheet of wind-harried water and the brightening pines, tapping his thumb softly against the glass. He stretched an arm to the handprint on the wall and covered it with his palm. The handprint of a child or of a very young girl, plump-fingered and careless. He got up and went to the table.

Bringing the lexicon down from the shelf he took out the sketches and laid them in a row with the portraits on either end and the little still life between them. It was crudely and effortfully made, six thick-traced curves drawn together into thorned stems ending in bunched-together, exaggerated blossoms. Voxlauer bent over the paper, bringing his face slowly toward it until his vision blurred. Tiny flakelets of charcoal spun and danced under his breath. He moved away. A pain stirred in his legs and he brought them stiffly together under the table, sliding the two portraits nearer to him. After a short time it subsided and he bent his head again over the sketches.

The portraits, for their part, were virtually invisible, as though the hand which had figured them had scarcely come in contact with the paper but had hovered instead in close ribboning circles just above it, bobbing and circling like a horsefly. Both seemed drawn from a single quivering thread curving forward and back again, gently spinning a likeness. The face in the first he recognized now as Else's and in the second the same face perhaps fifteen years younger smiled out at him from an open window, the long straight hair twisted into braids and the brow pulled back sharply as if in pride or doubt. The lines of the portrait thinned and gathered at the paper's edge into smoky, cobweb-figured nets, lightening and drifting leftward off the page. All three sketches were dated the preceding summer. He put them back into the lexicon and lay down on the pallet with his face against the cool plaster, picturing her. —How did I manage it? he said aloud.

One week later as Voxlauer was gathering wood in a stand of dead firs he saw Else walking on a logging track not fifty meters below him. A girl ran ahead of her on the wet spring turf, stopping now and again to look back and call something out with a laugh and a toss of her loose, coal-black hair. A few meters further on Else called the girl to her and they bent down together over a budding elderberry bush. He watched them a few moments longer, keeping back among the firs, then called out a hello and slid awkwardly down the slope. The girl's face as he drew near had the same frowning, half-friendly look he'd seen in the second portrait. —Ach! It's you, Herr Voxlauer, Else said, curtsying. —Back to average, I hope?

—They tell me I'll live to the play pump organ again, Fräulein, in the idiots' choir. The girl laughed at this. She stood a few steps past them up the road, toying with a knotted kerchief, watching him closely.

—You should meet Theresa, Oskar, Else said. —Resi, come here. This is Oskar. He lives in Opa's cottage now, and minds the ponds.

The girl smiled up at him. —You shot yourself in the knees, she said.

Voxlauer looked at Else.

—A funny business, Oskar, she said. —I had to tell somebody.

—I have brand-new knees now, said Voxlauer to the girl. —Fresh off the presses. He flexed his knees and cut a caper. —No need to worry. See?

—I wasn't worrying, said the girl. She extended a hand and he shook it solemnly.

The girl ran ahead of Else and Voxlauer as they walked, gathering pine needles from the track into her kerchief, mumbling to herself. They walked together measuredly and slowly, almost shyly now in the presence of the girl, and it seemed to Voxlauer for the second time that something had changed between them. He held his bag of kindling by its strap, whistling tonelessly and glancing at her every few moments. —You should have come by for those sketches, he said. —It's remarkable, the likeness. He looked again at the girl.

—I don't go into that cottage anymore, Herr Voxlauer. I've told you that already.

—Yes. You have.

—If you want me to have those drawings, you'll have to courier them down to me, I'm afraid. She smiled. —Something like the postman.

—I've been crippled till today, Fräulein. A tragic case study. Dragging myself around the cottage by my gums.

—With a bottle in each hand you don't leave yourself much option, Herr Voxlauer. She sighed. —I've seen enough to know.

He put out a hand and stopped her. —Is that all you've seen, Fräulein?

She smiled a little, raising her eyebrows at him. —I beg your pardon? What else should I have seen?

—All sorts of things, he said, still holding her by the arm. —I don't understand how you could have missed them. What's happening in town, for instance. What's happening to everybody. Don't you ever go to town?

The smile disappeared from her face and she looked at him as if he'd insulted her. After a moment she laughed. —You can't imagine what all I've seen. I don't like to go to town, it's true. In spite of this, I am not a hermit, Herr Voxlauer. Not by any stretch.

—Then maybe you'd explain things to me. I am one, as I'm

sure Herr Piedernig has told you. He hesitated, glancing up the road to where the girl was standing, watching them. —I've been away so long, because of this. What's happening. He paused again. —This and other things like it. I'm afraid to go anywhere. I can't go anywhere. He laughed. —I don't expect you to understand, Fräulein. Don't look so worried.

Else waited a long time to answer him, looking off into the trees. —What's happening now has never happened before, she said finally.

—There was a feeling I got from the war, he said—that I get now in town. It came to the Ukraine, too, a few years after I went there. But it began in the war. He stopped and took a breath. —That was one reason I stayed away. I was afraid to come back and find it here. I couldn't bear to come back and find that everything had changed. He waited until she turned again, frowning, to look at him, before he continued. —And it has. It has changed. You must see that.

—I don't know that anything has changed, in the way that you mean.

—Of course it has, Fräulein Bauer. Everything's changed. You know that very well. Why else would you be up here, for the love of Christ? Do you enjoy it so much up here in the woods? Are you perhaps taking the alpine cure?

As if in answer to his question, Else said:—What were your other reasons? She was looking not at him now, but at the girl. —For leaving, she added, when he didn't seem to understand her. —You must have had others.

A wind was coming up through the tops of the trees. The girl was standing with her head far back, looking at the sky.

—I did certain things that can't be undone, Voxlauer said, letting his eyes rest on Else. She was still watching the girl. —Have you ever done a thing like that?

Slowly she loosened her arm from his grip. —Yes, I have. I've done some things, and I know some others. I know what you did at the Holzer farm last Friday. She waited a moment for him to respond, then said:—Do you think so little of yourself, Herr Voxlauer?

Voxlauer opened his mouth to speak, made a little sound, then let it fall closed again. The girl had come closer and stood throwing pebbles at his ankles. —Those aren't my knees, he said, bending stiffly down to her. She turned to Else and silently handed her the handkerchief. —We'll be going soon, Resi, Else said. The girl cursed and ran off up the track. They began walking again with an arm's length between them.

—Does she live with you? said Voxlauer.

—She lives with her father's family in St. Marein.

—I thought I might have noticed her.

—Yes.

—I'd mistaken her for you in those sketches.

—Yes. Well, you didn't know about her until today, did you, Herr Voxlauer.

—No, I didn't. He smiled at her. —I'm a bit of a fool.

—And a drunk, she said, looking off into the trees. —And that's a shame, Herr Voxlauer, because otherwise we get along very nicely.

Voxlauer stopped short and took hold of her arm again. —Be careful, Fräulein. All gamekeepers are not alike.

—I deserved that, I suppose, she said, staring past him up the road.

—Don't confuse me with your father, that's all. Or with mine.

—What a habit you have of grabbing hold of a person, Else said expressionlessly, waiting for him to let go of her. They walked without speaking for a while. Where the track met the road she slowed slightly and took hold of his hand. The girl was waiting restlessly for them at the next turning. Else turned Voxlauer wordlessly to face her and looked straight up into his eyes, pushing her fingertips lightly into his ribs. Her face was unsmiling now and close to his.

—I won't confuse you, Herr Voxlauer, she whispered.

That first night it seemed to Voxlauer they were in the low cold attic of a house full of people with no idea what was happening above them. He would reach over and lay hold of her still form, put together of all the quiet dark suffering things of this world, and she would turn and stretch herself lazily in her sleep. She was unaware of his hand, unaware of the room, unaware even that she was suffering. Maybe she isn't, thought Voxlauer, taking in a breath. The thought seemed hollow and false at first but bloomed in him slowly, like a drink of wine. He sat up in the bed to look at her.

She slept with her knuckles to her mouth like a teething child, indifferent to everything but sleep. In the dull glow of the lamp she looked like something seen through silt-dark water. Gradually as Voxlauer watched her she became frightening to him, other-worldly, alien in her completeness. It seemed to him that if she awoke she would look at him calmly and he would die.

Her eyes as he watched them moved back and forth serenely under their heavy lids. The air whistled in her mouth. A scar ran the length of her side, relic of a childhood burn, and the rippled skin felt smooth and fossil-like under his hand. He ran his fingertips along it from her shoulder blade to her hip. Like the rest of her body it reminded him of water, of two stones clicking together at the bottom of a river. Her arm closed over it protectively. Her eyes opened.

—Give me a kiss, she said.

Slowly, haltingly, he bent to kiss her. She was looking up at him as he'd been afraid she would, calmly and deliberately, eyes still faraway with sleep. Sleepily she raised an arm and brought it to his neck and pulled him closer. Her lips were cool and dry and as he moved his mouth across them they drew together and slowly parted. Her breath came soft and noiseless against his skin and he felt a sudden tightness in his throat and brought his lips along her neck. She sighed. She was seemingly all things, smooth and whorled, soft and edged, light and dark. But she was not all things. She had a want. He sucked his breath in sharply and bent over her.

Again it seemed to him that they were in a tiny attic room. People were asleep beneath them and he could hear them groaning and creaking in their beds. She was holding his hips loosely in her hands like the reins of a cart and he was moving above her. The room continued dwindling, focusing itself into a grain of clear, white light. She was straining up to meet him, propping herself on her elbows. He was alive, alive! He was not afraid. All the past had been exploded. They were moving together in an absence of future and past. Light was there, sped up into a film reel of stuttering movement. A spare dry snow was falling all around them in the room. He looked out at it and cried.

In the early morning he was sitting at the edge of the bed, wide awake. She was awake also and talking to him and he felt calm and effortless.

—I'm walking shoulder to shoulder in a wide line of people, a search party, across a field of very tall grass. You're there, Oskar, and Walter and Herta are there, and so is my father, who is looking well. Our arms are linked together and we're moving step by step across the field. The line comes to a point with me and falls away on either side as far as I can see.

—We're walking?

She frowned. —Not so much walking, I think, as hovering. Gliding. The grass is well above our heads, more like bamboo, really, or very high reeds. The farther we go the harder it is to keep together. The woman next to me turns toward me and smiles. "Let go of my arm, Else," she says. "Go and find it." "Who?" I ask. "The baby," she whispers, her mouth close to my ear. I'm aware then suddenly of moving my legs and of a smell in the air like beeswax, or summer pollen.

She paused a moment, fingering the sheet.

—We've separated now into smaller groups and soon I've lost sight of everybody. A storm is building in the distance, black and horrible-looking, and I duck down under a bush to escape the wind. The grass is being beaten now in great swaths all around me. Close by on the ground I see someone else hiding, half hidden by the bush. I bend down closer and see a tiny gray man with the head of a sparrow.

—Christ! said Voxlauer, laughing.

—Listen, Oskar. Are you listening?

—Is it the baby?

She nodded. —He peers at me out of his frightened yellow eyes, then up at the sky. I'm filled all at once with a strange nervous happiness. "Lie down," I tell him. "The grass will cover you." He looks at me gratefully, then disappears.

Later I rejoin the others. I see nobody I recognize and begin to feel afraid. It's as if the line of people I knew has been replaced, though I begin to recognize some of the faces. They're all huddled together, discussing something in whispers. "Where have you been?" they ask. They seem very surprised to see me. "Hiding the little promise!" I laugh back at them. They turn away from me, beaten.

—Beaten? said Voxlauer, looking at her confusedly.

—Beaten, said Else, smiling.

Over the next days and weeks his feeling of blank surprise and shock consolidated itself into something understood and manageable even as each surprise led obliquely to the next like views in a baroque garden, distracting and bewildering him until he felt altogether lost in its immensity. That he could walk down at a given hour, cross the empty square at Pergau, turn up her drive and climb the villa steps to find her waiting for him in the narrow kitchen, calm and expectant, dumbfounded him each day as it had on the first. Often he would wonder secretly at his inability to get over his surprise. Am I so modest? he would ask, looking at himself in her parlor mirror late at night when she was sleeping. Do I think so little of myself? He would turn his body to the right and left, studying it in the light of the lamp: his pale, flat, bearded face, his wandering, distrustful eyes, his belly, his legs, his stooped, servile shoulders. Yes, he would think. I do think little of myself. Then it would come over him again, the slow, almost painfully acute surprise, the stubborn disbelief. And he'd laugh at his pitiful reflection in the dark.

—Look here, said Else.

They'd been walking along the valley road, shirtsleeved in the mid-April sun. She had stopped and let go of his arm and now stood bent over the stump of a fallen birch, holding the brush aside for him to see. With her free hand she pointed to a thing like a cloven oak leaf hanging from the tattered bark. —Look here, Oskar, she said.

Bending closer, he saw it was a moth of some kind, covered in silver fur, matted and slick like the pelt of an otter. Its head was hidden in a cowl of sulfur bristles. Bands of sulfur ran into pools along its abdomen, glowing dully against the silver. The bark curled away above it and it hung fixed in the shadow, motionless and gilded as an icon. —What is it? said Voxlauer, not knowing what to say to her.

Else took its wings between her fingers and pulled them open. The bands he'd imagined to be marks along the body now resolved themselves into bright yellow crescents on the underwings. The hooked black legs scrabbled wildly and the fern-shaped antennae batted and quivered against her thumbs. She held it up for his instruction, turning it slowly, as she might have for one of her schoolchildren. He nodded.

She was precious to him now, ridiculously so, more precious already after those few weeks than Anna had ever been. Any guilt he felt at this was eclipsed by his fear, not of her, precisely, but of the future: the future he'd seen the night of his accident, the future he was connected to again, against his will and intention, because of her. He could no more disconnect himself from it now than he could be rid of his surprise at the fact of her presence in his life each day. The image of Anna's face the day she died came to him suddenly, drawn and bloodless, grayer than the wallpaper behind it. No, he thought. I won't do it. I won't move upstream against the future anymore. I can't.

—Dove-of-the-moon, Else was saying brightly. —*Colias mnemosyne*. Very rare here so early. She held the wings spread between her thumbs now, like a cat's cradle. —I think we'll take it home with us, for Resi's box. Do you have a kerchief, Oskar?

—Oskar? she said again.

—Yes, of course. I have one here, said Voxlauer quickly, reaching into his pocket.

—Take it, said Else. —Carefully. Do you see this row of spots, here? Along the abdomen?

—Yes.

—Those are its breathing holes.

One morning, a week after the beginning of their time, they awoke to find everything under glass. The garden tinkled like a chandelier and the transparent crowns of the pines along the road glinted amber and turquoise in the early light. Else wore a blue cotton wrap over a calico dress and carried a jar of olives in a linen purse, passing it to him from time to time to hold. They went across the square in Pergau and out the cemetery road without meeting a single soul. A shallow mist lay on the roads and in the ditches. Where they met the main road curving up to Ryslavy's land a few boys out spading turf waved to them from across a field.

They continued lazily on to the junction, then bore right up the long slope to the colony. Everywhere branches sparkled and clacked together in the breeze. Coming out of the pines they saw Piedernig leading a ragged line of men across the meadow, his white crest bobbing beacon-like ahead of him as he walked. Halfway to the huts Else called out a greeting and the column stumbled to a halt.

—Hail to the patrol! Voxlauer called.

—Blessings, blessings! said Piedernig once they drew even with him. He frowned. —Where are your trouts, children?

—Best stick to roots and grubs, prophet, said Voxlauer, handing him the olive jar.

—You'll take what you get, Walter, said Else. —And praise us for it.

—I will at that, said Piedernig, bowing. He turned and waved the men on to the settlement. There were seven of them in all, somber and dirty-faced, in crudely made leather sandals made of three flat loops threaded into one another. A few greeted Else with a slight nod as they stepped past her. None of them were wearing clothes.

—Praise be to supper, first and foremost, at the present time, said Piedernig, carving the air into generous and equal portions with his cane.

They sat in the same room as before, around the same blanket, eating Else's olives on crumbling sourdough rolls. —How'd you come by this bread, Professor? asked Voxlauer between mouthfuls.

—Our own Herta made it, said Piedernig, nodding toward a squat, smiling woman to his left. Voxlauer recognized her vaguely as the frowning woman in the garden from his earlier visit.

—It's delicious, Herta, said Else. The woman shook her head bashfully and waved a fat round hand. It struck Voxlauer suddenly that she was the only one in the room who looked adequately fed.

—Our Frau Lederer doesn't know what to make of flattery, God bless her, said Piedernig, winking at Else. Herta shook her head again and stared fixedly down at the olive bowl, reddening a little.

Voxlauer looked around the room, at Piedernig and Herta and the rest, and at the blanket laid out between them. It was sparer than before, and the conversation quieter. —Where do the children eat? he asked, chewing.

Down the circle someone guffawed. —Oh, here and there, said Piedernig absently, waving a hand. —About.

—You don't know Walter's policy toward children yet, I see, said Herta. It was the first time she'd spoken.

—I can guess at it, said Voxlauer.

—Slander! said Piedernig, waving a hand dismissively. —Slander and defamation!

—I brought olives especially, Walter, said Else. —So you wouldn't have to share with your little urchins.

—You understand us pretty well, Fräulein, called a man from the kitchen. —Keep the little pilgrims skin and bones.

—Fat lambs make better Fascists, said Piedernig into his teacup.

—That's not always true, said Else.

—We defer to you, Fräulein, of course, said Piedernig. The others laughed.

The bread was passed again. Two small boys wandered in and ate sullenly from a bowl of dried apple peels. An older, cropped-haired woman Voxlauer didn't recognize was describing a visit to town.

—There were banners flapping everywhere, she was saying, glancing importantly round the circle. —Like during Republic Week, but on the houses, the cottages, even the better cattle stalls. Red and gray banners. Felt. And that huge pornographic cross. She paused a moment for effect, nodding at each of them in turn. —The illegals are marching in Villach tomorrow. With full state's honors.

Piedernig let out a low groan. He turned to Else. —Is this true?

—How should I know, Walter? said Else, staring down at the blanket.

Piedernig shrugged and waved a hand. —The march of progress, Oskar. There's no resisting it. We've lost three of our fattest citizens to the festivities already.

—A plump citizen is their easiest mark, the man called in from the kitchen.

Voxlauer looked slowly around the circle, dwelling for a moment or so on each of the assorted faces. —I'd judge the rest of you are in the clear then, he said finally.

—By the by: our bees are coming to, said Piedernig, as they took their bowls into the kitchen. —Care to honor us with an appraisal?

Voxlauer laughed. —I'd esteem it a solemn privilege. He glanced back over his shoulder.

—She's with Herta in the garden, said Piedernig, winking. —Never fear. He pulled open a cupboard and took out a tin of tobacco, raising a finger to his lips. —Come along now. Lend us your studied opinion.

The sun had thawed most of the morning's frost and water shone under the grass and on the roofs of the cabinets. As they neared them Voxlauer grew aware of a steady hum, electric and smooth, rising in pitch with each step they took forward. A second, louder hum sprang up suddenly like the starting of a generator as Piedernig stepped to the door of the first cabinet and pulled it open. Bees teemed out across the shelves, moving in wide, bewildered spirals, giving pattern to the noise. Voxlauer leaned in closer to the cabinet. The hive's paper face was completely obscured by the whirring, trembling bodies. A light breeze rose from their wings and played mildly on his face and hair. —Why don't they fly? he said.

—They're still mostly asleep, said Piedernig, pulling a wad of black tobacco from the tin and working it into his pipe bowl. —Watch now. He reached in and gathered a cluster of bees into his palm, closed his hand and shook it. —See that? What they want now is a shock to let them know winter is over. He grinned and lit his pipe. —Maybe I should tell them about the Anschluss.

—Christ, let them sleep, said Voxlauer.

They stood awhile and watched the bees, not speaking. —We're nearly finished here, Piedernig said.

Voxlauer smiled. —You mean your good work here is done.

—Ha! Yes. Exactly right. Piedernig was silent again for a time, sucking on his pipestem. After a while he struck a match, brought it up to the bowl of the pipe and said:—No. I mean finished. He let out a sigh. —This is not another country, Oskar.

Voxlauer laughed. —I know it isn't, Walter. I've been to other countries.

—I mean up here, you blessed fool. This valley.

—Yes. I know you do.

Piedernig was looking at him. —I know it, Walter, he repeated.

—And Ryslavy? Is he worried?

—I don't know. I don't think so.

Piedernig sucked his cheeks in doubtfully.

—He has money, said Voxlauer.

—I don't doubt it.

—Bribes should be worth as much to them as to anybody else. They can't all of them be such fanatics, can they?

—Yes. Well, said Piedernig, looking back toward the huts—it's the Monte for us, early fall at the latest. *Veritas, venitas, vicetas,* as the saying goes.

—Italy? said Voxlauer.

Piedernig laughed. —You've been away nearly twenty years, Oskar. I have it from irreproachable sources that the Italians are now our friends.

—I'm very relieved to hear it. Still—

—Move back a step now, there's a man, said Piedernig. He leaned in toward the cabinet and blew a thick jet of smoke onto the shelves. The column of sound ruptured suddenly and fell away as the bees funneled outward, beating and stinging the empty air. Voxlauer put up his hands and felt a bright rain of sparks across his wrists and knuckles. Piedernig took him by the collar and jerked him fiercely backward, cursing him.

—It's all right, said Voxlauer. —It's all right. It's beautiful.

—You're a queer one, aren't you? barked Piedernig, squinting into his face. —Are you stung badly?

—No. I'm all right, said Voxlauer. —I'm sorry, Professor, he said after a little pause.

—No harm done on my side, said Piedernig, still regarding him closely. —They certainly livened up obligingly, didn't they?

—Yes, said Voxlauer. —Yes, they did. He crouched down on the path, breathing heavily. —Yes. That was a surprise.

—Let's go find the ladies. Up you go, Gamekeeper.

They walked back past a row of empty pens and around the meetinghouse to the terraced garden. Else and Herta and another woman were there, leaning against the gate, talking and laughing.

—What happened to your hands? said Else as Voxlauer stepped up to her, rubbing his knuckles together and grinning.

—The best thing for that, said Herta—is fresh mayonnaise. Cold. In a compress.

Else laughed. —Mayonnaise?

Herta nodded solemnly. —Mayonnaise. It has to be cold, mind.

—I'm sure I don't have any, Herta, cold or otherwise. Mayonnaise gives me the hives.

—I'll do just fine without, I think, begging the ladies' pardons, said Voxlauer.

—Yes. You've done yourself just fine, without any help from anybody, haven't you? said Else, patting him on the hands. Everyone laughed.

—Why did he ask you about Villach? said Voxlauer. It was late in the day and the meadow as they crossed it was dark all along its edges. They crossed it slowly, their boots sloughing off in the thickening mud. Else walked in front, looking up now and again toward the head of the path. —Who? she said.

—Walter. He paused. —About the marching in Villach. If it was true.

—Oh. That, said Else. She made a little wave. —Probably because of my cousin, Kurt.

—What about him?

—He got into trouble. He had to leave.

They had reached the pines and now walked side by side down the steepening hill. —Without a word, she said, half to herself.

—What's that? said Voxlauer.

—He left us without a word. Kurt. In the middle of the night.

—Us?

—Us. Resi and myself.

Voxlauer slowed for a moment, but as Else kept walking he sped up again. She was looking down the slope into the woods, walking quickly.

—He took care of you, before he left? Your cousin? said Voxlauer, still half a step behind her.

—Yes.

—You and Resi.

—Yes, Oskar.

—Else?

—What?

Voxlauer hesitated, arranging the words carefully in his throat. —He's an illegal, is he, your cousin?

She nodded. —Yes, Oskar. He was. Until last month. Now he's just the opposite.

—He'll be coming back, then, Voxlauer said slowly.

—I wish he wouldn't.

Voxlauer was quiet for a time. —And the father?

—What about him?

—Where is he?

—With Kurt, wherever that is. I don't care.

—Ah.

She took a half step toward him. —Oskar—

—They were both of them illegals, were they? The two of them?

—Right, she said, turning back down the slope. —Lovely young garden-variety Black Shirts. The two of them together.

—That's a . . . a surprise, said Voxlauer.

—Is it, Oskar? Is it such a surprise?

They were standing now side by side looking in the same direction down the trail. Past a little rise they could see the rust-colored stripe of the junction road dimly through the trees and scrub.

—Who was he, then? said Voxlauer finally.

Else frowned slightly. —Who was who?

—The father.

—A boy, Oskar. That's all. She shrugged. —From Marein. His mother looks after Resi now.

Voxlauer was quiet again for a few moments. —Why is that?

She had begun walking again, stiff-legged and deliberate. He followed close behind her. They passed silently into a stand of elms showing their first hesitant green. Her steps in the brown leaf cover ahead of him made small brittle noises as she went, as though she were walking over waxed paper, or onionskin. He drew alongside her.

—Why is that? he repeated.

—What?

—Why does his mother look after her?

—Because I'm unfit, of course, Oskar. It's not right that I look after her. Is that what you wanted to know? I'm unfit. That's all. She was taken away from me.

—But why? he said again, unable to check himself. —What had you done?

—Oskar, she whispered, turning toward him. Her face was wet and she was trembling. —Can we stop this, Oskar? For God's sake? If we don't stop right away, I have to go. I'll have to go, Oskar. Do you hear?

He looked at her for a few seconds, then shut his eyes. The fear that he'd half forgotten in the last weeks rose and heaved under him again all at once and he felt weak-kneed as if from sudden vertigo. —Go where? he said finally, opening his eyes. But Else had begun walking again, moving away from him down the slope.

L ater that day, when Voxlauer arrived at the ponds, he found a pine-green sedan parked alongside the bridge and Ryslavy slumped over between the cottage steps and the woodpile. He picked up two splints from the pile and clacked them together next to Ryslavy's ear.

—Citizens of the Reich! This is your Führer speaking!

Ryslavy jerked violently awake, looking around him with wide-open, bulging eyes. Seeing Voxlauer he began cursing immediately. —You'll get yours, little friend. By God you'll get yours.

—I was just thinking about going to see you, Pauli. Tomorrow or the day after. And here you are laid out on my doorstep like a birthday present.

Ryslavy sat back against the wall. —Just you come a little closer, birthday boy.

—Thanks all the same, said Voxlauer. He leaned lightly against the woodpile. —I've been wondering about you a little.

—What, pray tell?

—I don't rightly know.

—No?

Voxlauer shrugged. —If you're still in business, I suppose.

—In business? said Ryslavy, eyes narrowing.

Voxlauer nodded.

Ryslavy studied him awhile longer, then let out a grunt.

—They haven't stopped drinking beer, if that's what you're getting at. Or started caring much who pours it for them.

—Still eating trout?

—They'll still eat mine, Oskar. Don't you worry. If I have any left to fry, that is. He looked toward the ponds accusingly.

Voxlauer took another splint from the woodpile and began knocking the dirt from his boots. —It's true I haven't been around so much lately.

—No?

Voxlauer grinned. —You come up here to sack me, Pauli?

—We'd just have you in town then. Thank you kindly.

—It wouldn't be so bad. I could help you lay sandbags.

—No thank you.

—Or courier your bribes, depending . . .

Ryslavy made a face. —On what?

Voxlauer scratched his chin. —Your plan of action. Your tactical agenda.

—I think we'll keep you in reserve for the moment, Oskar, if you've no objections. Seeing as how you appreciate your work.

—Is it so very obvious? said Voxlauer.

In the last light they went up and cast lines into the creek. Ryslavy lay with his head against a tussock of new grass, smoking and holding forth on selected topics. Occasionally he sat forward to check his line. Voxlauer had a second rod and was casting into a shallow eddy.

—They're no more socialists than I am, Ryslavy was saying. —If they're a workers' party then I'm a burr up a barmaid's ass.

—You wish you were.

—They went after the perfumed citizens straight off, no dilly-dallying. Old man Kattnig, Otto Probst, that new doctor moved into the Villa Walgram. Even came snuffling round *my* door, if you can believe it, that first week. Turned out I was a Zionist.

—If you're a Zionist, then I am a wheel of cheese, said Voxlauer, yawning.

—Believe me, Oskar. Nobody was more surprised than I was.

—I believe it very well.

—Came round your mother's house, naturally. Brought along some paperwork. Mentioned you, of course, I needn't say what regarding. She asked could any of them speak French.

Voxlauer said nothing.

—They want her, all right. Your Père too, rest his bones. "Your personal loss, et cetera, was a loss for all of Germany." She was grand, though. Asked did Germany feel the loss of all Austrian geniuses so deeply. That buggered 'em.

—They mentioned me?

—Hmm. Ryslavy nodded, fumbling with his pipe. —Toward the end.

—Well?

—"We sympathize with your shame, et cetera, Frau Voxlauer," et cetera. The paperwork came out again. A pardon or some such was hinted at. She told them to get pissed.

—Ah, said Voxlauer.

—For pity's sake don't club away like that. For pity's sake, Oskar. A little charity. Ryslavy took up his rod with a gesture of despair and arced it soundlessly out over the water. —These are graceful, delicate things we're after. Beautiful things.

—Floating sausages, said Voxlauer. —Bug-eyed gluttonous little fiends.

—Conversely, the favored food of your prophet, according to apostles Paul and Peter, said Ryslavy, raising a hand in benediction.

—I never knew! said Voxlauer thoughtfully. He reeled in his line and cast again. —Who's your favorite apostle, Pauli?

Ryslavy cursed picturesquely. —Speaking of which, that heap of kidneys is making things hot for me a little. Not to dirty the subject.

—Our boy Rindt of the greasy knickers?

—That's the one.

—Sopping piss off barstools not enough for him anymore, I guess.

Ryslavy shrugged. —Black Shirts drink free on Tuesday. He grinned crookedly. —The pan-German angle.

Voxlauer spat into the grass.

—Wish I'd thought of it myself, really.

—You did, Pauli. You couldn't stomach it, that's all.

Ryslavy laughed joylessly. —You expect me to work the pan-German maneuver, Oskar? Me? Paul Abraham Ryslavy, money-lender? Corrupter of womenfolks? The bandy-legged menace? He hunched over in the twilight, leering.

—Speaking of which, said Voxlauer. —Could you spare half a schilling?

—Very comic, said Ryslavy. He stared blankly out at the water.

—I thought not, said Voxlauer.

—You go to hell.

They cast quietly for a time. —Is it all so far gone, then? said Voxlauer quietly.

Ryslavy thumbed his nose. —They drink until they're pissed, then they toddle home. It's a happy time, really.

—We could all do with one of those.

Ryslavy moved his pipestem fondly from his right mouth corner to his left. —I'd say you've done all right, Oskar.

—What's that?

—You've done all right.

Voxlauer cast again. —What would you know about it.

—You'll notice, said Ryslavy—I haven't asked where you've been.

—I wasn't expecting you to.

—Still. I haven't asked.

—Shall I light you a candle, brother?

—Do you remember Sarah Tilsnigg? My second cousin?

Voxlauer didn't answer for a moment. —I might remember.

—You always did have a weakness for the mountain air. Had an effect on you like a pound of oysters.

—Leave off it, Pauli, for the love of God.

—What year was that? What summer?

—I don't remember. Eighteen hundred and three.

—We had fine summers up here, though, it's a fact.

—A few.

—I think of them all the time now. I must be getting old.

—That must be it.

—Père told those endless, wonderfully complicated fairy stories. Do you remember them?

—Some.

—What happened to him, Oskar? To go from such a normal life—go so all at once—

—It wasn't so all at once. You didn't see it, that's all. Maman kept things quiet.

—There were the problems with his pieces, I remember that much. His pieces not getting played, and so on. Don't say that wasn't a part of it.

—It was something inside of him, Pauli. In the brain. It wasn't the goddamned good-for-nothing pieces.

—What makes you so blessed sure?

—Because it's inside of me too, Pauli. That's why.

—Oh, said Ryslavy.

They sat awhile in silence. Ryslavy chewed his pipe. —Vulgo Holzer was broken into a few weeks back, he said. —Turned on its ass proper.

—Is that so?

—Just so you're careful, that's all, Oskar. These are chancy times.

—I've heard that already, said Voxlauer. —You'll be happy to know of a fellow deep thinker—

There was a hit on his line and he brought it in hard, with a whirring and buzzing of the reel. A fish no longer than a finger struggled fiercely against the hook. Voxlauer pulled it in, cursing.

—Sprats hit quickest just now, Ryslavy said, comfortable again. —The old ones drop lower, in my experience, when dark is coming on. A heavier plumb might clear it, maybe. Or a better floater. You might try one of those damselflies.

Voxlauer yanked the sprat from his line and threw it back. —You're bothering me tonight, Pauli.

Ryslavy sighed. —I bother myself, lately. He drew his rod back pensively. —You know about her family, I suppose?

—Enough.

—Not simple, is it.

—It's simple. Voxlauer cast again. —It's simple up here.

—Don't believe it, boy. It's no simpler up here than anywhere. Things take a bit longer to happen, that's all. Ryslavy jerked his head down valley. —Your nudists know that, you can bet. They won't be around much longer.

—Look at me, Pauli. I'm fully dressed.

—And thank God for it.

—I couldn't agree more.

Ryslavy leaned over, took Voxlauer's arm and shook it. —Don't make trouble for me, old man. I'm begging you now.

Voxlauer laughed. —Trouble, Pauli? You must not have looked at me too well just now. Am I worth fretting over?

—No, you jackass. I am. I'm worth fretting over for weeks.

—Fret away, then. You don't need my permission.

—Everyone knows who it was at the Holzer farm. The whole town knows it.

Voxlauer didn't answer. The creek had darkened now into a small cautious band of gray. The light above it was dim and gravel-colored.

—That seems very far away now, all of that, he said finally.

Ryslavy was quiet a moment. —Well, Oskar. It's your business, as you say. But for God's sake don't pay any more visits to the Holzer boys. Buy your butter in Pergau from now on.

—I just might at that, said Voxlauer.

It rained all that night and the next day and in the evening wide pink spots appeared on the sky and it grew clear and cold. Vox-lauer rapped on the window and watched Else move in the warm honeyed light of the kitchen toward the door. She fumbled a moment with the catch. —Fish still belly-down? she said, pushing open the screen.

—I never looked. He brushed the hair from her face and looped it carefully behind her ears. —Ryslavy was by. I think he'd sack me if his conscience would permit him. Lucky for me he's a sentimentalist.

—He can't sack you if he doesn't pay you, Oskar. You still think like a Bolshevik. She took his wrist and brought it along her mouth.

—He gives me a general amnesty, Fräulein. That's something. And then there are the fishes.

—Tsk, Oskar! What do *you* need an amnesty for, of all people.

—Oh, I've done terrible things, Fräulein.

—I know what you're thinking of, Herr Gamekeeper. Paul Ryslavy has no business giving out amnesties in that province.

—Well, said Voxlauer, shrugging. —He tries to look out for me.

She laughed slyly. —Some things nobody else can do for you, *Oskarchen*.

—If you say so, Fräulein. He paused a moment. —He doesn't seem to like you much. I suppose that's no surprise.

She made a face. —That man. He should nurture his friendships.

—He thinks he does.

—What does that mean?

—Well. He's paying enough insurance.

—I'm sure he is. To the wrong people.

—Most likely, said Voxlauer. He paused. —Who aren't the wrong people, then?

—I'm not. I am not the wrong people, said Else. She laughed. —You tell that to Ryslavy.

For supper they ate dumplings and tinned peaches and the last of the smoked sausages he'd stolen from the Holzer farm. They ate by a gas lantern in a corner of the kitchen with the house door creaking open on the dark, pouring schnapps from a little blue-green bottle into their tea. Else hummed under her breath, half mouthing the words to a nursery rhyme between sips. Her face glowed roundly in the lantern light.

—You're very quiet this evening, she said.

—So are you.

—I'm drunk.

Voxlauer looked at her. —You don't look drunk.

—Well, I am.

—A good feeling, isn't it. He smiled.

—Yes. Yes it is.

—I'm going to town tomorrow, he said, leaning back contentedly in his chair.

Else frowned. —What for?

—My mother. Pauli says she wants to see me.

She said nothing for a time, lowering her eyes to the table-
top, running her fingers restlessly along its rim. —Don't go just
now, Oskar.

—Why not?

—I don't know, she said, still frowning at the table.

—They don't care about me in town, Else.

—Did Ryslavy say that?

He waved a hand. —I'm going to see my mother. That's all,
Else. Just her.

Else took a sip of her tea. —What is it? Is something wrong?

—No. Nothing's wrong at all.

—Aside from everything that is, said Else.

Voxlauer sat on a bench on the verandah, looking out at the red
glare along the rooftops. —Well, Maman, he said. —The sun is
shining on your little town today.

She set a tray of sweet rolls down in front of him. —You look
ill, she said.

—Scurvy, say the specialists. Voxlauer sucked in his cheeks and
rolled back his eyes. —They tell me I'll have to take the Russian
cure.

—For heaven's sake, Oskar. She sat down tiredly in her chair.
He noticed for the first time an involuntary shaking of her head, a
constant slow avowal of disbelief. She let out a long, involuntary
breath. —Is she feeding you well, at least?

—Maman, he said. —Couldn't we sit quietly for a while?

—Yes, Oskar. I suppose.

The noon light passed through the screen of hanging ferns and
dappled the white wall and the table and the plates and cups. The
radio was on in the parlor and the garbled remains of an overture
carried out to them through the open doors.

—Do you recognize it? she said.

—Barely.

She kept quiet. —Verdi, he offered.

—Yes. That's right. You know, your Père and I—

—Is something wrong with the radio? said Voxlauer.

—What? Oh, the radio . . . she said, letting her voice trail away. Her lower lip began to tremble.

—That static. It's terrible.

She nodded. —An Italian station, sad to say. Udine. I couldn't bear any more Wagner preludes, or that Lortzing, saints preserve us.

—Who?

—Lortzing. A choirmaster or some such. From Linz. A great favorite of the new regime, apparently. A great lover of horns. She sighed.

Voxlauer smiled and took her cool, slack hand in his. —What was that about Verdi? he said.

That afternoon he took her walking through the garden and the new-budding orchard. She moved through the thick scrub unsteadily and had to be led by the arm and given many pauses to rest. They sat together on an iron bench by the groundskeeper's cottage and watched the setting sun tilting behind the ruin, lingering in its tines and arches. —I'm so tired now, Oskar, she said, leaning weightlessly against his shoulder.

—I was tired too, Maman. Very tired. But now I'm wide awake.

—You're so young yet. I've been tired now for ages. She sighed mildly. —Do you remember when you left? Do you? How young I was?

Voxlauer let out a hollow laugh. —Go on and say it.

—No. You're a good boy, Oskar. A sweet dear boy. My dear boy.

—Maman, he said hesitantly. —You're frightening me a little.

She sat without answering for a time. —Did Pauli tell you to come?

—Of course not.

—It doesn't matter. I'm happy to see you. She laid her arm across his. —I was hoping you might explain things to me.

—I was hoping the same of you, Maman. I haven't been to town in weeks.

—You're in love, she said simply.

Voxlauer said nothing. She raised her head partly off his shoulder and let out a breath.

—It seems we're part of Germany now, she said.

—Yes.

—Awful garbage in the papers.

—Yes.

—Is Pauli in trouble?

—No. I don't think so.

—He hasn't been to see me lately.

—I don't think he's in any trouble. Honestly.

—Ah, she said. She smiled strangely.

—Maman? he said. —What is it? Are you unwell?

—I don't understand, she said, as if in answer. She was shaking her head fiercely now and looking down at her lap.

—Maman, he said again. She took no notice of him.

—The day you left, Oskar, as Père and I took you to the station, I knew you'd be very different, a stranger almost, when you came back. I knew it. You might never come back at all, but if you did I knew that you'd be changed. The world would change you. I prepared for it every day after you'd gone. She paused a moment, breathing and thinking, rubbing her hands together. —What never occurred to me was that I'd be changed. And this place, she said, looking around her at the garden. —That this place would be changed. That Père would be gone from it, gone so utterly. And not just him. You couldn't find us here at all, any of us, if you looked. She let out a muted, pained sound, moving her hands as over the flat empty surface of a table, looking at him all at once confusedly, almost questioningly, eyes wandering from his face and then rushing gratefully back to it, remembering him.

—All these people, Oskar. All these people. I don't recognize anybody at all, now, on the street. And they don't recognize me. I never thought that could happen. Never. The streets are different also, and the houses. You must have noticed something, but you never said. I think about you so much now, Oskar. Every day. It must be terribly hard for you. God in heaven . . . She reached over and laid the knuckles of her left hand against his temple, as though checking him for fever. —God bless you, Oskar. My sweet sweet boy. Bless you. I wonder that you found your way back at all. Everything's so different. *Here* is different: old. Even your old mother, Oskar. Even her, God rest her.

—Maman, said Voxlauer. His voice cracked slightly. —Don't say that, Maman. Please.

—I don't understand anymore, Oskar. That's the shame of it. She paused. —I don't understand at all.

The light on the ruin was dull and purple and the walls and buttresses looked grander and less forgotten, prouder now, in silhouette. A warm wind came down from the woods and rustled through the garden, heavy with the smell of rain. —I've never understood, Maman, Voxlauer said after a long while.

On his way up from town he held to the quieter roads and transcribed a wide circle around the Holzer farm. He came off the ridge at the last of the pens and wound his way along the creek's northern bank into the spruce groves. In the younger stands the saplings clustered tightly together, round as fusilier's brushes, and whisked into him as he moved forward. The flat blue needles felt warm and fleshlike against his eyes. He walked in circles with his arms together and his head bowed low, coming down with each step into the dense, rubbery bristles. After a time he stopped and listened carefully to his breathing. A strong wind bowed the treetops. He leaned backward and stared up at the clouds, ribboning and trailing away into wisps toward the south.

A dull light billowed in the air, spreading into a mist along the ground. The creek was to his left. Two wet planks stuck out over the water braced on heaps of yellow stones. He went carefully down to them and started across. As he was midway over the water the planks gave suddenly, plunging his legs into the current. He yelled loudly from the cold, marveling even as he yelled at the way the sound vanished into the spruce rows like a pebble into a well. He waded to the far bank and climbed out and shucked off his boots, laughing at himself. The hollow small noise of the creek rose hesitantly upward. He wrung the water from his socks and dried his feet against the mossy ground.

He was crouching there awkwardly with his boots in his hands when he saw them, half a dozen meters upriver, leaning on their rifle stocks and watching him. The older son carried a chamois fawn slung over his shoulder and a loose tinkling clatter of rabbit traps like a purse below it. His brother stood a few paces behind him, shifting from foot to foot and grinning. Voxlauer stood up slowly. They separated and came down on either side of him, rustling purposefully through the branches as though flushing up a deer. When they reached him he was still trying to get his feet into the water-sotted boots.

—Going for a swim, citizen? said the older son, laying the traps down carefully. Voxlauer said nothing. The younger son stepped forward and leaned his rifle against a stump and eased the chamois off his brother's shoulders. —Go on, citizen. Speak freely, the older son said, not unkindly, leaning over slightly to let his load slip off onto the ground.

Voxlauer didn't answer. One of the boots was half on his needle-covered foot and the other was in his hands, dripping onto the turf.

—Here's a shy one, said the older son to his brother, leveling his rifle stock. The younger son nodded, blinking effortfully out of wide-set, cowlike eyes.

—Wait, said Voxlauer. The younger son had stepped around to the left and now swung his rifle hard into Voxlauer's side, splaying him out onto the moss. —Wait, Voxlauer gasped. The older son pressed a boot against Voxlauer's head and drove his face into the turf, cooing gently. His brother raised his rifle butt and brought it downward like a gaffing spade again and again onto Voxlauer's

back and shoulders. Voxlauer could see nothing for the dirt and
the sparks behind his eyes but he could taste the salt of his tears
and of his mucus and hear himself crying Wait :

Wait:

until finally they left him.

When they were gone Voxlauer rolled over onto his back and
looked up at the leaded-glass patterns of the branches with the
white clouds just behind them. Drops of dew fell from the branches
and streaked toward his face like chimney sparks, hissing and
crackling as they passed. He lay with head back and felt the warm
soft earth pulling him into it and was grateful. The air was very
still, pale and green as bottle glass, and he shut his eyes and listened to the *pat-pat-pat* of water dripping steadily onto the moss.
Now and then a drop would spatter against his eyelids in a halo of
blue or orange fire.

A spider had dug a small round burrow, about the width of
a child's finger, in the dirt near his elbow and lined the entrance
with a skirt of white silk. It sat drawn up in the burrow mouth,
motionless and intent. Voxlauer twitched a finger and it vanished
soundlessly.

They lay together on the pallet in the alcove in the close-fitting dark. Now and then Else would rise and shift the pillows under him or help him to sit up and cough into a white enamel bowl. He was talking almost without pause, gesturing with his hands in the air almost invisibly, the smell of rain coming through the open windows. There was the sound of rain against the shingles of the roof, and dripping from a gap above the stovepipe onto the floor. She listened to him from her corner of the bed and did not try to hush him or to coax him into sleeping. When he'd told her everything, all of it from the beginning, he lay his head back on the pillows and looked at her.

—That's all, he said. —That's everything I can think of.

—Tell me more about this Anna, said Else, drawing closer to him. —Was she like a mother to you?

—Very much, said Voxlauer. —Very much like a mother. He smiled. —With one or two noteworthy differences.

—Was she always running around behind you with Mercurochrome and a roll of tape, bandaging your cuts and so on?

—Hardly ever.

—I don't believe it.

—I didn't get into so much trouble in those days. I was a model Bolshevik.

—What did you do those fifteen years, to keep out of trouble? Mind the People's trout?

—Close enough. I grew the People's beets.

—Beets!

He nodded. —Beets and radishes.

She stared at him a moment, wide-eyed. —You know something. I've never had a beet.

—The worse for you, Fräulein. The beet is nature's omnibus.

—How so?

He raised four fingers, folding them down one by one as he spoke:—It vivifies. It fortifies. It regulates. It clears the bowels.

—Who would ever have imagined it. Such a modest-looking item. A cross between a pickle and an egg.

—Excellent, also, for staining gums and fingers, said Voxlauer. He lay back again and stared up at the rafters. —What a dreary little ash can of a cottage this is, he said sleepily.

—I asked you about Anna, said Else. —Pay attention.

Voxlauer took a breath. —Can there be anything I haven't told you yet?

—All sorts of things. She paused. —Ways we're different, for example.

—Every way I can think of, said Voxlauer, yawning.

Else turned wordlessly to look out the little window.

—Should I have said the two of you are just alike?

—What did you do together, the two of you?

—We grew beets.

—Is that all you did for fifteen years, grow your beets? All day and night? Don't you Bolsheviks ever take a holiday, in the name of God?

—We went back to her house twice a year. She had a phonograph. We played records on it.

—What kind of records?

He shrugged. —Operas. Operettas.

—Which operettas? Name them.

He looked at her. —You'll be asking me my catechism in a minute.

She smiled. —Go on, Oskar Voxlauer. Recite.

—*Fantiglio*. *The Bride of Cozumel*. *The Beggar's Feast Day*. Three or four others. None of my father's, if that's what you're wondering. Her taste ran more to works of the great Saxon Romantics. Not unlike our Führer.

Else waved this off. —Back to the topic. Any children?

Voxlauer shook his head.

—None?

—We did try, if it please the court.

—No children, said Else. —That's very sad.

—We loved each other, Voxlauer said tentatively.

—That's more important, of course. Any idiot can have children.

—That's true.

—I did.

—Yes.

—You do like Resi, don't you, Oskar.

He nodded.

—Do you like her?

—Very much. I like her very much.

—If you didn't like her you'd be turned out with the bedsheets first thing in the morning. You know that, I hope. Turned straight out without the smallest mercy.

—I love Resi like a sister, said Voxlauer solemnly. He coughed.

—That's fine. She looked at him a moment. —Do you need the bowl?

—No. Anything but that.

—Do you need it?

—Christ, no.

They lay quietly. Voxlauer felt himself drifting off again toward sleep.

—Do you think about her often? Else said.

He groaned quietly.

—Answer me!

—Not often.

—You said that you loved her.

—Yes. I think I did.

—You think?

—I loved her. I'd like to go to sleep.

—You loved her, or you think you did, said Else, grimacing. —But now you never think of her.

—That's right. You've summed it up perfectly.

—Think about her now. Wake up, Oskar! What was she like?

Voxlauer rolled onto his back. —Have you no pity?

—Speak or I'll get the bowl. Speak!

He was quiet a moment. —Strait-laced, he said finally. —Tall and thin. Pale. Serious. Bourgeois. Unhappy.

—Unhappy? said Else.

—Yes. Unhappy.

—Always?

—No. Not always. Sometimes she was so happy she couldn't sleep.

—Why? said Else after a little pause. —Why couldn't she sleep?

—I don't know.

—You don't know?

—She never said.

—"She never said"? What do you *mean* by that? She sat bolt upright in the dark. —What did you talk about then, all day long?

—You're very interested in her state of mind all of a sudden, said Voxlauer, rubbing his eyes.

She muttered something under her breath. —I just hope you talked to her, that's all.

He tried to turn toward her, then lay back gingerly on the pallet. —You didn't know her, did you, Else.

—You're right, of course. I'm sorry. She yawned.

—I did talk to her.

—Well, then.

—Let's talk about you for a while, he said, tapping her on the leg.

—Please, Oskar. She yawned again. —There's nothing to tell.

—I doubt that very much.

—I've never been to Russia. She brought a hand down over his face, closing his eyes. —I've never farmed state's beets. I've never been a Bolshevik.

—The worse for you, said Voxlauer. —Bolshevism is society's beet.

—Good night, Oskar, she said, drawing the blankets up over them.

—Is it time to sleep? said Voxlauer into the quiet.

S low and tidelike through the month of June the butterflies came and blanketed the valley. The first to appear were translucent and white and sat harbored on the road like an armada of paper ships, folding and unfolding. —Postilions, said Else, stepping into them so they rose up on either side of her, shimmering and unreal, like crepe-paper snowflakes in a country theater. On into midsummer they settled in every patch of light, ranged in bands along the Pergauer road in beams of late sun or drifting in loose columns across the fields. Caught in the hand they left a roan dust behind, iridescent and fine as pollen.

Soon after came the rest, mourning cloaks and swallowtails and purple moors, chess pieces and white apollos, peacock's-eyes and cyllabils and others whose names Voxlauer couldn't remember ever having known. He would follow Else down along the water and tell her stories as she stalked them with her net and killing jar, struggling to keep up with her as she ran ahead through the heavy brush, following the tip of her net as it dipped and circled above the reeds. Often he would realize as a story was half finished that he'd lost track of her completely. Coming out onto the road a short while later, scratched and dusty and grinning, the end of the net tucked down into the ether, she'd beg his forgiveness and ask him to start over again at the beginning. More often than not, he'd abandon the story, sigh and lie down in the grass and think of something else to tell her.

One morning as they were sitting by the creek together and he sat playing a fly line into the current he found himself staring at the back of her head, dappled and striped by the overhanging reeds.

—What is it? said Else after a minute or two had passed, turning round.

—Pauli says your cousin's come back, he said, reeling the line in carefully.

—Yes.

He looked at her. —You knew?

—His mother sent word he'd asked where I was living. I'm not sure what she told him.

—Ah, said Voxlauer.

Else kicked at the water with the heel of her boot. —She didn't say how long he was planning on staying. He might only have been passing. I'm not sure.

—He's head of the new Reichs-Commission, Voxlauer said slowly. —From Gressach to the Steyrmark. I think it's likely he'll be staying for quite a while.

—I've asked her to tell him not to come, Oskar. I've told her not to say where I am. I can't do more than that, can I?

—He'll know where you are. He knows already.

—Why do you say that? she said, looking away.

Voxlauer closed his eyes. —Because he's SS, Else. That's why.

She said nothing.

—You didn't tell me he was SS.

—You knew he was an illegal. She got up slowly from the bank. —Does it matter?

—It does matter. Yes. It matters.

—Well, Oskar: now you know. She stepped behind him and disappeared into the bushes, taking her net up as she passed. Voxlauer sat without moving for a long time, staring down at the water.

An hour later Else came back and set her net down by his shoulder. —Look here, Oskar. Reaching in with her tweezers she pulled out a dark blue set of wings veined and speckled with vermilion and purple. The under pair of wings glittered lazuli as she turned them. —There's room in Resi's box for one more, don't you think?

Resi came through the door first, hanging back in its lit frame. The evening sun behind her glowed in her dark mass of hair and erased any trace of childishness from her features. —Why are you here? she said, looking at Voxlauer. —I didn't ask you.

—No, you didn't, said Voxlauer, rising from the table. —Would you like me to go?

—Theresa, Else said, coming up the steps behind her. —Oskar's my good friend. He can come in very handy.

Resi looked at him again. He grinned stupidly at her, showing his missing teeth.

—How did *that* happen? said Resi, taking a half step backward.

—Robbers beat him, said Else, shooting a glance at Voxlauer.

—Friends of cousin Kurti's, said Voxlauer, still leering.

Resi laughed loudly, a shrill, malicious-sounding, boyish laugh. —I bet he could knock out all your teeth if he wanted.

—Most likely he could, said Voxlauer. He sighed. —Sometimes they fall out by themselves.

—You can stay, said Resi abruptly, crossing the room. Voxlauer bowed to her and sat down.

After dinner they sat Resi at the table and blindfolded her with a dish towel and told her to count to twenty. The evening light shone on her through the open door and Voxlauer could see her smiling to herself as they brought the boxes up from the bedroom. With her eyes covered by the cloth she looked less like Else, thinner-faced and darker. Again Voxlauer had the impression she was older than she was. —Happy twenty-eighth! said Else, slipping off the blindfold.

—I'm not twenty-eight, said Resi, smiling up at them suspiciously.

—Sure you are.

—I'm seven.

—Ah. Well. We'd best take these presents to a more mature young lady, then, said Voxlauer, picking up a box. Resi let out a shriek and clutched at his leg.

—Fräulein! Please! said Voxlauer, staring down at her aggrievedly. —A bit more decorum. You'll shatter my glass eye.

—Look to your presents now, Resi, Else said. —Ignore this man altogether.

—Tell him to give that back, said Resi, pointing at the box.

—*Voilà!* said Voxlauer, laying the box down on the table. —I was only keeping it safe for the mademoiselle.

—What is it? said Resi, looking past him at Else.

—Don't play the diva, mouse. Open your blessed boxes.

—For mademoiselle's convenience, said Voxlauer, extending a pair of scissors.

Resi took the scissors and snipped without ado through the twine. —Is this a ribbon? she asked, holding it up to her face.

—Close enough, Resi. Else leaned over the table and pulled the twine away from the box and held it open. Resi stood on her stool and pulled out a long black silk dress Voxlauer recognized after a moment as from the trousseau under the parlor window. She held the dress up to the light and studied it intently. —Are we going to a funeral? she asked, glancing uncertainly at Voxlauer.

—Funeral season begins next month, mademoiselle. A little patience.

—No one's going to any funerals, said Else, narrowing her eyes at him. —Next box, please, Resi. I swear I've never seen such a girl for dawdling.

—Don't rush me, Mama. Resi had taken up a smaller package now and was trying to slide the twine off all in one piece. Her small-boned face was set in an expression of fixed attention, her mouth twisting slightly as she worked. —Smells like a book, she announced, tearing the paper in a spiral. She looked at the cover a moment and grinned. —Bugs and flowers.

—So you won't always be pestering me, said Else. —Last one, now. She motioned excitedly to Voxlauer.

Voxlauer brought the box up onto the table, tapping significantly against its sides with his fingers. —It's wood, said Resi, eyes widening. —I'll do it, she said, pushing Else away. —I'm doing it, Mama.

—Help me please, she said a moment later, her small voice wavering. Else took the box by its corners and pulled the paper downward. Bright wings phosphoresced in the light from the window, darkening and shifting color as the box revolved. —*Ach!* Thank you, Mama! Resi said, taking Else's hand in that strange formal way of hers.

—You'll have to name them all, of course, said Else. —From the book. And say thank you to Oskar. He made the box.

After dinner the two of them sat late into the evening labeling specimens from Else's lexicon. Voxlauer said good night and walked slowly down the slope and up again through the little town. The air was still and warm and smelled of pine dust as always and the gables of the cliffs glowed a heavy violet behind it. The chittering of crickets accompanied him as far as the last fields, surging and ebbing and surging again, then faded gradually through the pines. Now and then a branch would snap close by the road and something would tumble away from him into the brush. For a long while he was unaware of his own breathing and when he did notice it again it seemed wonderfully untroubled to him. He walked purposefully and steadily and counted as many as seven steps between breaths. Everything on all sides was benevolent and mild. As the road straightened and leveled he closed his eyes and walked blindly forward, feeling his way upward through the dark.

The air above the ponds was filled with fluttering bodies, oblivious to his presence in their sightless dips and circlings, curving over the water in nervous, erratic arcs, tracing ancient, encrypted patterns across its surface. For a long time Voxlauer listened to their soft, parchment-like wingbeats, sitting on the bank and searching the surface of the pond for their reflections. At times they came close enough to him that he felt or imagined the pass of their fine-boned leathery wings against his face and his hair. When it grew too dark even to guess at them anymore he stood up clumsily from the bank and crossed the pilings.

. . .

A figure came up the road the next morning as Voxlauer sat on the stoop leafing through the *Selections from Goethe* he'd taken from the old house. Long before he could make out the features below the wicker hat brim he recognized the loose storklike gait and the deliberate, august advancement of the cane. He called out a hello as Piedernig drew even with the pilings.

—I don't believe I've had the pleasure yet of a house call, Professor. Would you do us the honor?

Piedernig bowed deeply. —With your permission, young Herr. With your kind and generous permission.

—Headed to the heath? said Voxlauer, leading him up to the cottage steps.

—I'll not deny it, said Piedernig. —What's more, I was hoping you might yourself be able to spare an hour.

—I might just. Voxlauer set the book down on the woodpile and pushed the door to the cottage closed. —I'd invite you in, Professor, but it isn't much to look at.

—I believe it implicitly, said Piedernig. He took Voxlauer's arm again and they crossed back to the road. They walked in silence for a number of minutes, Voxlauer adjusting his steps to Piedernig's more stately, level stride.

—I'd thought of stopping in at the farm for a few drams of Kirschbrannt on the way, if you've no objection, Piedernig said, smacking his lips.

—Ah. In that case, said Voxlauer, slowing.

—Eh? said Piedernig. The light of comprehension flickered across his face an instant or two later and he began to laugh. —No, no, Herr Voxlauer! he said, taking Voxlauer by the shoulders and coaxing him forward. —I'm no sadist. I'd forgotten your situation for a moment, that's all it was.

—You're still amicable with them, are you? Voxlauer said sullenly.

—With their schnapps, Oskar. With their schnapps I am amicable.

Voxlauer smiled. —I'm beginning to understand better about these walks of yours.

Piedernig raised a finger. —*Mens sana in corpore sano,* Herr Voxlauer, as you well know. In this case, he said, drawing his robes about him—something like last rites.

—How's that? said Voxlauer. —Are you infirm?

—Threatened with infirmity, you might say. We leave tomorrow for Monte Veritas. He spat resoundingly into the dirt. —Let the Black Shirts have this greasy country.

—Except for my little half acre, said Voxlauer.

—Ply them with enough trout and maybe they'll let you stay on, Herr Gamekeeper. In an advisory capacity.

—That would be fine, said Voxlauer. He paused a moment. —What should I advise them on?

—Any blessed thing you can think of. The eastern question, possibly. Absentee beekeeping.

—Are you trying to sabotage me, Professor?

They were just then passing the cabinets and they stopped a moment to watch a thin file of bees spiraling upward from the nearest of them. —Ever get any honey out of them, by the by? Piedernig said.

—About a mouthful, said Voxlauer. —Tasted terrible. He made a face. —Papery. Dusty.

Piedernig looked at him compassionately. —That's the shit of bees you ate, Oskar.

—The shit?

Piedernig nodded. —In plain country language.

Voxlauer was quiet a moment. —I thought honey was the shit of bees.

Piedernig clucked and shook his head. —No, not honey, Oskar. Not honey, he said, smiling from ear to ear.

They had come out of the spruce plantation and were passing the first of the two fenced-in pastures. A few head of oxen raised their heads idly to look at them. —This is close enough for me, said Voxlauer. He led Piederning off the road and into the trees.

—Where in God's name are you taking me? huffed Piedernig.

—I'm wanting my constitutional, lest you forget.

—Quietly, Professor, said Voxlauer. They climbed through a stand of saplings onto a weed-choked logging trail that skirted the edge of Ryslavy's woods and rose finally through thick full-grown trees to the clay road up to the heath. When they came onto open ground a half an hour later the noon sun was full above them, close and hot and white, and the country on all sides hung skirted in haze. Piedernig sat down promptly on a patch of sandy ground with his legs crossed beneath him and shut his eyes.

Voxlauer walked a few paces to where the view of town was clearest and shaded his face with a forearm. He stood a few minutes looking intently down the cross-cut slope at Niessen, half listening to Piedernig's mumblings and half to the sound of motor traffic on the toll road across the plain. —I can see your old school from here, Professor.

Piedernig exhaled melodiously and opened his eyes. —May it crumble into dust. He rose and brushed the sand from his robes. —I suppose you've been to town recently?

—Not too recently.

—I've yet to see it under the new management.

—The overall effect is very festive, said Voxlauer, still looking out across the valley. —Flags, posters, torches, all manner of public diversions. The charlatan in you will be deeply smitten.

Piedernig took a breath and held it, speaking the next few phrases wheezingly, like a man with the wind knocked out of him. —We're bound to lose some more of the faithful en route, of course. It can't be helped. Still: it's high time we left this backwater to its fate. Italy, Oskar! It's Italy for the likes of us.

—I've had enough Italy to last a while yet, said Voxlauer. —I don't believe things are so very different down there.

—Nonsense! said Piedernig good-naturedly. They stood quietly awhile, looking across the shadeless plain. After a time Piedernig let out his breath.

—Have I ever asked you why in hell you ever came back here?

—More than once.

—But you've never answered.

—I've always been a patriot, Walter. I thought you knew.

—Ha! said Piedernig.

—What route will you be taking, Professor? The toll road or the carriage road? The straight route or the scenic?

Piedernig made a fatalistic gesture. —We'll go slowly, I'll tell you that much. We're grossly overburdened. Top-heavy, as the saying goes, and bottom-broke. He sighed. —I'd hoped to drop the children off at some sort of public charity but the women wouldn't stand for it. I tried to explain to them, God knows! that children are a renewable commodity.

Voxlauer laughed. —I'm sorry, Walter. I don't believe you.

—That's your privilege, said Piedernig, arranging his robes again. —You wouldn't consider minding them awhile, would you? You might build a kennel for them somewhere. Or a camp of some sort, the way we did for the Serbs in the Great War. Would you consider it? They don't require much looking-after.

—I'm looking forward to a little peace and quiet, thanks all the same. Still, I'll miss you and your collection of basket cases. Else, too.

Piedernig coughed. —Else isn't coming, Oskar, worse luck for her.

—No. Of course not, said Voxlauer. —I meant that she'd miss you, as well. He frowned.

—Yes, said Piedernig, scratching the dirt distractedly with his cane. —You've met the father, then?

Voxlauer raised his eyebrows. —Whose father? Else's?

—No no, Oskar, said Piedernig. He paused. —The father of the girl.

—Ah, said Voxlauer. —No. No I haven't. He's not been heard from as yet.

—He hasn't?

—No.

—I see.

—The cousin has.

—The cousin. Yes, I'd heard, said Piedernig, clearing his throat. —You've met this cousin, then?

—I've not yet had that pleasure either.

Piedernig said nothing. Across the plain the sun caught the

windows of the onion-headed steeple of a church. —What church is that, straight across? Voxlauer said, squinting.

—I'm not sure. Ah—St. Marein, I think.

—Looks far away.

—Not far enough, said Piedernig. He looked at Voxlauer and grinned. —Italy, Oskar! he said, brandishing his cane like a hussar's saber. —Italy for vagabonds and fools!

—Rehearsing for Passport Control, are you?

—Passport Control? said Piedernig, stopping in mid-swing.

That afternoon Else came to the door as he was halfway up the steps and led him around the house to the garden gate. —The rhubarb is almost due, she said. —Look at that first row, and the one behind it. We'll have compote soon, and rhubarb tortes. All manner of cakes and delicacies. She beamed at him. —Where have you been?

—With Walter. He's leaving tomorrow. You know that, I suppose.

—Yes. He came by this morning. She bent over and pulled a clump of grass from among the cabbage heads along the fence. —Seemed in very high spirits.

—Some kind of spirits, said Voxlauer, smiling. —He wanted to go to the Holzer farm for schnapps. Asked if we'd mind minding the children for a year or two. I told him we weren't running any kind of game-preserve and he said that was perfectly obvious.

Else laughed. —He'd never manage without those brats of his. Not for a second. They're the only ones left with any sap in them, aside from Herta.

Voxlauer was quiet a moment. —Maybe we should go up tomorrow, to see them off. What do you think?

—You've grown fond of the old gasbag, haven't you? Don't pretend any different.

Voxlauer shrugged. —He's honest, Fräulein. I admire that in a fraud.

. . .

Going up the next morning they found them already on the road, the children first in an absurd procession driving a column of mud-caked goats ahead of them, the adults close behind, shuffling heel to heel like convicts, Piedernig and Herta last of all on a loose-axled cart pulled by mules. Voxlauer and Else stepped back from the road and waited for the dust to settle. Piedernig smiled down at them with weary dignity, wiping mock sweat from his brow with the hem of his moth-eaten riding coat. —Blessings, pilgrims! he said, both hands raised in benediction. Herta nodded to them stoically.

—Morning, all, said Else. —Morning to the collective! she called down the convoy. A chorus of mumbled greetings rose up in answer. —You're the pilgrims, Walter, she said brightly. —Oskar and I are as sedentary as they come.

—Off to stake your claim, Professor? said Voxlauer.

—Naturally, said Piedernig. —I've read my Cooper, child. A golden future awaits us in the west.

—Why head south, in that case?

—It's the spirit of the thing, Oskar, Else whispered.

—Quite right, Fräulein, quite right! Piedernig said, looking hard at Voxlauer. —The direction of course is immaterial, Herr Gamekeeper.

—I beg pardon, said Voxlauer. —Keep an eye out for the redskins.

—Wrong again, Oskar! The redskins will befriend us and teach us their ways.

—There's a different sort of tribe in power now, Professor, from what I've heard.

—Nonsense, Oskar! said Piedernig happily. —Fairy stories!

Else stepped forward and curtsied. —We brought you some very nice strawberries as a token of good riddance.

—No fishes, children? said Piedernig, looking sorrowful.

—You'll have to provide your own loaves and fishes from now on, Professor, said Voxlauer. —There's no getting around it for a man of your position.

—Walter thinks he has that all arranged, said Herta. She smiled down at Else.

—Good-bye, Fräulein, Piedernig said brightly. Of their own accord the two mules and the column of raggedly attired bodies began to move. —Mind those aborigines! said Voxlauer, reaching up a hand.

—Don't trouble yourself too much about *us,* said Piedernig, leaning over and taking it solemnly in passing. —Best look to yourselves awhile. Remember, Oskar: if they come for you, take them fishing.

—Duly noted, said Voxlauer.

Piedernig gave a shout and a huddle of boys who'd been lolling in the grass got up grudgingly and began to drive the goats and the cows down the road. In a few moments they were all of them gone in a clatter of iron pots and a cloud of sepia-tinted dust. For some time afterward the shouts of the children and the bleating of the animals carried back to them up the road, dimming and returning like water lapping against a pier. Then that, too, faded and Else and Voxlauer were alone.

The two of them spent that afternoon laying damp hay on the garden to keep down the weeds and clearing beds along the warm south wall for summer corn. As evening came the air cooled unexpectedly and they went inside to the parlor and took out the dog-eared tarok deck and tried to play. They kept at the game half-heartedly for an hour or so, not bothering to keep score, then sat dumbly at the table as night fell, uneasy for the first time in each other's company. The evening sun canted across the table and the cards and ran in soft pink streaks along the floorboards. They sat quietly looking across the floor at nothing, waiting, it seemed to Voxlauer, for something to happen. The last pale rays were just ebbing from the garden when they heard the shouts coming up the hillside.

He came calling her up the road, pushing his heavy olive-colored motorcycle in front of him. When he came within sight of the villa he left the bike idling and hung back at the edge of the fenced-in garden, watching the kitchen lamp being lit and her figure a moment later in the doorframe with the lamplight steady and full behind her. Seeing her he stopped a moment, muttering to himself, then went back to the motorcycle and started it and turned it to face the woods. He reached into the pocket of his riding jacket and fished out a shallow hinged-topped flask and tipped it back. Still cradling the flask, he leaned forward and switched on the headlamp and spun the handlebars back and forth, watching the ball of light arcing through the clay-colored trees. Then he shut off the motorcycle and walked back up the hill, all the while calling out to her: *Liesi!*

Voxlauer was still at the kitchen table, shuffling the tarok deck clumsily and cutting it and watching her stare out the window, rapt and breathless, her whole body tense with waiting. Finally she looked over at him. She opened her mouth once and closed it.

—Is it your cousin? he said tonelessly.

She nodded.

They were quiet a moment. The light of the motorcycle swung steeply across the kitchen and into the woods.

—He seems reluctant to come in, said Voxlauer. —Why is that?

—I don't know, said Else. —He knows you're here, she said after a pause.

—Ask him to come in. It's all right.

She looked at him again. —I don't know, Oskar.

—He's your cousin, isn't he? Shouldn't he like to meet me? I'd think he would. I'd think he would be curious.

Her mouth opened slowly. —Yes.

Voxlauer sat silently, holding the cards.

—Oskar—

—Yes?

She made a low sound, not moving her lips. The light passed again behind her. —I don't think I can not go to him, Oskar.

Voxlauer didn't answer. He remained sitting at the table as if she had said nothing, squaring the cards and laying them out in rows. From time to time the shouts carried up to the house. The lamp was to her right now so that as she stood at the kitchen window she was perfectly cast for Voxlauer in silhouette, like a mannequin in a dressmaker's window. Something gave in him suddenly and he wanted to stand close to her, to look out into the dark, to see what she was seeing. He closed his eyes. —Go then, he said a moment later, moving his chair back from the table. But she had already gone.

For six or seven days Voxlauer didn't see her. He moved purposelessly from day to day in a haze of dull bewilderment, keeping to the higher woods, eating and sleeping only rarely. Once each morning he would go down to the cottage to see if she had left any word for him and, finding none, would retreat again into the haze which hung everywhere on the roads and among the trees, waiting to readmit him. That she had gone out so strangely, left the kitchen without a word and stayed away that night while he waited for her at the table, shuffling cards and laying them out in rows, meant little to him after the first day had passed. After three more days his tiredness and confusion were such that he no longer cared what she had done and could see nothing so very terrible in what little he remembered. In spite of this the thought of simply walking down to the villa, finding her there and asking what had happened, he banished from his mind each morning as quickly as it came. The source of his unhappiness was obscure to him still and far away but was connected as if by a length of twine to that place. He could not go down to the villa without a sign from her: he was afraid. Some strange thing had happened there.

She came across him on the seventh morning. He'd been standing a long time in the middle of the road under Birker Heath, unsure of whether to go up or down. She looked drawn and pale and awkward as she approached him. He himself felt ragged and weather-beaten but drew himself up with a kind of pathetic pride and waited for her to speak.

—Hello, Oskar.

He nodded.

—You haven't been about.

—At the villa, you mean.

—The villa. The cottage. Anyplace.

He nodded again, helpless in the face of accounting to her. —Well. I've been busy up here—

—You look tired, she said.

—I am. Yes.

—Good God, Oskar. Where in hell have you been hiding? I've been everywhere trying to find you. I even went to town.

—I don't remember very well.

She stood without speaking for perhaps a minute. If she was angry or disgusted or relieved she showed not the slightest sign. She looked calm and tired, mortally tired, and resolved to something. —Were you heading up or down? she said.

—Up, said Voxlauer. He began to walk and she fell in beside him.

Farther up the slope where the grade made logging difficult the pines grew taller and more oddly shaped. Fingers of pink and yellow rock showed here and there through the thinning trees. The shoulder of the narrowing road, unused since the last logging forty years before, was washed sharply away at each inward curve and covered in many places by mud and debris. At the most recent washes where the mud was still soft, Voxlauer's and Piedernig's prints were still clearly visible, baked into sharp reddish-brown relief by the sun of the past week.

—Why did you say that, the other day? said Else.

Voxlauer rubbed his eyes. —The other day? What was it?

—About Walter. That he wasn't a liar.

—I don't know. I don't remember. He shook his head as though trying to clear it. —Never mind about that.

—Were you making a comparison?

—What?

—Were you comparing him to me? She was looking at him now, almost smiling.

Voxlauer stopped, blinking, staring at her. He shook his head. —I don't think you're a liar, Else.

—Oskar, she said, putting her hands on his shoulders. They stood in the road for another vague, pale stretch of time, leaning stiffly against each other. Voxlauer suddenly felt very weak. She had held him in front of her this way once before, he remembered: when she had told him she wouldn't confuse him. He drew her closer. He was standing over her now, bending slightly to accommodate her arms. —I haven't lied to you, Oskar, she said. —I told you about him, about what he did. I told you all of that.

—Yes, said Voxlauer slowly, not caring anymore. —You told me.

—I never hid any of that from you.

Voxlauer didn't answer.

—He's my family. All that's left. We grew up together.

—Yes. You've told me that.

—Resi needs him.

—He abandoned you both, said Voxlauer.

Else nodded. —Yes. You're right. She paused. —But I can forgive him that.

—And the other things he's done, Else? said Voxlauer, not

knowing himself what he was saying. —Can you forgive him those?

She frowned at this. It was difficult to talk, he knew, when they were both so tired. But still he found himself feeling nauseous at this new refusal of hers. —I don't know of anything else, she said slowly.

—I don't either. He took a breath. —But I can imagine very well.

She turned and took a half step down the hill. Her face when she looked at him again was pulled together queerly. —I came and found you, Oskar. I looked for you all week and came up today and found you and asked you how you were and where you'd been hiding and if you were tired or sick, just as if you were a baby. Doesn't that matter at all? Does it matter more to you what my cousin does? I don't know what my cousin does. She brought herself up short and ran the sleeve of her shirt across her face. —He's a policeman now. That's what he calls it. I haven't asked him yet what I should forgive him for.

—Where did you go with him?

—Walking.

—Where?

—To the spruce plantations, she said, straightening herself.

—It's not my business, said Voxlauer. —I'm sorry.

—That's all right.

Voxlauer let out a breath. —I told you he'd be coming.

—Yes, Oskar, she said. —And I told you he was someone who'd never have a place in the present for me. Only in the past. She came to him now, reaching up and laying a hand over his eyes. —In the past only, Oskar. But the past is important to me just now. And to Resi.

—I remember your saying that, said Voxlauer. —I remember thinking it was a strange thing to say about a cousin.

—Yes, she said, her hand still covering his eyes. —It's strange. The hand smelled lightly of cooking oil and dirty water. He opened his eyes under it and looked out through the bright red gaps between her fingers at the light on the road.

They began walking again and came out onto the heath not far from where he and Piedernig had stood the week before. Else had brought a little food with her, some goat cheese and a roll wrapped together in linen, and she crouched down now and spread the limp white cloth over the grass. —I'd thought this might turn into an expedition, looking for you, she said, directing him to sit down beside the cloth.

—Is it you, Mother? said Voxlauer, smiling weakly up at her. He was trembling from hunger and from nervousness and leaned back and drew his legs up to his chest. After a time the sun came out again from behind the clouds and he began to feel better. Else had laid out the food and arranged it and was at that moment unstopping a bottle of sweet-smelling cider. —Will you be partaking of spring's bounty this afternoon?

He lay himself down with his head on her lap and his feet pushing into the warm sun-bright grass. —I think I'll just lie here at present.

—When did you eat last?

—I don't know.

She cursed half under her breath. —You're always doing yourself harm, Oskar. How do you explain that to yourself, a fullgrown man?

—I'm easily swayed by public opinion, Fräulein.

—You're lucky I'm not.

—I know that. Voxlauer touched a hand to the small of her back. —I know that very well.

—You're shivering.

He looked up at her. Her hair fell down across his face, folding over him like a Chinese screen. —I'm afraid.

—So am I, Oskar. But not of Kurt.

—No?

She shook her head. —Something's happened to him. He's lost his confidence.

—Strange time for that.

—You don't understand. She cradled his head now in one of her hands, running the other absently through his hair. —He drinks now.

—Didn't he before?

—No. Never. He's hated drunks since I can remember.

The wind rustled through the grass. He drifted very close to sleep but her hair brushing across his face now and then kept him awake. —What are you afraid of, then? he said, opening his eyes.

—Everybody else.

—Ah! That I can understand.

—Can you? She tilted her head to look across the plain. Voxlauer watched her eyes travel carefully over the landscape point by point before eventually falling closed. —Why did you leave town? he said suddenly.

She drew her mouth sleepily into a smile. —I've just told you.

Later, as they were walking down from the heath, Else began talking again about her cousin. —Kurt hates them just as much as we do, she said. —Rindt keeps blathering away about Ryslavy, how something needs to be done. She cocked her head at him. —Kurti told him to see his own knickers were washed before sniffing down any of his neighbors'.

—They certainly could do with a rinse, said Voxlauer.

—And to wash his drawers next. Rindt was slack-jawed.

—I can picture that.

—Yes, Oskar. She tugged happily at his chin.

Over the tops of the pines the sky shone dull and white and the shadows on the road dimmed and disappeared altogether. Voxlauer walked with his eyes half closed, letting his light-headedness and hunger carry him down the road.

—He hates Ryslavy, though, said Else after a time.

—Is that any great surprise?

—I suppose not, she said. —He's always had that hatred. Of the Ryslavys especially, because of being beholden.

Voxlauer frowned a little. —What did he say, exactly?

She paused. —They're looking for a target.

—Who?

—Town. The Polizeihaus. Maybe both.

—What does that mean, a target?

—I don't know, Oskar. That was the word he used. He didn't explain. I let him talk. That was what he wanted.

—Yes? said Voxlauer. Time passed. They were on the valley road now, just above the plantations. —The thing to do now is to keep faceless, said Voxlauer suddenly, making a face at her.

—You won't be able to. He's already been to see your uncle. Your mother too.

—My mother? said Voxlauer.

She nodded. —Last week.

—What does he want with her?

—He's been living in Berlin these last five years. Going to the opera.

Voxlauer stared at her.

—Even *we* knew who your mother was, Oskar. And your father. You must know that. There's been nobody else famous ever to come out of Niessen. Or to end up in it, either, that I can think of.

—To end up in it, said Voxlauer. —Christ in heaven. He laughed.

—What's so funny about that?

—My father. Do you know what happened to my father?

She hesitated. —I think so, yes. He died.

—He shot himself. With a rifle. Here. Voxlauer pointed to his mouth.

Else stopped. —You never told me that.

—I thought you knew. Everybody does in town.

—In town, said Else, saying the words differently from the way he'd said them, calmly, almost affectionately.

Voxlauer began walking again. —My mother's ill. I don't want your cousin visiting her. Will you tell him?

—He wants to meet you.

He looked at her a moment. —Does he know what we do at night?

—More or less, she said, giving him a smile.

—Well. In that case, I suppose.

As they walked through the spruce groves and crossed over the creek Voxlauer glanced unconsciously from time to time over his shoulder. —What are you looking for? said Else.

He shrugged. —I don't know. Game of some kind, I suppose. I keep game, you know, Fräulein. Game is my bread and butter.

—You haven't found any, then, for about a week, by the looks of you. She reached a hand up under his shirt. —You're barely bones, she murmured into his ear.

Voxlauer sighed contentedly. —I'll get fat yet, he said. —I'm not in any hurry about it.

—Just make sure you don't disappear altogether, and your bread and butter with you.

—Remember your Hansel and Gretel, Fräulein. If you're bony they cook the other bugger.

—I remember it very well. I've been saving all my chicken bones.

—They'll parboil Rindt, first of all, Voxlauer shouted. —Keep an army in blubber.

Else frowned. —They're not cannibals, Oskar. Are they?

Voxlauer danced skeleton-like down the road.

A bright trill of brass greeted Voxlauer as he climbed the stairs of the old house. Maman was standing at the kitchen table cutting dough, humming along with each flourish like a newlywed bride.

Voxlauer stood in the hallway, watching her through the open door. —You look better than I feel, Maman, he said.

She looked up at him and nodded. —It's not all bad, Oskarchen.

—So you've always told me.

—Well. She seemed confused. —If I did, I was right, then.

He glanced toward the parlor. —I thought you'd had your fill of Brahms, he said, smiling.

—Yes, she said brightly. —This isn't Brahms.

He stared at her in blank surprise, saying nothing. She continued to fuss about the table, taking no further notice of him. When all of the dough had been cut into palm-sized squares she kneaded them back into a ball and began again from the beginning. He made no move from the doorway but stood motionless in its frame as if he were bolted to it, staring at her.

—Can I help at all, Maman? he said after a long while, stepping through the doorway. Looking around the kitchen he now saw piles of unwashed plates and cups and cooking pots covering the counters. The cabinet and the credenza were also open and filled to their furthest recesses with opened tins and boxes, silverware and newsprint and refuse of all shapes and descriptions. Staring from one corner of the room to another in his confusion, he thought at first the Holzer boys must have done it, come down in the night while she was sleeping, and he was filled with a sudden panic that they had done something to her. Then he looked over again at the table and saw that her hands were caked with dirt. She was looking at him now, confidently, the dough still massed together between her fingertips. —It's not all bad, Oskar, she repeated.

Voxlauer came over to the table and took hold of one of her hands to wipe it clean. It was damp and cool and lay limply in his grip, patient and unprotesting, as if nothing more was to be expected of it. —Come out with me to the verandah, Maman, he said, leading her into the stairwell.

They sat next to each other on the sagging cane couch, looking up at the sky. How many times we've sat this way together, Voxlauer thought. Maman gazed into the distance serenely, nodding her approval of all that she beheld. A warm breeze rustled the dahlias in the window boxes.

—I met a young man this week, she said. —About your age.
—My age?
She nodded.
—What did you talk about?
—He was here to visit.
—I see.
—A bit younger than you perhaps, Oskar, she said, appraising him.
—What did he want? He squeezed her hand gently. —Maman?
—Yes?
—Tell me what he wanted.
She leaned back on the couch, resting her head on the wall behind her. The nodding had given way now to a steady shudder. She seemed oblivious to it, however, gazing into the woods. Her face was tranquil. —Cold now toward night, she said after a while. —I'm not properly dressed.

Voxlauer stood up and went to the linen trunk and dug out an old gray blanket. —This young man, Maman, he said, coming back to the bench. —What did he want to talk about?

—Herr Bauer, she said. —An Obersturmführer. Imagine!

—Maman, he said, arranging the blanket, ducking down to catch her eye. —Please tell me what he wanted. Can you say?

—Wanted? She frowned. —I wouldn't know, Oskar. Some of them are quite decent.

—Maman.

—We talked about Berlin. He was there five years. Five years, Oskar! We talked about the opera.

—He was an illegal. A Nazi, Maman. That's why he left.

—Yes. She nodded her head emphatically. —Yes, he was.

—Maman, said Voxlauer, gripping her tightly by the shoulders, bringing his face down close to hers. —Look here at me. What is it? What? Can you answer? Tell me, Maman. You have to tell me. Tell me. I can't bear it.

When she didn't answer he knelt in front of her and took her hand. He stayed there for a long time as the light faded, waiting for her to tell him what was the matter. She sat smiling at him contentedly, interestedly, as though watching him from a great distance through glasses that were too weak for her. —Maman! he heard himself saying over and over. He felt then, staring up at her, as though he were calling out her name from a ship that was traveling quickly out to sea. Soon the point would come when he could no longer see her, not even as a speck against the shore, and he would give up calling. —Maman, he said again, almost to himself, weeping openly now in front of her.

Eventually a change came over her face and she sat up and took a long, deep breath.

—Oskar? she said, a trace of a shadow crossing her face. —What's wrong?

—Nothing, Maman. It's nothing.

This answer seemed to satisfy her. —I had a dream yesterday, she said, smiling down at him. —Would you like to hear it?

He nodded.

She took a shallow, girlish breath, repositioned herself on the couch almost coquettishly and began.

—I'm a tiny thing. A girl. She sighed. —Seven, or six. I'm going from the farm to Herbst's to sell cream. She paused a moment, lightly touching the side of her face. —The pail is knocking against my knees. It's very bright in town and everything is going slowly. Wagons and traps are passing on the street and the gentlemen all step off the curb to let me by. You're not alive yet, Oskar, she said, reaching for his hand.

—I know it, said Voxlauer.

—Your father passes by and tips his hat. He seems to be doing well. He has on his spectacles. I keep down the street with the pail, which is really very heavy and beginning to hurt my wrists. When I get to Herbst's the tables are all very crowded and I pick my way through them to the door. Everybody is quiet. The cups are clicking against the saucers. Werner Herbst and the children are waiting. They have horses saddled in the kitchen, drinking out of the kitchen sink. Two bay mares, Oskar, and a yellow pony.

She nodded quietly a moment, smiling in the recollected light of the dream. —Here are the horses! they say, pointing. —Do you want to ride or sing? I don't say anything at all but hold the pail out for them to see. Then I watch as they lead the horses around the tables between the customers with their drinks and their iced creams on their blue glass plates and canter off. They wave back to me once from the canal bridge. She paused, looking out now along the street. —They just ride away.

—And then?

—That's all, Oskar, she said kindly, as if to an easily disappointed child.

Voxlauer sat back on his heels. —What a pretty dream that is, Maman.

—Yes. I know. He left a note for you on the parlor table.

—What?

She gestured into the parlor. —On Père's composing table.

He stood up quickly and went in to the little desk and found a typewritten summons on stiff gray Polizeihaus stationery, stamped and embossed with various red and candlewax-colored seals. The signature at the bottom was jagged and fine, like a crack in an eggshell. Under it were printed the words "Kurt Elisabeth Bauer: Obersturmführer of the Schutzstaffel of the German Reich." Voxlauer slid the summons into his pocket, feeling the warp of its fibers a moment between his thumb and forefinger. When he came back to the verandah Maman was spitting onto the blanket and rubbing its corners together. —There's a stain on this blanket, she said quietly.

Voxlauer climbed the wide stucco steps of the Polizeihaus just before noon. Two brass pegs had been driven into the flaking yellow plaster above the entrance and a square felt banner hid each lintel corner. A black swastika on a red and white field fluttered gaudily between them. Two ribbons, frayed and speckled with watermarks, hung down limply to either side. Looking up at them Voxlauer was reminded of Christmas banners left out to rot over the winter. Through the propped-open doors a clerk watched him idly, looking down at his desk and then up at him again, as though sketching out his likeness. As Voxlauer entered he rose to his feet and saluted. —Heil Hitler.

—The same to you, said Voxlauer tonelessly, looking around the foyer. —I'm here to see Herr Bauer.

—I see, said the clerk. —To see the Obersturmführer. He smiled. —Are you here by appointment, Herr . . . ?

—Voxlauer. By invitation. He slid the balled-up summons across the desktop.

The clerk bent over and picked up the summons, smiling indulgently. Uncrumpling in his smooth white fingers, the paper made a noise like a sack of candy being opened. —Be seated, won't you, Herr Voxlauer? said the clerk. As Voxlauer went to sit he slipped gracefully around his desk and left the foyer.

Voxlauer eased himself into a padded rattan chair and scratched

at the tip of his nose with his thumb. The clerk's steps receded up
the stairwell. Outside the window a column of martins spiraled
over the canal and the freshly tarred street steamed and glistened
in the sun. A dank smell wafted through the open doors, sweet
with compost and oily water. A wrinkle-faced old woman passed
carrying a pail. A dray cart rattled by a short while later, piled high
with fresh-washed linens. Its driver tipped his hat cheerfully and
saluted.

After a quarter of an hour the clerk reappeared. —Obersturmführer Bauer is dedicating a playing field, he said, handing back the
wrinkled summons. —Pardon our confusion, Herr Voxlauer. This
is a very busy time.

Voxlauer looked down at the paper. —It does say one o'clock,
Tuesday the twenty-fifth, he said.

—Does it? said the clerk, blinking.

Voxlauer said nothing for a time. —Expecting him back soon?

The clerk blinked again, coyly, and shrugged his shoulders.
—Your guess is as good as mine, citizen.

—Could I leave a message? I'll be brief.

—If you must, Herr Voxlauer. The clerk pulled open a drawer
of the desk with a smooth, precise movement, stifling a yawn.
—What might this be regarding? he said. His thin blond hair was
slightly damp and stood out from the back of his head like the tail
of a canary. His otherwise perfect, featureless voice peaked and
fluttered over its r's and s's. He stared at Voxlauer, pen in hand.

—You're a Reichs-German, aren't you, said Voxlauer after a
moment.

—We all are, citizen, said the clerk impatiently, his cowlick rising danderlike behind him as he spoke. —Even in this sow's-milk
valley. Now then, he continued, pulling out a sheet of the heavy
gray stationery from the drawer and uncapping a pen. —What was
the message, in ten Reichs-German words or less? Be sure to talk
slowly enough, mind, so that I'll understand you. None of your
back-valley gibberish.

Voxlauer said nothing, watching the clerk's damp, white hands
tapping against the desktop.

—Come now, Herr Voxlauer! said the clerk after a moment,

smirking. —No message, after all, for the Obersturmführer? I'm confident that you can think of something. I've just put fresh ink into my pen, and I'm very eager to put it —

—Shove it up your ass, said Voxlauer. —And keep the hell away from my mother, you sons of bitches. He leaned forward slightly and lowered his voice. —With that first request I was addressing you specifically, you mincing, cow-faced bastard.

—Duly noted! the clerk said amicably, putting away the stationery with a neat click of the sliding drawer.

Voxlauer stood up slowly and hobbled out of the foyer and down the Polizeihaus steps. His leg had fallen asleep in the chair and the blood now trickled back into it, prickling and searing. He leaned back against the wall and raised the leg up and massaged it. Two more clerks had come down into the foyer and Voxlauer leaned back against the wall and listened to the noise of their chatter scored by fits of mule-like braying. He spat out a string of thick gray spittle and looked wearily down the street toward the toll road, waiting for the pain to lessen.

Up along the canal came a figure on a bicycle. Drawing closer, it broadened into the shape of a heavy man in a red-and-white-checkered shirt, open to the belly, and a freshly greased pair of lederhosen. The bicycle veered, slowed, and came to a halt a few meters away from Voxlauer. Its rider let out a knowing chuckle.

Voxlauer cursed quietly to himself. —Hello, Uncle, he said, still massaging his knees.

Gustl dismounted from his bicycle, grinning with his entire face. —Never too late for some of us, eh, nephew?

Voxlauer made to step into the road and winced. —Buy me a drink somewhere, would you, Gustl?

Gustl touched the side of his nose mischievously with a finger. —You just mind this machine for two halves of a minute, boy. I'll be back directly. He climbed up the Polizeihaus steps and went inside.

A minute later he reemerged, adjusting a band of black elastic above his left elbow. —Off we go now *and high time for it,* he whispered, taking back the bicycle. They walked purposefully down the Bischoffstrasse to the square, Gustl ringing the bicycle's bell at every passing citizen, tipping his hat to many of them, whistling all the while loudly and emphatically off-key.

—What are you in mourning for, Uncle? said Voxlauer, looking at the armband.

—Nothing, boy! Not one blessed thing! Gustl chuckled again and slid his arm merrily through Voxlauer's. —A little drink's the thing just now, I'd say. You look fairly parch-mouthed. No excuse for *that* in a man of sense and substance.

He led Voxlauer straight past Ryslavy's to the sun-spattered patio at Rindt's. —Now then. Let's set ourselves up out here under God's high heaven and force a little air into the icebox.

Voxlauer looked over his shoulder at the blank blue windows of the Niessener Hof. —Could we go inside?

—Ho-ho! said Gustl. —Naturally, Oskar. As you prefer. He leaned his bicycle absently against a lamppost and turned back toward Rindt's with a contented sigh.

—Aren't you going to lock it? said Voxlauer, pointing at the bicycle.

Gustl shrugged. —If you're troubled, nephew, I suppose. He waved Voxlauer on and turned back to the lamppost, producing a ring of jangling keys from a pocket of his lederhosen. —Go on in, Oskar! Stake our claim.

Voxlauer passed reluctantly through the iced-glass doors into the barroom. Werner Rindt was behind the bar as always, leaning on his wide, pillow-like elbows, halfheartedly toweling a row of steins. Two drunks sat on barstools just across from him, bobbing their heads and mumbling to each other. Most of the stools were occupied and a low, steady murmur hovered over them. The top of the bar was greasy and wet. Voxlauer found a vacant spot and leaned across it, motioning to the barmaid. —Two little mugs, Fräulein, he said.

Rindt and a few others had broken off their conversations to look at him. The barmaid nodded, keeping her eyes on the buttons of his shirt, and turned without once having met his eyes back to the taps. —Bring them over there, said Voxlauer, pointing to a table near the door. The barmaid bobbed her head slightly, busy at the taps.

He walked back at a leisurely pace along the bar, not looking at Rindt or at anyone else, went to the table and sat. The barmaid came almost before he'd pulled in his chair, set two mugs down in front of him and went quickly back to the bar. He took up the damp and mildewed list of specials and, feeling Rindt watching him, made a show of looking it over with morbid interest.

When he glanced up again Rindt had gone. Rindt's two drunks and a handful of others at the bar were still turned part of the way round, keeping him in view. A moment later the glass doors swung open and Gustl waddled through them. He looked carefully from face to face in the crowded and smoke-thick dining room, touching his hat brim now and again, and making out Voxlauer in the corner crossed quickly to the table. —Touch somber in here all of a sudden, he said with a wink.

—I took the liberty, said Voxlauer, indicating the mugs of beer.

—And right you were, said Gustl, raising his mug to his lips. An instant later he was coughing and retching and staring to the right and the left of him with outraged eyes. —What in *God's* name? he sputtered, holding his mug away from him at arm's length as though it might pollute him.

—I asked for beer.

—Well! Gustl grimaced and stood up from the table. —You sit tight here a minute, boy, and I'll see if I can locate some. He went back over to the bar and returned a short time later with two unopened bottles. —For safety's sake, he muttered sheepishly, pulling an opener from the breast pocket of his shirt. Voxlauer allowed himself a smile.

—They've a bit to learn here, I concede that, said Gustl, opening the first of the two bottles and setting it down on the table.

—We could easily have gone to Pauli's.

—Not so easily, actually, said Gustl, wrestling with the second bottle.

—The help's a damn sight better there. And they keep beer in their taps.

—Between you me and the bedpost, said Gustl, bringing the bottleneck up to his lips—the help improves here by the day. By-the-day, he repeated, tapping his nose.

—What are you doing for them, Uncle? said Voxlauer, holding his beer up to the light.

Gustl clucked and waved a finger. —You won't draw me into your stratagems that easily, my boy.

—Stratagems?

Gustl nodded, sipping cautiously from the sweating rim of his bottle. —Yes, Oskar. I said stratagems. I know what sort of society you've been keeping in those hills.

—Strictly Aryan society, Uncle. I'd swear an oath.

—Don't make light of this, Oskar. I try hard enough to keep the peace, Lord knows.

—What are you, Gustl? said Voxlauer, examining the armband more closely. It was the width of a palm and elastic and silken and looked as though it might have been fashioned out of a pair of women's stockings. —Some sort of policeman's helper?

—In a manner of speaking. They call us reservists.

—Ah. I understand now. Something like you were in the war.

—Something like that, I suppose, said Gustl, eyeing him suspiciously. —We maintain a presence. He smiled again and waggled one fat-upholstered forefinger. —So keep those nudists of yours in lederhosen.

Voxlauer laughed. —You can rest easy on that score, Uncle. My nudists have all gone down to Italy. In their finest pants and dresses.

Rindt was back at the bar, slopping glasses into a wooden pail. An ancient, wizen-faced man with eyes like the creases in a potato rose up from his stool as if to make an announcement, wavered a few moments in the air like a hand puppet, then collapsed back onto his stool. A round of laughter accompanied this event. Voxlauer raised his bottle toward Gustl, who was looking over at the drunk with something that might almost have passed for embarrassment. —To your good health, Uncle.

—I'd forgotten! said Gustl, grinning. —Of course, Oskar. Prost!

—Prost.

After a time Gustl looked meaningfully around the room. —Listen to me, Oskar. They're not going to go away. Are you listening? Look around you. These boys won't be leaving.

Voxlauer looked past Gustl at the tables and the bar. —They look as though they haven't left for weeks, he said.

Gustl studied him for a time. —When I saw you outside the Polizeihaus today I thought you'd had a breakthrough of some kind. I sincerely hoped so.

—Sorry to disappoint you, Uncle. I've broken some ribs, that's all.

—You're going wrong, Oskar, Gustl said quietly.

—Don't trouble yourself too much on my account, said Voxlauer, getting up a little stiffly from the table. He drained his bottle and set it down, along with half a schilling. —For the maid-of-the-bar, he said, looking calmly into Gustl's face. —See that she gets it, would you? The entire sum.

—I'm trying to explain something to you, Oskar, said Gustl, struggling to keep his voice low. —Sit down, you blessed idiot.

Voxlauer took up his coat and walked out into the daylight, waiting until the doors swung closed behind him to take a breath.

Crossing the square to the Niessener Hof Voxlauer found it locked and shuttered. He rapped on the glass and waited, peering in at the darkened coatroom. A minute or so later Emelia appeared.

—Good afternoon, Fräulein.

—Hello, Uncle, she said, not looking at him.

—Taking a holiday?

She nodded.

—I see, said Voxlauer. He was quiet a moment. Emelia stayed exactly as she was, the door partly open, the even dark behind her.

—The chief in? Voxlauer asked, smiling down at her penitently.

—In his office, she said, acknowledging his smile without moving any part of her face.

Ryslavy was sitting much as he had been that morning months

before, with his boots up on the desk and the cowhide chair tilted back under him, casting flies through the open office door into the kitchen. —Oh, it's you, he muttered.

Voxlauer ducked in between casts and sat himself down on a box overflowing with yellow invoices. —Is today a holiday for your people?

Ryslavy laughed. —You know I've never observed any of those, Oskar. Bad for business.

—I thought maybe state-imposed, said Voxlauer.

Ryslavy drew his arm back and cast again. —Ah! That's different. That's a different question altogether. He spun the reel back whirringly between his fingers. —You might say that a referendum has been held, Oskar. A quorum of the people has ruled that we might take a holiday.

—Rest for the wicked, I suppose.

Ryslavy turned to him suddenly. —What happened to your teeth, for the love of God?

—A referendum of the people.

—Frau Holzer's sons?

—In quorum.

Ryslavy whistled. —An able couple of boys.

—You might say.

—Smoke? said Ryslavy cheerfully. He tossed Voxlauer the tobacco tin without waiting for him to answer. —Smoke! he repeated. —Sterilize your gums. He waved at the far corner. —There's paper on the second shelf behind you. Under that minor continent of bills.

—This?

—No no, Oskar. That's the subcontinent at best. Farther to your left.

—Shall we stuff your briar, too, while the tin is open?

—I suppose I'd better, said Ryslavy, sighing heavily. He leaned back and put down the reel.

When Voxlauer had finished they smoked in silence. —Been to see Maman lately? he said after a time.

Ryslavy shook his head. —Not in ages. I've been meaning to. I'd thought of asking her for help, actually, he said, grinning a little. —What do you think, Oskar? She's still quite well thought of, you know, hereabouts. Our one solitary claim to Culture.

—"Culture," said Voxlauer, making a face.

—Laugh if you want, little man. Your mother was once a justly famous lady.

—My mother was an ensemble singer in operettas. A solo part thrown in here and there. Strictly bread-and-butter.

—Nonsense! She was a fine soprano.

—You never heard her, Pauli.

—I don't need to have heard her. You can see it. Even now, when she does nothing all day but roll her blessed balls of dough. It's the way she looks at you.

—I suppose you're right, said Voxlauer after a little pause.

—She sang in Berlin, Oskar.

—Once. She sang *once* in Berlin.

—Still. That counts for something.

—I'm worried about her.

Ryslavy sat forward slowly. —What is it?

Voxlauer let out a long breath. —I don't have any money.

—What do you mean?

—For a doctor.

Ryslavy drew a hand over his eyes. —How did this all happen? he said quietly. —All at once, from one day to the next? How, Oskar? He set the rod down cautiously beside him on the desk. —Should we have been keeping some sort of watch?

—Do you have any money?

—Ach! said Ryslavy. He shrugged. —Enough for a doctor, if it comes to that. But tell me what it is, for God's sake. Is it a stroke?

Voxlauer ashed his cigarette onto the floor. —You need to see her.

Ryslavy said nothing. Through the open door and the kitchen they could hear Emelia sorting bottles at the bar. —Quite a busy bee, that niece of mine, said Voxlauer. —I'm not altogether convinced she's yours.

—She's mine all right, worse luck for her. Did she tell you already, when you came in? I've taken her out of school.

—Why?

—You live a hermit's life, don't you, Oskar. I'd forgotten.

Voxlauer stared uncomprehendingly for an instant. —Is it so bad already? he said, the smile gone from his face.

—I'm a patient man. I give them six months, a year at best. They're idiots, Oskar. Garden-variety Punicellos. People in this town have never cared too much for circus comedy. They won't stand for it, in the long run.

—They seem to be standing for it beautifully.

—The trouble is with Rindt, mostly. Rindt and a handful of others. Anton Schröll, from the mill out in Greffen, and some Villachers I outbid five or six years back for wood rights. It has nothing to do with the Germans at all, really.

—They seem to think it does.

Ryslavy grinned. —They're particularly popular in the hills, as I think you've noticed.

—Yes. Well, they don't seem starved for attention down here, either.

—I've said already, Oskar. It'll pass. Ryslavy cast and reeled the line in slowly. It came snaking around the doorframe, trailing a black-and-turquoise-feathered fly. —It's just the waiting now that's killing me.

—Why don't you go, Pauli? Voxlauer said quietly.

Ryslavy looked at him soberly a few moments, then shook his head. —There's the land, for one thing.

—To hell with the land. Sell it.

—You buying?

—Plenty would. It's good timber.

Ryslavy sat for a while running the leader of the line back and forth across the floor, following it with his eyes. Finally he laughed. —Damn it, Oskar. I'll not sell to those sons of bitches.

—Others, then.

He laughed again. —Yes! Other sons of bitches.

—Others, that's all. Voxlauer watched the line as it ran in. —You might sell.

—Not me, said Ryslavy flatly.

Voxlauer said nothing for a long while, gazing fixedly at something over Ryslavy's shoulder.

Finally Ryslavy glanced at him. —What is it, Oskar? he said, raising his eyebrows. —Is there something outside?

—That rocket ship of yours, said Voxlauer, still looking out the window to where the Daimler stood in a parabola of shade, dark and proud and otherworldly. —Does it take very long to start?

They drove in a streak out past the canal and through the town gate and down the toll road at the fullest possible throttle between the bending, blurring willow rows. Voxlauer leaned out over the road with his face to the wind and his eyes tearing over and his hair whipping back and forth across his neck, gulping lungfuls of hot, steaming summer air. It tasted of cut green grass and dried cow dung and tar. Ryslavy let out long, stuttering whoops and beat against the hood with the flat of his hand. The shadows of the trees made perfect widening bands on the hood of the Daimler and flashed by in a cinematic flicker of white and black and green, bowing to let them pass. Flocks of starlings exploded upward from the fields and ruts and ditches. The Daimler rifled forward, banking smoothly as a biplane in the sudden dips and bends. At an abandoned mill they skidded sharply off the tar onto the split yellow clay of the Pergau road.

Leaving the plain the road narrowed and after a few curves the sun fell behind the walls of the valley. The road was wet in places from the past night's rains and at one curve they were forced to stop and haul a fallen sapling out of the roadway.

—Barricade us out, will they? Ryslavy bellowed. A few minutes later they passed through Pergau and rolled once, idling, around its empty square.

—This place is always deserted, said Voxlauer, shaking his head.

Ryslavy laughed. —Maybe they've all gone down to Italy.
—Or the Ukraine.
—Bolshevists, the lot of them, said Ryslavy, nodding fatuously.

—Greasy Yid-loving homosexual Gypsies. He sniffed. —Where should I drop you?

—The fishes will be missing me by now, I expect.

—I very much doubt it, said Ryslavy.

—Spend much time here, do you? Ryslavy said, kicking a half-empty tin of peas across the floor.

—Not so very much, said Voxlauer. He looked up from the hunting locker and made an all-encompassing wave. —Sit down wherever you like. My house is your house.

Ryslavy looked around him aggrievedly. —Smells like piss.

—Old man's piss, Pauli. The piss of the ancients. One develops a respect for it after a time.

—I'd rather not, said Ryslavy. He lowered himself cautiously onto the stove bench. —Do you have any quarterweights? Any decent sinkers?

—I thought you were using flies.

—I might do. Conversely, however—

—I'm looking, said Voxlauer. —A little patience. He brought out a battered lure case. —Have a look in this. Voxlauer brought the case over to the bench and turned to the stove and began to fill it.

—These'll do, said Ryslavy a minute or so later, snapping the case shut.

As he set the kettle to boil, Voxlauer watched him through the porthole struggling up the bank on bowed legs with the tackle box in his left hand and the two reels in his right, gasping for air like a great hairy carp. It seemed to Voxlauer he could make out Ryslavy's lips quite clearly forming passionate chains of curse words in the dwindling light, fine and lovingly crafted insults sent out in all directions to every living creature. He watched until he disappeared into the first cluster of pines above the bridge, then went back to the little table and sat quietly waiting for the water to boil, exploring the sockets of his missing teeth with the tip of his tongue. After drinking the coffee he went up and found Ryslavy sitting sullenly on his heels with his rod held stiff as a broom handle out over the water. —Too late a start, Ryslavy called out preemptively.

Voxlauer stretched himself out unconcernedly in the grass. —I thought the later the better, in the afternoons.

—Yes, but not in June, Oskar. Ryslavy spat into the creek. —Never in June, he said, more tentatively. A moment or two later he prodded a stone into the water with his boot.

—That ought to rouse 'em.

Ryslavy dipped the tip of his rod into the current. —Never question my methods, Oskar. Never doubt them.

Voxlauer propped himself up on his elbows in the grass. —Pauli.

—Present.

—Tell me about the old man.

Ryslavy reeled in and cast again. —He's dead.

—And yet his memory somehow lingers.

Ryslavy snorted. —Try turning out your sheets.

—You remind me of Maman, Pauli. Have a little mercy.

Ryslavy played the line out, fixing his eyes on the toes of his boots. He coughed once, cleared his throat and spat again into the water. Voxlauer lay back down and looked up at the sky, waiting for him to begin.

—He was run out of town, said Ryslavy finally.

—Why?

—I couldn't say.

—I doubt that very much.

Ryslavy shrugged. —He was strange. Nobody trusted him. His wife drowned in the middle of winter and they told him to leave town. He'd drunk with us for thirty years, so Papa in his unholy goodness offered him the cottage. He was a drunk, Oskar. A drunk. That's all. They wanted him out of town, old man Herbst and Papa and the rest of them. So he brought himself up here, and his children with him. On the back of a Burmese elephant for all I know or care.

—Did you say children?

—Your lady friend and her cousin.

—Kurt was with them?

Ryslavy nodded. —For a while.

—When was this?

—Five years after you left. Six. The war had been over about five years.

Voxlauer was quiet a moment. —Did you know them?

—No.

—You must have known them.

Ryslavy threw the rod angrily against the bank. —Why are you asking me these questions, Oskar? I wish I hadn't. I wish to hell I didn't know them now. They hated Papa for throwing table scraps to her ass-scratcher of a father and they hate me too, now, the both of them. Don't think I don't know it. Kurt Bauer would murder me if he could. The two of them would, together, and the little girl with them. Christ, Oskar! Why in hell should I tell you anything?

—I'm sorry, Pauli. I've been wondering about them a little, that's all.

Ryslavy laughed and said something to himself that Voxlauer didn't catch.

—What was that?

—Look to Kurt Bauer for the answers, I said.

Voxlauer took a breath. —Kurt and Else are not the same person, Pauli. I don't need to tell you, of all people, that they knew each other long before any of this had come into anybody's—

—He was an illegal already, they'd killed the Chancellor already by the time she got that child, Ryslavy said, spitting the words out. —You ask *him* about her politics, Oskar. Ask him about her views. Ryslavy let out a sour, tight-voiced laugh. —I should be thanking you, really, Oskar. You're in such a privileged position to find out what they're going to do to me.

—What was that you said about the child? said Voxlauer, his voice wavering slightly.

• • •

It rained that night, hard and even, and in the morning every puddle in the road hid a palm-sized toad floating as still as a leaf in its muddy shallows. Voxlauer knew them well from boyhood summers and knew too that when caught in the hand they showed their bright yellow undersides and bled a dark, poisonous-looking ink from tiny vents along their ribs. —India bottle, he said aloud. He caught one and wrapped it in a kerchief and took it with him in his shirt pocket to the villa.

As he came into the garden voices carried to him from an open window and he stopped a moment. Else's voice, Resi's, and another he didn't recognize. The dampness of the kerchief in his pocket formed a cool dull crescent against his chest and he could feel the toad gasping and scrabbling through the cloth. He breathed in and went the last few steps up to the screen door and pushed it open.

—Oh! said Else, looking up and smiling.

—Good morning, said Voxlauer.

—Oskar, this is Kurti, Else said, rising.

The man had been sitting at the table but now he rose as well and turned to Voxlauer, his face in an easy grin.

—Kurti: Oskar, said Else.

—A very great pleasure, said the man. He made a little pantomime of clicking his heels together and saluting. Resi laughed.

His hair was reddish and very thick but his eyes were the same as Else's, dark and heavy-lidded, and his skin was smooth and brown. He was slight and clean-shaven and looked barely over twenty. —Kurt Freiherr von Bauer, he said, extending a hand.

—*Ach,* stop it, Kurti! laughed Else. Her voice sounded brittle. —Please pay him no mind at all, Oskar.

—Oskar Baron von Voxlauer, said Voxlauer. He took the hand Kurt held out to him and shook it.

—Pleased to meet Your Grace, said Kurt, his hand firm in Voxlauer's. —Ouch, Herr Voxlauer! A perfect logger's handshake. The genuine article.

—And yet I've never logged, said Voxlauer.

—Show him your teeth, Oskar! Resi whispered.

—I have something better to show, said Voxlauer, going to the table. He took the kerchief out of his pocket and set it down. The toad struggled under the wetted cloth. Voxlauer undid the kerchief with a flourish.

—What is it? said Resi, taking a quick step backward. —What is it?

—An inkpot, said Voxlauer. He flipped the toad over onto its back and stroked its quivering belly with his thumb. Beads of black sprang up up and down its ribs.

—Nasty, said Resi, sucking in her breath.

—I wrote messages with these, in my spying days, said Voxlauer. —The ink dries invisible. You run over its belly with a spoon. He glanced over at Kurt and Else. —Didn't you ever use them? How did you write down your secrets, the two of you?

Else laughed. —I'm sure we didn't have any secrets, Oskar.

—Of course we did, Kurt said. —We don't remember them anymore, cousin, that's all.

Resi had taken the spoon from Voxlauer's hand and was holding it cautiously under her nose. —Is it poison?

—The tears of an enchanted prince, more likely, said Else, puckering her lips.

—Just the smallest kiss will do, said Voxlauer, holding the scrabbling toad down to her.

—I'll never! Resi squealed, ducking behind the table.

—Very well, then, said Voxlauer. He bowed and stepped to the door. —He'll have to wait for some more willing maiden, I suppose. Such a pity.

—We have no sympathy for you, Baron! Kurt called out through the screen.

—None expected, Voxlauer answered, stepping down the steps, the toad cool and slippery and beginning to struggle again in his hands.

—Good-bye, inkpot! Resi yelled.

A few days later Kurt brought Resi on his motorcycle and the four of them walked meanderingly through the pines, stooping low along piles of brush, hunting chanterelles. Here and there on the damp ground a cluster would glimmer through the needles, cool and luminous as a vein of ore, and Resi would run ahead and pull them up and arrange them carefully on the ground in rows. A thin film of oil shimmered along their rims and in the grooves of their undersides and caught the weak light under the trees. Else found the most, letting out a low quick cry and pointing them out to Resi, or stooping down in a patched summer dress wet from the damp ground and the dew. She unscrewed them with a small soft pop and threw them one by one into the sack Voxlauer carried with him, flicking dirt at him solemnly after each toss. Kurt kept far ahead of them, hunched over like an ape, hands wandering down and around the tree trunks as he went. Resi followed close behind, shrieking with happiness. After a time he snatched her up and settled her onto his shoulders and the two of them disappeared into the brush.

The sound of laughter carried back through the pines and the latticed sun as Voxlauer stood with the half-filled sack, damp and heavy and smelling of moss, waiting for Else to come with another armful from a stand of younger trees. She came out a minute or so later, bent over almost double to pass under the branches, rolling down a fold of her dress to show him the bright heap of chanterelles. Seeing her coming down to him proudly and happily he felt a tightness in his throat that ached and tightened even further as another peal of laughter carried back to them.

—They do get on, the two of them, don't they, Else said, raising the fold of her dress up over the sack and dropping the chanterelles in all at once. —Feel abandoned?

Voxlauer shrugged. —Ties of blood, Fräulein. There's just no getting around them.

—You should talk to him, Oskar. I'd like for you to talk to him.

Voxlauer fished a mushroom out of the sack and sniffed at it.

—Should I not let him come up? she said. —Is that what you think?

—He'd come up just the same. Whether or not you asked him.

—He's not after *you*, if that's your worry. He's told me.

Voxlauer hung back a moment. —He said that?

She nodded.

—When?

—This morning.

—So he's only just decided, said Voxlauer, starting to walk again.

He felt her coming up behind him. —He's still just a boy, really. You have to understand that. Prideful and stubborn as a boy.

—A boy? said Voxlauer, stopping short.

Else looked away immediately. —I know what you're thinking now, she said, setting her features defiantly, even scornfully. —I know what you'll say next.

—That's a lie you just told, Else. That's a lie. You know it is.

—Oskar—

—Don't start lying to me now, because of him.

Else brought a hand slowly to her mouth and bit it. Voxlauer watched her as if from a great distance and she, for her part, seemed to have forgotten him entirely. Eventually she roused herself and said:—Yes, Oskar. It was a lie. She slid her arm under his and curled her hand around his shoulder. —Please don't let's talk about him again. Will you promise me? I don't think I can stand it.

Sometime later they came to the creek and found Kurt and Resi sprawled out against each other in the shade. Resi lay on her side with her head in Kurt's lap and her legs scissored into his. Kurt's eyes opened as they came down and he raised a finger conspiratorially to his lips. —Can you take over, Liesi? he whispered. —I'd like to go for a walk with Oskar.

Else nodded, avoiding Voxlauer's look. Kurt slid out carefully from under Resi's legs and climbed to where Voxlauer was standing. —Come along, Oskar! he said, striking Voxlauer playfully on the shoulder.

—Why here? said Voxlauer, looking down into the muddy water.

Kurt stood with his hands in his pockets, surveying the cottage with the woods behind it. His thick hair stirred lightly in the wind.

He shrugged. —One place is as good as another. I had fine times here as a boy.

—So did I.

—Did you? Kurt frowned slightly, wrinkling his nose. —I can't say I remember you.

—I'm not surprised. You'd have been less than a glimmer.

—Ah yes! Of course, Kurt said, bringing a hand up into his hair and patting it down nervously. He shaded his eyes with the same hand and looked toward the cottage. —I like you, Oskar, he said suddenly.

—Does that mean no more beatings, Obersturmführer?

Kurt looked at Voxlauer, blinking at him slowly, squinting now and again, as if to make him out more clearly. —I'd pictured you darker, somehow. More heavyset. He puffed out his chest. —More of a woodsman.

—You're exactly as I pictured you, said Voxlauer.

—Pardon me for not believing you. I hardly look the type. Kurt cocked his head, still squinting. —*You* do, though, actually, in your weather-beaten way.

—Yes? What type is that?

—The lover, Kurt said softly.

Voxlauer said nothing. Kurt watched him awhile longer, head cocked strangely to one side, then leaned forward and put a hand on his shoulder. —I'm not threatening you, Oskar.

—No?

Kurt shook his head. —Not in the slightest. Though I don't expect you to believe me yet.

—I'd like to believe you, Obersturmführer. Very much. But first I'd have to understand you.

—It's really very simple, Kurt said, his face very close now, wide-eyed and sincere. —I wanted to thank you, Oskar. That's why we're here.

Voxlauer laughed, fighting the urge to take a step backward. —*Thank* me? What in hell for?

—For allowing this to happen. My time with Else. This . . . reunion.

—I had nothing to do with that, Obersturmführer. Believe me.

—Never mind. Accept my thanks anyway, cousin-in-law, if you can bear to.

Voxlauer looked at him for a long moment, studying his round, freckled, boyish face, smooth-featured and impossible to decipher, before raising his shoulders once and letting them fall. —All right, he said.

Kurt took a deep breath. —When I called on your mother with that summons note, Oskar, he said, turning again to face the water—I'd determined to make clear to you the fact of my return. I had every intention of threatening you then. You are suspected of being a Bolshevist and a spy. Your choice of occupation is highly suspect and your motive for hiding yourself away in this muddy little corner of nowhere equally so. Of course, on that last count I was privy to a certain knowledge. He grimaced. —The thought of my cousin consorting with such a person sickened me to my innermost self. I resolved to meet with you face-to-face and to make this understood.

—What stopped you?

—I had my reasons at that time, Herr Voxlauer, for avoiding this valley.

—I see.

—Do you? Good. Don't trouble yourself any further about them. It might not be too much to say that they saved you a great deal of suffering.

—I'm grateful, said Voxlauer. He paused, wheezing slightly, feeling a weakness building in his chest. Please let it not come just yet. Please not just yet, he thought. He stepped back and to one side, feeling light and unsteady on his feet.

—Now, Oskar, we've made our peace. Else has made things clear to me as best she can and you and I have had this very important talk. I've thanked you for welcoming me hospitably, I might even say charitably, back to this valley. And you've accepted my thanks.

—I see, Voxlauer said, feeling the ground underneath him settle.

—Yes. In the shade of his hand Kurt's expression changed slightly. —My role in town is to serve as the mouthpiece of the party that made me, Oskar, and little else besides. I had hoped, firmly *intended,* in fact, that up here I might begin to have a different purpose. He let out a sigh. —What do you think? Would that be possible?

Voxlauer said nothing for a long moment. —What purpose?

Kurt's eyes were clear and patient. —You have your ideas about illegals and the unification and your ideas are very well known to me. Does that surprise you?

Voxlauer shook his head.

—I have my own problems with the unification. Kurt took a step back, as if to see him better. —Yes; I thought that might give you pause. Shall I tell you what they are?

—Please.

—It may appear to you, Voxlauer, that the unification movement has made me a powerful man. I don't fault anyone for that assumption, you least of all, but the fact is that I have been made a fool of. He waved his fingers in the air. —Things were said and written and alluded to, *promises,* I suppose you'd say, meant to keep me happy and committed to my work, which was often very dangerous. Of these many promises not a single one was kept. I never wanted to return this way, as some kind of . . .

His voice drifted off. —Are you listening to me at all, Voxlauer?

—I'm listening.

Kurt sighed. —It wasn't going to *happen* this way, that's all. The old guard, all the old illegals pensioned off, farmed out into the hills, Reichs-German fops in every post. This wasn't what any of us wanted for this country. Ever. We were coming as equals to the Reich, not as some bastard colony. The Austrians were to have positions. *I,* he said, tapping himself on the breastbone—*I* was to have a position, Voxlauer. A real one. I would have rearranged things in this stinking country of ours, I can tell you. You wouldn't have recognized it.

—I don't recognize it now, said Voxlauer.

—What is it you think about me? That I hate the Jews? I've known many in my life that I've liked well. I'm an intelligent man,

Oskar. I reserve the right to judge every man's Jewishness, such as it is, for myself.

—I congratulate you.

—Just the same I admire strength in a man, Oskar, and I despise all forms of cunning. I think I may safely say that I hate cunning more than any other human failing. I hate it with a blind and unrelenting hate. You make a mistake, for example, if you think your Herr Ryslavy is suffering for any other reason. I am not a brute, Oskar, or a fanatic. But neither am I a fool.

—I never thought you were, Obersturmführer.

—Call me Kurt, for heaven's sake, Oskar. Kurt coughed. —We're practically family.

—You're not a fool, Kurt.

Kurt was still watching him. —Understand, Oskar, that when I come on these visits I come in my civilian dress. My uniform stays behind in my rooms, thank Christ, airing out on a little wooden peg. He breathed in deeply. —We're outside of history here, the four of us.

—If I was a Red you'd have had me killed anyway.

—Maybe so, said Kurt. —Eventually. But only for the sin of bringing history into this valley.

—What is there, exactly, between you and Else now, aside from history? said Voxlauer carefully.

—Blood, of course, Kurt said, stepping away from the bank. —The *girl*, Oskar. Some small sense of the future. Doesn't the future matter to you at all?

—It matters, said Voxlauer. —It's beginning to.

—And you ask what binds me to my only cousin? You're wonderfully dense at times, Voxlauer, for a man of the great outdoors.

—I didn't ask you that, said Voxlauer, squinting at him against the glare. —I asked what there was between you.

—There's you, Herr Voxlauer, first of all, Kurt said brightly, starting toward the cottage. Voxlauer hung back very briefly, playing with the idea of striking off into the pines. Watching Kurt's small-boned frame moving jerkily over the marshy ground, his thick reddish hair pressed imperfectly down onto his head, Voxlauer saw him for one fleeting instant as a young boy, walking with that same gait in pond-sodden clothes toward that same cottage, empty-headed and self-assured. Whatever menace he'd held vanished utterly in that instant. He was wonderful to watch, moving awkwardly across the meadow, as lovely in his way as Else was: her complement. Resi, too, corresponded to them absolutely. As he began to walk forward the thought came to Voxlauer that it might be best, after all, to keep out of such a perfect picture.

Reaching the door first, Kurt glanced over his shoulder before trying the handle. Voxlauer held the keys up and jangled them. Kurt shook his head good-naturedly.

—It's a strange sort of floating peace you've made for yourself up here, Voxlauer. You must feel very satisfied, holed up in your little patch of woods.

Voxlauer came slowly up the steps. —It's not my patch of woods. You know that very well.

—Come now, cousin-in-law! Confess! All alone up here, uncomplicated by politics, no one to watch over you; you must feel wonderfully free!

—I have someone to watch over me, Obersturmführer. Have you forgotten?

Kurt only shrugged his shoulders. —*Are* you a Red, Oskar? he said almost wistfully.

—Does that word have a meaning up here, outside of history? Voxlauer brought his shoulder against the door and pushed it open.

—Ah! You're a wily bastard, aren't you! Kurt said appreciatively. He leaned forward to peer past Voxlauer into the gloom. —What did you leave behind with the Bolsheviks, you wily bastard? A girl? A wife? Family?

—A wife, said Voxlauer, stepping away from the door to let Kurt pass. —No family.

—And I have a family without a wife! We make quite a pair, don't we.

—You have the future, said Voxlauer, smiling. —You have the Reich.

Kurt paused in mid-stride, looking back at him thoughtfully.
—When I was in Berlin, Voxlauer, during the term of my exile, I
watched our cause gaining momentum hour by hour. A beautiful
thing, beautiful, to have a cause, especially when you are lonely. We
nursed it together like midwives, the best of us, and the people who
scorned it or hindered it gradually fell away. Some tried, when it
was far too late, to recast themselves as our comrades. He pursed
his lips. —That's not your idea, is it?

—Would it work? said Voxlauer.

—We'll see, Kurt said, ducking under the lintel. —May I enter?

When he'd searched the cottage to his satisfaction Kurt sat down at
the table and flipped idly through the sketches. —These are by the
old man, these two, he said, holding up the portraits. —I remember when he did them.

—The one on the left's of Resi, said Voxlauer, leaning against
the doorframe.

—Yes. I recognize her mother in it.

—Not her father?

Kurt frowned. —No, not her father so much.

—Where is he now?

—He left.

—A friend of yours?

—He was. Yes. We went away together.

—I see.

—She still thinks of me as a deserter, doesn't she, Kurt said
quietly.

Voxlauer didn't answer.

—What do you think, Oskar? You're no stranger to it, after all.

—To what?

Kurt grinned. —Desertion, of course.

—I don't actually cherish an opinion on the subject, Voxlauer
said tightly.

—No? Tell me something, Herr Voxlauer, said Kurt, looking

around the room. —What was it drove you to hide away up here in this filthy hole? He let the sketches flutter one by one onto the table. —What was it, Voxlauer? He paused a moment. —Shame?

Voxlauer went to the door and held it open. —I suppose it was, he said. —But not the sort you'd understand, Obersturmführer.

THE ILLEGALS

AUGUST 1938

The morning of the day we shot Chancellor Dollfuss a rally was announced over the radio. *The usual selection of bureaucrats would speak, followed by assorted Home Front mannequins, and finally Dollfuss himself, on the thirteen-inch brass platform he brought with him to all his speeches, sometime in the early evening. The Brown Shirts were planning to attend with their smoke bombs and their broom handles and we said nothing to discourage them. "Let's just keep them in the dark for the time being," said our operations chief, Glass, grinning at no one in particular from his couch by the teletype. "It's their natural condition." One of the younger boys guffawed. Glass leaned back and continued to wait for word from Berlin with absolute serenity, hands folded neatly in his lap. As I watched him I reminded myself again how much I admired his carefree air. The rest of us stood awkwardly about the office, glancing skittishly at one another, waiting for Glass to nod off as he always did after breakfast so we could stop holding in our excitement. I walked with measured slowness to the window. In the courtyard the boys were filing in lazily in twos and threes.*

We spent the rest of the morning strangely bored, playing tarok, watching Glass twitch and mumble in his sleep and dreaming up titles for ourselves in the postputsch government. I was elected minister of cultural sanitation or some such silliness. The putsch was still nothing more than fantasy to us. Street brawls and so on were for the Brown Shirts; we fancied ourselves an elite. A few of us had been hunting with our fathers and knew how to handle, load and fire a rifle. One or two of us had even shot a deer.

Glass was the fat sly old uncle we were all desperate to impress. I had impressed him most thus far, largely through flattery, and thus was allowed to eavesdrop from time to time on his affairs, to spy on the other boys and to order them about when Glass himself was occupied or napping. At present there was nothing to be done but wait. Rain came down from the north shortly after ten, darkening the pavements. I played cards for a while, grew distracted, lost a little money. At noon the wire came from Berlin giving us our mandate.

Glass cabled the Brown Shirts straightaway with select details: a full and total putsch, signed into being by the Chancellor himself, whose abduction that afternoon he, Glass, was personally overseeing; seizure of rail and tramway lines, and radio; immediate opening of the border to Bavaria with the assistance of the Republic's own Home Guard, already secretly sworn in allegiance to the Führer. In short, the complete incorporation, within thirty-six hours, of the Austrian Republic into the Greater German Reich. The Brown Shirts were furious, of course—it all came as a complete surprise to them. The telephone rang in seconds. I could hear the local SA brass screaming like Gypsies one after the other in Glass's ear, refusing to back us. There was talk of double-dealings, provocateurship, even treason. They wanted a line straight to Himmler. Glass, needless to say, was tickled.

"There's no such thing as a direct line to the SS Führer," Glass cooed, rolling his eyes at me. "If you'd like to protest to the Home Council, comrades . . ." He was still on the line when the first trucks arrived. Hearing them rolling in, he excused himself blithely and hung up the receiver. At that point we still had confidence the army would back us, and the Brown Shirts must have, too, or else figured us done for. Not that they would have warned us in any event. The Brown Shirts had their own plans for Dollfuss; execution by broom handle, most likely. We should have expected them to auction us off to the highest bidder. As it was, they sold us to the first one they could find.

One of Glass's more recent protégés knocked shyly on the office door, holding our disguises. We got into them quickly, no longer trying to choke back our excitement, giggling at our reflections in the hallway mirror like toddlers in a Nativity play. I was dressed as a lieutenant in the State Police, in creased, pleated grays and blacks; Glass had selected a Civil Guard's uniform for himself, although he was not actually coming with us. "The spirit of the thing and so on, Bauer," he said, struggling to wedge his calves into the knickerbockers. "They wouldn't take me in the Guards, you know, back in '23."

"With all due respect, Hauptsturmführer, I'd not have taken you either," I heard myself answer. I should have recognized it right away as an omen. Glass wrinkled his brow for the briefest of moments, then broke without warning into his infamous titter, poking me merrily in the ribs. Eventually he got himself into his uniform and we went down to look the rest of the boys over. We found them lounging along the cars, suited up and waiting—thirty in police blacks, sixty-five more dressed as foot soldiers in the Civil Guard. Glass glanced quickly down the line and turned back to me, his face flushed with pleasure. "There you are, Bauer," he said, taking me by the shoulder. "Bastard sons of the Republic, to a man." I spat demonstratively on the ground.

Once the boys had been reviewed we walked slowly back across the courtyard. "By the way, Obersturmführer," Glass said when we were almost to the stairwell, bringing out a roll of mimeographs: "Your partner in crime Spengler's artistry. What's your verdict?"

I looked over the sheets, onto which a crude sketch of the Chancellery floor plan had been copied. Glass kept quiet, watching me. I felt a vague twinge of something like roadsickness while flipping through them, trying to make sense of the thickly traced diagrams and the dense chicken-scratches of script. "They're a disaster, Hauptsturmführer," I said.

Glass let out another titter. "Nonsense! Just take them round, Bauer, there's a boy. You'll manage. You're all fine soldiers."

"Listen to me, Hauptsturmführer. Spengler is not a fine soldier. Not at all. Spengler is a—"

"We all know very well what Spengler is, Bauer. Spengler is the *very type we need to bring our plan to fruition. Spengler is what we call a man of action."*

"Spengler is a . . . a child, Hauptsturmführer. Surely you must—"

"All the more reason for you to ride with him this afternoon, Bauer," Glass said curtly. "We have absolute confidence in your judgment."

"What?"

"Rolling in one quarter hour," said Glass, no longer looking at me. He spun on his heels, clownish, dandylike. "Just keep Spengler on his hind legs, Bauer; the rest will follow."

He went into the stairwell then and waved me on about my business. I have a clear memory of him there, just inside the doors, the midday light glistening on his immaculate pomade. The next time I saw him he was tied to a chair with wire cord, pleading for his life as best he could through a blood-and-spit–soaked piece of rag.

"Heil Hitler, Bauer," Glass called out as he was halfway up the stairs.

"Heil Hitler," I answered, saluting his retreating backside.

I found Spengler slumped against the hood of one of the trucks, nattering with Little Ernst, the driver. He was dressed, like me, as a lieutenant of the police, but the uniform was far too small for him and he'd left the shirt flapping open. He stood and saluted as I came up, shifting his weight uncomfortably like a field hand in his Sunday best, dense brown hairs pushing out through his open shirtfront. Recognizing me, he let out a grunt. "Well, I'll be buggered," he said, flashing his gap-toothed boxer's grin. "I almost took you for the genuine article, Biddlebauer."

I smiled thinly, holding up the roll of mimeographs. "This your doing, Heinrich?"

"Hup," said Spengler, snapping to attention. "Straight copied from memory, officer."

"Is that so?" I turned to Ernst and smiled. "Is it your feeling, comrade, that a chimp with a runny ass could have done any better? If we'd handed him Dollfuss's own prick for a fountain pen?"

"I can't say he would have, Obersturmführer."

"Ah! Very grand," muttered Spengler. He looked me over slowly and appraisingly. "I believe you're riding with us on today's outing, paper jockey. Under our motherly protection." His thick hand lolled against his pistol butt.

I looked at Ernst again. "Is this man my mother, Ernst?"

"Not to my knowledge, Obersturmführer."

Spengler let out a carefully timed belch. Whatever point Glass was making in choosing him to head the attack was lost on me entirely. In spite of his stupidity, or perhaps because of it, I was afraid of him, and I realized this clearly as I returned his stare. "Go ahead; have your cracks, Biddlebauer," Spengler muttered. "You're riding in my car today, just the same."

We stood a moment, looking at each other. "They'll get us in, all right," Spengler said after a time, jerking his chin toward the mimeographs.

"They just might, Heinrich. Seeing as how we're going in through the big brass doors, just like every other enemy of the people." Ernst did his best to suppress a chuckle. "See you in a quarter hour, brothers," I said, stepping down to the next group of boys.

When the cars were all lined up and idling, Glass leaned out of the office window to bestow his blessing. Our sedan was the first of seven, with five trucks following after. I glanced at my watch; it was fifteen minutes after three. Glass beamed down at us a moment, then made a shooing-away motion with his hands, as one might to a flock of pigeons, and we were off. We rolled around the block very quietly, then swung out onto the Ring and navigated through moderate traffic to the Ballhausplatz. On the way we checked our pistols and loaded them and Spengler fussed with the chest flap of his uniform. We took care to avoid the Hofburg-side façade of the chancellery and pulled up instead at the northwest corner, along the Church of the Minorites, parking well against the curb like model citizens. Our car and the six others carrying mock policemen emptied out onto the pavement. The boys dressed as Civil Guards were to wait another ten minutes before following us, locking the courtyard gates as they came in. Spengler reviewed the boys coolly. "You could use a shine, officer," he said, glancing down at my boots.

Staring into Spengler's face, I saw a tiny insect, a gnat, perhaps, or a flea, crawl out of his hair. As I looked on, it made its way painstakingly across his forehead, found a deep, sun-battered furrow and vanished into it. The nausea I'd felt earlier looking at the mimeographs returned at once full force and I reached toward Spengler to keep from falling over. "I feel sick, Heinrich," I whispered.

Spengler laughed and stepped away from me. "Of course you feel sick, Biddlebauer," he said, loudly and for the benefit of all present. "Best to wait here with the cars, I think. Try not to make any messes."

"Shut up, Spengler, for Christ's sake."

"On my word, boys!" Spengler crowed, holding his rifle up. But instead of the promised word he simply raised the rifle above his head and let it fall.

The sound of an engine laboring up the steep grade woke them early one morning at the beginning of August. —It's your landlord, said Else, drawing aside the window shade. She made a face.

—I've gone to Italy, said Voxlauer, hiding his head under the sheets.

—Not without me, you haven't. Up and into your britches. She was rummaging through the clothes trunk, letting skirts and slips and stockings fall lightly through her fingers. He listened to the rustle of her nightshirt over the floor and the slap of her bare feet on the kitchen steps. He pulled the coverlet back and watched as she peered out the kitchen window. A moment later she undid the latch and a light breeze swept down to him.

—Herr Ryslavy! Such a rare privilege.

—Fräulein Bauer. Good morning. I'm sorry to disturb you.

—Not at all. Else stood still for an instant, squinting. —What time is it?

—I need to speak to Oskar. Is he here?

She swung the door open. —Come inside.

—Thank you, Fräulein.

She opened a cupboard. —Have you had any breakfast?

—Yes. Thank you.

—Cup of tea?

—No. You're very kind.

Else sat down and smiled flatly. Voxlauer could see only the back of Ryslavy's head from the parlor. He was fidgeting with the drawstring of the blinds and humming to himself.

—Would you like a drink, perhaps, Herr Ryslavy?

—No, thank you. He looked about him all at once, remembering his manners. —Very pretty house you have here. Tranquil.

—That's right; you've never visited, Else said.

Ryslavy didn't answer. Else sat with her arms folded, watching him.

—Hello, Pauli! said Voxlauer, stepping up into the kitchen. —Where's the fire?

Ryslavy grimaced and shifted in his chair. —I need you to come down, Oskar. Voxlauer looked back and forth between the two of them, buttoning up his shirt. —Something's happened, he said stupidly after a moment.

Ryslavy stood up and bowed to Else. —Sorry again for disturbing you, Fräulein.

—Not at all. Could you tell us what's wrong, please?

—Is it my mother? said Voxlauer. —If it is, then—

Ryslavy shook his head from side to side. —It's nothing like that, Oskar.

The glass-fronted awning was gutted and splayed open and the window boxes facing the square hung down in all directions like the leaves of a fire-wilted bush. Crushed glass covered the foyer and curled in from each charred, battered window frame in sparkling arabesques. The bar was blistered and discolored and each stool lay hacked into sections and scattered across the floor. A wide dark stain ran from the bar into the kitchen. —Whose blood is that? said Voxlauer.

Ryslavy shrugged. —I don't know. Not a person's, I don't think.

—Where's Emelia?

—A friend's in St. Marein.

Else stood in the vestibule, looking around her. —Who would do such a thing?

Ryslavy glanced at Voxlauer. —I'm sure I wouldn't know, Fräulein.

—But I would, Herr Ryslavy? You're perfectly right. She walked past them and stepped carefully behind the bar. —There's more blood back here, she said.

—An even trade, Ryslavy said, grinning crookedly. —The blood of a sheep for everything I own.

—Where were you? said Else.

—Trying to keep the kegs from boiling, said Ryslavy, pointing to the cellar door.

—Nobody came down after you?

—No, Fräulein. I had a pistol.

Voxlauer looked at him. —You had a pistol?

—As far as anybody knew. Ryslavy leaned back against the bar. —They weren't trying to murder me, Oskar. Just the business.

—What was it, Pauli? Weren't you paying your fees?

—Ach! What fees, Oskar? No one's paying any blessed fees. He paused, passing a hand across his eyes. —I was open an hour or two on Sunday. A few people came.

Else came round from behind the bar. —I found one lonely old beer.

—We'll be drinking from the bottle, I expect, said Voxlauer. Ryslavy shot him a wounded look.

—Who was it? Did you see? said Else.

—Rindt, Maier, Kroyacher, Fuchs. There were more outside. Breischa, I'm fairly sure. Welinek.

—Welinek? The schoolteacher?

Ryslavy nodded.

—Might as well have been red injuns, said Voxlauer.

—How did you put the fire out? said Else, turning the bottle back and forth on the top of the bar.

—Werner Hirt came and brought his sons. Old man Herbst came. The fire wagon too, after a little while.

—People actually came?

Ryslavy smiled. —They're decent, civic-minded citizens at bottom, Fräulein. And their houses stand flush up next to this one.

They were quiet for a time. —Old man Herbst's still alive, that gassy bastard? said Voxlauer. Ryslavy didn't answer.

They spent the afternoon sweeping the glass into burlap sacks and nailing quartered crates over the windows. At six o'clock Else came back with lye powder for the floor and a pot of warm *pastaciutta* and poppy rolls. Ryslavy went down to the cellar for wine. Voxlauer and Else righted a table and brought three stools from the kitchen. —I went and saw Kurt, she said furtively. —He says he knew. But he wasn't part of it.

—You'll have to explain that to me sometime, Fräulein, said Voxlauer. —When we're both of us feeling patient.

After dinner Ryslavy brought out a pack of cards and a second and a third bottle of wine and they played Pagat by the light of a gas lantern set on the bar. A window at the far end of the room was open and through it the lights of the square threw the shadows of passersby onto the ceiling. The shadows began near to life size at the far corner but grew huge and grotesque as they passed overhead. Voxlauer was convinced he could recognize some of them. He felt light-headed. —Lots of people out strolling tonight, he said.

Ryslavy nodded, staring down at his cards.

—You should charge half a schilling admission, said Voxlauer. He turned to Else. —You might mention it to your cousin.

—Oskar has to have his jokes, said Else.

—I know it all too well, Fräulein, said Ryslavy, slurring a little as he spoke.

—Don't call her Fräulein like that, said Voxlauer.

—You're drunk, said Ryslavy, eyes still on his cards.

—Pagat! announced Voxlauer, dropping the card face upward onto the table.

Ryslavy shook his head. —These are troubled times, Fräulein.

—We'll have our satisfaction yet, Herr Ryslavy. A little patience.

Voxlauer shuffled next and dealt. They studied their hands in silence.

—I'll call out a three-game, said Ryslavy. He raised a finger. —The Jew stands alone. *Semper solo.*

—It's you and me, then, Fräulein, against the undesirable, said Voxlauer. —We have society's mandate.

—Shit-eaters! Ryslavy yelled, lunging up from the table. —Shit-eating sons of bitches!

—Time for bed, said Voxlauer, rising. He caught up with Ryslavy at the door to the kitchen and shepherded him in a loose wobbling arc past the bar to the foot of the stairs.

—Good night, dear Fräulein. Dear dear Fräulein. Ryslavy made a halfhearted attempt to climb the bottommost step and looked sideways at Voxlauer. —Oskar, he muttered. —You have a beautiful wife.

—And you have very pretty trout, said Voxlauer. —Up.

—Take any room, said Ryslavy, lurching forward. —Take the bridal suite.

—None of these units qualify, I'm afraid, said Voxlauer, guiding him up to the landing. —Do you need me to make a light?

—Get back to your Pagat, old kid. Get back, you old billy goat.

—Good night, then, you drunken ass. Dream something about Christmas.

—I like Good Friday better, Ryslavy shouted. —Tell that to those sons of whores and donkeys! Tell them *that*!

—Most likely they've heard already, said Voxlauer, dragging him by his collar up the stairs.

—You should have let him rant, said Else as Voxlauer came down the stairs. —He has a right, poor bastard. She was sitting at the bar, looking out through the ruined foyer. She straightened herself slightly as he came near.

—You've certainly changed allegiances suddenly.

—Allegiances?

—You can't have it both ways, Fräulein.

She frowned. —Why are you saying this?

—You can't be for Pauli and your cousin both. That's all.

—Did I say I was for either of them? I said Pauli had a right. No more than that.

—They can't both of them have a right. Can they?

She didn't answer for a time. —I want to go back to the valley, Oskar, she said.

The glow of the streetlamps fell in pale wavering rectangles across the bar. Voxlauer stood in the dark drunkenly, watching her.

—Let's get out of here, at least, she said, slipping down from her barstool.

"Remember," I said to the boys as they filed past me. "You're policemen." No one paid much attention. They trooped without a word around the corner to the wide-open brass doors of the chancellery, their badly fitted uniforms sagging and billowing as they went. They were all of them young boys, good at following orders and strong and dumb as posts. I followed them as quickly as I could around the corner.

We had no trouble getting past the first brace of guards. There were seven of them in the courtyard, all together in a huddle, smoking cigarettes by an iron rack for bicycles. One of them asked me the time as we came in. Spengler immediately stepped over to him.

"Where's the cabinet room, brother?"

"What cabinet room?" the guard said, frowning.

"A little joke," I said, moving between the guard and Spengler.

"What's this about?" another guard said curiously, coming over.

"You're all under arrest," said Spengler, ramming his rifle into

the first guard's ribs. "Urnngh," groaned the guard, bending over. The rest laid down their rifles immediately and raised their hands. We left ten boys there and went in with the rest, Spengler looking down at his floor plan all the while with a puzzled expression, turning it this way and that like a French postcard. "Give me that thing," I snapped, snatching it away from him. To my surprise he shot me a grateful look.

"A left here, then," I said, moving past him at the top of the stairs.

"Maybe we should ask another guard for directions," said Little Ernst, coming up behind us.

"You shut your mouth, Ernst," Spengler muttered. "Where to, Bauer?"

"Past those," I said, pointing down the corridor to a cluster of guards in bright red uniforms with panicked expressions on their faces. Spengler lowered his rifle and fired into them without slowing. The second from the left spun hard into the wall, clutched his stomach and slumped over without making the slightest sound. I had never seen anyone shot before and I remember looking at the back of Spengler's head with sudden envy. The other nine guards laid down their guns and knelt as one man wordlessly onto the carpet.

"There's patriotism for you," Spengler crowed. Ernst and the other boys collected the rifles, moved the guards to one side of the corridor and shoved their faces against the tiles. Spengler was already at the leather-padded doors behind them. He glanced back at us, gave a stiff-necked little nod and kicked them open. Behind the doors was a cluttered anteroom and beyond it three men in uniforms of state at a long oaken table. Dollfuss sat on an elevated chair between the other two. He raised his hands with deliberate, self-conscious dignity and they followed suit. "On your feet," said Spengler, fiddling with his rifle's safety catch.

The three of them stood immediately. They were all slight of build, but Dollfuss was a true miniature; with his hands raised in the air he looked like a child of eight wearing a paste-on mustache.

"Where are the rest?" said Spengler, pointing to the empty chairs.

"Gone," said Dollfuss.

No one spoke for a moment. "Well? Are you going to murder us here, at the cabinet-room table?" Dollfuss said, looking at each of us in turn. A trace of a smile played around his mouth.

"Quiet!" Spengler yelled. He began pacing up and down the long room, staring furiously at the carpet. Twenty or so of the boys had now crowded in behind us. An isolated gunshot carried in from the hall and Spengler drew himself up at the sound of it. "Search them, Bauer," he said, gesturing peevishly at the ministers.

The Home Guard adjutant, Ley, had a single-shot gentleman's pistol hidden in the lining of his smoking vest. The security secretary, ironically enough, was completely unarmed. Dollfuss had a pearl-handled jackknife in his waistcoat pocket; he let me take it only after looking me sternly in the eye. "That knife was given me by the Duke of all of Italy, little brother. See that you treat it with respect."

"You shut your mouth," Spengler hissed, pushing me aside. "Jew-lover! Dwarf! Save the drama for your abdication, little Napoleon! Save it for your Duce!"

"Spengler," I whispered, jerking my head toward the ante-room. Three more shots had sounded.

Dollfuss leaned forward now, his dark eyes twinkling. "Spengler? Is that your name?" He smiled indulgently. "You, Spengler, will be hanging in the Rathausplatz by noon tomorrow, like a side of beef."

Spengler furrowed his brow and came purposefully around the table. I had seen this expression on his face before, many times, and knew what it meant. Dollfuss had turned, statesmanlike, to address the assembled. "I have no sympathy for the Jewish cause . . ." he began. I stepped forward before Spengler could reach him and hit him flush across the base of his skull with the butt of Ley's pistol; he sighed once and fell weightlessly against me. "Right, then," said Spengler. We carried Dollfuss to a small adjoining room and herded the two ministers in after him, sitting them down on a bench with their faces to the cracked, dust-covered paneling and their hands clasped behind their backs. Dollfuss collapsed silently in one of the corners. I sat on the floor with a few of the boys and waited for him to come to, wondering idly what his knife might bring from a collector. After some minutes, the security secretary raised his hand and asked politely if he might have a glass of water. I stood up, straightened my jacket and told him he could drink after he'd resigned. A few of the boys giggled.

I found Spengler in the anteroom talking to the Brown Shirts on the telephone. "We've taken the radio!" he said to me gleefully, his hand covering the receiver. "South Station! The barracks! Everything!" This was a lie, of course, but neither of us knew it then. Right away I felt a tremendous surge of relief. We weren't alone. There were others, higher authorities, in command. The highest. We were their willing agents, no more than that, but no less, either. Even Spengler, lunatic that he was. I reached out a hand and patted him tentatively on the shoulder. He beamed at me an instant longer, then brought the receiver back to his face and began chattering away at it. Through the propped-open doors I could see the guards still lying facedown on the tiles, whispering to each other. "I'm going for a walk," I said. "Sieg Heil to those brave hearts."

"Hold on, Seppl," said Spengler, laying the receiver against his shoulder. He waved me back toward the conference room. "Go in and turn that radio on, Bauer. They're going to announce us soon."

I said nothing.

"Go on!"

"I have to piss."

Spengler sighed. "Pick any corner then, but be quick about it. Dibbern went over there, I think. On some old entente protocols."

I stepped over to the heap of files he had pointed at and undid the pants of my uniform. I sniffed. "Dibbern did this? On his own?"

Spengler hung up the receiver. "He had help. Halberstadt and three or four others. Get on with it already, for the love of Christ!"

I leaned back and closed my eyes. "Could you give us some privacy, Heinrich?"

Spengler laughed. "You're a funny fish, aren't you, Biddle-bauer. Glass did tell me to keep you in my sights. I'm not sure I could leave you here in good conscience."

"All right, then, Spenglerchen. Watch closely. This is how we do it in the Schutzstaffel."

Spengler got up from the narrow desk, showing the gaps in his teeth again. "I'm going, Bauer, I'm going. But don't be too long, little fish." He went out and shut the door.

I relaxed and let the piss trickle down the side of the filing cabinet, onto the thick-piled carpet that ran from one wall to the other. It mixed with the overall musklike reek of the anteroom and dampened it a little. Through the partition I could hear the buzz of the conference room's immense radio. Gradually as I listened another sound rose up behind it, a low rumbling vibration that ran up my spine from somewhere under the floor. I pulled up my policeman's pants and listened.

The noise grew higher and higher in pitch, then stopped altogether. I stepped into the corridor: the guards on the floor had felt it too and looked up at me. A boy I knew only vaguely was there, keeping watch. "Did you feel any of that rumbling just now, Willi?" I asked him.

He looked at me blankly. "No, Obersturmführer."

I knelt down by one of the guards and tapped him on the back. "What was that just now, citizen?"

The guard only shook his head. I stood up and turned back to the boy. "In case Herr Spengler happens to ask for me, I'll be downstairs. Watch this crew carefully, now. No gossiping."

I went downstairs cautiously, as if Spengler might yet call me back, and crossed the lobby to a small barred window with a view of the Ballhausplatz. I glanced out the window once, shut my eyes tightly a moment, then looked again, this time letting out a quiet groan. Directly outside the courtyard gate four khaki-colored armored cars stood idling, ringed by three full Home Guard battalions, a Civil Guards unit and what looked to be the entire police force of the city. Gray-shirted underofficers moved through the waiting rows like prize drones in a beehive, buzzing purposefully together for a moment wherever their paths happened to intersect. Across the square a small civilian crowd had gathered, gaping at the cars and pointing up at the chancellery windows, laughing and calling things out in small, shrill voices to the soldiers. I stepped back from the window, stood still a moment, then ran down another short flight of steps to the lobby. Civil Guard shirts were everywhere, milling aimlessly about; no one seemed the least *bit troubled by the circus going on outside. Just then a cadet of mine wandered by and I grabbed him by the collar. "What's the matter with you, Klintzer? Haven't you looked out the window lately?"*

The cadet gaped at me. "We'd heard negotiations were under way, Obersturmführer . . ."

"Why has no one informed me of this? Or Comrade Spengler?"

"We have, Obersturmführer," he said, looking at me strangely now.

Else and Voxlauer walked arm in arm across the square, past the darkened shopwindows, under the cracked stucco wall of the cloister and out over the arched stone bridge and the reflectionless water of the canal. At the edge of the mill field they stopped, searching in the tussocked grass for the path across. Soft white clusters of light drifted quietly above the grass, resolving themselves into groups of sheep before drifting slowly off again into the dark. —I can hear the mill wheel, Else said.

Voxlauer stepped forward into the field and felt for bare ground with his boot soles. The lights of St. Marein glittered like scraps of tinsel at the edge of the plain. He moved carefully toward the silhouetted willow trees, waiting now and then for her footfall behind him in the grass. —What's St. Marein like? he said when they were halfway across the field.

—I haven't spent much time there, Else said, catching hold of his hand.

—I thought you'd lived there.

—You must be thinking of Resi. Resi lives there now.

—With her father's family?

—Come along now, Else said, running ahead into the trees.

Voxlauer hung back a moment, squinting along the ground, then followed cautiously after her. —Can you see? he called. The sound of the mill brook came very loudly now and under it was the creaking and rumbling of the wheel.

—They've left it going! Else yelled.

Voxlauer made for her voice in the dark. —Do they ever turn it off?

He was close beside her suddenly. —Have you never been to a mill before, Oskar? she said.

—Of course I have. He smiled. —But never at night.

She took his arm and led him up a narrow ramp clogged with debris to the steps of the mill. The huge dark wheel turned massively on its hub and drew up cords of light with a noise like the creaking of a ship at sea. It seemed to Voxlauer as he stood above it an ancient, almost prehistoric thing.

—I practically lived here for a time, said Else.

—Here?

She nodded. —In love with the miller's boy.

—Ah, said Voxlauer. He reached for the slick wooden handrail. —What happened?

—Resi.

—And the boy?

—He left when Kurt left. She shrugged.

Voxlauer looked down at the water. —No bad blood between them?

—The Cause, Oskar! You're forgetting the Cause. It's what makes them fanatics, remember. You'll never understand them without it.

—I don't want to understand them.

—But they want to understand *you*, Herr Voxlauer. Kurt Bauer does. Terribly. She stepped forward and kissed him on the chin. —What makes you such a gloomy citizen? Why aren't you more civil? Didn't your Maman teach you any manners? Are you a Bolshevist? A secret agent? A Jew-lover? She dropped her voice low. —Do you fancy the little boys?

—No, no, no and no, said Voxlauer, leaning in to kiss her.

—That's only four of five.

—Say that again about my mother, he whispered.

They crossed back over the weir and walked along the riverbank to the toll road, then turned and followed it out to the station and the long ramp of earth where the rails came down from the gorge at the northern end of the plain. A train loaded high with timber was just passing through the station when they reached the tracks. As it came toward them it rose magisterially above the plain, canting and rumbling, its red and blue hitch lights swaying and clanking from side to side. They watched it make the slow curve to the mouth of the gorge and vanish into it one car at a time. —Are we getting our timber from Italy now? said Voxlauer.

—Kurt says they're our new Reichs-partners.

—Ah, said Voxlauer. —They'll be Fascisti at Monte Veritas, then, before too long.

—There'll be Fascisti everywhere. We'll be Fascisti, too.

—I don't care anymore. I'm tired. That sounds lovely.

The last lights of the train disappeared into the trees. They walked toward the station. —He'd sign on, wouldn't he? said Voxlauer after a time. —If it came to that?

—Who?

—Piedernig. Don't you think he would?

—Without a doubt, Else said, taking his arm. —You're sweet to worry about that old con artist.

—I'm not worried about him, exactly, said Voxlauer. —Just wondering what it would take.

—Fresh fillet of trout. A little flattery.

—I don't think our friends are the flattering kind.

—Of course they are. They're *all* the flattering kind.

—I hadn't noticed.

—You have to give them some sort of encouragement now and again, that's all.

A boy in tar-blackened overalls walked up the tracks toward them, stopped, bent down and began hammering at a rail switch. A watery blue light flickered on the platform. Two more boys, slightly older than the first, leaned sleepily against the station wall cradling automatic rifles. —Children's hour, said Voxlauer, sticking his thumb into his mouth.

—Shh! Let's go up to the road.

On the way back to the square they went around the canal and passed Maman's orchard and the old house. A light was burning on the verandah.

—Care to face the jury? said Voxlauer.

—Not at two in the morning, thank you. I'd be sure to get death by hanging.

—Not at all. She'll be relieved we're not in bed.

—I wish I were, said Else, yawning. —Does Ryslavy have a room for us?

—You'll be happy to know we've been promised the newly-wed's suite.

—I am. I'm very happy to know it.

—There's a catch, of course. There isn't any.

Else sighed. —Well. I can't imagine what we'd be doing in one, anyhow. I'm safeguarding my virtue for the Heavenly Host.

—Is that so?

—It is. Or the Lamb of God, possibly.

—Ah. The Lamb.

—Or the Red Army. Whichever happens to come first.

—The Red Army has arrived, Fräulein, said Voxlauer, catching her by the waist.

—Saints protect us! The times we live in.

—Sweet times, said Voxlauer. —Glorious times.

—We have our own town, don't we, Oskar.

Voxlauer nodded. —Our own city-state. Our own republic.

They walked on, keeping alongside each other in the dark. —I'm still afraid, she said, running her hand up and down his arm as if to comfort him. —I've just decided not to pay attention anymore.

—That's very wise, said Voxlauer, drawing her closer.

I ran back upstairs as fast as my legs would carry me. I found Spengler in the conference room with fifteen of the boys, swaying boorishly to the radio. Through the crackle and hiss a light polka was audible. "They announced it!" he said grandly. "Then we sang the Horst Wessel." He looked around him from one to another of the boys, making as if to wipe away a tear. Gradually his eyes drifted back to me. "Where have you been hiding yourself, Biddlebauer?"

I stood looking at him, speechless. "Are you drunk?" I got out finally.

Spengler's huge head bobbed busily to the polka. "What's that?"

"There's bulls and Home Front everywhere," I said slowly, stressing every word. "There are four tanks on the front steps, Gruppenleiter." I spread my arms wide. "Tanks, Heinrich—"

"We've phoned in our demands," Spengler said tranquilly. "Sit down already, Bauer, for heaven's sake. You're making everybody antsy."

With that he turned back to the radio. The boys stood around the room in various attitudes of uneasiness, looking from him to me and back again. "Could I have a word, Gruppenleiter?" I said.

Spengler straightened, his back still turned to me. "I thought you wanted to be left alone."

"I'm done pissing now, Gruppenleiter. Come and see."

"Would you like that?" he said, winking at the boys. "All right then, Obersturmführer. Let's go have a look." He stood up, cracked his back and switched off the radio, to the loud objections of all present. We went into the little anteroom where the sour reek had very much intensified.

Spengler leaned back comfortably against a desktop, arms folded. "Now then. What is it you want, exactly, Bauer? A hall pass? A pardon? A change of drawers?"

"Where's the army, Heinrich?" I said, very quietly.

Spengler raised his eyebrows. "The army?"

"They were supposed to be here by now, if you remember. The army. And the Brown Shirts, Heinrich. Where are they? Weren't they supposed to put in an appearance?" I could feel my voice rising to a squeak. "Have they decided to stay at home, Heinrich? Is it the ninety-six of us now, versus the Republic?"

Spengler looked at me for a time, half smiling, then shrugged his shoulders.

"We're surrounded by the Home Guard, you idiot! There's not enough blessed room on the Ballhausplatz for all of them. Where for Christ's sake is the goddamned shit-eating army? Where is it?" I jumped up and down on the heaps of loose files, gasping and stuttering like a baby; the entire scene played itself out like a cabaret routine. "Where are they?" I shouted, slipping on the folders, scattering documents of every variety across the carpet. "Where, Heinrich? Where?"

Spengler regarded me coldly for a long moment. "Last I heard, they were setting up sniper's posts, Bauer. On the roof of the Home Ministry."

I stared at him, nauseous again and dizzy with disbelief. A knock came on the cabinet-room door and a crony of Spengler's ducked his head into the room. "The Home Guard minister insists that he speak to you, Gruppenleiter."

Spengler's grin returned at once. "That's fine. Come along then, Bauer, if you're finished. Let's go hear the news."

Ley sat just as we'd left him, straight-backed, staring at the wall unblinkingly, hands arranged elegantly in his lap. As we entered the room Dollfuss roused himself briefly, mumbled something, then fell slack again. Spengler tapped Ley on the collar.

Ley turned slowly to face us. He looked us over dutifully and intently, but at the same time with marked indifference, as though neither of our faces need especially be remembered. Spengler shifted from foot to foot, unwilling to be the first to speak. "What was it you wanted, Herr Minister?" he said. "A glass of water, perhaps?"

Ley let out a sigh. "That a revolution should be run by two such perfect half-wits," he said very clearly, as if for his colleagues' benefit. The secretary of security said nothing; Dollfuss moaned loudly in his corner, to all appearances utterly lost to the world. I squatted down before Ley's bench. "Has nobody told you yet? Adolf Hitler leads this revolution. We poor half-wits only carry out his orders."

"The worse for him."

"The worse for you, I'd say, Herr Minister."

"Yes," said Ley. "That's all very fine. I'd like to speak with you in private now, Herr Gruppenleiter," he said, turning abruptly to Spengler.

The security secretary sat forward, trying to speak, but was seized by a violent fit of coughing. "What's the meaning of this, Emil?" he managed to wheeze. Ley simply leaned over and put a finger to the old man's mouth. "You have problems with my Home Guard, I understand," he said, keeping his eyes on Spengler.

"Figured that out all on our own, did we?" Spengler said, glancing at me.

Ley waved a hand. "A guess, Herr Spengler. Nothing more. I thought I'd heard the sound of trucks." He paused a moment, smiling politely. "Not the best position to be in, I'd imagine—"

"Get to the point," I interrupted.

Ley paused a moment. The security secretary was still hacking and shuddering next to him. "A word with you in private, if I might, Herr Spengler," Ley repeated.

I kept quiet, watching them both. The vaudeville quality was building minute by minute. The Home Guard were, as far as I'd understood anything, supposed to be fighting shoulder to shoulder alongside the Brown Shirts at key points across the city; instead they were mustered in full force of arms just outside the window, sharpening their bayonets. Their commander-in-chief, who by rights should have been tearing his hair out by the roots at that very moment, railing at the faithlessness of his troops, was in fact sitting before us with his legs comfortably crossed, smiling at Spengler with a look of profound personal satisfaction. Whatever Glass's deal had been it had obviously crumbled, and we were powerless. To this day I have no idea why Ley chose not to warn Dollfuss earlier, but of this I'm certain: everything that happened that day did so according to his whim.

The idea took hold of me briefly to get through to Glass on the telephone, but I decided to wait a little longer before I took that risk. Spengler looked at Ley another moment, then shrugged his shoulders. Two boys helped Ley to his feet. I sat down on the bench he'd just risen from, next to the secretary of security, and watched the boys lead him out of the room. The paneled door swung smoothly shut behind them.

. . .

—Arise, therefore, and walk! said Ryslavy, throwing back the bed-sheets. —Ah! Excuse me, Fräulein.

—Christ above, said Voxlauer. —'Tis the dead again risen.

—What time is it? said Else, yawning.

—Breakfast time, said Ryslavy, beaming down at them. —No time for dallying.

—This is the newlywed service, you son of a pig?

—The Fräulein may sleep on if she wishes. You, however, are no newlywed. Take a look at yourself if you have any questions.

—I'd rather not, said Voxlauer, rubbing his eyes.

They ate the remains of the previous night's supper in the bar-room. The sun was already beating down on the square and they sat over their cups of coffee watching a troop of uniformed boys assembling a podium in front of the fountain. A tepid wind was blowing. The Kärnten state colors hung from bent birch poles over the platform and above them fluttered the long, gaudy banner of the Reich. A man in a brown uniform, cinched and pleated at the waist, called directions to the boys from Rindt's patio. As the three of them watched he sat down gingerly in a chair and began fanning himself with a newspaper. The boys were uncrating a public-address system from a row of orange boxes.

—What is it? said Voxlauer, squinting. —Is it a Bible Youth meeting?

—SA, said Ryslavy.

—Brown Shirts? Those children?

—He's looking at us, said Else.

—Who?

—The head boy. The dandy.

The man had taken off his peaked brown cap and sat shading his eyes, his head turned toward the glassless barroom windows.

—Do you know him? said Voxlauer.

—I don't think so. She craned her neck forward. —It almost looks as though he's smiling.

—Wave to him, said Voxlauer.

Else rose slightly from her seat and waved. The man sat bolt upright and turned his head back toward the boys, who were now unpacking microphone stands and rolls of thick blue wire from the crates.

—Must not like women much, said Ryslavy. —No great surprise.

—That's not the miller's boy, is it? said Voxlauer.

Else gave him a crooked smile. —When he arrives, Oskar, I'll let you know.

Later that day the two of them walked to the old house. —She knows everything about you already, said Voxlauer, unlatching the garden gate. —It's useless to feel nervous. The doors of fate have long since clanged shut on you forever.

Else laughed. —Why bring me at all, then?

—To be honest, I could use the company. He swung the gate open and raised a finger to his lips. —Be as quiet as you can. It's a game we play.

—A game?

—Shh!

—She's an old woman, Oskar.

—You just wait.

When they reached the house she was waiting for them on the verandah. —I heard you coming over the bridge, she called down happily.

—I've brought somebody with me, Maman.

—Yes, yes. Come along upstairs.

They climbed to the landing and waited for her to shuffle to the blue-paned stairwell door and draw the bolt. —I hadn't known you were coming, she said to Else. —But I heard you on the bridge.

—Yes, Maman. You always do, said Voxlauer.

—Come in! Come in and sit.

—Is there any tea?

—There's still some, I think. Yes! There's tea, Maman said after a moment, more confidently.

Voxlauer looked at the tea set laid out painstakingly on the table and the bone-china plates arrayed in neat arrow-shaped regiments across the carpet. —Did you have company today, Maman?

Maman raised her eyebrows. —No, Oskar. Not today.

—Those are lovely plates, said Else, smiling.

—Yes. Don't touch them.

—Oh! No, said Else. —I wouldn't. She glanced at Voxlauer.

—Maman. We'll need cups at least, for the tea.

—That's right, Oskar. Go and get them from the cabinet.

—Which one?

—The cabinet, Oskar. The *cabinet*. In the kitchen.

—All right, Maman. Sit down, now. I'm going.

When Voxlauer came back Else and Maman were sitting at the parlor table. Maman was holding a saucer up to the light. —How beautiful, Else was saying.

—Yes. Oskar broke most of these, the little monster.

—You must have me confused with some other little monster, Maman, said Voxlauer. She looked up and smiled at him as he set the cups and teapot down before her. Voxlauer poured the tea.

—Where did you come by these? she said after a time, studying her cup intently.

—From the kitchen, Maman, said Voxlauer after a little pause.

—Yes, that's where they're kept. There's marble cake in the cupboard.

—Should I get it? said Voxlauer, rising.

—Yes. And the sugar.

—I have it here, said Else. —Here you are, Frau Voxlauer.

—Oh! Yes. Never mind, Oskar. She blinked at Else. —Oskar was born here. In this house.

—Yes?

Maman nodded gravely. —He was. She paused for an instant. —December 11, 1902. At the bottom of the stairs.

—Halfway out the door already, said Voxlauer, taking the sugar from her.

—The war took him when he was very young.

—I'm still alive, Maman.

—Yes, Oskar. And then to Russia, she said, raising her teacup.

—Oh, yes, said Else.

Voxlauer went out again into the kitchen, opening the cabinet and cupboard doors methodically one after another. Else and Maman sat across from one another at the table. After a time Maman shifted heavily in her chair and let out a sigh.

—You and I, she said, taking Else's hand. She paused. —They go away. We sit here and wait for them. And we get old, don't we, Irma? Don't we get old?

—What are you doing out there, Oskar? Else called.

—I couldn't find any cake, said Voxlauer, coming back into the room.

Maman nodded. —It's just as well. I've gotten fat.

—No you haven't, said Voxlauer, crouching down next to her and looking nervously up into her face, the corners of his mouth twisting involuntarily into a smile. His voice when he spoke was as high-pitched as a child's, and the embarrassment he felt at his sudden fear was a child's as well. He was angry, bitterly angry at being embarrassed in this way. His voice twisted and balled up in his throat and he couldn't make a noise. —Maman, he said finally. —You're not fat at all. You're thin as a breath.

She shrugged her narrow shoulders and patted lightly with her palms at her ravelling bun of hair. —I'm glad you've come back, anyway, Oskar. She nodded again. —I certainly am. I'm very glad.

—I'm glad of that too, said Else, taking her hand. Voxlauer was already standing.

An hour later, as they stepped out of the Niessener Hof with Ryslavy, the square was already full of people. Old faces familiar to Voxlauer looked out uncertainly from rows of younger faces fixed in proud solemnity. Rindt, his grease-flecked tapper's bib tucked sharply through a wide brown leather belt, made the rounds with a platter of yellow beer. Here and there a gray or black uniform stood out among the linen jackets and dirndl dresses.

—Where are the guests of honor? said Else.

—Guests of honor are always late.

—We won't have any trouble recognizing them, at any rate, she said. —They'll be dressed in harvest colors.

—I'll be in my cellar, if anybody asks, said Ryslavy. —Call me if that fat bastard runs out of beer.

—In case you've forgotten, Pauli, said Voxlauer—we drank your last bottle yesterday.

—I might have a case or two somewhere, tucked away, said Ryslavy. He bowed to them gravely and stepped back into the ruins of his foyer.

As Voxlauer and Else moved into the crowd a rift opened on the east side of the square and the first wedge of SA marched in, alternating kick steps like horses in trap, holding their rifle stocks diagonally out in front of them. —We used to call that Gypsy-marching, back in my time, said Voxlauer, smiling to himself at the irony of it. Else was a few paces in front of him and didn't answer.

A man in a peaked, black-fronted hat, like a chauffeur's cap, called out commands from the little podium, rocking back and forth excitedly on his heels. The SA themselves were hatless and their cropped, tanned heads rotated briskly in execution of the drills. Here and there in the crowd arms were spontaneously raised in excited Heils. Elsewhere men were drinking beer and laughing and ignoring the SA altogether.

Voxlauer followed behind Else, who was making her way steadily through the spectators to the northwestern corner of the square. The upper floors of the houses were hung with crimson flags and banners. Those who hadn't been given flags had hung capes and dresses and bedsheets from their windows. The ruin had been decorated with torches and a long red banner with reticulated trim now graced the leftmost of its arches. Else waited for Voxlauer on the Polizeihaus steps.

Column after column of SA filed into the square from its eastern side, forcing the onlookers back onto the curbs. The platform was filling rapidly with officers. A fat, five-pointed star of brown now fulminated in the square, spinning like a leaf caught in a gentle current. The crowd, too, appeared to be twisting along its edges. The black-capped officer surveyed the square a moment, stamped his heels with satisfaction, then stepped back from the podium. Grudgingly the bodies came to rest. —It's almost beautiful, said Else, looking down at Voxlauer from her place above him on the steps.

—Do you think so?

—No. But it is a thing to see. It's so very strange.

—Are you still afraid?

—Oh! said Else suddenly, looking past him.

A man in a black field jacket approached the podium with both arms raised. He began to speak into the microphone and his voice seemed to intermingle with its hum, trembling over the massed heads of the crowd and carrying back in waves of half-articulated sound to the platform. The sound spread over the square like an awning, making everything but listening impossible. It kept on and fell back on itself and brightened and became louder and louder. At predetermined points the voice would cease, and the crowd would answer in quick joyous bursts of noise. The speaker would acknowledge the crowd with a brief, careless salute and the Brown Shirts would respond with a deafening chorus of Sieg Heils.

—Blessed Christ, it's loud, a woman next to Voxlauer said.

Voxlauer didn't look at her. He was looking at the podium.

—Look! said Else.

—I am, said Voxlauer.

—Look who it is.

—I know. I see him.

On the platform Kurt was smiling now and lifting his arms.

My feelings about the putsch had changed. I was no longer think-ing of it in terms of success or failure; I knew now that it could only end badly. I sat a long while on the bench in the little room, thinking only about my own skin. The secretary of security made regular requests for glasses of water, which were just as regularly ignored by myself and the two other boys on watch. Eventually Dollfuss sat up in his corner and mumbled a few words in what might have been Italian. An idea came to me then, or the start of one, and I stood up from the bench.

Going out the paneled door to the cabinet room, I found Spengler and Ley huddled together at the far end of the table, plotting away in their very best church whispers. Neither looked up as I passed. I went to the sideboard and took down the decanter of brandy and poured out a generous snifter, golden and amber-smelling. Ley and Spengler kept right on with their conference. I tipped my head back, downed the brandy and filled the glass a second time. The bottle was very old and clouded over and smelled faintly of cork and mildew. Above the sideboard hung a portrait of some earlier, more normal-sized head of state flanked by his thirteen ministers, examining a weighty-looking sheaf of yellow papers. A muffled, static hum, like the buzzing on a telephone line, rose out of the radio. I stood at the cabinet a moment longer, trying to make out what Ley and Spengler were whispering, then put the bottle down and walked back to the table over the thick-loomed Persian carpet. "Our man's come to," I announced in my shrillest, most military tone of voice.

Spengler glanced up at me. "Has he? Well, Herr Minister! Let's go have a look!"

The two of them stood up from the table, overflowing with mutual goodwill. I pointed at the minister. "Pardon my curiosity, Heinrich, but shouldn't this one be in the dunce's corner, with the other dunces?"

Spengler took a deep breath, mustered his resources and smiled the most patronizing smile he was capable of. Even I was surprised by its effectiveness. "No no, Bauer. Herr Ley is our new minister of war."

Ley stepped out from behind Spengler and patted me on the shoulder. "With all due regard, Obersturmführer, you might learn to treat your representatives in government with a slight bit more civility. After you, my commandant!" he said, turning again to Spengler. It was all I could do to avoid being ill.

"Come on out, boys!" Spengler called, opening the door. The two boys I'd left on guard came out, looking at us questioningly. Little Ernst and some others came in at the same time from the anteroom, sensing that something was about to happen. Ley went in to Dollfuss first and I made a move to follow but Spengler

held me back. "We won't be needing you just now, Bauer," he said softly.

"What won't you be needing me for, Heinrich?" I asked. Spengler only blinked and pulled the little door firmly closed behind him.

After a few seconds Ley's voice sounded dimly through the paneling. I listened for a while with my ear pressed to the keyhole, all thought of saving face with the rest of the boys abandoned, then glanced back to where they stood in a loose half-circle, watching me. After a moment or two Little Ernst stepped over. "Ley's bought himself in right neatly, hasn't he?"

"He's bought himself time, that's all. Take a look downstairs, will you, Ernst? And take all these Bolshevists here with you. Go on," I said, pointing at the other boys, who were watching us even more intently now.

Ernst clicked his tongue against his teeth for a few seconds, not answering. "As you say, Obersturmführer," he said thoughtfully after a moment. Something in his tone had changed, and I watched this change register, slowly but surely, with the others. I pretended not to notice and slapped Ernst cheerfully on the back as he went out. They know something's gone wrong, or is going wrong now, I thought. As soon as I was alone I crossed the room and poured myself another snifter.

Standing under the portrait sipping at my brandy, I tried again to think. Could this have been the way Glass wanted it? That seemed suddenly very likely. I forgot Spengler and Dollfuss and Ley and the rest of it and imagined Glass reclining that very moment on his couch by the teletype, sleepy and content, or speeding away in his apple-green Horch convertible, a present from the Reichsführer-SS himself, through the flat wheat and fir-covered hills to the border.

One week later, as Voxlauer was working in the villa's garden, the sound of Kurt's motorcycle carried up to him. He stood slowly and leaned his shovel against the fence and looked at Else through the parlor window. She motioned to him to come, made another gesture he wasn't able to decipher, then stepped away from the glass. Voxlauer swung open the low gate and stood for perhaps half a minute in the house's shadow, leaning against the cool dark wall and looking down at his hands. By the time the sound drew even with the house and stopped he was breathing quietly. —Hello, Kurt, he said, stepping around the house into the sunlight.

—Sieg Heil, Oskar! said Kurt, giving Voxlauer a mock salute. —Is Her Ladyship receiving visitors? I have no appointment.

—I wouldn't presume to say.

—Here I am, said Else, coming to the door.

The three of them stood silently for a few moments, Voxlauer and Kurt at the edge of the drive, Else on the steps. —Might I come inside? Kurt said finally.

Else reached for the door handle, then stopped. —Where are you going, Oskar?

—I thought I might take a walk.

—I'd rather you stayed. Or let us come with you.

—Let the man go, for heaven's sake, said Kurt.

—I'd like to come, Else said. —Would you mind very much?

Kurt kept his eyes on the ground.

—No, said Voxlauer, slowly. —I suppose I wouldn't mind.

Else came down the steps, much relieved, and took them both by the arm, letting the screen door slam shut behind her. —Where shall we go?

—The ponds? Kurt offered.

—I'd thought possibly the Kugel-tree, said Voxlauer.

Else clapped her hands together. —Yes! The Kugel-tree, Kurti. We've never been there yet, the three of us.

—I've never been at all, that I can remember.

Else began walking. Kurt waved Voxlauer past him. —After you, Voxlauer. I have the cavalry in my saddlebags. A little malted hops.

—Courtesy of the Niessener Hof?

—Now, Oskar! Kurt said, waggling a finger. —I was dedicating a football green in Treibach on the evening in question. No court of my peers would convict me.

—I'm sure of that.

—Don't be angry with me, Oskar. Please. I brought Ischinger's this time, still cold from Rindt's greasy icebox. Kurt brought out the bottles. —What's more, I didn't pay him for it.

—Well, in that case, said Voxlauer. —I'll go find a place for them inside, away from the beasts of the field.

The light was just leaving the top of the ridge when they reached the tree, a perfect globe of evergreen suspended above the yellow rock and the slope of woods falling away to the south and west. Voxlauer had caught up with them halfway to the ridge and Else had noticed the smell of beer on his breath but had said nothing. Now they stood looking down into the valley, the three of them side by side, catching their breath. Peach-colored bands of sunlight drew softly down into the pines. —What a funny old shrub, Kurt said, squinting up at it.

—Don't make light of the Kugel-tree, Kurti.

—I'm only saying, Liesi. It looks like a jelly bean.

—Or a Reichs-German, in profile, murmured Voxlauer.

Kurt let out a deep sigh. —For all our sakes, cousin-in-law, I prefer to leave my ideology in town.

—Is that where you've left it?

A silence followed. —Papa did bring us here once, said Else after a time. —Do you really not remember?

Kurt let out a snort. —He never. He'd have burst half his blood vessels.

—This was before, Kurti. He took us with him everywhere.

—The only place he ever took me was the Niessener Hof. But he took me there very regularly.

—Don't be an ass. You're *trying* not to remember.

—Stowed me away, first thing, in some piss-smelling corner. Sat and guzzled and messed himself for days on end.

—Well, Kurti. That's family, said Else, leaning back against the tree. —Our family, at least.

—Yes. Our family, said Kurt, looking at her.

—You forgot Resi, said Voxlauer.

—What?

—To bring her.

—Oskar, Kurt said patiently. —I see Resi nearly every day.

—I don't, said Else.

—Yes. Of course. I'm sorry, Liesi.

She looked away. —That's all right. Just bring her along next time.

—Of course, said Kurt. He shaded his eyes.

—That is, if you're not too busy preserving law and order, said Voxlauer.

—Oskar! said Else.

—I'm only saying. That would keep a person busy, I'd think. What with accidents and fires and so on. He paused a moment. —Does it?

Kurt let out a sigh. —Does it what, Oskar?

—Does it keep you very busy?

Else was looking at him now with a mixture of sadness and alarm. Kurt took a very long time to answer. Up between the trees, falteringly at first but then steadily louder, came the low clattering rumble of a truck. —I have no need of starting any fires, Voxlauer, Kurt said.

—Or of putting any out, either, I suppose, said Voxlauer, feeling his hands balling in spite of themselves into fists, his arms stiffening at his sides. He kept still, waiting for the feeling to pass, feeling the alcohol in his arms and shoulders, waiting as he always did for nothing to begin happening again. Then, as always, the feeling faded as quickly as it came. His arms relaxed.

The noise of another truck carried up to them, and another. —Where could all those trucks be going? said Else.

—God knows, said Voxlauer. He tilted his head back to look at the sky, then let his eyes move down slowly to take in the two of them, leaning shoulder to shoulder against the mottled trunk. In the failing light, with their deep-set dark eyes and soft, childlike faces, they looked as alike as two cameos in a locket. Kurt was smiling at him oddly. —You mean you haven't heard the news? Neither of you?

—What news? said Voxlauer.

—Ryslavy's sold his trees.

Voxlauer looked at Kurt a long moment in silence. —Say that again, he said.

—I think you heard me, Oskar, Kurt said, turning to Else. —Ryslavy—he began, and was about to go on when Voxlauer stepped forward and shoved him hard into the tree so the back of his head made a sharp, percussive crack like the popping of a fire-cracker against the wood and he let out a groan and toppled over. —*Oskar!* Else shrieked. Voxlauer gripped Kurt's head by the hair and tilted his ashen face back and screamed into it. He himself could not make out what he was screaming but he saw the face receding further into its ashenness and that was enough. It was enough that the noise was coming from him and that he, Kurt, was suffering under it. The world all around them both had grown pale and dull and slowly he himself became detached from the noise and dull and colorless like everything else and then suddenly very calm. After a time he became aware of Else's hand on his shoulder.

—Let it be, Oskar, she was saying, almost tenderly. She took hold of him firmly by his shirtsleeves and he allowed himself to be pulled back from Kurt, who was now lying against the base of the tree. He let her sit him down and watched as she stood and looked down at him an instant longer, holding her breath and knitting her face together as though he were something entirely new to her now and strange. —Kurt, he heard her saying a moment later, crouch-ing not before him any longer but alongside Kurt's legs, shaking them carefully and calling out a name:—Kurt.

—Let's lay him out on the grass, said Voxlauer. Else looked up at him again with that same look, not disgusted so much as curi-ous, as though he'd transformed before her eyes into a rare species of tropical bird. —All right, she said after a moment. Voxlauer knelt beside her. They spread Kurt out with his jacket folded under his head and wiped the blood from his nose with a kerchief. He sputtered and coughed. —Voxlauer, he said effortfully after a time.

Voxlauer leaned over. —Yes.

—I forgive you, Voxlauer, Kurt said slowly, licking the corners of his mouth.

—I haven't asked you to.

Kurt nodded, looking past Voxlauer into the grass. —You're forgiven.

—I'm not sure that lies within your powers, Obersturmführer.

—Yes, said Kurt, sitting up slowly. —Now I want to go.

They led him down with many pauses through the pines, holding him at his wrists and shoulders. At the road he shrugged them off and began to move more surely, still wavering every few steps. Now and again he stopped and shook his head bemusedly. —Who'd have thought it. Oskar Voxlauer, he said, smiling down at the ground as though at some private joke.

At the villa Kurt stopped again and pressed a finger to the back of his skull. He winced. —Who would ever have thought of it. Eh, Else?

Else neither answered him nor looked at him as he spoke. She was not looking at Voxlauer, either, but away from both of them, staring back up at the line of trees as if trying to recollect where they'd been. Voxlauer watched her a moment helplessly before turning slowly to the steps.

As he made to go into the house Kurt put out a hand and stopped him. —I'd not try that again, Oskar. I'd not try that again, boy.

Voxlauer said nothing, looking him in the eyes.

—Let it be, Kurti, Else said. —Oskar's sorry.

—Yes, yes. He's forgiven already, Liesi. Still—Kurt said, closing his eyes a moment and taking a half step backward. —Still. I'd not try that again. He opened his eyes and stared at Voxlauer. —What do *you* say, Oskar?

—You go on back to town, said Voxlauer.

—No! said Else, furious now. —You come inside, Kurti. Let's get you straightened up. Kurt nodded weakly.

—He's coming along inside, Oskar, Else said.

Voxlauer didn't say anything for a moment. —I'll get some water, he said, going around the house.

—You're forgiven, Oskar! Kurt called after him.

. . .

As I stood leaning over the sideboard two shots pealed out one after the other and quivered for a moment in the empty room, darkening and condensing along the ceiling. I stood perfectly still for a long time, cradling the cut-glass decanter. Then I let it fall and ran around the table to the paneled door and forced it open. Ley was the first to turn toward me, blood down his shirtfront in bright, gaudy streaks. Spengler looked up at me for the space of a few seconds with that puzzled expression I knew so well. He clucked to himself and put away his pistol. "Oh, it's you, Bauer," he said, getting to his feet.

I looked down to where Dollfuss lay on the floor, twin jets spurting from his neck in bright pulsed arcs, his child's mouth opening and closing. Light from the window caught the blood and lit it an impossible, garish shade of purple. I closed the door behind me. We stood a few moments longer watching Dollfuss struggling like a fish at the bottom of a boat before I could think clearly enough to form a sentence.

"Where's the security secretary?"

Spengler jerked his thumb behind him.

The secretary sat huddled against the wall, tapping at it with his fingers. "They were trying to break out," said Spengler, pointing to an iron shutter.

"Through there?" I said. The shutter was thick and rust-covered and riveted shut. It looked like the door of a pharaoh's tomb.

Spengler nodded. The secretary was looking about him now, his eyes traveling up and down the walls. He let out a whimper. Ley crossed over and knelt down beside him. "Be quiet now, Josef," he said gently, taking him by the shoulder. Spengler was looking at me, one eyebrow slightly raised, as if to ask me whether I was game.

"I'm game," I said quietly.

Spengler grunted. "How loud were the shots?"

"Loud. The boys in the corridor heard something definitely."

He frowned. "Go and explain things to them. Nicely. They were going for the shutter," he repeated, still watching me closely.

"I heard you the first time, Heinrich," I said, going to the door.

Ernst and three other boys were on the other side. "He's dead all right, fellows," *I said, leading them to the table.*

"Dollfuss?" *asked Ernst.*

I nodded, watching the fact of it sink in to them. "Going for the shutter. Two shots. One wide, one through the neck."

"Who was it?"

I made my face as blank as possible. "Who do you think?"

"We'll never make it out now, will we?" *said one of the boys, letting out a short clipped laugh.*

Ernst turned on him violently. "You didn't come here to get out, Willi. Or did you?"

"No, Unterscharführer!" *the boy said hurriedly, snapping to attention. Ernst waved him off with a disgusted look.* "How is it in there?" *he said, trying to look past me.*

"Messy."

"And with you, Obersturmführer? Does the sun still shine on your behind?"

"Little Ernst! I'm deeply moved by your concern. Only you mustn't fret on my account. We have other worries. Run along now and break the news to the boys downstairs. Don't go shouting it out any windows."

He hesitated for an instant. "Is Ley still inside?"

"Do your duty, Scharführer," *I said.* "Heil Hitler."

"Heil Hitler!" *said Ernst loudly, saluting. The boys filed after him in a state of complete bewilderment, saluting me hurriedly as they went. I spent the next few minutes at the conference table, staring at the somber-toned row of chancellors, trying not to think about anything specific. After a time, I rose and went to a window and looked out. More Home Guards were assembled on the curb, pushing the gendarmerie back against the cast-iron fence of the Volksgarten. I watched them for a minute or so, ordered neatly into eight-by-twenty-man standing units, the look on their faces identical, I was sure, to the look mine had worn at ten o'clock that morning in Glass's office. From time to time a closed brown car would round the corner from the Ring and pull up at the curb. The car always pulled away a moment later and this or that wedge of troops pressed back to accommodate another officer. The columns extended side by side the full length of the block and farther around the corners, blocking the entire Löwelstrasse and God knows how many side streets afterward. Looking down from the quiet of the cabinet room, I felt as though I were watching the newsreel playing before the feature in a lavish, cavernous, empty theater. A moment later as I reached for the curtain a piece of molding above the window ledge exploded with a crack and fell away in a cloud of white-blue powder. I dropped flat onto the floor as though I'd been hit and crept back across the parquet to the carpet.*

When I came back into the little room Dollfuss was under a yellow sheet taken from God knows where, his stockinged feet peeking out at one of its ends. The security secretary had quieted and sat slumped over his bench, staring down at the floor between his shoe heels. Ley and Spengler sat on stools in the opposite corner. No one looked up as I entered.

I let my eyes rest awhile on Dollfuss, saying nothing to disturb the quiet. His feet pointed directly at me as I stood in the door. I was gripped all at once by a superstitious feeling and took a tiny, discreet step to the left.

After Kurt had gone Else and Voxlauer sat at the kitchen table looking out through the screen door at the dark. —If I'd thought that would happen, Else said. —If I'd ever thought something like that would happen.

Voxlauer sat forward with one leg pulled up under the chair, his arms lying heavily on the table. —So they've finally managed it, those sons of whores and bitches, he said.

—Yes, said Else tiredly. —Yes, Oskar, they have. There wasn't a thing we could have done about it.

—There was, said Voxlauer, nodding. —There was.

—What could we have done?

—Anything, he said after a time.

—The things you've seen fit to do haven't helped at all. Are you listening to me? Not in any way. She let her breath out heavily and leaned back in her chair.

Voxlauer didn't answer.

—Today, she went on. —Do you think you helped anybody today? Me? Pauli? Any one of us?

—I could have.

—How the hell could you have helped us?

—I could have pushed harder, said Voxlauer.

She cursed at him and sat forward. —Don't you understand a thing? Haven't you realized yet that Kurt's the only reason we've been allowed to have a life up here at all? Who in hell would it have helped if you'd pushed harder? The Polizeihaus?

—Me, Else. It would have helped me.

—Where did you learn to help yourself that way? She waited. —In the war?

—I told you what I learned in the war.

Her expression changed slightly. They were both of them quiet. —I'm sorry, Oskar, she said a moment later, taking hold of his arm.

—You go to hell, said Voxlauer.

She flinched as if he had hit her. Somewhere outside the door the tops of two trees were sawing together in the wind. —Why would you say something like that to me, Oskar? she said.

Voxlauer let out a slow, steady breath.

—Oskar?

—You were there with me. At the Niessener Hof. Weren't you there?

She closed her eyes. —What happened there, that was everybody, the whole town. Not just Kurt. Everybody. What could we have done to stop it? She paused a long moment, frowning to herself, then sat forward suddenly and took hold of his hand again. —What we can do is try to live. Outlast it. It can't go on and on this way forever. I'm sure it can't.

—Of course it can. Why couldn't it?

She sighed. —That's all that I can do, anyway. All I can do is wait. Or go away. I can't do anything else.

—They're forcing him to sell. He paused. —Else—

—I know it.

—And that doesn't trouble you at all, in a cousin? He was forcing the words out now, almost spitting them. —Doesn't that upset you? No? He gripped the edges of the table. —Don't you have any right and wrong in you? What more can you possibly want?

She stood up from the table. —I want to see Resi. I want to see my little girl. I'm not sure he'll let me anymore, after what you did. Is that all right to want, Oskar? You'll allow me that? The both of you? She quivered there a moment between the table and the door, vacant and unreal-seeming in spite of her grief, hands opening and closing on empty air. —That's all I've wanted now for seven years. She swallowed and took a breath. —For all this time I've barely had it. She stopped again, then said:—He didn't bring her today. You saw.

—No, said Voxlauer. —He didn't bring her.

Else turned and pressed her face against the screen. —She was supposed to come to stay. Did you know that? The rest of the summer, until school. And now she won't.

—Why is that?

Else shook her head. —Go to him, she said pleadingly. —Make friends with him again, Oskar. Please.

He sat perfectly still. —Not till you answer me.

She turned back to the screen and was quiet. Finally she said: —She won't come because he can keep her from coming. She won't come because of who he is.

—Obersturmführer, you mean?

—Her father. He's her father, she said, bringing a hand up to her mouth.

—Why could you not tell me this? Voxlauer said softly. —I'd already guessed.

—Because I knew you. Because I knew what you would think of me. Because if I had had a child—she was talking quickly now, on the verge again of anger, looking not at him but at the floor, the chairs, the screen door, all about her—Because I knew what you would think of *me*, having a child by such a man. Because I knew what kind of man he was. Because—

—What kind of man? said Voxlauer.

She stopped short. —What?

—You told me before, when I asked, that you didn't know.

That you didn't know what kind of man he was. That you didn't know what it was he did. He paused to take a breath. —Was that a lie?

—Oskar, she said, crouching down beside his chair and taking hold of his arm. It was very dark in the room but he could see that her eyes were wet and she was trembling. Her hand on his arm was trembling too, moving up and down slowly from his wrist to his elbow. —Please, she said, breathing stutteringly. —Say you'll go to him—

—You go to hell, said Voxlauer, getting up from the chair. He stepped past her where she crouched with her hand still trailing toward him and took up his coat. She made a low sound as he stepped past her and reached for the back of the chair to steady herself. Voxlauer pulled open the screen of the door and a stirring of warm air came into the room, rousing him as if out of a heavy sleep.

One hour later he was kneeling by the bank of the lower pond, pressing his fingers into the warm mud and breathing in the smell of the grass and the floating pollen. The water lapped shyly against the reeds. He moved further along the bank to a low bluff of gravel and washed his hands. A trout broke the surface close by, to his left. When his hands felt clean he stood and walked over the wet ground to the cottage.

The cottage gave off a low white hum as it had when he'd first seen it, glowing white against the flat blue slope like chalk against a blackboard. Long ago, now, he thought. How much simpler things were then. I was unhappy. He smiled. The cottage door hung slightly open. He stepped inside and felt about him for the table and chair, then sat down facing the vague blue rhombus of the door and waited.

Before long the first tracings of gray crept under the shutters and the room began to fill with a tentative yellow light. Voxlauer got up from the chair and opened the shutters, then sat down as before. After another hour he stood up stiffly and went down the steps and out to the road. The sweet damp smell of the ponds rose up to him as he passed the standing water. Midges and damselflies, reticulate and green, spun before him in fiery arabesques over the grass. As he watched them razor-thin streaks of light appeared in the wake of their serpentines and the ground underneath darkened suddenly, as though in an eclipse. Voxlauer ducked quickly down into the shadow of the pines and clenched his eyes shut. The ground fell away under his feet and rose up like a swinging door and fell away and he knelt down in a depression at the edge of the woods and doubled over till his face was pressed into the dust. His breath came more and more painfully and a cord of bile surged into his mouth and clung there, frothing and clotting against his lips. He lay down and pressed his arms against his sides. Beneath the smell of the bile a fine dry smell, comforting and close, crept up from the sun-warmed needles. He curled into a ball and sank slowly into the earth.

After a measureless length of time his breath came back to him and he was able to raise himself from the ground and spit out the rest of the bile. He sat forward and propped himself on his elbows and waited for his eyes to focus. The bile glistened in a puddle at his side. Gathering up a handful of needles and dirt, he covered it over, then brushed the needles from his clothes and climbed to the road.

At the road Voxlauer stood for a time with his head tipped back, helping his sight to clear by following the clouds from west to east, then turned down valley. He walked slowly through the trees from sunspot to sunspot, lingering in each for a moment or two with his arms close against his sides, shivering. At the junction he hesitated briefly, glancing up again at the sky, then went left up the trail to the meadow and the colony.

The huts stood bright and unchanged on the far side of the grass, half in shadow and half in weak, cloud-muted sunshine. A few fluttering rags still hung from lines strung between them. He moved toward them over the dew-heavy grass, the water seeping into his boots. All around the huts was a deep vibrating quiet. That's a strange sound that quiet makes, thought Voxlauer. Like the sound of a train going into a tunnel, if you took away the noise of the rails. His footfalls as he began to move again seemed amplified by the clapboard walls around him and echoed grotesquely along the hard-packed ground. At the small circle of tamped earth at the center of the colony he hesitated, looking to his right and left.

The little pen to one side stood empty now and derelict and the wall of the terraced garden buckled in along its length where the soil had run out in the late spring rains. A few cracked plates jutted like sun-bleached bones out from the mud. By the garden wall he found a few turnips not yet turned up by deer and he ate them gratefully. His stomach hurt with a constant quiet pain. He leaned sideways with his cheek against the warm slate of the wall and closed his eyes.

The noise of a door clattering shut roused him a short while later. The sun had moved more completely now into the low bank of clouds and a steady wind was coming down off the cliffs. He slid from the wall and found the door of the meetinghouse swinging on its hinges, burls of dust floating and settling and swirling up again on the floor of the narrow entryway. Pushing on the door, he went into the little hall, which was pleasantly cool and desolate. A ring of water stains darkened the smooth plank floor where once a supper had been held. Many suppers, thought Voxlauer. Yes. But one especially. He remembered Else's voice as it had sounded to him that first day, before she had ever whispered to him in desire or shouted at him or spoken his name, before he had known even the smallest thing about her. He stood remembering the room as it had looked then. A moth-gnawed blanket huddled now in one corner like a sleeping child. He thought of the blanket that had lain on the floor that day, the food in wooden bowls, the circle of nervous, jaundiced faces. Crossing to the blanket he pulled it up and uncovered the husked-out carcass of a mouse.

Passing through the other rooms he found nothing beyond some straw pallets thrown together in an alcove and the faint lingering smell of unwashed bodies. In the pantry a few sunflower seeds lay scattered along a high shelf and he put them one by one into his mouth, feeling worryless and numb. He looked out a long time at the bright blue beehouses as they changed hue almost imperceptibly in the fading light. After a time he went out through the hall and down the steps and around the house to them. A dark stream of bees came and went from a vent at the bottom of each door, silently and flickeringly, like light from a cinema projector. A few meters from the cabinets Voxlauer stopped and watched them funnel out and upward as though blown from a tiny puckered mouth. Everything was bright and still and silent. He moved his arm slowly toward the cabinet and felt nothing but coolness and a shivering in the air. All at once, as though shut off by a switch, the line of bees disappeared. The flickering had stopped. The cabinet doors hung slackly open, revealing the lifeless hives. Voxlauer looked about him, blinking. The sound of wind came down to him as always through the pines.

"Where are his shoes?" I asked after a moment.

"I have them here," said Spengler.

I flirted momentarily with the idea of asking why Spengler had the shoes but said instead: "There are still Home Guard troops and bulls everywhere, Heinrich. They have sharpshooters now. I was almost just given a full state pardon, if you take my meaning."

Spengler furrowed his brow at this. He glanced at Ley. "Well?"

Ley got to his feet and began buttoning up his jacket. "I suppose I'd best go out to them," he said, as casually as he could.

I stared at Spengler. "You're not really going to let him waltz out of here, are you, Heinrich? With only the secretary of security left for us to haggle over?"

Spengler smiled at Ley, ignoring me completely. "Go on, Herr Minister. Go on out. Inform your men."

I stared at them both, my mind a perfect blank. After a moment or two I realized I was holding the door for Ley and pushed it closed. "Could you possibly be such an idiot, Heinrich?" I managed to stutter. He continued to pay me no mind whatsoever. Ley put on his yellow minister's cap and stepped to the door, turning to Spengler at the last moment and bowing. "Long live your revolution, Herr Spengler," he said, touching his cap.

Spengler said nothing. Ley bowed once more and walked serenely out of the room.

"Just a minute!" Spengler shouted. Ley reappeared after a few seconds, frowning very slightly. "Yes?"

"Take old granddad here along with you," Spengler said, pointing at the secretary of security, who looked up at us with an expression of amazement and rose uncertainly to his feet.

"Heinrich," I pleaded.

"I'm tired of looking at you, granddad," Spengler said kindly. The secretary hesitated the briefest instant, perhaps debating whether or not to take a bow, then shuffled quickly after his colleague, already vanished around the doorframe. I watched Spengler as he watched them go. "Why, Heinrich, for the love of God?"

Spengler shrugged. "One old man more or less. If you must know, I really was tired of looking at him, the ugly bugger."

"I meant why shoot Dollfuss? Why? Do you honestly believe that Ley won't cross us?"

Spengler shrugged again.

"Are you trying to kill yourself, Heinrich?" My voice had a far-off, hollow sound, like the rattling of two peas in a rubbish can.

Spengler only grimaced. He seemed hypnotized, or drunk, or half asleep. "Control yourself, Bauer. Eh? We have the Home Guard, don't we?"

"The Home Guard just left, Heinrich. With the secretary of security."

"The secretary of security," Spengler repeated. He laughed. "Is that what he was, the old gasbag?"

Just then I was able to see an angel of death hovering quite clearly above Spengler's left shoulder, opening like an umbrella. I saw it quite clearly. I closed my eyes, rubbed them and looked again. It was still there, much larger already, spreading now to take in the entire room. The nausea I'd felt earlier in the day hit me all at once and buckled me over against the wall. Spengler, for his part, took no notice of anything. He was busy reloading his pistol, sliding each greased green cartridge into its barrel with nurturing care. I took my eyes away from him and stared again at the blood-caked sheet covering Dollfuss's tiny body.

"I'm going to check on Little Ernst and the boys," I said, feeling behind me for the door handle.

Spengler glanced up. "Is that necessary?"

"I think so. Yes."

"All right," he said. I backed slowly out of the room and shut the door.

The conference room was abandoned. I went out through the reeking reception room to the corridor. Little Ernst had disappeared. Three boys I recognized only vaguely were there, leaning sleepily on their rifle stocks. The chancellery guards lay face down, just as they'd been before, but all of the tension seemed to have gone out of their bodies. Seeing me, the boys drew themselves to attention.

I raised my arm automatically in return, glancing again at the guards on the floor as I went by. When I was almost past them I stopped short. "Did you kill these men?" I said to the nearest boy.

"Yes, Obersturmführer."

I sighed very deeply. "Why? Why did you kill them?"

The boy looked at me confusedly. "They were making noises, Obersturmführer." He hesitated, scratching the back of his neck. "We told them two or three times to stop."

I stepped very close to him. He was sixteen, seventeen at the oldest. Wide pink blotches of acne decorated his cheeks. "This is a suicide pact you've all drawn up together. Is that it?"

He looked down at his feet for a time without answering. "No, Obersturmführer."

"Take these corpses downstairs, in-the-name-of-Christ!"

The boys nodded and said that they would and thanked me and saluted and clicked their heels. The one I'd spoken to looked troubled. "Downstairs where, Obersturmführer?"

The guards lay together in a slack brown pile with their hands still folded neatly against the backs of their heads. Some of them had wide round bloodstains on the backs of their shirts; some of them only looked asleep. The others looked to have been shot in the stomach and there was a huge amount of blood all around them on the floor. "Anywhere downstairs," I said after a time. "Do you think you can manage them now without too much trouble?"

One of the other of the boys smiled. "Oh yes, Obersturm-führer." He was tall and had a clipped brown mustache and might have been as old as nineteen. "We can manage them now."

As Voxlauer walked down to Pergau a cool rain began to fall. He wrapped the honeycomb he'd cut from the hives in a handkerchief of Else's he'd found in a pocket of his coat and hurried through the town. Coming up the drive he slowed to a crawl and then stopped altogether. She was in the garden, working on the hinges of the gate, and he felt himself overcome by a sudden fear of facing her out of doors. He turned and went a short distance down and waited until he heard the clatter of the screen, then walked slowly up the drive again, wondering what he could possibly say to her.

She was in the kitchen, washing her hands in a pressed-tin bowl. At his knock on the door she shifted slightly and granted him a weary smile. —You've brought something, she said, almost to herself. She took up a dish towel and dried her hands. —Aren't you coming in?

Voxlauer opened the screen door, hanging back uncertainly in its frame, one foot still on the topmost step. —What do you have there? said Else.

He set the parcel down next to her without looking her in the eyes and went and sat mutely and penitently at the kitchen table. He heard her behind him pulling away the folds of the handker-chief and letting out a sigh, whether of relief or pleasure or resig-nation he would not have ventured to guess. A short while later she came to the table with the honeycomb on a china plate.

—The bees disappeared, said Voxlauer.

—What?

—All of a sudden.

—Oskar? she said, putting the plate down. —What is it?

—I don't know, he said, still not able to look at her. —I didn't come back for you to take care of me, he said after a moment.

Else smiled. —But you always come back sick, don't you. It

must be a very shabby, disease-infested place you go to, when you run away.

—I hate that goddamned cottage, said Voxlauer, smiling faintly.

She laughed a little and crossed over to the table and took him by the hair. —Oskar Voxlauer! she said after a moment, tugging his head back and forth. —By all rights you should be on the blacklist.

—I thought I was already.

—Not *theirs*. Mine. I have one of my own.

—I can't think who would be on it, if not me.

—Yes. She laid her hand against his forehead. —I think you have a fever, she said after a moment. —I'm sure of it.

—I don't care. Please don't forgive me this easily, Else. I couldn't stand it.

—Where did you sleep last night? she said, ignoring him. —Down a rabbit hole?

—In a casket, said Voxlauer. —Did I tell you . . . He let his voice trail away.

—What is it?

—I feel dizzy.

Else sighed. —Don't run out like that again. I was up half the night. You'll ruin my looks if you're not careful.

—I went up to the colony.

—The colony?

—There's the proof, he said, pointing at the honey.

—Why there, of all places? What's left to see?

Voxlauer didn't answer for a time. Her hands on his temples lay smooth as polished wood and he was afraid if he said anything she might remove them. —A mouse, he said finally.

—And bees.

—Yes. But they disappeared. I told you before—

—Go to bed, Herr Gamekeeper. She raised his head and smoothed the hair back from his face. —You go to bed now.

—It's just past noon, said Voxlauer, sitting up.

—That's never stopped you before, has it? said Else. —I'll come with you, if you want.

—In that case, said Voxlauer, following bashfully behind her.

. . .

Sometime after dark he woke alone in the bed with a light streaming over the kitchen steps. He heard voices in the kitchen: Else's and a man's. He sat on the edge of the bed, dressing quietly without lighting the lamp. They were talking in a low monotone, his voice often indistinguishable from hers. Voxlauer finished dressing and went up the steps. —Oh! Hello, Pauli, he said after a moment, smiling confusedly.

—Oskar . . . Ryslavy said. He rose awkwardly from his place at the table.

Voxlauer looked from him to Else. —Why didn't anybody wake me?

—You were fast asleep, said Else.

—What's going on? said Voxlauer. —What are you two plotting?

—Oh, Oskar, said Ryslavy quietly.

Maman lay stretched out on a linen-covered plank over two wooden sawhorses in the parlor. A faint dew had gathered on her waxen upper lip. Voxlauer bent over and brought his face down close to hers. She looked younger now than before, younger and finer-featured and in some strange way more alive. But she was not, not at all. He laid his hands on hers and felt the rigor in them. A vague odor of lilac hung in the room. He turned round to Ryslavy. —Did you have her perfumed?

—I don't think so, said Ryslavy. He stood a bit behind, shifting from foot to foot.

—You can go, Pauli.

—What? Ah! Of course, Ryslavy murmured. He went out.

The coffin lay behind her under the window, the lid propped against its side. He looked down at her. In the light from the shaded lamp she glowed dully, as though cast in bronze. He reached out again to touch her face through the parted veil. Then he drew the veil closed again and left her.

—I mean to pay for all of this, he said, finding Ryslavy sitting on a low stool in the kitchen, staring at a bottle of beer.

—*Ach*, Oskar. Allow me this little thing.

—There was no need for any trimmings. She wouldn't have wanted them.

—Trimmings? Ryslavy said, frowning.

—That casket. The cosmetics.

—This is her last time, Oskar. Allow me this one thing. I don't think she would have minded.

—Goddamn it, Pauli. Look after your own goddamned business.

—I'd rather not, Ryslavy said, staring down at his feet.

They sat silently for a time. —She was kind to me, God bless her, Ryslavy said. —Kinder than all the rest of them piled together.

—I mean to pay you, Pauli. Voxlauer took a breath. —I'm set on it.

Ryslavy said nothing. He passed the bottle to Voxlauer and Voxlauer tipped it back.

—God knows she always did right by us, Oskar. God knows, Ryslavy said. —She was a goddamned saint in my eyes. He shook his head slowly. —Not that I have much use for saints, needless—

—Can't you leave me alone a little while? Voxlauer murmured.

—All right, Oskar. Ryslavy stood. —I'll come round in a bit.

—That's fine.

After Ryslavy left he sat well into the night, cradling the empty bottle. There were more bottles in the cellar but he had no strength to get them. The house with all its rooms seemed far larger now without her in it. But she was in it, in the parlor, laid out in charcoal-colored silk. The thought came to him suddenly that he had never spent a night in the house by himself. He sat quietly on the stool, looking into the bedroom. He felt younger than he could ever remember feeling. A weak candle beam from the parlor played over the floorboards.

He woke early the next morning to footfalls on the stairs and the sound of women's voices. He let them go around through the vestibule into the parlor, listening through the bedroom. —The candles have gone out, one of the women said. They whispered together for a time before reciting grace for the dead in a flowing mumble and stepping out again into the stairwell.

When they had gone Voxlauer raised himself from the stool and went in to see her. Her veil was parted and the window shade pulled partly up, letting sunlight fall in a broad, flat band across the floor. He pulled down the shades and closed her veil and sat down on the piano bench. Before long another set of footfalls carried to him from under the vestibule door. He let them come as he had the others, not minding the commotion of their voices. There were three this time, a gaunt, shambling man and two women, ancient and pale, dressed in the stern black silks and white bonnets of the preceding century. When they saw him there at the piano in the dark they stood still for a moment, then dipped their heads respectfully. The man stepped over to him and held out a pale and liver-spotted hand.

—Jürgen Schuffner, Herr Voxlauer, if you please. He paused. —You don't remember me, I'm sure.

—I remember you, said Voxlauer. He smiled. —You work at the mill.

The man let out a little laugh. —Years ago, Your Honor. Years ago. I remember your visits, though, very well. Your Honor loved to visit that mill as a little Herr.

—You sifted the flour, said Voxlauer. —With a two-handed sieve.

—I did, and other things. The man paused, turning his hat brim thoughtfully in his hands. —She was the right kind, Your Honor's mother. A lady in all cardinals. Of a different time, I always thought, if you'll pardon my so saying. A different time altogether.

—She often said the same, said Voxlauer.

The women were moving around the body slowly, murmuring to themselves and setting down small, gilt-bottomed candles. That's how they do it in the hills, thought Voxlauer. Even now. I wonder which valley they come out of. Dirt-poor, most likely. Look at his suit, their dresses. I'd like to touch them if I could. Watching the women and listening to the queer old-fashioned pleasantries of the man he felt transported suddenly into the sepia-toned flatness of a daguerreotype. The feeling was strange but not unpleasant, like a slow, warm immersion in muddy water.

—You'll not see many like that anymore, if Your Honor pleases, the man was saying. —She was the right kind, was your mother. The grandest kind.

—I'd never thought of her as grand, Herr Schuffner. Formal-mannered, possibly.

—Well. Your Honor wouldn't, being her son.

—Did you have far to come?

The man shrugged. —Down from In der Höll. Your Honor wouldn't likely remember to place it.

—I remember it very well. That's a fair piece of travel.

The man shrugged again. After a time he nodded. —She kept her contract with us long after Your Honor's uncle had gone over to those stinking Yids in Ammern, he said finally, as though in answer to a question.

—Well. If it's any consolation to you, he lived to regret it, said Voxlauer.

The man snorted. —He always was a weather-watcher, your uncle, if you don't mind my saying.

—I don't mind.

—He about?

—What?

—The uncle. Is he about?

—I haven't seen him.

—He'll get his bill, said the man, dropping his voice low. —*His* kind always have.

—Everybody gets their bill, Herr Schuffner, said Voxlauer. —We'll get ours, too, before much longer.

—As you say, Your Honor. Well now. He inclined his head again and lifted his hat slightly as a signal to the women, who were rustling around the body. —If there's anything you might be need-ing, we'd feel privileged.

—The burial is on Thursday, said Voxlauer.

—We'll have to be going back up directly, I'm afraid. Thanks to the Herr, though, all the same. The women came up now behind him, beneficent and smooth-faced. They curtsied.

—Yes. Well, good-bye then, Herr Schuffner, said Voxlauer.

—Good-bye the ladies. The women curtsied again, eyes downcast, and followed the man with a rustling of petticoats out of the room and down the stairwell.

The rest of the day people came in twos or threes, mostly quietly, up the stairwell and past him, moving stiff-jointedly around the body or sitting for a time on the bench he'd carried in from the verandah, moving their lips soundlessly and quickly. Most stayed only a few minutes, mumbling and bowing to him and moving on. And always more behind, the muted, sustained murmur of their voices, the steady bustle on the stairs. The men bowed as they passed him, most of them, and removed their hats. The women took him briefly by the hand. Ryslavy came in the early evening.

—Well? he said, looking sideways at the casket.

—I've just been sitting here all day, said Voxlauer.

—Come on out of here. You look like you're waiting your turn.

—Watch yourself, Pauli. I just might beat you to the ribbon.

—Scant chance of that. You've a good dozen more years of self-abuse ahead of you, little man. He took Voxlauer by the elbow.

—Come along. You'll be depressing me in another minute.

Voxlauer shook his head. —I'm waiting here.

—What for?

He waved a hand. —A state visit. Condolences.

—Else told me what happened last week. Scant chance of that either, I'd say.

—Yes. He got a shock, didn't he, the Obersturmführer.

—I'll say he did, you blessed idiot. Ryslavy grinned.

—Both of us did.

—Ach! Come off it, Oskar.

—Is it true what I hear?

Ryslavy's grin faded. —What's that?

—That you've finally dropped your pants to them.

—To hell with you. To hell with you, Oskar Voxlauer. Ryslavy's face worked and stiffened. —You're a damn fool. You think things through like a goddamned wet-assed baby. He bent low over Voxlauer. His breath reeked of wine. —You've let Kurt Bauer do your thinking for you. That's what you've done.

—*I've* let him? said Voxlauer. —You've got things turned around a little, I'd say. You're the one with his pants at his knees.

—There's no talking to you, Ryslavy said, almost too quietly to hear. —There's no good in it.

—Don't talk to me, then, said Voxlauer, turning away. A few seconds later he heard the bright slam of the stairwell door.

I waited for the boys to lift the first of the bodies and start with them down the stairs, keeping my face expressionless. I'd decided to escape even before I saw the angel over Spengler's shoulder but I knew now that it had to happen soon. I had no idea how to manage it, only that first impulse to send the boys down. I heard them grunting on the staircase, cursing as they missed their footing on the marble steps.

At the end of the corridor a tall leaded-glass window looked out over the Ring, and to the left of it, half hidden by drapes, a small open stairwell led to the topmost floor. Through the window I saw quivering, dark-edged shapes running together and dissolving silently in all directions. I couldn't make any of the shapes out clearly but I knew their significance well enough. I pulled the drapes aside and ran upstairs.

At the top of the stairwell a high, mansard-roofed passage began, bounded on either side by mesh enclosures filled to the rafters with unmarked, gothic-looking crates. A dull brackish light filtered down through skylights. I walked along the passage to a soot-stained window the size and shape of a bicycle wheel and pushed it open very gently. It turned smoothly on cross-hinges and through it I saw the lieutenant general of the gendarmerie, on the chancellery steps, give the order to storm the building.

The window was tucked high into the façade, just above the main set of double doors, and I was able to watch as they were battered open with a small wooden ram by a group of six men without the slightest trouble. An instant later a swarm of gray-shirted Home Guards poured in. There was a sudden wave of sound, smooth at first, then breaking into facets, and a puff of black smoke rose slowly up the façade toward me. Through the smoke came the steady chatter of gunfire. I looked across the Ring at the crowd that had gathered along the margins of the park, and marveled at its utter lack of fear; any stray bullet could have reached it. I smiled at this thought for a moment, feeling for a few seconds invisible and cunning, then ducked my head in and ran down the passageway.

At the other end, by the stairwell, was a second window, identical to the first except that it was locked and painted over. I could hear shouts and gunshots echoing up the stairwell and the sound of more doors being battered in. I slipped furtively down the stairs and rearranged the drapes in an attempt to hide the stairwell, then ran full speed back up to the window. Its cross-hinges were caked with rust and clotted greenish-yellow paint, cracked and ancient. I looked around for a loose brick or some other thing to smash the lock, then stopped myself all at once and stared up at the skylights.

There were twenty of them running the length of the passage; they were narrow and deeply recessed, but looked as though they might let a man through if he was desperate enough. The walls of the enclosures came within an arm's length of the roof beams. I went from one enclosure to the next, testing each gate. Reports of rifle fire came from time to time through the floor, often seemingly right below me, but the large-scale fighting appeared already to have ended. The sixteenth or seventeenth gate swung inward unprotestingly and I stepped into the enclosure and tested the strength of the wire mesh with my boot. It bent sharply under my weight, leaving the perfect impression of a toehold. I cursed and bent the mesh back carefully.

By now I was beginning to feel the first stirrings of panic. I knelt and examined the crates more closely. They had red stenciled numbers on them and were made of a light, waxy wood, but looked as though they might support my weight if I stepped very lightly. I lifted the nearest by its corners and was overjoyed to find it less heavy than I'd expected. I stacked them quickly and quietly into a column under the skylight, glancing down the passageway every few seconds, whispering little chants of encouragement to myself as I worked.

When I was nearly done, I heard the sound of footfalls on the stairs; it passed after a moment and I kept on with my work. At one point I dropped a crate that must have held cutlery or tuning forks or some other horribly clanging, metallic things; I crouched down behind the column and waited a long time without so much as taking a breath. But no one came after all and I finished the stack, pulled the gate shut, threw the latch with my fingertips and climbed carefully to the skylight. It opened easily and I stuck my head out a moment later into the drizzling gray air.

The next morning three men came from the diocese and nodded to Voxlauer and laid the body in the casket and arranged its unwilling limbs and fastened the lid down with screws. They carried her through the middle of town to the cemetery chapel, a bare, plank-roofed, whitewashed little room, open along its townward side like a box at the opera. Thirty or forty people were gathered in front in long dark coats and bustled dresses. Most of them were very old. Gustl was there. Ryslavy was there, looking pale and weather-beaten. Six or seven SS were there in their parade finery but Kurt Bauer was not among them. The priest hobbled meekly around the little stage swinging his copper censer. Voxlauer recalled his shallow docile face dimly from childhood services. He sang in a flutter of reedy, false notes at the casket.

—*Odore celesti pascat animam tuam Deus.*

When the singing was over a muted chorus of amens rose up from the assembled and the service began. It went on a very long time with everybody staring down at the ground in front of them. —*Pater, et Filius, et Spiritus Sanctus,* said the priest at the end of it. —Amen.

—Amen, the crowd repeated. The SS remained quiet.

The priest then turned to Voxlauer. —If anyone should like to say words at this time, he said.

Making Gustl out to the left of the stage, Voxlauer spoke his name.

Gustl nodded with an air of highborn detachment and shuffled up the stairs. Once beside the casket he stood solemnly a moment, eyes raised toward heaven, then gave a melancholy little sigh. —Fellow mourners, he began.

The priest stepped back from the casket and dropped his head. His narrow pale chin pressed against his wattled neck and his eyelids fluttered. —Fellow mourners, said Gustl again, clearing his throat.

Voxlauer sought out Ryslavy's face in the crowd and winked at him. Ryslavy looked away. Gustl's sad mild voice stirred like a dying summer breeze through the assembled. Voxlauer watched him bobbing on his short legs, spreading his arms out as he spoke and bringing them in again a moment later like some sort of flightless bird. After a time he looked more closely at the mass of faces, none of which he seemed to recognize. Ryslavy stared morosely ahead of him, muttering to himself, scratching the back of his neck and tugging at his collar. Occasionally a nervous smile would crimp his mouth along its left side. He glanced at Voxlauer, raised an eyebrow, then dipped his head to stare again at nothing.

—. . . and commend her soul into a more placid harbor, said Gustl quietly. —Amen.

—Amen, said the priest, opening his eyes but leaving his head bowed low against his windpipe. Gustl bowed gravely and stepped away from the casket. He patted Voxlauer encouragingly on the shoulder as he passed. A brief, expectant silence followed.

—Paul Ryslavy, said Voxlauer carefully.

Ryslavy looked up, startled. A murmuring rose among the crowd.

—Customarily, at this time, the son might say a few words, offered the priest. A few of the mourners made a show of beginning to button up their coats.

—A family time, Oskar, Gustl whispered.

—Yes, Uncle. We'd like to ask Paul Ryslavy to speak, said Voxlauer, more loudly. —There he is. Come up, Herr Ryslavy, if you would.

Ryslavy stepped out of the crowd and moved haltingly up to the casket. A number of mourners, the younger men especially, had put on their hats and stood ready to leave. The SS remained perfectly at attention, their eyes fixed on a point slightly to Voxlauer's left. Let them stand at attention for him, thought Voxlauer, watching Ryslavy straighten himself and cough a little into his sleeve. He looks terrible, he thought, glancing from Ryslavy back out at the crowd. So much the better.

Ryslavy stood at the casket surveying the fidgeting assembly. —Fellow mourners, he began, sucking in his breath. —We are gathered together today to . . . ah . . . say good-bye now and forever to a beautiful spirit . . .

Voxlauer looked from one to another of them all the while. They were staring at Ryslavy and the priest with awkward, disappointed faces. The SS were looking at Voxlauer almost fondly. They must have come for this, he thought. Well then, let them enjoy it. Let them do what they came here to do.

—We cared for her . . . ah, each of us in different ways. Each in keeping with our particular, ah, relationship . . . Ryslavy looked from one to another of them, breaking into a grin. —As for me, I loved her something like a stepson.

Loud murmurs arose. —That makes some of you piss your pants, I know, Ryslavy said. He looked over at Voxlauer and guffawed.

—This man is drunk, the priest said, stepping forward.

—This man paid your fee, grandfather, said Voxlauer, taking the priest's arm. —You let him alone.

—. . . like a cherished aunt, Ryslavy was saying, untroubled now by the priest or the mourners, slurring his words together. —Better yet, a governess—

—That's enough, said Gustl violently. Five SS were behind him. Ryslavy stopped in mid-sentence and stood half turned, regarding all of them with calm disdain.

—You've had your turn to speak already, Uncle, Voxlauer said.

—That's as may be, Oskar. That's as may be—

—A disgusting misuse of the occasion, all considered, the SS officer behind Gustl interrupted, stepping forward impatiently.

Voxlauer recognized him now as the towheaded clerk from his visit to the Polizeihaus. —A pretty little Jew speech, he said shrilly, turning to address the crowd. He stood parallel to Ryslavy, just at his shoulder; the two of them might have been joint speakers at a lecture. Ryslavy was leaning away from him now, watching him, the expression on his face set and unchanging.

—The love of Yids and Gypsies for our wives and mothers is well known, the officer said. Someone in the crowd began to jeer. Voxlauer stood still one brief instant longer, looking from one face to the other. No one seemed to be laughing yet, or even smiling. Ryslavy had fallen back into the crowd, watching with the rest of them. Those who had made a show of leaving during his speech had returned and now crowded in on all sides, craning their necks to see. There seemed to be many more of them than before. The older mourners stared at the stage in simple disbelief. Gustl was nowhere to be seen. The officer had just taken a breath and was about to go on.

Voxlauer stepped over to him. The officer checked himself and looked up into Voxlauer's face, smiling. Vaguely Voxlauer was aware of the other men pressed close around him.

—If you say one more word over my mother's body, I'll kill you, Voxlauer said.

The officer's smile widened. He wants me to do this, thought Voxlauer, looking into the narrow face, reddening subtly along the jawline. He wants me to do this and I will. I will do what he wants.

—Herr Wiedehopp! Herr Wiedehopp! Please! It was Gustl's voice, close at hand, sycophantic. Voxlauer could see nothing but the flush-cheeked face in front of him. The face turned slightly.

—Since when have you called me by that name, little comrade? the face said, not smiling any longer.

I will hit him, thought Voxlauer. Let it happen now. He saw the events of the last five months running together like rails dovetailing into a station, converging inevitably toward the moment and the act, concrete and inescapable. —Go away, Gustl, he said.

Gustl ignored him. —Please, Herr Oberführer. Look at all the people. The officer glanced grudgingly about him. —I'll stop this now. This minute. Please. Move the boys away, Herr Oberführer. I'll put an end to it.

There was a brief pause. Gustl still stood between them. The other four SS were nothing now but a circle of starched black cloth and silver buttons. Voxlauer peered out between the uniforms, looking for Ryslavy. He felt calm in that moment, almost content. Ryslavy seemed to have gone. Gustl and the officer were talking together quietly, their heads almost touching.

After a time the officer looked up and moved away from Gustl. —Disperse this crowd, he said, stepping past Voxlauer indifferently.

The three men from the diocese remained behind, waiting for Voxlauer beside the casket. Voxlauer moved tiredly to his corner and took hold of it and they began to walk. They walked measuredly, entirely alone now, down the canting rows of headstones with the casket heavy and awkward between them. At the grave it was laid on joists of unvarnished yellow wood looped together with canvas strips. After a perfunctory pause the joists were pulled away and the casket lowered. One end touched bottom before the other and made a soft thump, like the jostling of a boat against a pier. Sliding on the cushions, Voxlauer thought. The priest appeared again and made a slow baroque sign of the cross over the opening.

—Dora Anna-Marie Voxlauer, said the priest with his reedy voice. —*Pulvis es, et in Pulverem revertaris.* Amen. He lowered his hand and left without glancing once at Voxlauer. The three attendants lingered, waiting for the customary schilling, then finally left as well, grumbling to each other.

Voxlauer looked down at the casket with the canvas runners still trailing onto the cemetery lawn. —Far away from here, he said.

A few minutes later Gustl came puffing down the row. Passing the grave, he glanced down briefly, then took Voxlauer by the shoulder. —Come along now, you godforsaken lunatic. Let's you and I find us a mug and a table and sit down behind it and have ourselves a conference. A little meeting of the minds.

Voxlauer blinked. —Haven't you given up on me yet, officer?

Gustl didn't answer but steered him quickly down the row and out the cemetery gate. Voxlauer let himself be pulled along by the crook of his arm like a truant schoolboy, past the lumberyards and the mill and across the mill brook and the canal, past a long row of lumber trucks idling on the road above the gymnasium. —Where could those trucks be heading, I wonder? Voxlauer said.

—Great plans are afoot, Gustl said, tapping the side of his nose. —There'll be great work to be done soon. Man's work, Oskar. *Construction.*

—I see. Voxlauer was quiet for a time, looking over at the trucks. —What is it we're to be constructing, Uncle?

—The future, said Gustl, beaming.

—The future, said Voxlauer. —Who would have guessed.

—Don't play the innocent, Oskar. It's not attractive in a man of middle years, this coyness.

—I'm not playing at anything, Uncle. I don't have the spirit for it.

Gustl looked at him crookedly. —Not still waving the Red flag, are you, nephew?

—The Red flag? said Voxlauer, smiling in spite of himself.

—Nobody thinks your way anymore, do you understand? Not a soul. You must see that yourself. Today, at least, you must have seen it. You nearly got yourself plucked and gutted.

—They didn't think my way back in Cherkassy either, if it makes you feel any better, Uncle. Nobody has ever thought "my way," as you put it so nicely. Not even in Red Russia. I'd be a bigger fool than even you think to expect anybody to start now.

—I like to think *I've* thought your way, said Gustl slowly. —I'd like to think I have some notion of your take on things.

—Would you, Gustl? Voxlauer stopped short in the middle of the road. —What exactly would it get you, you old arse-licker?

Gustl reddened. —Go on! Have your fun with me, a tired old man. I know how you think. You think like your father, that goddamned tea-sipper. A man of the people, are you, because you made faces at your French tutors? Not for one minute. You're another would-be lord of the manor without a house and stables. Another bed-wetter. Another holy martyr. He spat passionately onto the curb. —Know what the people want, do you? You don't know any more than he did, with his blessed goddamned Kaiser and his tailored pants.

—You can think what you like about it, said Voxlauer.

—He wanted a private peace, too, remember. Above everybody. Nobody was good enough to change *his* knickers, either. Not even your mother, God rest her. And where did it get him? Where did it get him, after everything?

—Some people are good enough to change my knickers, Uncle.

—You want to end up like the old fool? Is that it?

—No, said Voxlauer, taking a breath. —But then he was mad, wasn't he, my father. Voxlauer put a finger to his skull and tapped it. —And I, on the other hand, am very sane. Too right in the head for my own good, most likely. He laughed. —Bless you, Uncle, for asking me that question. I've been waiting nearly my whole life to answer it.

Gustl stood in front of him now suddenly, almost clownishly, holding out a fat red hand. —Come down to Rindt's with me, Oskar. One last favor to your old uncle. He held his hand out straight at Voxlauer's chest, opening and closing his stubby fingers. —They'll be drinking to your health before closing. I promise you. Let's us bring them round together, you and I. He paused. —I won't ask again.

—Thanks all the same, said Voxlauer, looking up the street.

—How's that?

—I said no. No thank you, Gustl. Not today.

Gustl's hand was still outstretched, flapping clumsily in the air like a poorly managed puppet. His face was a flat and lifeless shade of white. —Perhaps it's for the best, he said quietly after a time.

—Yes. Maybe so.

The hand fell. —Take care, then, nephew. Try to keep out of sight.

—You keep out of trouble yourself, said Voxlauer. He waved Gustl off down the empty street.

. . .

I stayed on the chancellery roof three days and nights, drinking water from the gutters when it rained and hiding in the shadow of the chimneys from the full heat of day. I felt grateful, in spite of myself, to Almighty Providence for the fact that the putsch had been planned for the summer months. No one came through the sky-lights after me; I doubt now whether the attic was ever searched. By the second day I realized no one was likely to be coming and I felt a vague amazement at the thought. I thought often, as well, about the vision I'd had in the little room, how it had been reserved for me and me alone, and wondered whether Spengler was already dead.

By the second night the patrols had let up on the Ring and I felt very weak. Sometime late in the third night I woke with a hor-rible last-ditch thirst, an unbearable burning in my mouth and my windpipe. I slid across the damp tiles to my skylight and pushed it open and felt around with my foot for the top of the column of crates. They were still where I'd piled them and I scuttled down their ricketing length onto the floor, then stood leaning against them to steady myself, waiting for the spots to clear from my eyes. After a long time my sight was no better but I decided to carry on. I groped my way to the stairwell and went down. Before pulling aside the drapes at the bottom, I listened without moving until I was close to fainting; all I heard was my own breathing, shallow and rushed, and a faraway humming noise.

The long corridor was empty. I took off my boots and walked along the carpet past the conference hall and the chancellor's rooms, past the place where the bodies of the guards had lain, to the head of the marble stairs leading down to the lobby. It was very dark on the stairs but a faint glow came in from the streetlamps. The cut-glass chandeliers flickered dimly. I sat awhile at the top of the stairs, waiting for the night watch to pass on its rounds. After a few minutes a man came out from beneath me and made a haphaz-ard circuit of the lobby. I watched him through the banister, look-ing behind me now and again and tying my bootlaces. Eventually he was gone and I hurried down the stairs. The doors that had been battered open by the gendarmes were only poorly closed and I pushed one of them open and walked out through the courtyard into the open air.

After leafing through the early-morning papers and learning to my profound relief that all conspirators, with the exception of Glass, were officially in police custody, I decided to buy a ticket for the next train to Bavaria at the main counter of the Westbahnhof like any other tourist. Before going to the station, I stopped at the house of a friend and supporter, a philology student at the university, to change into a plain brown suit I'd left there. My friend was very surprised to see me and confessed with a guilty look that he'd thrown away all the clothes I'd given him for fear of being arrested. As there was nothing else to be done, I helped myself to some clothes of his, a very handsome pair of spats and a suit of lightweight summer twill, and took twenty dog-eared marks to replace the hundred-schilling note I'd left in the pocket of my coat. He was a good boy really, of simple means, et cetera. His father was a draftsman in an engineering firm and a long-term supporter of the cause. He offered me his passport as well, but I saw no reason not to travel with my own.

I boarded the Munich Express without a care in the world, rolling cozily into Bavaria in the first-class car, chatting about football matches and stomach trouble and politics and the latest styles of hats. My companions were mostly businesspeople of one kind or another, heavy sober-eyed men very worried over the state of international affairs. Every aspect of international affairs worried them, of course, but mainly they seemed worried about the possibility of a British trade embargo, or a "commodities freeze," as a result of the Dollfuss affair. I was hard put to put on a somber face, giddy as I'd begun to feel the farther we traveled from Vienna, but I made a concerted effort—otherwise it would all have seemed just too ridiculously easy. I was asked whether as an Austrian, a neutral party, as it were, I thought an embargo might occur and I allowed that I thought it very likely. They shook their heads gravely at this and clucked at one another. A bristle-haired, mustachioed banker from the Berchtesgaden Chamber of Commerce, returning from a spa holiday with his tubercular-looking wife, asked me what it was *that had brought me into Germany.* "The assassination of the Austrian Chancellor," *I answered.*

"Of course," *he said, nodding sympathetically.* "Are you very affected?"

"I should say so, mein Herr. I am."

"Did you know the Chancellor well?" *asked the wife.*

"Tut, Berthe!" *said her husband.* "I apologize for my wife's indelicacies, Herr Bauer."

I waved this off. "Not very well, to be honest," *I said, turning to her.* "But I was present at his execution. He died like a fish." *I rolled my eyes and made gulping noises at them across the aisle.*

"Good gracious!" *said the wife. She seemed not at all taken aback. After a moment she glanced over at her husband, who was looking me over from top to bottom, his baggy-lidded eyes suddenly open very wide.* "What exactly do you mean, Herr Bauer?" *the wife whispered after a breathless little pause.*

I was still wearing my policeman's shirt under the borrowed suit and I unbuttoned the jacket without further ado and showed it to them. They were incredulous at first, of course, but by the time the train pulled into the station at Munich I had convinced them completely and won my first admirers. I was to stay as an honored guest at their town house in the old city for a period of "convalescence," *however long that might be.* "We are not only patriots of the Reich but patriots of all of Germany!" *my host declared, perilously close to tears. His wife wept freely as she escorted me down the platform, flushed with excitement at the prospect of sheltering a* "freedom fighter," *as I was newly christened.* "Just think of it, Gottfried!" *she said over and over.*

A man with a car was waiting for us outside the station and we climbed inside and rolled off down the avenue. My hostess asked with infinite gentleness if I wanted the top up or down and I answered: "Down." *The afternoon was hazy and warm. We drove at a slow, stately pace through the university, across the Isar and along the bank past one beautiful villa after another. I was overcome gradually by fatigue and happiness and a vast upsurging of relief. I fell asleep in the front passenger seat of the sedan beside the driver and woke sometime the next morning in a sun-flooded* room on a canopied bed, happier than I'd ever been since leaving Niessen. I lay in bed, staring at the intricate plaster moldings of the ceiling, thinking idly about the future.

I'd been awake for not quite an hour when a knock came on the gilt-rimmed, ebony-paneled door and a girl entered carrying a tray of Berchtner rolls and a pot of steaming chocolate. I stared at her. She crossed the room without a word and unclapped the copper legs of the tray, positioning it over my lap. Then she poured a cup of chocolate, set it down, took a few steps back and watched attentively while I ate. I talked to her a little between mouthfuls and learned that my patrons were away from the house and wouldn't return till the following evening. I was to avail myself of every conceivable comfort. I looked again at the girl, who was small and firmly built, with cropped blond hair and thick-fingered, nervous hands. "Flutter about much, do they, our hosts?" I asked her. She shrugged and stared down at her feet, which were ever so slightly pigeon-toed. I decided to devote myself to the chocolate and the rolls and to ignore her.

The girl stayed put, however, watching me. Every now and again she scuffed the floor restlessly with a heel, making a noise like the squeaking of a wooden hinge.

"Well? What is it?" I asked finally, setting down my cup.

She reddened a little. "Is it true?"

"Is what true?"

"Are you one of them?" she paused. ". . . The Legion?"

"What are you talking about, little sister?"

The girl frowned. "Reichsführer Göring's Grand Austrian Legion," she said slowly. "Are you one of them or not? I have a bet."

I looked her over a moment. She was very pretty. I had never heard of any Grand Austrian Legion and was dead certain no such group had ever existed. "Absolutely," I said, pouring myself more chocolate.

Leaving town that last time Voxlauer walked slowly, committing each relevant detail to memory in a way he hadn't thought to when first he'd left. The thick slow water of the canal, the three mortared bridges, the Bahnhofstrasse and the square, the double-steepled cathedral with the ruin just above it. The Niessener Hof, now shut down and abandoned. A few people at the far end of the square in the shadow of the fountain, talking in pleasant deep-toned voices and calling a joke up every so often to the open windows of a house a short way up the hill.

The light was just withdrawing from the rooftops as Voxlauer climbed through the tangled summer brush to the ruin for a look across the plain. The three great windows were smothered with ivy, purple and evening-colored, and the roofs of town glimmered a blunt red behind them like stones in a dried-out riverbed. Another train piled high with timber cantilevered its way northward. Voxlauer sat in the grass with his back to the crumbling wall and watched the cool lid of the sky drop forgivingly over the earth. As he had twice before, he felt a vague foreknowledge taking shape within him like a swell building at sea, silently and slowly, gathering itself into a wave. He waited for a time with his eyes tightly closed to see if it would come, but it was still far away, small and dim and unremarkable. A short while later he climbed down and walked through the ruin into the pines.

He woke the next morning on the pallet with the daylight full and bright in the little alcove. His mind was empty and content, like a wide, shallow saucer full of milk, and he lay a long time watching dust motes eddy in the window beams, easing himself slowly into wakefulness. Gradually, one at a time, the events of the past days came and settled on the surface of his awareness and dissolved in it, dispersing a still, quiet sadness that made his body feel heavy-limbed and bloodless under the sheets. An hour passed before he was able to stand and cross the damp floorboards to the cottage door and throw it open, squinting upward at the slate-blue sky. It was already very hot and the steps shone painfully in the sun. Voxlauer took off his shirt and pants and went down along the pond bank to where the water reflected the sky's color most gently, lacing it with a livid green. Then he let himself fall slackly into the shallows.

He floated face downward with his arms trailing into the green as long as he could without breathing, listening to the far-off, bellows-like sounds coming up through the water, as though the whole of the world were breathing in his ears. Slowly he began to forget. Long thin filaments of bubbles swayed here and there above the green heaving curtain below him. The water was ice cold and soon he felt himself begin to shiver. He rolled onto his back and pushed his face above the surface of the pond. The air felt oily on his skin. A vibration made itself heard, loudening very gradually, and after a time a motorcycle came into view. Its driver saw Voxlauer in the water and held up a hand. Voxlauer found his footing and stood up slowly.

—Morning, Voxlauer! Kurt said cheerily, pulling up before him on the far side of the pond. —You were quite a sight there, bobbing up and down. I'd nearly made up my mind to jump in and rescue you.

—I hope you weren't in too much of a conflict about it.

—Ha, Voxlauer! Touché. Kurt pulled off his gloves one finger at a time. —Are you busy?

—I did have some rather pressing business, said Voxlauer, looking toward his clothes in the grass.

—I'll wait in the bunker, then, out of reverence for your modesty.

Kurt gunned his engine and rolled up the bank, bringing the cycle carefully over the pilings to the cottage steps. Voxlauer walked in through the shallows to his clothes. When he came to the cottage he found Kurt sitting at the three-legged table, looking around him doubtfully. —None too cozy, Herr Gamekeeper, he said, clicking his tongue against his teeth.

—I don't spend so much time here.

—I'm sure of that. Kurt laughed. —I don't blame you, either. This place has never been anything but a filthy hole. He spat into a corner. —Well. What was good enough for the old bastard, I suppose.

—I've taken your uncle for a model in all things, Obersturmführer.

—Bashing the stuffing out of me was a step in the right direction then. Kurt stood up suddenly. —Where do you keep the whiskey?

—That what the old man drank?

—When he had it. He wasn't choosy. Kurt looked around the room again, crossing after a time to the little alcove. —Here's where he breathed his last, the sorry bugger.

—I'd heard it was in a snowbank.

Kurt shook his head. —You don't know the Jews yet, do you, Oskar, though you spend so much time around them. You accept their stories with touching goodwill and faith. Maybe that's why they find you such a useful mule. He sighed. —Come for a walk.

—Where?

—To the reliquary.

—Are we going on a pilgrimage?

—Don't be a jackass, Voxlauer. I haven't the patience for it anymore. Just come along. He glanced a final time around the room. —God, I loathe this place.

Voxlauer followed him out the door. —Are we walking? he said, seeing Kurt step past the motorcycle.

—That's right, cousin-in-law! I thought we might enact the stations of the cross.

—You go first.

Kurt let out a metallic laugh. —Surely you're not superstitious. God has long since been declared dead in Russia.

—It's not that, said Voxlauer. —I'd just rather not carry your burden for you, Obersturmführer.

Kurt laughed again. —You're being reactionary, Voxlauer. I have no Christ complexes. On the other hand, I'm nobody's mule, either. His voice dropped to a whisper. —Between us, Oskar, I'm a realist.

—Is that so? said Voxlauer, stopping short.

—It is, Kurt said proudly. —Are you surprised?

—Amazed at the coincidence, that's all. It just so happens I'm a realist, too.

Kurt looked up the road a moment. —You're a slippery fish, Voxlauer, he said admiringly. —I'll say that for you.

—I get it from the trout, Obersturmführer, Voxlauer said.

.   .   .

The slatted steps of the reliquary were bowed and needle-covered and as he followed Kurt inside Voxlauer felt again for a moment the presence of the premonition that was building under his feet. The little paper Virgin flickered in its candlelit alcove, dug back deep from the invading daylight, sequestered behind a screen of yellowed lace. In front of the alcove stood eight rows of backless wooden pews, cracked and ricketed from long neglect, and in the third of these rows Kurt sat down gingerly, stretching his legs sideways into the aisle. The wood groaned under his weight and a little eddy of yellow dust rose into the air behind him. —Come on, Voxlauer! he called. —There's plenty of room up front here, near the Blessed Mother.

Voxlauer came hesitantly down the aisle, stooping to avoid the lowest-hanging shingles. —I wouldn't say plenty, he said, squeezing into a pew.

—Yes. I do remember it as roomier, from the old days.

—Well. You were probably alone those times, said Voxlauer, composing himself painfully on the bench.

Kurt laughed and leaned across the aisle, his face pulled into a leer. —I wasn't alone those times either, cousin-in-law.

—What do you want? Tell me what you want, Kurt. Don't bat me back and forth like a half-dead bird.

—Fair enough, Voxlauer. First of all I want you to know something, Kurt said mildly, leaning back to gaze up at the rafters. —I want you to know this: I've forgiven you completely.

Voxlauer let out a little laugh. —I thought you forgave me last week.

—I'm not talking about that silliness. Kurt waved his hand impatiently, as though brushing away a fly. —For other things.

—What have I done?

—Oskar! Kurt said, wringing his hands theatrically, looking to his right and left in helpless appeal, rocking backward and forward on the bench. —*Oskar!* he shouted, raising his eyes to heaven. —Oskar! What *haven't* you done?

Voxlauer said nothing. They sat silently, looking at each other through the heat and the sun-ribboned dust.

—Did Else ever bring you here? Kurt said after a time.

—Whatever you're going to do to me, Kurt, do it.

Kurt raised his eyebrows. —*Do* to you, Voxlauer? *Do* to you? It's not so simple as that. First of all I'm going to talk to you. And you're going to listen.

—Start talking then. Start saying something.

Kurt sat back for a moment, looking at Voxlauer with something almost approaching tenderness. He sighed. —I know that you consider me a burden to your peace of mind, Voxlauer. I know that. I want you to know that you're a burden to me also.

—Don't think about me, then.

—Ha! I'd like not to, Voxlauer. I'd like that very much. But there doesn't seem to be any avoiding it lately. You keep wriggling yourself into the public eye.

—I can't help where the public eye is pointed, Obersturmführer.

Kurt got to his feet now and began pacing up and down the aisle. —Yes you can, Voxlauer. Yes you can. He stopped at Voxlauer's pew and leaned across it. —You could look to your own a little while, Voxlauer. I'd advise you to most urgently.

—My own? said Voxlauer.

—That's right. Conceive of that, if you can, for the briefest moment. Looking to your own. Not making a sideshow of your every defect of character. Not parading your Jew relations at every public assembly. Not starting fights and getting drunk and vandalizing the homes of private citizens. Looking instead to your very own hearth and family. Can you picture that at all?

Voxlauer was quiet a moment, squinting into the candlelight surrounding the little Virgin. —But I'm an orphan, he said.

Kurt was on him before he'd finished, seizing him by the collar, shoving him hard against the back of the pew and hissing into his face. Voxlauer could smell Kurt's breath, hot and bitter, and feel it against the lids of his closed eyes.

—Don't trifle with me, Oskar, Kurt hissed. —Don't trifle with me now, because you can't. Look at me. *Look* at me, you goddamned derelict. I represent the present and I represent the future. The authority I act upon will endure for a thousand years. A *thousand years*, you piss-swiller. Look around you for an instant. Look! Who do you have behind you? A flicker of a smile passed across his face. —You have my cousin. Only her. And that won't be enough, Voxlauer. I promise you it won't.

Voxlauer waited calmly until Kurt had finished. —Would you like another walk with your cousin, Obersturmführer? Is that what you want?

Kurt jerked back violently, letting go of his collar, taking a half step back across the aisle. —This is not about her, Voxlauer. We're not talking about *her*.

—If so, you should talk to your cousin about it. Not to me.

—*Listen* to me! For the first time Voxlauer noticed the butt of a small-caliber pistol jutting from Kurt's trouser pocket. —Listen to me, Voxlauer. You're losing friends quicker than a leper in a bathhouse and you barely had any to start with. *Mother-of-Christ!* Even your own uncle wants you gone and forgotten. Kurt shook his head. —We had a long talk together, he and I.

—Old Gustl, said Voxlauer.

—You see? You haven't a leg to stand on, Voxlauer. You haven't a goddamned buggered prayer.

—Oh, I'll be all right, Obersturmführer. Don't you worry about me.

Kurt stared hard at Voxlauer a few seconds, frowning very slightly, then composed himself and sat down again at his pew. —We ran into some indigents on the toll road a few weeks back, he said quietly, leaning forward to examine the pew in front of him. —Twenty-seven or so odd citizens. Dandied up as if for a Roman holiday. He broke into a wide, freckle-bordered smile. —Saw fit to mention that they knew my cousin, of all people. Talked the most frightful gibberish. We found them in a cornfield, eating straight off the blessed stalks, chanting and carrying on like a pack of blessed monkeys. I'd never seen the like. He paused a moment. —Friends of yours, possibly?

Voxlauer let out a long, low moan. —What do you want, Kurt? What? You already have the land, for the love of God. All of it. His voice rattled. —Is there no shame in you?

—Ha! said Kurt. —Best to stick to your rods and fishes, old-timer. There's nothing that I want. He ran his thumbnail up and down the pew, raising jets of orange dust. —I have plenty of shame, in point of fact. Plenty. But nothing to be ashamed of. That's my dilemma.

—Tell me what you want. I'll do it, Kurt. You only have to tell me, said Voxlauer. His voice had fallen to a whisper. —But tell me now.

Kurt was next to him again, taking his shoulder kindly. —Calm yourself, Voxlauer. We didn't formally arrest them. They're in protective custody, that's all. Some locals in Arnoldstein were less than enchanted by their share-the-wealth policy. They were half starved when we brought them in.

Voxlauer passed a hand over his face. —Why say anything to me about it, then?

—It can't go on this way, Voxlauer. Kurt gave his shoulder a little squeeze.

They sat a moment in perfect silence. —Would you harm Else in any way? Voxlauer murmured.

—Listen, Voxlauer! *Listen!* Kurt was standing over him and stumbling a little from side to side, arms flailing crazily toward the rafters as though pulled and jerked by wires. —It's *you* we're here to talk about, Voxlauer. You, not her. The State versus Oskar Voxlauer, deserter, son of the famous shotgun suicide, toady to Bolshevists, Yid-loving bastard. Hearings postponed since 1918. This is your turn on the stand, Voxlauer. Hers will come.

—I want to know about Paul Ryslavy.

—Paul Ryslavy is a Jew and a homosexual. I promise you he won't get less than he deserves.

—You haven't done anything yet, then.

Kurt waved a hand impatiently. —The charges against you, Voxlauer, are long and detailed. He rustled imaginary pages. —Suppose you began with a brief statement.

Voxlauer took a breath. —What was it you hoped to gain by bringing me up here, Kurt? Were you hoping to make me afraid? If so, then you're a goddamned fool.

—A fool? said Kurt, half smiling.

—I've been a coward my entire life. Everything I've ever done was done out of fear, and everything I've seen has taught me to be more afraid with each passing minute. The only thing that kept me safe was believing that I was dead already, and I stopped believing that four months ago. Since that time I've been scared nearly out of my mind. There's not one thing you could teach me about fear. Do you understand? Not one blessed thing. Voxlauer leaned a little to one side, struggling to catch his breath. —I'd kill you right now if I could. You are lower in my eyes than a maggot and I'd like nothing better than to see you laid out dead in front of me. But I'm afraid of you, Kurt, and so I can't. I don't have the head or the stomach for it and because of that I deserve to die. That's all; that's all you'll ever make me say. If you have any more questions for me I hope you choke to death on them.

Voxlauer sank back against the brittle wood. The light was ebbing from the chapel, gilding the pews and the dust and the slow-moving air. A sparrow flew in the door and up to the rafters. Somewhere close by sheep were bawling. Kurt had taken out his pistol.

—If you're going to shoot me with that thing, do it, Voxlauer said, getting to his feet. —I'm not sitting here any longer.

Kurt glanced up at him. —Where in hell do you think you're going?

—Straight to the villa, said Voxlauer. —Straight to your cousin's house. Straight into bed.

Kurt said nothing for a moment. —Listen to me, Voxlauer, he said as Voxlauer stepped past him, in an altogether different voice from the one he'd used before. A quiet voice, tentative, almost pleading. Voxlauer stopped. Kurt had sat down a third time. With his head bent forward and his back half turned to Voxlauer he looked like nothing so much as a farmhand struggling through his evening prayers. His flat, thick hair hung down in front, shadowing his face. —War is coming, Voxlauer, he said, almost in a whisper.

—War? said Voxlauer. He felt again at that moment the presence of a vague fear, curling forward on the periphery of thought, building itself into a certainty. It was coming on even as Kurt sat watching him, bringing itself silently and inevitably to life. —War? said Voxlauer, trying to bring his attention back to the dust-filled room.

Kurt looked at him almost sheepishly, the smile gone altogether from his face. He nodded. —War is coming, Voxlauer, he said again. —Bad things happen under cover of war. Terrible things. To good men, worse men, and even, sometimes, to better women. He laughed at this, letting his shoulders slump forward. He laughed without breaking into a smile, the laugh defeated and hollow, more a clarion of blank despair than of victory or malice or even pride. —Terrible things, Voxlauer, he repeated. —And I'm not going to raise a finger to stop any of them.

Then suddenly Voxlauer knew what would happen.

That afternoon I set out to find Brigadenführer Mittling, our liaison to Himmler and poor dead Spengler's second cousin. I'd read in that morning's paper about the Führer's disavowal of our putsch, his claim to the English and Italian press that our actions had in no way been directed or encouraged by the Reich, and I needed to talk to someone about it right away. It's possible that he truly didn't know about us—we'd only had Himmler's assurances, with Mittling as middleman, that the operation had his approval and blessing. To this day I'm none the wiser. But I've certainly never faulted the Führer for saying what he had to say to keep the foreign observers mollified, to keep France, in particular, from starting another war before we were sufficiently rearmed. I've certainly never faulted him, but on that particular day I needed to talk to somebody about it quickly.

It was pointless to talk to the girl, or the other servants in the house, or the banker and his wife, either, should they eventually reappear. I had to go to Mittling. The problem with going to Mittling was that I'd never seen him or spoken to him directly. I didn't even know his Christian name. Glass guarded each communiqué from Munich jealously and burned each day's total in the lavatory sink before retiring. Not even Spengler had been allowed free contact with his cousin, though that may, in fact, have been Mittling's own preference; there was little love lost between them.

Once every morning in the month before the putsch the phone would ring, Glass would answer it, and the rest of us would file quietly out into the hall. There was a second receiver in a filing room a few doors down and when the door was unlocked I'd sometimes slip in and pick it up. Mostly they talked about money and Himmler, how there was never enough of the one and always too much of the other. They made bland, forgettable jokes about one or another of the boys, most often Spengler, and in general talked as little business as possible. Mittling was a Sudeten German and spoke with a cloying, timorous accent, as though his mouth was full of marzipan. It had been his idea that we dress as policemen. "One Black Shirt's as good as another," he'd said, tittering.

"Ha!" Glass had answered. "Very good, Brigadenführer."

I left my hosts' house in the afternoon and walked across the wide stone bridge to the center of town. Dust rose thickly from the cobbles; countless sedans and wagons rattled by. Everyone seemed almost laughably industrious and carefree. Excitement was everywhere in the air—a new, fierce optimism. This was the Germany I'd imagined for myself from the earliest days of the movement, clear-eyed, secure in its future and hard at work, and I felt at home in it. I'd never before been to another country; there seemed to be many more bicycles in Bavaria, and more convertibles.

As I passed into the Altstadt, throngs of housewives bustled past on the narrow walks, humming to themselves benevolently. The light on all the streets was warm and gilded. My heart fluttered in my chest and I realized for the first time that I'd escaped something horrible and entered into something fine. I broke into an idiotic, unembarrassed grin, laughing and bowing to people as I passed. I had only to look at the posters and handbills everywhere around me, on the streetlamps and sides of houses, to know that I was free. Even the thought of Niessen and all I'd lost seemed dim and insignificant to me then.

The offices of the SS were in a peach-colored building off the Königsplatz, a short stroll from the center of town, and I found it without much trouble. I was nervous, oddly enough, coming to the gate, and I stood awhile looking up at the yellow roof and marveling at its cheeriness. After a time, a guard came out of the gatehouse and asked me in an unconcerned tone of voice what I was looking at.

"Your building," I answered. "It's wonderfully put together."

"Oh," said the guard. "Student of architecture, are you?"

"Not exactly. I'm an Obersturmführer of Reichsführer Göring's Grand Austrian Legion." I clicked my heels as best I could in the low-cut spats I'd taken from the banker's shoe closet. "I'm here for Brigadenführer Mittling."

The guard straightened immediately and stared at me. "You'd best come right inside then, Obersturmführer."

He took me through the gate, into the building through chipped fluted double doors, and up a broad unpainted staircase to a second pair of doors with a newly painted swastika-and-eagle-recumbent on each wing. He rapped once, waited, then rapped again and stepped back at attention. I fell in beside him, conscious suddenly of my rumpled suit.

A small bespectacled man stuck his head out. "Well, Peter? Who is this citizen?" I recognized the marzipan voice immediately.

"An Austrian, Brigadenführer. An Obersturmführer from the 'Göring Legion,' whatever in God's name that is."

"Is that so?" said the man with a faint flicker of interest. He looked me over more carefully. "Are those policeman's castaways you have on under your jacket, Obersturmführer?"

"They are, Herr Mittling. Standartenführer Glass sends his regards."

"Does he," said Mittling, not smiling anymore.

I said nothing, unsure of myself suddenly. I'd thought for some reason that Glass's name would be a welcome one in Munich in spite of the fiasco, that as oily as he was he'd naturally not be held accountable for any of it. But Glass was clearly in disfavor. I supposed I must be, now, as well. I cursed my luck.

"Come along inside," said Mittling, heaving a little sigh. He looked like nothing so much as an underpaid, exhausted file clerk, waddling ahead of me with his self-pitying air. In spite of my new-found worries, I found myself grinning as I followed him down a narrow unlit corridor to a cramped, cluttered suite of thick-walled office rooms subdivided into alcoves, coated uniformly with plaster flakes and dust. "We've only just moved in," said Mittling out of the corner of his mouth, motioning me toward a chair. "Charm-

ing, isn't it?" he said, gesturing to a small leaded-glass window giving onto a tree-lined courtyard.

"It's very charming in general, here in the Reich."

"We like to think so," Mittling said blandly. He sat down at his desk and began rifling through a drawer. "Now then: who did you say you were? Forstner? Galicek? Bauer?"

"Bauer, Brigadenführer."

"Do you smoke, Bauer?"

"I do, Brigadenführer."

"That's a nasty habit," he said, his face creasing slightly. I'd forgotten his particularly joyless sense of comedy.

"Yes. I suppose it is, Brigadenführer."

"Well." He paused. "Suppose you tell me how you managed it, then. I'm very curious."

"Managed it, Brigadenführer?"

"Yes, Bauer: managed it. Made it from the chancellery in Vienna all the way to my office without getting hanged, shot or, as far as I can tell from the admittedly brief span of our acquaintance, made in any way untidy. How you managed it."

I said nothing, thinking how to represent my part in the whole blessed farce. Mittling leaned forward, puckering his mouth.

"Unclench yourself, for Christ's sake, Bauer. Herr Glass taught you wonderfully bad strategy, I'm afraid, and even worse manners." He sighed again, gently, and offered me a cigarette from a brown Bakelite case. "Indulge me, Bauer. You're among friends. Let's have the unabridged version."

I said nothing for a moment. Then, to my great surprise, I gave it to him, more or less in its entirety. I made no attempt to condense events or cast Spengler or anyone else in any particular light. Suspicious as he was of unadorned truth, Mittling was sharp enough to sense a lie three times out of four, and besides I felt for some reason at that particular moment like giving him exactly what he wanted. It took me less than an hour to tell it all. When I'd finished, Mittling fished out a cigarette for himself and lit it. "That's quite an epic," he said, exhaling. He looked at me expressionlessly for a time. "Some would call what you did desertion, Bauer. Most would."

I returned his look as calmly as I could. "What's to become of Spengler and the other boys?"

"What's to become of them? They're already dead by hanging, boy. This very morning, coincidentally, at six o'clock. With all attendant pomp and ceremony." His eyes twinkled briefly. "A far better question, I'd say, is what's to become of you, Kurt Bauer. Don't you agree?"

We sat in silence again for perhaps half a minute. Mittling drummed on the desktop with his fingertips.

"Let them call it desertion then, if they like," I said.

Mittling smiled at this. "That's right. Let them call it desertion, Bauer," he said quietly . "If they like." He took a telephone from another drawer of his desk and leaned over to plug it into a socket. "Would you mind stepping into the hall for a moment, Obersturmführer?"

"Not at all, Brigadenführer." I stepped into the corridor and shut the door behind me. I stood just outside, feeling light-headed, listening to the indecipherable buzz of Mittling's voice and the sound of typing echoing from some other room, trying to form a theory as to what might happen to me. I was nervous at first, leaning uncomfortably against the wall, but my nervousness soon passed. I hadn't yet had a chance to ask Mittling about the Führer's disavowal and I had a premonition that chance might never come, but that didn't matter any longer. When the door opened and Mittling waved me in I knew that chapter was a dead one for me now, my questions about it irrelevant, even morbid. A new chapter was beginning.

Mittling stood at the window, looking into the courtyard. "We're in a bit of a predicament over you, Bauer, as I'm sure you can well imagine. You're not a fool, clearly enough, whatever else you may be." He dug a finger into his nose, held it there a moment, then drew it out, examining it absently. "The Führer has denied any complicity in the Dollfuss business, and therefore any connection to you."

"I know that, Brigadenführer."

Mittling appraised me coldly. "Do you? All the better." He paused a long while, staring at a package of unopened stationery to the left of his folded hands. "We're sending you to Berlin tonight on the nine-o'clock express."

I swallowed hard to keep back my surprise. "I have no clothes but these, Brigadenführer—"

"They'll do," said Mittling, busy at his desk.

"Is there no uniform or clean shirt for me here?" I swallowed again.

Mittling arched his eyebrows. "You're not going there to meet the Führer, Bauer, if that's what you're dirtying your pants over."

Coming down from the reliquary in the failing light Voxlauer saw them, lolling at the edge of the spruce plantation in the high unbending grass, looking for all the world like a sketch from an album of country reminiscences. That they'd been lying in wait for him for some time he had no doubt. They were sprawled in the grass, caps tipped forward over their eyes, passing a wineskin back and forth between them. Voxlauer bowed to them as he went by. The younger brother took the skin and looking at Voxlauer took a long, calculated draft, letting the wine spray noisily against the back of his throat. The older one wasn't looking at him at all but gazing instead back up the valley, scratching his bare and sunburnt belly in deliberate, lazy circles, as if hoping somehow to provoke him. Their rifles lay beside them in the grass. Voxlauer passed within a meter of where they lay and looked them both full in the face but they seemed suddenly not to see him. A few moments later he'd left them behind him to wait in the even, indifferent dark.

—Something's going to happen, said Voxlauer, stepping into the kitchen.

Else looked up from the table. —Has Kurt been up to see you?

—Just now. Was he here, too?

She nodded. Her eyes were small and red. —I'm frightened now, Oskar. I can't not notice any longer.

—Something's happened to Pauli. Or is about to.

—Who's Pauli? said Resi, coming up from the bedroom.

—No one, mouse. Go to sleep.

—He *is* someone, said Voxlauer sharply.

—Hello, Oskar, said Resi, letting out a yawn. She stood between them sleepily, leaning against the counter. —Can I sit?

—I know he's somebody, Oskar. Christ in heaven, remember who you're talking to. Go on back to bed, Resi, Else said, half turning toward the counter. —Go on. She turned back to Voxlauer, taking his hand and squeezing it. —I want to leave. I want to leave tomorrow.

—A few more days, Else. A little while longer. Let me find out about Pauli.

—Who's Pauli? said Resi again, looking back at them hopefully from the top of the stairs.

Else spun angrily in her chair. —You go to sleep this instant! This instant, Fräulein! *Go!*

Resi went. They sat silently at the table. Resi was humming to herself as she dressed for bed and the sound of her humming carried faintly up to them. —I had a terrrible talk with Kurti today, Else said.

—He brought Resi?

She nodded. —He talked about you as though you were dead, she said, running her hands along the edge of the table.

Voxlauer was quiet for a time. —Where would we go?

—I don't know. She smiled weakly. —Tyrol?

—Tyrol would be all right. Except for the Tyroleans.

—Where, then?

Voxlauer shrugged. —Not Italy. Not east, either, if we can help it.

—It doesn't matter, really, does it? said Else.

—No. I suppose it doesn't.

One half hour later they went down the steps and crossed on tiptoe to the bed. Resi was curled on the parlor couch, whistling tunelessly. Voxlauer leaned over tiredly and unlaced his boots. Else ran her fingertips along his scalp, over his forehead and his eyes.

—Thank you, he said in a whisper.

Else gave him a light kiss on the neck. He drew in a long and grateful breath. Opening his eyes he saw Resi watching from the couch.

—Aren't you a peach? he said, smiling at her crookedly.

—Leave us alone for a little while, mouse.

—What for? said Resi, giggling.

—Evil spoilt child, said Voxlauer.

—Suffer the little children, Oskar, said Else. —Suffer them. The Good Book tells us to.

—Damn the Good Book, said Voxlauer, falling back onto the bed.

Resi's eyes widened. —Mama!

—Shh, mouse, said Else. —Don't bother us just now. The springs chirped sweetly as she lay down next to him. He felt the shifting of the mattress as she turned onto her side and the unbelievable fineness of her hair against his face and neck. —Good night, Voxlauer, she breathed into his ear.

In Berlin I found myself quite the celebrity for a time. Mittling had friends very high up in the brass and they took to me at once. I was put on display that very week at all the most exclusive cocktail parties.

"The Bolshevists have their pet subversive movements, of course, in every nest," one bird-faced general with hair the color of dirty wool said to me, waving his sherry glass in my face like a baton. "Spain, Italy, the Argentine. Now, by God, we have ours!" He held on to my arm tightly, teetering a little.

"I'm sure you're right, General."

"That Dollfuss affair was regrettable. But you'll have your time yet, son. Your golden moment. What do you say?"

"I hope to, General. Watch yourself."

"Thank you, my boy. Very kind. Blood of Christ! If we had fifty more like you . . ."

It was the same everywhere I went, particularly with the drunks. Himmler never came to these parties but I received a brief note from him through Schellenberg, the Brigadenführer for foreign intelligence, instructing me to work closely with both of them in preparation for "the intersection of public policy with what is dearest on the international front to all our hearts." The only work I seemed to be doing, however, was to go to six or seven endlessly dull cocktail parties every evening.

The purported need for secrecy in smuggling me from one salon to the next worked on everyone like an aphrodisiac. I was moved about the city like a theater prop those first few weeks, gawking at everything from the wings. Here at last was a great city, a German city, fully ecstatic over the Cause. People addressed me by my full title of Obersturmführer, Austria SS, although it was now of course meaningless, and flattered me in a thousand other ways. There was some talk from Schellenberg and certain others of actually forming an Austrian Legion, unifying the various bands of illegals that had fled across the border in the weeks following the putsch, but I quickly realized that greener fields lay elsewhere. Already it was too crowded in the middle brass, too many ambitious young officers and not enough room for them in the Reich bureaucracy. Expansion was inevitable. When the annexation happened it was clear enough it would be Reichs-Germans, not Austrians, filling the posts. Positions would be open to Reichs-Germans and to Reichs-Germans only. So, with help, I became one.

An old Junker heiress took me into her house in the first glow of my celebrity and outfitted me in the clothes of her late husband, whom she fancied me to resemble. Maria von Lohn was a well-preserved sixty-five; I slept with her only once, after which she sent me away in a fit of melodrama and self-reproach. I took up with her daughter-in-law, Lotte, and occasionally with Liesl the chambermaid, who came from the Rhineland and was obliging and very generously put together. I stayed in the von Lohn house three years. The arrangement had something of the bedroom farce about it that kept me, by and large, in very high spirits. I'm not sure where else I could have gone after the novelty of my story faded, and it faded quickly enough.

Lotte, the daughter-in-law, was married to Gustav, a high-ranking general in the Waffen-SS who was often away from Berlin.

It was through him, or through her, to be more accurate, that I became a citizen of the Reich. Through the indulgence of certain fortunately placed friends of the family, a plea for asylum was made on my behalf. My dearest hope, it was explained, was to become a German. This, of course, was absolutely true.

"Like our Führer," Lotte would say, wrinkling her nose at me. "A fugitive from your Austrianhood!" Lotte was not a great patriot. "I'm sure he had a woman behind him, too, the sly bastard."

"He only has his secretary, darling. Fräulein Braun."

"Pah, Kurtchen! Secretary. Pah!" She made an obscene gesture with her hand and let out a giggle.

"Please, Lotte."

Lotte sat up at once, frowning. She'd been lolling at the edge of the bed, watching me dress in front of her heavy pier glass. "Look at yourself, Herr Bauer! Another tight-lipped citizen of the Reich. I liked you better when you were from the territories." She laughed to herself in that high, sparrow-like way she had. I can still hear it, dry and chittering and unhappy, girlish and middle-aged at once. A drinker's laugh. When I try to remember her face now it escapes me, fittingly enough. But that laugh I remember very well.

"I have a meeting with the Reichsführer-SS today, not that you'd care," I said, straightening my tie.

"Little Heinrich Himmler, of the pince-nez?"

"That's the one."

"He'll have need of you to 'off' someone or other," said Lotte, falling back onto the bed. "That's what murderers say in America. It's from a picture, not that you'd care. Edward G. Robinson."

"You and your America," I said, still looking myself over in the glass.

"You're being exceptionally peacock-like today, Kurtchen," said Lotte, twisting her mouth disapprovingly.

I smiled patiently at her reflection. "I've waited for this for an eternity, darling. You know I have."

"You look silly in Papa's clothes."

"Mama doesn't think so."

"Mama is a senile old cow."

I looked at her again and saw that she was glaring at me. I turned around. "I'm not going to 'off' anybody," I said. "Honestly, Lottchen."

"Promise?"

I raised my right hand in solemn oath. Lotte cursed me and slid back under the covers. She always looked much younger than she was, I remember, in spite of the fact that she was near to permanently hungover. She had freckles across her cheeks like a girl of seventeen; in fact she was nearer to forty. "Get out of here, peacock!" she clucked at me, already beginning to smile. I bowed and took my hat up from the floor.

The Schutzstaffel High Command was housed during that time in an unobtrusive gray building down the avenue from the newly built Air Palace. The boys at the gate knew me well by then and waved me through without ceremony. *They think I've come here to see old Schellenberg,* I thought, and the idea filled me with a deep and secret happiness. One of the clerks at the lobby desk, a nephew of Lotte's who passed the time dropping a bewildering variety of innuendos about my connection to the von Lohns, smiled at me as I passed, and I was sorely tempted to inquire as to the location of the Reichsführer's new suite of offices, but of course I knew exactly where they were. Passing the desk and turning without hesitation to the left-hand of the two stairwells, I had the satisfaction of feeling everyone's eyes on me, widening, or so I imagined, with growing astonishment as I stated my business to the sentry at the top of the stairs and was wordlessly allowed to pass. The doors closed on all of them a moment later.

The hallway was immaculate, its concrete and tile floor polished to mirror-brightness, so I was very much surprised, at the end of it, to find the Reichsführer's front office in even worse disarray than Mittling's had been. Papers and photographs of all sizes spilled from dog-eared, water-speckled folders and littered the floor between chairs set at strange and irrational angles to the walls. I watched a clerk sift through a massive pile of manila envelopes at the foot of a three-legged table for the space of almost a minute *before recovering the presence of mind to clear my throat. The clerk looked up at me blankly, muttered a grudging pleasantry and reached up to the intercom button set into the wall above his desk. A very long time later the black-and-white-checked door of the inner office opened slightly, seemingly of its own accord, and the clerk waved me on. I cautiously pushed the door open.*

Himmler's office, in turn, proved very much like the hallway: a high-ceilinged rectangular room furnished only with three straight-backed farmer's chairs and a narrow steel-topped desk, from which two high, square windows looked out onto the street. The uniform of a captain of the Waffen-SS hung from a coatrack. The Reichs-führer himself was nowhere to be seen. I stood stiffly in front of the desk, in anticipation of his appearance, but after a number of minutes drifted over to the windows and finally to the uniform. I was holding one of the boots to my foot when Himmler entered, so quietly I gave a little cry of surprise when he spoke my name.

"Obersturmführer Kurt E. Bauer," said Himmler, peering at me nearsightedly. "The last of our unsung freedom fighters. That is how you see yourself, am I correct? The hope of our as-yet-fettered south?" He drew his lips together not unkindly. The expression on his face, one of myopic, schoolteacherly attentiveness, was deeply unnerving. His eyes were so tiny behind their bottle-glass lenses that you could never make out precisely where they were pointed. Innocuous, colorless, well-intentioned eyes. I shook my head.

"Not at all, Reichsführer. I'm sure the south has long forgotten me."

"Well. Let's hope so." Himmler smiled. "Please be seated now, Herr Bauer. Please. That's better." He paused. "We hear good things about you, in circles. You've made yourself some very devoted friends. Vocal friends."

"I try to be worthy of them, Reichsführer."

"Yes," he said, less benevolently. "I'm sure of that." He sat a moment lost in thought, his breath whistling through his nose. "You're a citizen of the Reich now, I understand."

"Yes, Reichsführer."

"Please, Herr Bauer. This is a casual visit. Herr Himmler will do between us for the moment."

"Yes, of course," I said, biting back my disappointment. "Of course, Herr Himmler."

Himmler smiled. "You did good work, Bauer, in your brigade. What's more, you lived to tell about it."

"I've lived to tell no-one about it, Herr Himmler."

He smiled again, settling back in his chair. "Yes. We know that very well."

Both of us were silent. Himmler seemed to look down at his desktop, on which lay an assortment of passport-sized photographs, and at the next moment past me toward the uniform.

"It's a shame to see you in a common suit, Bauer," he said finally. "What's more, yours doesn't fit very well."

I shifted uneasily in my chair. "I know it doesn't, Reichsführer."

"We'd like to see you in a uniform again."

I said nothing, struggling to hold in my excitement. Himmler was squinting at me patiently, apparently expecting some sort of a response, running a slender upturned finger along his clipped blond mustache. I thought of the state portrait we'd had of him in Vienna, above Glass's cherished couch. What an inaccurate picture! I thought. He isn't at all an ugly man.

Himmler was still watching me. After a few moments more, his expression changed; he seemed to have decided something to his satisfaction. "We have a man in protective custody at present," he said, sitting forward. "A former Party man. Former Schutzstaffel. We'd all of us appreciate it deeply if you would visit with him, in your civilian capacity only"—here Himmler smiled faintly—"and try to talk some sense into him. He's become violent recently, and given us no end of worry. The two of you, believe it or not, have had certain shared experiences." He paused a moment. "Lately our man has been plagued by suicidal thoughts. I don't mind telling you, Bauer, we're at our wit's end. Our little fraternity has always had a difficult time smoothing over these crises of confidence among its own, as I'm sure you're abundantly aware . . ."

I nodded.

"I've often found," he continued, "that a no-nonsense conference of some kind, conducted, of course, in absolute and total privacy, is the one hope for betterment in such cases." He paused a moment, patting down his mustache. "What's your opinion, Bauer, as a private citizen?"

"I quite agree, Reichsführer. Private solutions are always best."

"Not always, Bauer. Not always. Sometimes the more public the solution the better." He frowned very slightly. "But not in this case."

"This man . . . he's an Austrian?"

Himmler nodded with an air of deep regret. We regarded one another for the briefest possible interval in silence. His squint was more severe than usual, his eyes almost completely hidden, and I had the distinct impression he'd lost sight of me altogether. Sensing that our appointment was at an end, I rose.

"Thank you for your time, Reichsführer. I'll report back with the result of the conference."

Himmler waved a hand. "Quite unnecessary, Obersturmführer. Quite unnecessary." He smiled one last time, then took up a glossy brown folder and began leafing through it. "Weidemann, just outside, will explain things to you further. Heil Hitler."

"Heil Hitler." I pulled the door closed as quietly as possible behind me.

The next time I saw Himmler he was riding down the Ring in an open sedan at the Führer's side, waving to the adoring crowd, smiling myopically out at them and nodding his small pale unassuming head, blinking uncomfortably in the noonday light. I was three cars ahead of him, looking back along the bright black motorcade with a mixture of exultation and remorse and pride, sensing on all sides of me the noises and the colors and the smells of the city I'd always known I would return to and claim.

Two days later Ryslavy's sedan rumbled up the drive. It was loaded high with parcels and crates and dust rose in the noontime sun where its back axle scudded against the gravel. Voxlauer was in the garden. By the time he came round the side of the house Else was already at the door.

Ryslavy tapped the horn once, stepped out of the car and saluted. —Sturmführer Apfelschnapps reporting for assignment!

Else laughed. —We've been worried about you, Herr Ryslavy.

—What's the meaning of all this? said Voxlauer, pointing at the crates and boxes.

Ryslavy shrugged. —Call it tax evasion.

—That's not what I call it.

Else came partway down the steps. —Come inside, both of you. I'll make a pot of coffee.

—That's not necessary, Fräulein, thank you, said Ryslavy. He paused. —I thought Oskar might like to come up to the ponds.

—We'll have the coffee afterward. On our way down, said Voxlauer.

—Oh, said Else, more quietly. She went back inside.

—Is she offended? Ryslavy whispered.

—Not half as much as I am, said Voxlauer. —Get in the car.

Going back around the hood Ryslavy took out a steel hoop of keys and began sorting through them. The overloaded rear of the sedan was covered in a creased canvas tarpaulin tied down with looped-together leather belts. It bulged and billowed frighteningly.

—Like a circus tent, said Voxlauer, tugging doubtfully on the canvas.

—What's that?

—Are you figuring to join the circus, Pauli?

Ryslavy didn't seem to hear. He was flushed and his hands moved restlessly along the door of the sedan. —I thought I'd have a look at them one last time, he said cheerily. —Not enough time to fish, of course. But I'd like to have a look at them just the same, the little ingrates. His eyes as he fumbled with the door handle seemed vague and unfocused.

—Are you in any state, Pauli? said Voxlauer, his hand on the half-opened passenger door. —I hope you are aware I am entrusting you with my life.

—Cold sober, Oskar, Ryslavy said, bringing a finger slowly up to the tip of his nose. Voxlauer climbed into the car and slid over to unlock the other door.

—Voilà! Ryslavy said triumphantly as the door opened, holding a small copper-colored key aloft. —Now we're off, boy. Now we're rolling.

The engine bucked to life and the sedan lurched violently forward with a noise like the firing of artillery, nearly shearing off the end post of the garden fence before coming to rest at a steepening of the lawn. Ryslavy cursed and spun the sedan around and suddenly they were rolling down the dappled drive, gathering speed, Ryslavy rocking back and forth impatiently behind the wheel. In another moment they were out onto the road and catapulting up the valley, tires stuttering furiously over the slanting ruts. —Not so fast, Pauli, for Jesus' sake! Voxlauer shouted.

—What's that? said Ryslavy.

—Mother of Christ, Pauli!

Ryslavy grinned. —Hold tight, Oskar. Here comes a tricky piece, if I remember. The car lurched left and shuddered into a sliding curve. —Mind those boxes, Ryslavy yelled. He shifted down with all his weight and leaned fiercely into the wheel.

—Dear precious Christ! Voxlauer gasped over and over, half covering his eyes. The curve seemed to ribbon ahead of them into infinity. He clutched wildly at the seat back and at the handle of the door, an identical ribbon of nausea uncoiling in his bowels. But then they were out of it suddenly, out of the pines and rolling gently along the pond bank, the blur of white along the right side coming smoothly into focus and resolving itself into a line of birches. Ryslavy killed the motor and they floated effortlessly alongside the flat, green water.

—Yes, that was fast, said Ryslavy, beaming.

Voxlauer said nothing, filling his lungs with air.

—Don't be angry with me, Oskar. Indulge me my little excesses.

—Stop the car, said Voxlauer, thowing his door open and leaning out over the road. Ryslavy slowed the car and he jumped onto the sunlit grass, stumbling a little.

—Hold on! Ryslavy shouted. —Hold on a minute! He leaned down and pulled the hand brake and scrambled out of the car. Voxlauer was walking away from him up the road.

—Oskar! Stop! I want you to come with me! *Oskar!*

Voxlauer stopped walking. —To hell with you, Pauli. I'm not getting back into that death barge.

—You can't stay here. Ryslavy looked meaningfully about him at the water and the trees. —None of this is mine anymore.

—Yes, that's right, Pauli. You've given it to them.

—*Sold* it to them, Oskar. *Sold* it to them. For a nice fat cube of butter, too, I don't mind telling you.

—Don't lie to me, Pauli. They robbed you blind.

Ryslavy didn't answer. —Has anybody been up yet? he said finally, looking over at the cottage.

Voxlauer shrugged. —A few logging trucks.

—Have you talked to anybody?

Voxlauer nodded.

—Who?

—A fairly high-ranking officer of the police, said Voxlauer. —He's promised me a thorough investigation.

Ryslavy shook his head. —Why you had to pick that girl, out of all of the attractive and well-cultivated women of this valley, I'll never know. He smiled sourly. —She hasn't brought us very much luck, you must admit.

Voxlauer looked at him. —You're not honestly going to put any of this on her head, are you?

—No, no. Of course not. Ignore me.

—I'd better, while I still have the chance, said Voxlauer. He was quiet a moment, looking at the car. —The truth is, I'm not so sure you'll make it.

Ryslavy nodded and looked back at the car almost penitently. —Still. You'll let me go, won't you?

—Yes, said Voxlauer. —It looks as though I will.

—You won't come? That's your final word?

—Tell the truth for once, Pauli. You don't want us both along. Three of us, with Else's girl.

—Of course I do, said Ryslavy, looking flustered.

They stood a moment looking at each other.

—What's to become of you? said Voxlauer.

—We have family in Budapest. We have family in Nuremberg. I

was thinking Budapest, maybe, said Ryslavy. He cleared his throat. —By the by: I've been forbidden to leave town. Ever heard anything so jackassed?

—Parting is such sweet sorrow for them. They're probably missing you already.

—They want me to throw pies at, I think, on holidays. That's the only way I can explain it.

—I'll never understand these monkeys, said Voxlauer, sighing.

They were quiet again for a while. —I'd guessed you'd be headed down to Italy, said Voxlauer, squinting into the water.

—Italy? That's comic, Oskar. They've already had purges in Milan.

Voxlauer laughed. —You're thinking of the Communists, Pauli. Communists have purges. Fascists have rallies.

—Fascists have purges, I'm sure, when the fancy takes them, said Ryslavy. —What's the blessed difference?

—Communists have purges, said Voxlauer. —That's the difference.

They began walking slowly back to the car. —Where's your daughter now?

—At the mother-in-law's.

—You'd best be getting on, then.

Ryslavy nodded. —I'll drop you at the villa.

—You go on, said Voxlauer. —I said I wasn't getting back into that sarcophagus.

—Get into the blessed car. Don't insult me.

—Begone from my sight! said Voxlauer, waving his arms.

They stood by the hood of the sedan, looking at each other in embarrassment. —You're fired, said Ryslavy finally, opening the driver's-side door and putting a boot up on the fender.

—Good-bye, Pauli.

—Good-bye, Ryslavy said, getting in.

—Kurt is coming up today, Voxlauer said quickly, looking Ryslavy in the eye. —On his motorcycle.

—Up this road?

Voxlauer nodded.

Ryslavy said nothing for a moment. —When?

—Soon. About this time, Voxlauer said. —He'll be alone, he added after a little pause.

Ryslavy was staring at him from inside the car with the door still open, understanding what he was saying fully and absolutely but looking at him in confusion just the same. Another moment went by. —Well. Good-bye, Oskar, Ryslavy said again, very quietly, reaching out to close the door of the sedan.

—Yes, said Voxlauer, stepping back.

Ryslavy pulled the door closed and waved once through the dust-caked window. He started the engine and sounded the horn and drove up to the pilings and turned back down the valley road. He let the car gradually gain momentum, waving again as he passed, and rolled down the sun-flecked road into the trees.

—Careful in the curves, Voxlauer called after him.

The sedan took me on unfamiliar roads through the suburbs of the city, past the new Alfred Rosenberg Housing Authority on the south bank of the river, past the site of the Air Rally Stadium, out through the fir-covered hills of Oberwiessen, low and crumpled together, to the ruins of the old Weimar Gasworks. I'd been given a pocket-sized .20 caliber handgun—a society lady's pistol, really— a slim box of cartridges, a roll of gagging tape and a flashlight, all in a plain yellow box. The box was too big for its contents and they rattled and slid about more and more noisily as we turned onto ever-smaller roads. The rattling might have bothered me at another time but now it seemed insignificant and far away. I was about to do something I had never done before.

The gasworks were arranged in a loose half-circle in the middle of the woods. At a green sliding door in the side of the nearest building the car skidded to a halt and I stepped out into the twilight, looking around me calmly. The drive from the center of town had been a short one, but I'd had more than enough time to compose myself. "Is this it? This one?" I asked the driver. He nodded without turning to look.

The door was padlocked and I walked around the building to a decrepit slate-roofed cottage just behind the gasworks. It was stained a uniform brown from decades of smoke and soot, and the windows were almost completely blacked over, but I saw a dim light coming from one of the ground-floor rooms. I went to the door and turned the handle and found it unlocked. A naked light-bulb was burning in the filthy soot-covered stairwell, illuminating great continent-shaped water stains on the wallpaper. I stood at the foot of the staircase a moment, listening. Then I walked to the end of the shabby little hall and stepped into a tiny unlit room in which a man was sitting tied to a chair by the neck, hands and ankles with loops of bailing wire. It was hazy in the room, and dark, but I recognized him just the same. It was Glass.

Voxlauer walked down through the dwindling light patterns, kicking up the ever-present red clay dust under his heels. Blackflies glittered on the road and climbed to the scent of him and buzzed and worried around his ears. He could hear the steady noise of water to his right and the rustling of the heavy boughs on every side. Past the colony junction he began to hum a half-remembered air, a song his father had favored in the evenings. He heard again for a moment the bright accompaniment of the piano and saw his mother in the doorway, playful and at ease, announcing supper. The color of the scene was sepia and gold and reminded him of the photographs he'd sorted through that first day back, ages ago already, in the old house. He imagined Maman herself now as a sort of photograph, lucent and serene, composed and unchanging for all time. The questions that had harried him for the past hour, of what might happen that day and the next, receded under this image like fever chills beneath a quilt. As he walked into Pergau he felt calm and resolved.

When he arrived at the villa Else was sitting on the steps with a broom across her lap, the folds of her housedress hanging over the gravel. It was an old dress, worn through in patches and coal-colored. —You can't come up yet, she said tiredly. —I've put this entire shack under quarantine.

—That explains the black dress, said Voxlauer. —Or has somebody passed on?

—Very comic. It was blue before I started sweeping, if that says anything to you. A heap of gray dust lined the entranceway behind her.

Voxlauer came to the steps and put a hand to her forehead. Her hair was damp. —Should we go for a walk, till the air clears a little? he said.

—Where's Pauli?

—He's gone.

Else sighed and stood up slowly and fetched a dustpan from the kitchen. She swept the dust into it and carried it around the corner of the house. Then she undid her housedress and stepped out of it and wiped her face and neck a few times and shook her head. —God knows what I'm cleaning for anyway, if we're leaving tomorrow. Maybe I don't quite believe it yet.

—I don't either.

—Hard to imagine, isn't it? She took his hand and led him back down the drive. —I sent Resi down an hour ago. On a bus.

—A bus? What bus? said Voxlauer, raising his eyebrows.

—The new Reichs-bus, Oskar. Pergau–Niessen–St. Marein. They've only just started it.

—May it run for a thousand years.

—May it run for the next few days before dropping into a ditch, and I'll be satisfied. She took his arm.

They walked on through the little town, past the churchyard and square, lifeless-looking as always, to the down-valley road. —Where are we going? Voxlauer asked when they'd come to the last of the outlying fields. —Up to the ridge?

—Let's keep on this way, said Else.

—I'd rather go to the ridge, said Voxlauer, slowing.

—We haven't walked this way in ages. Come along, Herr Gamekeeper!

They continued down as the road narrowed to little better than a mule track, steep-ditched and slashed with gullies, snaking sharply through the trees. Voxlauer began to feel the first stir-

rings of fear. —So he's gone, then, said Else, looking back at him.
—Pauli, I mean.

—He is. Yes.

—And he still holds me to blame for it all, does he? She smiled.
—I suppose there's no point in asking why.

—He doesn't hold you to any blame, Else.

—It's a strange way to leave if he doesn't. He barely tipped
his hat.

—He offered to take us with him.

—Should we have gone?

Voxlauer nodded. —Yes. We should have.

—But you didn't want to, either.

Voxlauer was quiet a moment. —I suppose I didn't.

—We'll be all right, said Else. —Don't you think so? I think we
will.

They walked farther to a washed-out curve with a view over
the trees and lingered there for a time, looking up at the cliffs. The
colony meadow shone in a ray of sun and above it a round, shadowed opening hung starkly in the light, black and partially veiled
by pine scrub.

—See the cave? said Else. She pointed. —There, just under the
rocks?

—I'd heard an old loony used to live there.

—Years ago, yes. None of us ever saw him. Papa said he did,
but Papa used to make up all sorts of horrible stories to make us
behave. There was smoke sometimes, though, in the evenings. In
the daytime too, in winter.

—You never wanted to pay him a visit?

Else laughed. —We were afraid to, of course. Kurt especially.
We drew pictures of him to make up for it. He looked a little bit
like you, actually, only three or four meters taller, with a walking
stick made out of an old butter churn. And a broken stovepipe hat.

—That's more or less how I picture myself.

—On your off days, Oskar, she said, patting him on the cheek.
—Kurt tried to find him once, when we were a little older. He
went up to the cave in the middle of the night with a candle, a box

of matches and a spade, but all he found was a pile of tattered women's dresses. Had nightmares for weeks after.

—About the dresses?

—About the man, I think, said Else. She laughed.

They began walking slowly around the bend. —Piedernig knew him, said Voxlauer.

—I can't think how he would have. This was before—

Voxlauer stopped suddenly. —What's that sound?

—What sound?

He held up a hand. —Listen.

The whine of an engine spiraled upward through the pines, high and keening as a bandsaw. The pines dampened the sound and smoothed it. It kept constant and dull and grew louder with each step as they followed it down the hill. Underneath and behind the keening was another sound, dimmer and harder to identify. It might not have been a sound at all but it quivered as a sound would along the ground and made them hurry forward. They came into a glade and the noise spread and brightened to a flat wail all around them, hanging on the air like a shield of shivering, spinning glass. Voxlauer covered his ears and began to run. Else was already running as fast as she could, screaming to him to hurry.

Where the road met the creek and fell back into the pines a wheel spun above the ditch in a cloud of blue-black smoke. Coming up behind Else Voxlauer saw the shape of the wheel and the smoke around it and knew already what had happened. As they drew nearer he saw the rest of the machine, broken and inverted, and the body underneath pressed down deep into the grass.

In the three days before his death Kurt spoke almost not at all, breath coming to him in sharp splintered gasps that seemed chipped as they came from a hard, glasslike column of air. Else brought food to him, cups of broth and bits of milk-soaked bread that he almost always refused. Occasionally Voxlauer would see the two of them whispering together. Catching sight of him from a corner of his eye, Kurt would stop and look over at him for a long moment, his face calm and blank.

The windows were kept open on the warm summer air and every so often Kurt would take a deeper breath than usual and sigh mildly, like an old man unlacing a heavy pair of boots. He would lie quietly for hours then, barely breathing, until his chest would seize and blood would well in a froth over his tongue and lips. From the kitchen Voxlauer would hear him choking and rush down to help Else turn him onto his side. As they took hold of him he would scream and curse them both until his breath was gone, then once it was done quiet again into an uneasy, effortful state of rest. Within the hour he would be asleep, breathing shallowly through his nose, and they would steal two or three hours' fitful sleep themselves, waking always to the sound of Kurt flailing back and forth across the bed.

As soon as Kurt had been laid out Voxlauer sent word to the hospital in Niessen and the Polizeihaus. The next morning a doctor and the little SS officer from the funeral, both dressed in olive-colored field jackets and matching jodhpurs, pulled up in a beautiful jet-black Horch convertible with two uniformed SS privates in the back holding an elaborate folding stretcher across their knees. The doctor and the officer came briskly to the house and rapped on the screen door. The two privates waited by the car, staring up at the house.

—Else Bauer? the doctor said as Else came to the door.

—Yes. She looked at the officer, behind her at Voxlauer, then back to the doctor. —Come in, she said after a moment.

The officer turned to the two privates and made a little gesture. They brought the stretcher from the car and set it on the grass. As he stepped in after the doctor, he caught sight of Voxlauer and stopped in mid-stride.

—Who is this person? said the officer, frowning slightly.

—A friend of the family, said Else. —Are you coming downstairs?

The officer remained motionless.

—It *is* my cousin you've come for? said Else, already halfway down the steps.

The officer didn't answer. Else went down with the doctor. The officer and Voxlauer stood a shoulder's width apart just inside the door, studying each other. —Is that for me? said Voxlauer, looking at the two privates crouched in the grass over the stretcher.

—I couldn't say, Herr Voxlauer. Are you ill?

—I'm tired, said Voxlauer, sitting down at the table. —Shouldn't you be attending to something or other?

—I'm not needed downstairs at present, said the officer, taking a packet of cigarettes from his shirt pocket. —Peaceful up here, he said in his faint Reichs-German accent, a cigarette dangling slantwise from his mouth.

—Not lately, said Voxlauer.

—Of course, said the officer.

Voxlauer drummed his fingers against the table.

—Regarding the accident, said the officer. —Any thoughts worth mentioning?

—None.

—Pass anyone on the roadway yesterday evening? Anyone at all?

Voxlauer sighed. —You'd have it much easier if I owned so much as a wheelbarrow, wouldn't you.

—I'm asking for your testimony, Herr Voxlauer. Surely that must have some significance, even to you. You're a reliable witness, aren't you? Clear-headed? Unsentimental? Sober?

—You'd not much like the testimony I'd give.

—Oh! I'm sure we would, Herr Voxlauer. I'm sure we'd all like to hear your testimony very much, should you feel inclined to give it to us. If not, however, we can certainly follow things to a satisfactory conclusion without your help.

Voxlauer said nothing.

—Do you? said the officer.

—Do I what?

—Do you feel so inclined?

Voxlauer looked out through the screen door, breathing in the sharp dusky smell of the burning cigarette and the heavy, grass-scented sweetness everywhere behind it. —I feel inclined to live, he said.

The officer smiled and looked down at his fingernails. —Really? That surprises me, I must say. I'm almost beginning to think the Obersturmführer was wrong about you after all, God rest him.

—The Obersturmführer's not dead yet, I believe.

—He is to us, the officer said, letting the words fall out of his narrow mouth one by one, distinct from one another and perfectly formed. —Listen closely now, Herr Voxlauer. My predecessor may, as one of his countless whims, have extended to you some small measure of protection but that protection is now at an end. It has already been decided by an authority greater than my own to regard his death as an assassination on behalf of Jewish interests, and to take the accused, once he has been recovered, to a full and public trial. Your testimony might prove of some slight interest to said authority. Alternatively, you may be tried as a collaborator and hanged. Do you follow me?

—I follow, said Voxlauer, very quietly.

—And?

—I've told you already. I want to live.

The officer shrugged his shoulders. A moment later the doctor and Else came upstairs.

—They can't move him, Else said, taking Voxlauer's hand and gripping it.

—I've been invited to give a statement at the Polizeihaus, said Voxlauer. —I explained to the officer here that we're much too busy.

—Yes, that's right, said Else, turning to the officer. —He doesn't have to go with you just now, does he?

—Well. If he's needed here, with the Obersturmführer, said the officer, still looking at Voxlauer.

They stood without speaking, the four of them, for the briefest of instants in the narrow room. Then the doctor heaved a deep professional sigh and ran a kerchief over his damp flushed jowls. —The Obersturmführer needs time to recover his air, he said. He glanced at Voxlauer. —Don't move him any more than necessary. He's at an extremely delicate stage in his recovery.

—I've just come to that conclusion myself, said Voxlauer.

—Can you leave him something for the pain, at least? said Else.

The doctor looked at her in surprise. —Herr Bauer is a soldier of the Schutzstaffel, Fräulein, he said flatly. He glanced over at the officer and coughed. The officer put out his cigarette hurriedly and went to the door.

—Good day to you, Fräulein, said the doctor. He and the SS man bowed once more and went down the steps to the Horch and herded the two privates into it and drove away, leaving the stretcher half assembled on the drive.

Voxlauer shuttered the room against the midday heat and took the pan of blood-spattered urine from beside the bed and arranged the pillows and the sheets. Kurt stared dazedly up at him. With eyes half closed and the lamplight behind him the resemblance to Else was full and utter: the round, smooth face, solemn and androgynous, the wide dark pupils, the heavy lids. His eyes followed Voxlauer as he moved around the bed. —Else? he murmured. He let his eyes fall closed completely, then opened them all at once, frowning. —Else, he repeated.

—She's here, said Voxlauer.

Else came barefooted from the kitchen, smoothing the hair back from her face. Kurt's eyes saw her, focused briefly, then fell closed again. —He asked for you, said Voxlauer, moving away.

—Kurti? Else said. Kurt's eyes opened and closed.

—They didn't even change the poultices, she said, looking over her shoulder at Voxlauer.

Kurt smiled at this and made a low sound, midway between a croak and a laugh, lifting a hand and waving it in the air. —Let it be, he said hoarsely. —Let it.

—Else, he said a moment later, opening his eyes very wide.

Else sat down by the bed and leaned over. Kurt said something too quietly for Voxlauer to hear. Else took Kurt's hand in hers and held it, whispering. As she whispered to him his body arched suddenly and he began groaning and sputtering, kicking angrily at the sheets and twisting his head from side to side. —Oskar! Else cried. Voxlauer came quickly and together they lifted Kurt and turned him over. The blood had already begun to pool in his mouth and he leaned his head down slackly and let it dribble out through his teeth. —I'll get the pan, said Voxlauer, running to the kitchen.

In the kitchen he cast about a moment for the pan before finding it. When he came back down into the bedroom Kurt had quieted and was breathing in even, steady gasps. His face glowed sallowly in the light coming through the shutters. Else sat motionless at the foot of the bed, staring dumbly ahead of her. Her hand lay on Kurt's forearm. Kurt was looking at Voxlauer. He took his arm from Else's and beckoned to him. —Voxlauer, he mouthed silently.

Voxlauer came and crouched by the bed.

—There you are, Voxlauer. The whites of Kurt's eyes shone against his yellow face. His left eye socket was running and bruised and the ball had begun to darken around its edges. He let out a sigh.

—What is it? Else said, taking hold of his arm again.

Kurt's eyes wandered up to hers. —Go away a minute, Liesi.

Else hesitated, opening her mouth to speak, then stood without a word and left. Kurt's eyes were wide and luminous as he watched her. He turned them back slowly, unwillingly, to rest on Voxlauer.

—The time's come for me to tell you my regrets, cousin-in-law. Kurt motioned to the stool.

The sound of Else taking dishes from the cupboard carried from the kitchen. —I'm not interested in your regrets, Kurt, he said.

Kurt attempted another laugh, a raw, hacking croak that collapsed on itself immediately. —I don't believe you, he wheezed.

—That's your privilege, said Voxlauer, getting to his feet.

—Two of your friends from the colony are dead.

Voxlauer stopped short, staring at the shutters.

—That's better. Kurt took a breath. —Now sit quietly a minute.

—Else! Voxlauer called.

—No! Don't call her! Listen to me, Voxlauer! I don't want her. *Voxlauer!*

—Else! Voxlauer called again. He saw her silhouette now through the slats of the shutters, bending over something in the garden.

—Keep her away from me, Voxlauer, Kurt gasped. Voxlauer looked down at him straining desperately to meet his eyes, baring his teeth from the pain and effort of holding himself up. Just like one of my fits, Voxlauer thought, watching the blood rushing to Kurt's face. He felt no pity or concern, only a remote, sterile curiosity at the tenacity of the life still animating the body propped tremblingly before him. Something in the abjectness of Kurt's features or in his own faraway state of mind made him think of the soldier he'd killed long ago in the Isonzo. Decades later, near the end of his own life, he would think of those two moments, standing over the deserter in the snow with the military police on all sides, and crouching at the foot of the bed as Kurt suffered through his last few conscious breaths, as connected by a wire that ran through all the moments in between, fixing them in precise order, like glass beads on a string. He waited another drawn-out, deliberate moment before speaking.

—All right, Kurt. Lie back now. I'll listen.

—I'm dying, Kurt said feebly, falling back onto the sheets like a wooden effigy.

Voxlauer said nothing. The screen door banged as Else came back inside.

—Go now, Kurt murmured, his eyes losing focus.

Voxlauer stepped away. Kurt's eyes had closed and his forehead was beaded over with sweat. —Voxlauer! he said loudly as Voxlauer was halfway across the room.

—Yes, Kurt? said Voxlauer, coming back to the bed. But Kurt turned his head and waved him impatiently away.

Two days later they woke to find his body crumpled like a sheet of paper, thighs drawn in against the wound in his chest, head turned into the bed, one arm drawn in and one flung wide over the sweat- and blood-soaked bedcovers. Voxlauer reached out a hand and passed it over the blanched, ungiving skin, cool and mottled over with tiny blots. He bent down and with a great effort straightened the tucked and stiffened legs and pulled the sheets over them. Else hung back by the kitchen steps. A warm breeze carried through the open windows, moving the hair on the back of Kurt's head lightly, ruffling it and smoothing it down again exactly as it would the hair on a living body. Voxlauer bent over the bed and took in a breath but smelled only the faint scent of sweat and the morning damp. Then he stepped away from the body and went past Else up the kitchen steps and out of the house.

Thin wisps of cloud were massing into a palisade above the cliffs and he stood just outside the doorway, watching them. In Pergau the green copper steeple caught the first tentative rays of light and held them fast. A high bending file of rooks rose from it like a standard, thinning as he watched into a fine, dark thread. After a while Else came out and sat next to him on the steps. They sat wordlessly, looking across the valley. Nothing in her face or in her way of sitting beside him would have led anyone to believe that she was suffering. A short time later she stood and went back inside.

That afternoon as they were wrapping Kurt's body in the bedding Else straightened suddenly, frowning, and went to the window. —Someone's coming up the drive, she whispered.

—Who is it?

She turned to him, furious, a finger pressed against her lips. —Shut your mouth!

He said nothing for a moment, standing transfixed by the bed, a corner of the bedsheet still in his hands. —Do you want me to go look?

She shook her head. —I'll go. You stay down here. And keep quiet, Oskar, for God's sake.

She crossed the floor silently and ran up the kitchen steps. The screen door squeaked as she leaned against it.

—It's the Holzer boys, she called down a moment later.

Voxlauer sucked in his breath.

—Wait—the mother's with them. Come up here, Oskar. Have a look.

He climbed the kitchen steps haltingly and stood well behind her in the doorway. The sons had stopped a few paces from the house and stood on either side of their mother, sullen-faced and restless.

—Evening, Fräulein Bauer, Frau Holzer said, curtsying. The sons nicked their heads.

—Evening to you, Else said. —What do you want?

—We'd like to see him, if you please, said the long-haired son. —The Obersturmführer.

—He's dead.

—Yes, Fräulein. We'd like to see him.

—My cousin is to have a full state service at the Niessener Dom. There'll be more than enough opportunity to see him then.

—I can't spare my boys for any sort of services, Frau Holzer said deferentially, keeping her eyes at the level of Else's hips.

—There's a frightful amount of work to be done, and I'm precious little good alone. She paused a brief instant, fingering the sides of her dress as if debating whether to curtsy again, still unwilling to raise her eyes. —If there were any possibility, Fräulein, any at all, we'd take it as a kindness. I'll speak for their behavior, if that's any worry, she added, glancing furtively at Voxlauer.

Else looked back at him and raised her eyebrows. The sons were looking at him as well, staring at him out of their wide-set eyes, whether threateningly or plaintively he neither knew nor cared. He wondered very briefly at his sudden equanimity.

—For all I care, he said, turning back into the house.

—All right, said Else. —Come in, then, the three of you. We're just getting him ready to be taken to town.

Frau Holzer nodded gratefully, already coming up the steps. —Thank you kindly, Fräulein. If I can be of any help at all, I've tended to a fair number of the departed—

—We were nearly done, thank you, said Else, holding the screen door open to them.

Voxlauer leaned back against the counter as they passed down into the bedroom, much as he'd done when the doctor and the SS man had visited three days previous, and waited for them to be gone again. How things would change now that Kurt was dead he had no idea, but to pass the time he forced himself to think about what might happen. We'll find out now if he was keeping us safe, the way he claimed, he thought. Keeping *me* safe, he corrected himself. That Else was out of danger, the widow of a great man, had been clear already in the way the doctor and the SS officer had spoken to her. She can live like my mother lived now, if she chooses, thought Voxlauer, smiling a little to himself.

It's a good thing he's dead, though, he thought. That's certain. Anything might have happened if he'd lived.

A few minutes later they were out on the steps with the afternoon light all around them. At the bottommost step Frau Holzer paused, fidgeting again with the hem of her dress.

—Thank you kindly, Fräulein. She hesitated a moment further, beaming up at Else, her face creased into a bright motherly bundle of goodwill. —And you, Herr Voxlauer? she said, leaning to one side of Else to catch his eye. —Won't you be coming up again for milk?

—Not blessed likely, said Voxlauer, looking at the sons.

—Yes. Well, she said quietly, stepping down.

The sons were already at the head of the drive, dragging their feet impatiently in the dirt. —Good evening, said Else, pulling the screen door closed.

—Good evening, Frau Holzer said, treading carefully on the grass. —Good evening, she said again, suddenly much aged, her sons loping ahead of her along the ditch. At the first bend of the drive they waited, feral again with the dense woods behind them, looking warily back at the villa and the shut screen door. As their mother drew even with them they straightened somewhat and fell in behind her. A moment later they vanished, all three of them, into the top-lit green.

That night Else and Voxlauer climbed to the ridge with the starlight stuttering down through the pines and lines of resin shining wetly on each trunk like ropes of pearls. A mist rose up from the valley floor, sloughing off under the cliffs. At the foot of the Kugel-tree they spread out the old army coat that had once been Anna's husband's and sat wrapped in it, shivering against each other, looking down toward town and passing a tin cup of Birnen-schnapps between them. Heat lightning flickered far away to the south, over the Dolomites and the plain of Italy and the sea. Now and again the town bells thudded, four soft fluid peals followed by deeper tolls to mark the hour. The old tree's limbs cracked and murmured. They passed the schnapps carefully back and forth until it was gone. A few minutes later, Else said:

—I think they did it.

Voxlauer looked sideways at her profile, blurred, close to his eyes. —Who?

—They. Them. Pauli and his daughter.

Voxlauer turned his face away from her. The wind was building in the south and the sounds from the tree above them grew steadily louder. He thought about Pauli on the day he left, his strangeness, his recklessness and the overloaded car. He thought about the premonition that had come to him so suddenly in the reliquary, the look on Kurt's face as he leaned across the pew and the decision he'd made, keeping his decision hidden even to himself, walking down to the villa afterward. Finally he said: —Pauli may have. Emelia wasn't in the car. Remember?

Else looked at him a moment in confusion. Then all at once she understood and said:—Ach! That isn't what I meant at all. I meant *did it*. Got away. She craned her neck upward and kissed him, breath sweet and resinous from the schnapps.

—Oh, said Voxlauer.

She turned her head again to look down the slope. —They'll hang it on Pauli, though, won't they? Of course they will. Because he's gone.

—Maybe they're right to hang it on him.

—Yes. Maybe, Else said. She rearranged the coat around her. —It doesn't matter now.

—I knew it would happen, Else. With Kurt that last time. In the chapel.

—What?

—That Kurt would die. I saw it plain as day.

—Don't talk that way, Oskar. What good is talk like that?

—I only felt that I should tell you. He was quiet a moment. —I wanted it to happen.

—Enough! she said fiercely, pulling at his beard. —Enough of that kind of nonsense. I won't stand for any more of it. Her fingers closed tightly against his jaw. —Promise me now. Not another word.

—All right, said Voxlauer. —All right! Jesus!

They leaned back again and watched the weather coming. —What will we do now? said Else quietly.

—I haven't the faintest idea, said Voxlauer, taking the cup from her. Else said nothing.

—Else?

—Present.

—What do you recommend?

A Note About the Author

John Wray was born in Washington, D.C., in 1971, the son of an Austrian mother and an American father, and has divided his time between the two countries. Currently he lives in Brooklyn. This is his first novel.

A Note on the Type

The text of this book was set in Sabon, a typeface designed by Jan Tschichold (1902–1974), the well-known German typographer. Based loosely on the original designs by Claude Garamond (c. 1480–1561), Sabon is unique in that it was explicitly designed for hot-metal composition on both the Monotype and Linotype machines as well as for filmsetting. Designed in 1966 in Frankfurt, Sabon was named for the famous Lyons punch cutter Jacques Sabon, who is thought to have brought some of Garamond's matrices to Frankfurt.

Composed by Creative Graphics,
Allentown, Pennsylvania

Printed and bound by Quebecor Printing,
Fairfield, Pennsylvania

Designed by Ralph Fowler